CAITLIN
FROM THE FILES OF THE
OFFICE OF PARANORMAL RESEARCH
BOOK 3

Terence West

CAITLIN
FROM THE FILES OF THE
OFFICE OF PARANORMAL RESEARCH
BOOK 3

DOUBLE DRAGON

Chapter One

A lone drop of water fell from somewhere above. It splattered against his forehead and ran down over the bridge of his nose, finally pooling under the tip. Letting his head fall forward, he shook the drop free. A spasm of pain arced up his neck from the deep wounds on both sides. He wondered how much blood he had lost. His thoughts were beginning to lose coherence as his mind became increasingly muddy. His body was bruised and broken. He tried to take a deep breath but stopped. It was too painful. He felt a cough welling up in his throat but did his best to stifle it.

Pressing his eyelids tightly together, he tried to relax his eyes. He could feel a bruise high on his right cheek with a small laceration running through it. His arms had gradually become numb from inactivity. They were chained to the wall above his head, his wrists bound together by two iron cuffs. A long, taut chain connected them high on the wall. He couldn't remember how long he had been a prisoner here as the days and nights bled into each other in this dark place. He slowly opened his eyes. There was a thin strip of light bleeding from under a far door, barely enough to illuminate the room.

Through the haze behind his eyes, he could vaguely remember being brought here and why. It had been his fault. As a flash of fear gripped him, he remembered his companion. Was she alive? Holding his breath for a moment, he listened for any sounds of life. The silence became deafening. Only the slight creak of his restraining chains filled his ears. His head fell forward in defeat. She was dead and he was next, but the point was moot. Without her, he was already dead.

He needed to relax for a moment, but his predicament made that almost impossible. He was standing flat-footed on the floor with his arms raised straight above. Little leeway was allowed in this position. Shuffling his feet back against the wall, he pushed up onto the balls of his feet until he was standing on the tips of his toes. He let out a long sigh as the pressure was taken off his wrists. He could feel how raw they were. Even the slightest movement of the restraints stung the wounds.

Cane was completely naked. His captors had taken joy in ripping his clothes from his body and exposing his pale flesh. They had taken care of some of the wounds on his body, especially those on his chest and upper thighs. Cotton bandages were being held in place by generous amounts of tape. He found it odd they would even attempt to take care of him. They were keeping him alive just to watch him die.

A cough shattered the silence followed by the rattle of chains and a soft moan in the darkness. Zachary Cane perked up his ears as a look of hopefulness crossed his face. "Lydia?"

There was another cough, but no reply.

"Lydia, are you okay?" Cane asked again. His voice sounded strange in his own ears. It was slightly younger, and his British accent was a bit thicker. He cleared his throat. Maybe he was going mad—the combination of constant darkness, pain, and blood loss had a way of doing that to a person—but something about this entire situation wasn't right....

"No," came Lydia's voice. It was weak and engorged with pain. "I'm dying. How do you think I feel?" A cough interrupted her anger. It gurgled from deep within her lungs, bringing blood with it. She could taste on her lips. Leaning her head back slowly, she found it increasingly difficult to catch her breath. Her lungs were filling with fluid. She was slowly drowning.

Lydia Katran wasn't pinned to the wall as Cane was, instead, her captors had chained her feet and hands to the floor. She was stuck with her legs crossed behind her and her palms flat on the floor in front of her. Her back ached, but there was no way for her to sit up or lie down. As with Cane, she was completely naked except for a scrap of her shirt that hung from her collar. Her long brown hair, matted with blood and dirt, hung over her face in a mess. The smell of blood was beginning to make her nauseous, but that was the least of her problems. "They'll come for us," she said after a moment.

Cane furrowed his brow. "Lydia," he said cautiously, "I don't think anyone's going to bloody find us here. We really screwed up this time," he said more to himself than her.

Lydia threw her head back trying to get the hair out of her face. "Have faith in the God and Goddess," she rasped. "They will find a way to free us. My coven knows we came here."

Cane remained quiet for a long time. Lydia knew he didn't believe in any kind of God, or Goddess for that matter, and that he only tolerated her Wiccan beliefs. It was strange. He was an avid believer in the supernatural, magick included, but he refused to believe a higher power could exist. She forced a smile. Cane was a riddle, wrapped in an enigma and tucked nicely in a basket of fish and chips.

"I don't think even your mates could bust us out of 'ere," Cane said finally.

"You have to have faith," Lydia's voice was filled with wheezes and pops, but she still managed to bring a small amount of comfort to Cane. "I may still be a new initiate, but I have felt their power. We will be rescued soon."

Cane ran his tongue over his dry, cracked lips. It had been some time since any liquid had touched them. If there were to be a rescue, surely it would have happened by now. He didn't want to voice his doubts to Lydia, but he had the nagging feeling an attempt had already been made, and their captors had wiped out the coven. It was just a feeling. He hoped to Hell he was wrong. Taking a deep breath, he felt a twinge of pain run up his side. Cane gritted his teeth, fighting the urge to cry out. After a moment, the pain began to subside, returning the familiar numbness. As he relaxed his jaw, he scanned the room with his eyes. He was barely able to make out a few dim shapes in the room, but it wasn't enough to allay his worries. As his eyes stopped on the small sliver of light at the base of the door, his heart begin to race. A pair of shadows passed through the light. Someone, or something was there, just outside…waiting.

He perked his ears at the slight sound of the

door handle being grasped. Pushing up as high as he could on his toes, he leaned his body forward and pulled on the chains. Every muscle in his upper body strained against the iron shackles. He heard them creak and groan in protest, but it wasn't enough to break free. There was nowhere for him to go, no way he could get to Lydia.

He listened to the door mechanism click. A burst of light blinded him temporarily as the door was thrown open. Turning his head away, he continued to listen. There was nothing. No footfalls and no whispered voices. Not even the sound of moving fabric could be heard. The sharp scent of a woman's cologne suddenly stung his nostrils. Opening his eyes slowly, he faced front with hesitation. He could make out a woman's form, her face shadowed by the backlight. It looked as if a glowing yellow aura surrounded her entire body, but Cane knew it was just the light spilling in from the hallway just beyond the open door.

"How's my pet feeling this morning?" a soft voice asked.

Cane ignored her, but kept his vision trained on her.

The woman leaned close, pressing her hand gently against his chest. She moved her fingernails softly through his chest hair. "I see someone's grumpy today," she said. Cane wasn't quite sure, but he could make out the slightest Gaelic accent in her voice. It was barely perceptible.

She glanced over her shoulder and nodded. The room was instantly filled with a hard, white light. Cane clamped his eyelids shut as he turned his head away. He had been in the dark so long, the light hurt him. Opening his watering eyes again, he blinked rapidly as he tried to adjust. Slowly, everything in the room came into focus. They were in a wine cellar. Tall shelves lined the far walls filled with bottles of numerous label and vintage. The floor was covered with deep, red tile, but he could still make out several bloodstains below himself and Lydia. The room was much smaller than he had estimated, measuring probably ninety to one hundred square feet.

Looking up, Cane could see two men standing on either side of the open door. They were dressed casually, but impeccably. Both were clean-shaven and appeared to be of Caucasian and Hispanic—respectively—descent, but seemed extraordinarily pale in the light. Their eyes had a slight yellow tint to them.

Cane returned his attention to the woman in front of him. She was beautiful. Long, wavy, red hair hung down around her face, terminating just below her shoulders. Her eyes were lush and as green as sea foam. They almost appeared white as the light danced off them. There was nary a blemish or scar visible anywhere on her face. Her alabaster skin was flawless, appearing very much like porcelain. The blood red lipstick she was wearing on her full lips and dark eye shadow complimented her perfectly.

Her body, wrapped in a tight black dress that ended just above her knees, was equally impressive. She could easily have passed as a model or movie star. Her breasts appeared firm and full, but weren't

10

overly large. She was definitely fit and trim, and Cane would describe her body type as "athletic". The beautiful curves of her hips gave way to long, slender legs. He glanced down at her hand, which was still firmly against his chest. They were immaculate to the very tips of the sharp nails painted almost the same color as her lips. A pair of black heels and a long, dark brown leather jacket completed the package.

She pulled the corners of her mouth up into a seductive smile, barely exposing her flawless white teeth. "I'm going to give you a choice tonight," she breathed. She leaned close to his ear. "Do you want to die first, or second?"

Cane remained silent.

She ran her hand up his chest to his throat and stopped. Curling her fingers over, she sunk the tips of her fingernails viciously into his flesh. Cane gasped, but remained resolute. "Let me ask you again, pet. Do you want to watch us abuse the witch, or would you rather go first?" She dug her nails a bit deeper producing a bead of blood.

"Why don't you sod off?" Cane growled through gritted teeth.

The woman smiled. "Fine. The witch is first." She lifted her free hand and snapped her fingers. Her two men moved quickly toward Lydia. Dropping to their knees on either side of her, they held still for a moment just watching her. Then, with movements so fast it was hard for Cane to track, they were on her. Lydia screamed in pain and terror as the first man grabbed a fistful of her hair and yanked her head back. The second man straddled her crossed legs, pressing his cupped hands against her breasts. The two men paused and looked back at the woman. A smile crossed their faces as she nodded.

Tossing his head back, the second man opened his mouth wide. Cane watched in horror as the man's canine teeth grew into fangs. Snapping around, the second man bent down and ran his tongue over Lydia's right breast and nipple. Lydia struggled vainly to get away but the men easily overpowered her. The second man turned his head back slightly to watch Cane's reaction. His eyes were changing into a deep, mustard yellow as an evil smile grew on his lips. Grabbing her breast again with his pale hand, he exposed his fangs and bit into her flesh. She screamed in pain, but it quickly died in her throat as the first man bit into her neck. Lydia's head fell back as a moan escaped her lips as the two men worked over her.

Cane turned away from the sight. Anger burned in his eyes as he stared at his captor. "Vampire," he hissed.

The woman laughed. "Human," she said mockingly. She slowly pushed herself against Cane's naked body, grinding her hips slowly between his legs. "You know," she smiled, exposing her own fangs, "even though you die when we feed, most victims find it quite," she paused for effect, "pleasurable. Look at your woman. She's loving every minute of it," she whispered. "If she could move her legs, she would probably spread them wide for—"

"You bitch!" Cane yelled as he lashed forward,

barely missing the woman's face. She was too fast for him. He struggled angrily against his restraints.

The woman pressed her finger against Cane's lips. "That wasn't very gentlemanly. You should save the dirty talk for when we're alone," she laughed. She pulled slightly away from Cane. He watched as her eyes dissolved to yellow and her iris and pupil quickly vanished. "It's your turn, love. Try to relax."

Lunging forward, she pressed her mouth to Cane's neck, just below his jaw. She drug the tips of her razor sharp fangs over his skin, then with one push, bit down. He felt both pop through his flesh. Pain radiated out in every direction as she removed her fangs from the holes she had just created. She worked the tip of her tongue around what felt to Cane like gaping craters. Quickly, the pain subsided as a wave of pleasure began to wash over him. The woman pressed herself firmly against him as she moved her hands up his body. Cain's eyes rolled back in his head and the light around him began to fade, but he didn't care. If he could move his arms, he would return the embrace. The analytical portion of his brain realized her bite had triggered a kind of euphoria in his brain, but he didn't care. He hoped she would never stop touching him.... He felt his life begin to slip away.

* * *

Cane sat straight up in bed. His heart pounding, he immediately moved his hand to his neck and let out a long sigh of relief. Propping himself up on his hands, he took a deep breath and tried to calm down. Glancing to his right, he saw the familiar red

13

glow of his alarm clock. It was a little after three in the morning. His entire apartment was still dark. He looked down at his bed. His sheets and comforter were in a state of disarray. It was a dream, he reassured himself, but he knew the awful truth. He reached for the glass of water he kept next to his bed. Lifting it to his lips, he took a long drink of the clear, cool liquid, then deposited it back onto the nightstand.

Lying back down in bed, he pulled the covers up to his stomach. He briefly wondered how Lydia was. Now that they were back on speaking terms, they had been talking much more often. He would have to call her first thing in the morning. Cane ran his hand through his graying hair as he closed his eyes. He needed to get some sleep. He couldn't waste any more time dwelling in the past, awake or asleep.

* * *

A wave of dark clouds rolled in overhead muting out the sunlight. They were heavy, ready at any moment to let loose their precious, watery cargo. Wind whipped through the bare branches of trees, lifting dead leaves from the ground and continuing on its way. Winter was nearing, but it hadn't yet slipped its icy fingers around the landscape. The numerous shades of green had gradually turned to the reds, golds and yellows of the season.

It was a time of death, but as everything eased into deep winter slumber, they knew they would experience rebirth. It was the great wheel, the cycle of life, ever turning…but then that was all new age garbage, wasn't it? Things die. It wasn't some grand plan, or another step in God's plan, it was just death. Everything on this planet was placed here with its clock already ticking. Humans are, in every sense, born to die. That is the way of life, and if anyone tells you differently, they are a fool.

They knew better. They had unlocked the great mystery of the universe in their few years: God does not exist. There is no plan for each of us, no spiritual will or fate keeping us on a predestined path. The only answer is to live now and enjoy what you can because there is nothing waiting for us at the end of our journeys. No pearly gates, no tunnel of light, only a wooden box buried six feet beneath the ground.

Black cloth billowed around them as they moved through the foggy streets of London. Some would call them outcasts, but they disagreed with the label. Religion, morality, these trappings did not touch them. They were animals, and this was the way they wanted it. They moved freely through 'the savage garden of life', to quote their favorite literary character, partaking in all the joys they could. Nothing was beyond their capabilities. They were free.

Side by side moved three women and two men, all clad in the color of night. They weaved in and out of the fog that hung on the old cobblestone streets. Each had taken their appearance to the extreme. Strands of red, green, purple, white and orange streaked through their hair while silver piercings dotted their faces. Their skin was pale, not having glimpsed the sunlight in some time, and their eyes, covered with contact lenses, were more intense shades of normal colors. These were so-called "Modern Vampires". Creatures of the night who were still very much alive, yet adhered to a vampire-like lifestyle almost as if it were a religion. Most would think of them as blood fetishes, or a cult of blood worshipers, but to them, this was not the case. This was as close to being a vampire as they could get, but that was all about to change.

For each, what drew them to the lifestyle was different. Perhaps it was a general affection for the night, the lure of possible immortality, or something much more personal. For others, it had become a much more sinister pursuit. A vampire's life meant the end of rules, the end of the laws of men. These "vampires" took the lifestyle to the extreme and some even killed. These were the outcasts of the modern Vampire society, and thankfully, rare.

Blood was the currency of their realm. For some, it had become secondary to the lifestyle, but it was still important to most. Since a majority of the Modern Vampires are still law-abiding citizens, they simply can't walk out onto the street, grab a victim and drink their blood. They have instead evolved unique ways to satisfy this lust. A pack of Modern Vampires generally has two to three "donors". These are people, who for some reason— be it the pleasure they receive from being cut and having their blood drank, or the need to satisfy their own dark cravings—allow the vampires to "feed" off them. And for most, a system of checks and balances are in place for donors and vampires so that no disease can be transmitted. Each vampire will take only a little and it's generally part of a sex act. They have no actual physical need for the life sustaining liquid, but some, much like a fetishist, receive a drug-like high from the experience, while others claim it keeps them young by slowing down the aging process. Whatever the ultimate reason, it was what defined who they were.

They were vampires in every sense of the word, except one: all were still very much alive. Tonight, however, that would all change. The coven had a plan that would take them to the other side. Another coven in the area had discovered something…incredible. If it were true, it would mean the fulfillment of their dark fruitions. The plans had been made and all was in order. Tonight, they would become. The five were moving side by side, taking large, confident strides. Ego oozed from each, as they knew instinctively they were better than the "normals" they passed on the street. They were a pack of wolves on the hunt. One of the two men took the lead and stopped. Spinning around, he grinned at the others with his porcelain fangs.

"Let's get crazy."

He was simply known as Zeke. His chosen vampiric name was Ezekiel, taken from the Christian faith he detested. Every drop of blood he drank was his way of dishonoring the name and the religion. Zeke was dressed in a long, black leather trench coat that licked at the heels of his thick boots. The right lapel was decorated with several silver pins, including an atheist's cross and a small skull with rubies set in the eye sockets. His skintight shirt was made entirely of a stretchy mesh that revealed and highlighted his extraordinarily fit chest. A tattered pair of leather pants were plastered to his legs. His short, messy hair was jet black with a few wisps of red hanging down over his forehead and the pair of oval, rose-tinted sunglasses he always wore. His face was long and gaunt with well-defined cheekbones. A long goatee hung down from his chin almost to his chest and was dyed the same color black as his hair. Several piercings hung in his left ear, attached by a thin silver chain to another in his left nostril.

He was the unspoken leader of the pack, an honor he had earned through seniority. Zeke had recruited most of his group, or "sired" as he liked to call it, through a blood ritual. At twenty-three, he was also the oldest of the group. His fascination with vampires held its roots in his childhood. He had been inadvertently introduced to the concept while watching television one afternoon. To this day, he could still remember the film's title, who it starred, what channel it was on, and the time of afternoon he watched it with his eyes open for the first time. Given a little bit of time, he could also probably tell you the complete meteorological conditions for the day in question as well. It was the moment of his rebirth when he became aware there was much more between Heaven and Hell than ever revealed to him.

Zeke had been born a sickly child, suffering from severe allergies, asthma, and eczema. It was hard for him to lead a normal childhood, but that didn't stop him from trying. The time he tried out for the basketball team in junior high had left him

18

bedridden for an entire week due to a massive asthma attack during the third game of the season. That was a difficult lesson for him to learn. He knew he could never participate in extracurricular athletics, even with the comprehensive medical treatment he was enduring. Through his formative years in high school, his general mental stability worsened—although he would say he finally began to understand the path that lay before him. He began to suffer through intense periods of depression that only worsened his feelings of isolation and loneliness. It was then he met the woman who would change his life.

He was a senior and she a freshman. The first time he set his eyes on her, Zeke knew this was his Gothic Queen. She revealed to him that she was a vampire, and needed blood to survive. This was music to Zeke's ears. He willingly became her donor in hopes he would eventually be changed himself. This was his chance to get away from the pills, the diseases that plagued his entire early life. He would live forever in a place sickness could no longer touch him. She was the miracle cure he had been seeking his entire life.

It was the night of his eighteenth birthday that he first gave in to her dark temptations. On the small bed in his room while his parents were out of town, she drank his blood for the first time. At first, there was the need to hide what they were doing. He would cut the inside of his bottom lip with a razor blade so she could feed. After a while, though, all pretenses were abandoned. Cuts began to appear on his upper arms and back, and a few even showed up on his neck—for which he still bore the scars.

Soon their duo became more as members were taken into the fold. What had begun as an intimate connection between the two was perverted into something different, something darker. But as with everything in high school, an end came even for this tightly knit group. People moved away, harsh words were said and addictions became all consuming. Zeke lost his hold on the vampire world. He was back to being himself, and that frightened him. In an act of desperation, he contacted a group of vampires in London via the Internet. He dropped out of college in the States and hopped a ship to England. There he met up with his new group, but wasn't immediately accepted. Through several acts of initiation, including blood rites and outright crimes, he finally became one of their ranks.

Zeke found a job working at a blood bank as the night watchman—an idea he remembered from that very first vampire movie he ever watched. From there, he could supply fresh blood to the group while maintaining a steady income that paid for the small flat he lived in alone. He was finally living the life he wanted. During his voyage by ship to London, he had seen his last sunrise and sunset. He never turned back. Through several power struggles and machinations, he came to lead this "coven" of vampires. He immediately trimmed down the size of the group, keeping only the true believers. They were:

Ina, a lithe shadow of a woman had blonde hair with multiple black streaks dyed in it. Of the group, she was easily the most stunning as a vampire. Her porcelain fangs were always pearly white and flawless and she wore a pair of contacts that actually made her eyes look completely black. Ina—who was born Christina, but had taken Christ out of her name—was the daughter of a rich South African Industrialist. Work and money had never been an issue for her as her father provided anything she wanted without question. She lived in a small manor on the outskirts of London and was attending Oxford with her major being medicine. Ina had been a welcome addition to the group because of her medical knowledge. She could stitch wounds that had been cut too deeply, draw blood effectively, and administer basic health care (illegally, of course) to those in the coven who could not afford it.

Ina had begun her vampire life by visiting several themed clubs inside the city. As her visits became more frequent, she found herself falling into the lifestyle, but would never consider taking the blood of another. One night as she walked home from the club, she was attacked and raped by a man who claimed he was a vampire. As she struggled to get free, she bit into his bottom lip. His blood mingled in an open wound he had given her. From that night, the transformation of her psyche began. In that moment, she became a vampire. The old Christina was gone, leaving only Ina. She never pressed charges against the man as she felt this was the turning point of her life. Then there was:

Wrack, Zeke's second-in-command. She was almost as tall as him, with beautiful, curly red hair that tonight, she had up behind her head revealing two small scars on the left side of her neck. Her story was similar to that of Zeke's. Always an outsider, she longed for something more. She differed in the fact she was actually running from the law. The coven she had been a part of back in the States had taken the game too far, too early. She and two girlfriends had assaulted a female neighbor and killed her. They had taken her blood in the ultimate act of vampirism. Her two friends had been arrested and charged, but Wrack had stolen money and escaped to Canada. From there, her flight had taken her to unknown parts and finally, to London. She was immediately accepted into the coven by Zeke and placed in charge due to her sordid history. He claimed she was the most vampire-like of them all. With her deep blue eyes, she knew she was intimidating to the younger members of the coven, and sometimes, even to Zeke. She was dangerous and they all knew it. One of Wrack's closest confidants in the coven was:

Seraph, a raven-haired woman with a large angel tattoo on her back. She came from a very religious family, but had begun to rebel early. She saw her family members dying of diseases like cancer and emphysema, while others just succumbed to their addictions, such as drugs or alcohol. At the age of eleven, she was placed in foster care as her biological mother committed suicide and no relatives would take her. She wondered how a God of infinite love could do this to a child. Hatred grew of Him and all things He represented. She sought to become the one thing that was most unlike Him: a vampire. This creature represented the very essence of evil in the world. It took whatever it wanted and killed indiscriminately and yet it faced no repercussions as it lived forever. Not even God could take the vampire from this place. It was beyond reproach. It was everything she wanted to be. At seventeen, she took her chosen name, Seraph, and had that representation etched permanently on her back. She was a fallen angel. In her younger years, she had lived in His light and basked in His glory, but somewhere along the way, He had turned His back on her. Seraph hated God, and she would do everything in her power to bring pain and suffering on those who spoke his name with reverence. Seraph was the lover of:

Priest. As the newest recruit of the coven, it was his duty to screen new candidates and make sure everything was in order for rituals and feedings. Priest, a young man of twenty-two years with dyed, spiky green hair, was the only English native of the coven. Born and raised in London, he had fallen in with several vampire and occult sects at an early age. Like Zeke, he was first a donor, but had finally been "sired" himself. Seminary school had been his home for the past few years as he trained to follow the path of God and become an ordained Catholic minister. This career choice was entirely his parents'. As a way to rebel and find his true calling, he joined and eventually became High Priest of an occult sect. When his dark secrets were found out, he was tossed out of the seminary. From there, he hopped from sect to sect without much luck until joining with Zeke.

"What did you have in mind, Zeke?" Ina asked seductively. It was no secret that she wanted him.

He was the very epitome of the vampire to her. The two had partaken in blood rights together, but Zeke had never taken it any further (although she always offered). It always seemed like he was waiting for someone, perhaps a lover from his past.

"Tonight marks a new beginning for us all," Zeke replied grandly. Grabbing a nearby light pole, he lifted himself above the rest of the coven. "Tonight, we shuffle off our mortal coils and take our well-deserved rank among the undead." He smiled, his fangs glinting in the moonlight. "Let's send it off with a bang!"

Cheers erupted from the coven.

"Before we make contact with the other side tonight," an evil grin spread across Zeke's face, "let's burn this fucking town to the ground." Reaching into his coat, he produced a small silver lighter. "I think we have a few extra Molotov cocktails," he said, pointing to the large duffel bag over Priest's shoulder.

Priest reached into his bag and produced a small beer bottle filled with motor oil, gasoline and a long cloth fuse. He tossed it with a smile to Zeke. "The honor is yours, mate."

Clicking open the lighter, Zeke stepped down off the light pole and lit the fuse. Running into the street yelling, he lifted the explosive high above his head. Rearing back, he tossed the bottle with all his strength at a small jewelry store window. The bottle crashed through the glass, shattering on the floor inside. Flames erupted and quickly began to engulf the store. With a scream of victory, Zeke pulled several items out through the broken window as alarms blared and returned to the group. He passed out the rings and necklaces among the women of the coven and grabbed another cocktail from Priest.

Zeke lit the fuse and tossed it.

* * *

She stirred in her creaky chair for the first time in days. Her skeletal fingers scraped against the wooden arms of the chair as she slowly stood up. Not too fast, she warned herself. It had been almost a full year since the last time she tried this, but it was a special occasion. Everything was beginning to fall into place and align in her favor. Soon, she would be free of this wretched, broken-down hovel, free to walk under the silvery glow of the moonlight again and bask in its glory. It had been far too long.

She stopped as she felt a trickle of blood run down from her forehead over what was left of her nose. Lifting her hand, she wiped away the blood and applied pressure. Her skin had become so thin and brittle, it could barely contain her bones anymore. Slowly lowering her hand, she looked at the deep red substance on her fingertips. She fought the overwhelming urge to lick it off, as it would do her no good. Only one thing could save her now, and it was the very thing about to be delivered to her.

She stood in front of a window looking out over the sandy landscape. It was hot and miserable here, making it very difficult to rest during the days, but this was what her body in its weakened condition needed. She couldn't survive in any other climate, but soon, none of that would matter and she would be restored to her former glory. All she needed was patience. Something she had proved to have an excess of in the past thirty years.

Chapter Two

"Nice of you to finally join us," Nick Bishop said. His smile faded as he watched his team leader enter the room.

Cane walked into their office and sat down at his desk without retort. His face was stern and focused as if he were deep in thought. The black clothes he wore obviously reflected his mood, as did the dark pair of sunglasses hiding his eyes. Glancing down at the stack of file folders on his desk, he lifted one off the top and flipped it open. He began to chew through the report inside.

The entire team—what was left of it—had already assembled this morning, and for some time, had been sitting at their desks chatting over coffee and doughnuts. Nick Bishop, the youngest member of the Office of Paranormal Research, sat to Cane's right. He was clad in a red and black v-neck shirt, a pair of dark slacks and his trademark leather jacket. He was usually clean-shaven, but this morning, he had opted for a more "rugged" look. Dawn, however, thought he just looked scruffy.

Dawn Lassiter was to Cane's immediate left. She was leaning back in her chair with her legs crossed on the desk. Behind Cane and Chairman Thomas Weiss, Dawn had the most seniority of anyone in the company. She had been there almost from the very beginning. Today, she was wearing a white blouse and a dark blue skirt that hung just past her knees. Her long, curly dark hair was pulled up behind her head, allowing only a few wisps to frame her slender face. She took a long sip from her coffee mug and returned it to her lap where she cradled it with both hands. She smiled at her friend. "Doughnut for your thoughts."

Cane slowly looked up from the file at Dawn. A quizzical look passed over his face. "I'm sorry, what did you say?"

Dawn pulled her legs off the desk and swiveled to face Cane. "Are you okay this morning?"

Cane nodded. "I'm fine. Just didn't get a lot of sleep last night."

"A woman?" Bishop prodded.

Pulling off his sunglasses, Cane rubbed his eyes with the heels of his hands. "You could say that."

"Tell us," Dawn said after another sip from her cup.

"It's nothing," Cane assured them, "just bad dreams. Let's get to work," he said, quickly changing the subject.

"We received a call from Lydia this morning," Bishop started.

"How is she?" Cane asked, mentally scolding himself for forgetting to call her.

"Everything in Seattle is good, and she says Kelley is recovering nicely," Bishop reported. "She may be able to rejoin the team soon."

Kelley Windel, the fourth member of Cane's team, was currently under the care of Lydia Katran, a Wiccan High Priestess. Earlier in the year, Kelley had actually been declared dead, then her body had been possessed by a powerful group of Witches known as "The Abydos Triad", effectively bringing her back to life. After the spirit of the Witch was exorcised from Kelley's body, she fell into a state of

28

shock that could only be cured magically as her mind and body began to fuse back together. It had been almost six months now, and she was still in Lydia's care. Cane wondered if he would ever have his teammate back, but he didn't want to rush things. Her health was much more important than anything else.

"That's good news," Cane said. A shadow of a smile passed over his face, but vanished as quickly as it came. "Did you get to talk to her?"

"No," Bishop said regretfully. "She was in meditation with Lydia's coven at the time. Lydia promised she would have Kelley call us the first chance she had."

Cane nodded.

"Lydia also said she spoke to Hayden yesterday," Bishop added.

Cane leaned back in his chair. "How's the head of our first branch office holding up?"

Bishop smiled. "She said he's having a blast. He and Django are investigating a Bigfoot sighting just outside Seattle. He showed Lydia the plaster molds he made of the footprints he found," Bishop chuckled.

Cane finally let loose with a full smile. "Chairman Weiss is even happy with their progress reports. They've been doing some good work around Seattle. I'm glad the Chairman took my advice and started a branch there."

"I think it was more than your advice that made the Chairman make up his mind," Dawn reminded him. After all, she was the one who originally proposed the idea.

"So noted." Cane laughed. He had almost called in sick today, but now he was glad he came. "Let's get to work," he said for the second time.

Dawn sat aside her coffee and scooted up to her desk. Pulling a plain yellow notepad from her top desk drawer, she scribbled the date and time at the top. Bishop, much less organized, dug into the small pack he kept in his bottom drawer until he successfully fished out a steno notebook with a black pen stuffed into the spiral binding. Flipping it open, he leafed through several pages until he came to a blank one. Setting it flat on his desk, he propped himself up on his elbows.

Cane dropped the file folder flat on his desk and lifted out several pages of reports. Handing one each to Dawn and Bishop, he kept one for himself. "What we're looking at here," he said addressing his team, "appears to be poltergeist activity. If you'll turn to page—"

"Wow, look at that place," Bishop was already a step ahead of him. "It looks like a tornado hit it."

Cane nodded as he looked over the photos of the damage. "This is a small condominium in Georgetown. Two separate units, but only one has reported any activity. As you can see from the photos, the place is trashed."

"Witness interview?" Dawn asked.

"No," Cane said slowly. "Jill Hodge's team took these photos last week. They were called away on another case before they could complete the investigation."

"So it was dropped in our lap," Bishop added.

"Essentially," Cane agreed. "I want to check

the place out this afternoon. Do we have anything else scheduled?"

Dawn checked her day planner. "Nope. We're free."

"Good," Cane said, standing up. "I want this one done by the book. Bish, you research the location, see if it has a history. Dawn, why don't you run a background check on the current occupants? Find out if they show up in our database, or anyone else's for that matter."

"You thinking telekinesis?" Dawn asked.

Cane rubbed his chin. "It's possible. They could be causing the manifestations and not even know it. Either way, I don't want to walk into this place blind. I'll start rounding up the standard equipment from storage." He looked at Dawn and then Bishop. He knew he couldn't do this without them. "Let's get on this one."

* * *

Wind was whipping through the streets of Budapest, Hungary. Night had fallen several hours ago, leaving only the moon and lampposts to light the streets. Landlocked deep in the heart of central Europe, Hungary was one of the more prosperous republics and the streets and buildings of its capital city reflected that. Ancient castles, citadels built during the Russian occupation, and monuments still dominated the skyline of much of the city, as tall spires reached toward the heavens. As with most cities of this age, the old world was butting up against the new, creating a unique mixture of architecture and culture that could be found nowhere else in the world. An amber hue dominated the city's nights, as yellow lights reflected off worn ancient structures.

He stood on the far side of the Elisabeth Bridge, looking over the Danube River shrouded in darkness. On the far side, he could see the Buda Castle, stretching off magnificently just above the bank. The yellow tinted lights of the bridge and castle were reflecting in the calm waters of the river, creating a murky double of the city. This was his first visit to Budapest and he hoped it would not be his last, but he was here on business. All else was secondary.

He was a Wraith. It was their job to blend into the shadows, to make the darkness their own. They had, over time, become as much denizens of the night as the quarry they hunted—a result of their dedication. Dressed almost entirely in gray and black, he worked alone, a dark rider on a pale horse. He wiped a bit of dirt off the black, wool trench coat he was wearing, making sure not to expose its precious cargo. He was part of the Gwyliad Wriaeth—translated in English as the "White Guard"—an ancient Celtic order of warriors. An elite sect of hunters trained to fight back the darkness encroaching across the land. In addition to multiple fighting techniques, each Wraith was a devout practitioner of the ancient Celtic religion. It was an effective combination against the warriors of the undead.

He was Brother Marcus Specter of the White Guard. His body and mind had been honed into a weapon as lethal as the wooden stake he kept in his jacket. His entire life consisted of training to fight the creatures of the night: vampires. He was the ultimate machine of destruction, even more so than the killers he tracked. He peered out at the world through glistening blue eyes that hinted at the great power within, but never gave away too much. In the tradition of his order, his dark brown hair was cropped close to his head. A single long braid hung from the right sideburn and was swept behind his ear; it had a specific set of colored bands around it, signifying the completion of a training regimen or the death of a vampire. Specter's braid, which hung to the center of his chest, had fifty-six colored bands on it. They represented the number of vampires he had killed thus far in his career. It was an impressive number, even for a Wraith. A Wraith usually didn't live long enough to record twenty kills.

Specter glanced out over the glimmering Danube River. Over the past few nights, several bodies had been recovered from the river in this area. He theorized that his quarry had been killing in the city and dumping the bodies here to dispose of them. Specter had been tracking this particular vampire for three months now. The trail had started in northern France, wound down through Spain and finally led here. Most vampires, he had learned through experience, liked to take up roots in one place and settle into a routine. It was the last remnant of their human side showing. People needed routines to make sense of their lives—monsters did not. Specter knew he was tracking a monster.

He glanced up at the partially covered moon,

still no sign of his target. Reaching into his jacket pocket, he pulled out a pack of filterless cigarettes. He shook his head as he pulled one out with his teeth. He had acquired this disgusting habit some time ago while working in the field. It was generally frowned on for a Wraith to put a harmful substance, especially a drug, into their body. It was said to take the edge off, and that went against principles of their training, but Marcus didn't care. It made him feel human…something severely lacking in his life and training. Producing a small pack of matches, he struck one and took a long drag. Tossing the spent match away, he moved away from his vantage point toward several benches aligned next to the river.

Sitting down, he crossed his legs and slipped one of his arms over the back of the bench. Flicking the ashes off his cigarette, he took another hit, inhaling the thick smoke. He blew it quickly out the corner of his mouth as he watched the bank of the river. The opposite side was heavily populated. A museum sat below Buda Castle, its exterior showing off the Roman influence in its architecture. Several tall columns stood at the top of a set of stairs that helped protect the entrance. In times of war, that would have been a spectacular vantage point to hold off invading armies, but Specter knew it was purely decorative having been built less than sixty years ago.

Stop.

He held his breath and focused. There was movement just below him. Specter dropped his cigarette to the ground and crushed it out with the toe of his shoe. Exhaling the last puff, he began to lean forward, his eyes intently focused on a bit of brush about three feet from the river bank. Resting his elbows on his knees, he watched and waited. This was the moment he had been waiting for. He started to reach his hand into his jacket as he stood.

Snap.

His heart sank. Specter knew in an instant it was behind him. Spinning around with all his strength, Specter drew his wooden stake and came face to face with a gleaming pair of white fangs. With speed and strength far beyond a human's, the vampire blocked Specter's attack and was upon him.

Leaping over the bench, the vampire wrapped his clawed fingers around Specter's shoulder and pushed. The two spilled to the ground, but the vampire was still in control. Springing to his feet with superhuman speed and agility, he kicked Specter hard in the ribs sending him sailing into a nearby bench. The force of the impact shattered the wooden bench, leaving Specter lying in a pile of debris.

Specter's mind and focus remained sharp despite the pain. Rolling away from the jagged hunks of wood, he snapped up onto the balls of his feet and focused on the vampire. It had climbed up on Specter's original seat and was perched on the back. He cocked his head slightly and smiled at Specter. He was thin, much thinner than Specter, and looked no older than eighteen years. He was clad in black leather and a white t-shirt and was wearing a pair of round, rose-tinted sunglasses. His dark, curly hair hung just below his chiseled chin.

"Specter," the vampire hissed. "If I had known it was you the Guard sent after me, I would have come out to play much sooner."

Marcus stood from his crouch and pulled off his jacket revealing the black Kevlar body armor beneath designed to look like a human chest with defined pectoral areas and abdominal muscles. His trusty wooden stake, complete with handmade metal hilt, sat in a holster to the left of his armor. His arms were bare from the shoulder down, exposing the swirling pattern of his black tribal tattoos which terminated just above his elbows. He nodded once at the vampire. "Ash," he said slowly.

"Why did they send you after me?" Ash asked, his fangs barely visible beneath his lips. "Did they hope I would finish you this time?"

Specter remained silent, his intense eyes focused on Ash.

Ash stood up on the back of the bench, perfectly balanced. "Not in a talkative mood? That's fine by me." He spread his arms wide. "Let's play." With one fluid motion, he crouched again and leapt from his perch.

Specter was ready for the attack. Leaning to the left, he whipped his right arm up to deflect. Swinging across with his left, he hit Ash squarely in the temple as he careened by. Ash hit the ground, skidding to a stop. He lifted his head just as his blood began to gush from the wound. He glanced at Specter in anger as he felt the inch deep cut that ran from his temple back into his hair. Specter smiled and lifted his left hand displaying the black ring on his index finger. A sharp, jagged barb protruded from it.

Specter laughed. "New toy."

Ash, not amused, charged again. He stopped flatfooted and threw a combination of punches. Specter blocked or dodged all but one, which landed just left of his chin. His head snapped back as stars twinkled briefly in his eyes. Recovering, he ducked the followup and retaliated. Dropping his head down, he punched Ash hard in the gut, doubling the vampire over. Specter straightened up as quickly as he could, head butting Ash. The vampire reeled backwards trying to regain his composure. Specter pressed the attack. He delivered a vicious right left combination to Ash's face, then finished with a solid kick to his kneecap. Ash's leg buckled backwards. Specter could hear tendons snapping as the vampire crumbled to the ground. Specter was simply too much for him.

Ash cried out in pain as Specter hovered over him. "I've had a little practice since we first met, Ash," Specter admitted with a note of satisfaction underpinning his voice. "You never had a chance." He drew his stake.

Ash looked up at the Wraith with fear in his eyes. He had lived for one hundred and fifty years, and it was all going to end here. "Please," he whimpered. "Don't do this, Specter. I don't want to die." Ash held up his open hands in an act of surrender. "Please...."

Specter shook his head. "Show a little dignity, Ash." With a move almost too fast for the human eye to follow, he flipped the stake around in his hand and drove it deep into the vampire's heart and took a step back. Ash's hands wrapped around the metal hilt of the stake as his head fell back. An inhuman scream escaped his lips as blue flame engulfed his body from the inside out. In a matter of seconds, only a pile of ashes remained while a few red-hot cinders floated on the wind.

"Fifty-seven."

Retrieving his stake, Specter pushed it firmly into its holster and lifted his discarded jacket. Turning away, he let out a long breath and set off into the night.

* * *

Three hulking men stood in front of a large metal door, its frame littered with locks and chains of every kind. The gleam of the new gold and silver metals looked odd against the backdrop of the rundown surroundings featuring holes in the drywall and trash and debris scattered about the wooden floor. This place, long since abandoned, was a former meat-processing plant deep in the heart of the industrial district of London. Large meat hooks still hung from the ceiling, swaying lightly in the drafty conditions. The wooden floor, built before many health standards were placed in effect, still bore multiple bloodstains under the hooks and around the wooden doors. It had been forgotten, much to the delight of its current occupants, a coven of modern vampires. They had set up shop in the two-story building almost two years ago, transforming it into their lair. Multi-colored graffiti marked the once drab gray walls and all the windows were painted black. Candles, many burned down, were melted to every free surface in the building.

This coven, by contrast, was much, much larger than Zeke's. Consisting of well over fifty members, this was the dominant coven of the area. They had taken to calling themselves "The Order of the Crimson Moon"; in reference to the blood moon—a lunar eclipse—that was the sacred night for many of their rituals and gatherings. The Order of the Crimson Moon was led by a woman known as Ice. She was so named because of her bleached white skin and perfectly white hair that hung to her lower back. The only natural color left in her face was her slightly bluish lips, and deep, emerald, green eyes. By candlelight, she was said to look like a ghost hovering in the gloom. She wore only shades of white and green, matching her eyes and adding to her namesake.

Ice was at times a ruthless leader, while at others she could be one of the most creative and compassionate of the coven. It was said she had actually killed two members of her coven in a fit of rage. The rumor also held she still had the skulls hidden within her private sanctuary inside the plant. Whether this was true was never proven, but somehow, the rumor had propagated and become a full-fledged legend among the London vampire community. Unless you were a member of Ice's coven, or were trying to get recruited, she was one to avoid.

She appeared out of the darkness carrying an unlit white candle in her hand. She moved lithely across the floor, never making a sound, toward her three guards. Stopping just shy of them, she pursed her lips exposing the tips of her porcelain fangs. Leaning over slightly, she dipped the wick of her candle into the flame of another's and held it up. She took another step. "How's our guest?" she breathed.

The first guard was a tall black man wearing a knee-length leather trench coat. He smiled. "Still unconscious."

"And still restrained," the second guard, a man wearing entirely black denim added. "I don't think he'll be able to break loose before the ritual, Mistress."

Ice's eyes narrowed. "What do you know of the ritual?"

The denim clad guard knew he had misspoken. "Just what I've heard in rumors, Mistress," he stammered, addressing her formally. Even though he was a full foot taller than Ice, she still intimidated him. It was not so much Ice herself, but with a snap of her fingers, she could easily turn the other two guards on him. They were both his friends, but they would fight him with the same savage intensity they would show anyone else.

Each guard was handpicked by Ice for their loyalty, strength and intelligence. On their foreheads, just above their brows, each bore a small crescent moon tattoo that not only signified they were among the higher echelon of the Order, but that they were Ice's personal guards. There were less than ten in the entire Order, and in most cases, they accompanied her. In this case, however, they were guarding something much more important than any of them realized.

40

"I know only what I have heard, Mistress," the guard stammered.

"And what is that?" Ice hissed.

"That the man we are guarding is to be used in tonight's ritual. Why or how, I don't know."

Ice stared at the guard for a long moment. He felt as if she was peering into his very soul with her green eyes. He tried to remain dignified, but a bead of sweat rolling down his forehead gave him away. Ice took a long breath and patted the man on the shoulder. "Very good."

The guard felt a wave of relief.

"Don't speak of this to anyone," Ice warned. "This is far too important to be lost on account of loose lips. That man in there," she pointed to the metal door, "will change all our lives. Remember that."

Each man nodded slowly once, respectfully.

Turning away, Ice blew out her candle and retreated into the darkness, satisfied her wishes would be met. Tonight would be a turning point for the Order of the Crimson Moon. Everything would change, and she would be remembered as the one who brought it about. Her name would long be remembered in the annals of Modern Vampires.

Chapter Three

"There's no ghost here," Bishop said as he stared in awe at the condo.

Essentially one big house, it was divided down the middle, making two separate units. Both had identical entrances, the same square patch of green grass and accompanying one car garage. The right unit was in immaculate condition. The grass, flowers, and condo itself looked beautifully maintained—the pride of the owner, or renter in this case, was easily self-evident. The left unit was another story all together. The yard, with sporadic dead spots and large patches of crab grass, was strewn with children's toys and gaudy lawn ornaments. Several tall yellow plastic sunflowers lined the sidewalk, while a herd of lawn gnomes had taken up residence below the front window. Several whirligigs clacked noisily on the roof above them.

"How do you know?" Dawn asked in bemusement.

"Because I wouldn't be caught dead here," Bishop laughed.

Cane groaned at the horrible joke. Moving past his companions, he headed for the front door. Each had a small pack slung over their shoulder containing the various pieces of equipment they would require for the investigation. The contents included the now standard Electromagnetic Field (EMF) Meter, thirty-five millimeter camera, flashlight, digital thermometer, air ion counter and a fresh notepad. These were the traditional tools of ghost hunters. The EMF Meter was the most commonly used tool as most hunters now believed that ghosts were no more than hallucinations caused by dense electromagnetic fields conflicting with the brain. This, however, was not the stance of the Office of Paranormal Research.

Cane stepped up on the front stoop and raised his hand. He paused with his closed fist in front of the door, unwilling to knock.

"What's the matter?' Dawn asked from just behind him.

"I was just thinking," he said slowly, "if the outside of the house is any indication of what we'll find inside, we may never be able to accurately document any phenomenon."

Dawn smiled. "We'll just have to risk it." She reached past Cane and knocked on the door.

Cane cocked his head and shot her a dirty look.

They heard a voice from inside yelling for them to hold on. Each listened intently to the various bangs and thuds as the resident approached the door. There was one final thud just inside the door followed by a muted streak of profanity. Bishop bit his lip to stop the laughter. The door finally opened revealing an elderly woman in a light blue jumpsuit that would have been more at home in the 1970's. Cane watched in amazement as a small candelabrum whizzed past her head. The woman paid it no attention.

Cane lifted the small notepad he was carrying and flipped it open. "Good morning. Are you Miss..." he ran his finger down his page of notes quickly, then stopped, "Jenkins?"

The woman nodded. "I'm Eleanor Jenkins."

Cane extended his hand. "My name is Zachary Cane, and I'm with the Office of Paranormal Research. These are my associates," he motioned behind him, "Dawn Lassiter and Nick Bishop. Are you the one who originally reported the supernatural activity in the home?"

Eleanor smiled and shook her head. "No, that was my daughter. I'm just here babysitting the grandkids today."

"Do you mind if we come in and take a look around?" Cane asked.

Eleanor stepped outside and closed the door behind her. She lowered her voice. "Are you here to get rid of that damned ghost?"

"We're here to investigate," Cane answered, "but we'll do what we can."

The woman craned her neck around as if to check if she was being eavesdropped on. She pressed her lips nervously together as she placed a hand on Cane's shoulder. "We've tried everything short of an exorcism. He won't go away."

"'He', ma'am?" Bishop asked.

"Raul," Eleanor whispered, "the ghost."

"The ghost's name is Raul?" Dawn asked as a wisp of amusement grew on her face.

Eleanor nodded. "He's told us so."

"Has," Bishop took a moment to roll the name around in his mouth, "Raul presented a danger to any of your family?"

"No," Eleanor said slowly, "he's just a pain in the ass mostly."

She heard one of her grandchildren screaming.

Turning around, she pushed through the front door and charged into the living room with Cane and his team in tow. The four stopped just inside the living room. Awe immediately set in for the team as they watched a small boy, he couldn't have been more than nine or ten years old, hovering motionlessly in the air. The toys he had just been playing with were orbiting around him. In the far corner, hidden behind a green recliner, sat a small girl—his little sister—curled up with her teddy bear. She was obviously the source of the scream. Bishop flipped his pack off his shoulder and unzipped it. He quickly dug out his camera, EMF Meter and digital recorder. Handing the camera to Dawn, he flipped on the EMF Meter and recorder while taking a step toward the boy.

Eleanor pushed him aside and walked right up to the boy. In a huff, she placed her hands on her hips. "Raul," she said firmly, "put Jack down."

Dawn lifted her camera and quickly began snapping photos while Bishop logged several readings.

Eleanor stomped her foot. "Raul," she said again, "we've told you not to play with the children." She watched as her grandson remained paralyzed in the air. Eleanor became angry. She pointed over her shoulder. "Do you see these people? They're here to get rid of you!"

A sinking feeling hit Cane as he quickly lifted his hands and patted the air. "Hold on, we're just researchers," he corrected.

Jack suddenly fell to the floor in a heap with his toys. A very succinct growl could be heard rolling throughout the house. The boy looked up at his grandmother with fear in his eyes. Running forward with a speed surprising for her age, Eleanor scooped her grandkids off the floor and headed for the door.

Cane watched in amazement as Eleanor raced outside and shut the door behind her. "I guess we're on our own," he concluded after a moment.

Dawn nodded. "I think Raul's pissed."

A metal skillet whipped past Cane's head and slammed against the living room wall. The entire team hit the deck. "What was your first clue?" Cane asked sarcastically.

Bishop held up his EMF Meter. "These readings are incredible!" The yellow plastic device was ripped from his hand by an unseen force. "Hey!" He watched it lift up into the air, spin around twice, and finally disintegrate before his eyes. "Those things are expensive, Raul!" Bishop yelled.

"Don't talk to it," Dawn warned.

"Why not?"

Above their heads, a vortex of random objects was beginning to form. They watched as pictures were ripped from the wall and knickknacks were uprooted from their displays. The vortex began to swirl faster.

Dawn pointed above her head. "That's why."

* * *

Zeke and his coven stood shrouded in darkness. They looked down onto the abandoned plant that housed the Order of the Crimson Moon from a nearby rooftop. Zeke was perched on the ledge with a pair of small spyglasses scanning from window to window. He let out a long breath and set the glasses aside. He turned back to his coven.

"Are you sure they have it in there?" Wrack asked.

Zeke nodded. "My sources are reliable." Was he trying to convince the other coven members, or himself? Even he was unsure. All he knew was that he wanted this. It was everything he dreamed about. He glanced up at Priest. "How's our supply of cocktails?"

Priest checked his duffel bag quickly. "After our little party downtown, we're at about half our original supply. That should be enough, though."

Zeke smiled. "More than enough." He took a few steps away from the coven, then sharply turned. He looked back over at his friends. "I can't lie to you," he said after a moment, "I expect people to die tonight. Be it members of the other coven or us, I know we're not all going to make it back. I will completely understand if any of you choose not to accompany me. If we succeed, we will have the one thing we all dream about, but if we fail, we could spend the rest of our lives as fugitives." He took a breath. "It's up to you. Are you with me?"

Ina stepped forward and wrapped her arms around Zeke. "I would follow you into the very flames of hell if you asked me to."

He returned the hug then pulled away. "Thank you." Zeke turned his attention to the rest of the coven.

Priest stepped forward. "This little party wouldn't be very fun without the cocktails, and since I'm carrying them, I guess I'm in."

"Me too," Seraph sounded off without hesitation.

Each turned to look at Wrack. She was biting her fingernails as she weighed the question. She was already a fugitive from the law. She wasn't sure if she wanted to complicate matters. Taking a deep breath, she lifted her face to the sky. If they succeeded and the rumors were true, she would never have to worry again. If they weren't...Wrack stopped herself. She had to believe. She returned her attention to her coven mates. "I'm in."

Zack reached out and patted Wrack on the shoulder with a smile on his face. "We face them together," he said with a hint of excitement in his voice.

"Can I make a personal request?" Ina asked.

Zeke nodded.

"If anyone sees that bitch, Ice, kill her on the spot."

The comment caught Zeke off-guard for a moment, but he quickly began laughing. "What did she do to you?"

Ina brushed off the question. "It's personal. Just trust me, she needs to die."

Zeke nodded. "We'll see what we can do. Does everyone know the plan?" He waited for each to acknowledge. "All right, we're in business. Let's get to where we need to be. Tonight, we become!"

Splitting up, Zeke, Ina and Wrack made their way down a fire escape to street level with several Molotov cocktails each, while Seraph and Priest remained on the rooftop with the remainder. Each knew the plan inside and out. Several nights during the previous week it was all they had talked about. Priest had even gone so far as to scout the plant in the early hours of the morning when the others were sleeping. He knew exactly what he needed to hit, and if the plan held true, when.

Zeke, Ina, and Wrack stood outside the plant's main entrance. It was marked with a fading crescent moon just above the door. To each side, there were large windows. These were their targets. If Zeke's information held true, their objective would be in no danger from the napalm bombs. Zeke took a step forward and turned around. He nodded at Priest and Seraph.

Priest smiled. Reaching down, he took the hand of his lover, Seraph. "Ready, love?"

Seraph giggled. Lifting a bottle, she lit the fuse and handed it to Priest. "I've never been more ready."

Priest cocked the bottle back with his arm and released. He watched it sail through the air toward the plant's façade, flames leaping off the fuse. He lifted his arms into the air to signal a goal as the bottle crashed through the large window left of the door. Immediately, flames erupted inside, releasing an orange glow through the shattered window.

Zeke tossed his bottle through the second window at the same time. Inside, he could hear screams and frantic shouting as the flames spread. Reaching into his leather jacket, he pulled two small, white buds out and slid them into his ears. Tapping the play button on his MP3 player, he waited for the first song to load up. As he watched the flames erupt from the windows, his ears were assaulted by a cacophony of dark lyrics, heavy drumbeats and buzzing electric guitars. Lifting his sunglasses from his shirt collar, he slowly slid them on. He was ready.

The front door slammed open as dozens of Crimson Moon coven members spilled out in terror. Zeke watched as one, totally engulfed in flames, staggered out the door and fell into a nearby puddle in an effort to put himself out. Fire rained down around them as Priest and Seraph bombarded the rival coven members with cocktails. Lighting another cocktail, he, Ina, and Wrack charged into the plant. Fire raged on all sides of them as the napalm had spread across the wooden floors and up the walls. Three men dressed in black were frantically trying to put out the fires with blankets and buckets of water. Zeke unloaded his bottle in the middle of them. The glass smashed on the floor and the homemade napalm inside splattered, instantly catching fire. The flames engulfed the three men. Ina spun and tossed her bottle in the opposite direction cutting off that section of the building. Quickly moving past the three screaming men, Zack led his group toward their target.

On the rooftop above, Priest and Seraph were completing their end of the plan. Priest pointed down at a group standing outside the plant watching in horror as it burned. Seraph nodded, and with an evil cackle, she launched a cocktail in their direction. Burning napalm shot out in every direction like water spilling from a glass. The group screamed as they fell backward to avoid the fire. Priest launched a second volley at the front door. It was their job to keep anyone who came outside from heading back in, they knew Zeke, Ina, and Wrack would be up to their ass in enough angry coven members without having more coming in.

Wrack spun around a corner and skidded to a stop. Her eyes widened as she saw at least six men and women charging her direction. Tossing her cocktail straight up in the air, she backpedaled quickly to stop Zeke and Ina. Turning around, she pushed both to the floor. The bottle shattered against the floor, but in Wrack's haste, she had neglected to light the fuse. Unlit napalm splattered over the rival coven members, but didn't stop their charge. Zeke looked up to see them bearing down angrily on them. Thinking quickly, he pulled his silver Zippo from his pocket and lit it. Rolling up onto his knees, he flipped the lighter at the attackers. The first two men lit up like torches. They both began to flail wildly, accidentally catching three more of their companions on fire.

Zeke and his team took the opportunity and raced around the pyre. Zeke patted Wrack on the back as they ran. "Next time, make sure you light it."

Coming around another corner, they stopped. Rows of tall, white candles lined the entire hall and a long, black carpet had been laid down the center. The entire area was bathed in a beautiful yellow orange light that seemed to wash over the hall like the tide. At the end of it, Zeke spotted his quarry—a large metal door with a Red Crescent moon painted on it. Two large, wooden tables on either side of the door had been arranged with dozens of white candles and black cloths that spilled onto the floor. Even the rusty meat hooks hanging from the ceiling were put to use. A wooden circle with more candles hung from each. The room was unguarded.

Zeke turned to look at his two companions. Each felt a sense of awe at the sight, but a strong feeling of foreboding also hung over them. "This doesn't feel right," he finally stated.

Ina nodded. "Agreed."

"Maybe the guards left to help put out the fires," Wrack offered. "That makes sense, doesn't it?"

Zeke thought for a moment, "It does." He took a deep breath. "We've come this far…."

The three, walking side by side, moved down the black carpet toward the door. They were cautious, each holding a cocktail tightly in their hands. Anticipation set in as they neared the door. Zeke stopped his music and popped the buds from his ears. Sliding them back into his jacket, he strained his ears. Ina, as she brushed a bit of her hair out of her face, was also on high alert, but she was beginning to suffer from the heat in the room. The hundreds of candles had turned the hall into a furnace with no ventilation. As they neared the door, Wrack tightened her grip on her bottle and held her lighter at the ready. This was it.

Zeke stopped and lifted his hand. Slowly, he placed it on the metal door. The cool metal comforted him. Taking a breath, he pressed his ear to the door and listened. Inside, he could hear nothing. Perhaps the door was too thick, he thought. He took a step back and examined the door. This was obviously the entrance to the plant's old freezer. There were no windows on the door, only a round thermometer that showed the temperature inside. He glanced at the reading. It was slightly below room temperature, but nowhere near what the freezer could handle. Along the right side of the door were several newly installed locks. This puzzled Zeke. The Crimson Moon coven had gone to great lengths to secure this door, but all the locks were open.

"What do you think?" he asked.

Wrack shrugged. "This is weird."

"Perhaps our plan worked even better than we'd hoped," Ina offered. "This is exactly what we wanted."

Zeke sighed, "I know, but—"

Ina didn't wait for his argument. Reaching around Zeke, she pulled the freezer door open.

The cold, gray steel of the door was replicated inside on the floors and walls. The freezer was immense, measuring at least twenty-five feet long. It had been polished so every surface shined and showed a reflection. In the center of the room stood what looked like a concrete sarcophagus. It was flat gray and appeared to be extremely thick. Taking a step inside, Ina scanned the room, then motioned for the others to join her.

"I think we've found what we were looking for," she said encouragingly. She started to move toward the sarcophagus, when a hand grabbed her arm. She spun around to see Zeke stopping her.

"Wait," he said softly. "We all go together."

A moment of rage flared inside her, but she

quickly let it go. "What's wrong with you? This is all you've ever wanted, and now it's right in front of you! How can you be so calm?"

"I'm just as excited as you are, but we still need to be cautious. Who knows what kind of idiotic booby traps Ice has set up in here?" Zeke glanced up at the sarcophagus. "Let's take it slow—together."

The trio moved slowly along the sarcophagus. Ina estimated it was at least seven feet long and probably four feet at its widest point. The top of it was slightly above her shoulders. As they reached the top, each had to take a moment to catch their breath. Wrack took an uneasy step back, but Zeke and Ina held their positions. Jutting from an opening in the top was the head of a creature. Its features were mostly humanoid, but it was unlike anything they had ever seen, with skin a solid shade of gray and appearing smooth and shiny, much like that of a shark's. The nose was nonexistent; only two flat triangular holes remained. The eyes were closed under heavy eyelids, while the ears were slightly larger and pointed. The creature's head and neck were hairless. Its mouth was twisted up into a hateful sneer exposing its gleaming white fangs. A second slab of concrete that had been slipped over its forehead was holding down the head.

"What the hell is that?" Wrack asked.

"It's a vampire. A real one."

The three spun around to see a similar looking creature pressed against the wall just inside the door dressed entirely in white. The creature's eyes were an eerie shade of gold. Two streaks of blood were running down its chin. It was cowering. It was afraid.

"Who are you?" Zeke asked. He squeezed his bottle a little tighter in his hand. "Or, what are you?"

The creature glanced down at its open hands. "I had no idea I looked like this. Do I look exactly like he does?"

Zeke nodded. "Pretty close."

The creature turned to face the wall. "As you can see, I don't have a reflection anymore."

The situation became instantly clear in Zeke's mind. "I guess the question I should be asking is 'who were you'?"

The creature turned back to face Zeke. "Ice." She took a step toward the trio and her image began to change. Like a ripple in a pond, her gray skin was replaced by the more familiar white of Ice's. As the ripple passed over her face, the distinguished visage of the woman appeared, as did her long white hair. She stopped. "What just happened? I feel very strange now, as if my entire body is tingling."

"You look like Ice again," Zeke offered. "You just changed right before our eyes."

Ice glanced down at her hands again and a smile crossed her face. "Wonderful." Her composure and confidence quickly returned.

Ina had heard enough. "What the hell is going on here?"

Ice smiled at the sight of her old friend. "It's good to see you again, Ina. How've you been?"

"Answer my question," Ina pushed.

Ice's smile faded. "Don't feign ignorance, my

dear. You know exactly what I did, because you came here to do the same thing. I drank from the vampire, and I am now one myself. It was really that simple. I feel…powerful."

Zeke stepped forward. "Are you going to stop us?"

"Surprisingly," Ice began, "no, but understand that I could."

"Why?" Zeke asked.

"I'm really not sure," Ice admitted. "I have this nagging voice in the back of my mind that says, 'let them drink'."

Zeke smiled broadly. "Will you show us what you did?"

Ice nodded. Moving around the sarcophagus, she lifted a wine glass and a razorblade. Moving to Zeke's side, she handed him both items. "Just slit the vampire's throat and catch the blood in the glass. Simple enough."

"How much do I drink?" Zeke asked nervously as he eyed the immobilized vampire in front of him.

Ice smiled and licked her lips. "As much as you can."

"How did your coven come into the possession of this guy anyway?" Zeke asked, nervously wasting time.

"We became aware of a pattern of killings around London that looked suspiciously like a vampire was committing them," Ice answered. "We figured out this gentleman's pattern, ambushed and drugged him with elephant tranquilizers, end of story. Now drink." She pushed his hand containing the razorblade toward the vampire's throat. "He's

56

out cold," Ice added. "Just do it. Or do you not want to be one of us?"

Zeke steeled his nerves as Ina and Wrack looked on. Dropping down to one knee, he held the razorblade just above the vampire's throat. Looking from the creature to Ice, he took a deep breath. Turning back, he pressed the blade into the soft flesh just below the creature's jaw and pulled. With one swift motion, he laid an artery open. Blood spilled from the gaping wound. Its consistency was not that of normal blood, but more like water flowing smoothly. Zeke lifted up the glass to catch the precious red fluid. He watched in amazement as the glass quickly filled to the rim. Standing up, he took a step back and held the glass up.

"It's better when it's warm," Ice warned him.

Lifting the glass to his lips, Zeke closed his eyes. He could feel the warmth of the blood radiating from the sides of the glass. It was now or never. Tilting the glass back, he opened his mouth and drank deeply. The fluid stung his mouth and throat as he swallowed it down. It felt like thousands of tiny daggers were punching into his flesh and then branching out like burning roots into his body. Lifting the glass up, Zeke felt the last bit of blood splash into his mouth. Ice pulled the glass away from him and set it on the ground. He couldn't tell what she was saying, but Zeke could see her mouth moving. The world started to become hazy, and in that moment, he felt Ina and Wrack each grab one of his arms. The three fell to the ground as the first wave of pain hit Zeke.

Ina watched as Zeke doubled over. His skin felt

hot to the touch as they tried to restrain him. Zeke writhed in agony as he cried out. His speech was incoherent, but the pain was easily evident.

Ina turned to Ice angrily. "What have you done to him?"

Ice laughed. "Only what he wanted."

Zeke ripped his arms free of their grasp, but they quickly had him again. His back arched and his mouth shot open. Inside, they could see his pristine porcelain fangs. Ina watched in horror as a crack suddenly appeared on his right fang. There was a sound much like metal scraping against dry ice coming from his mouth. The high-pitched whine grew in intensity until the porcelain shattered. Ina watched in amazement as new fangs quickly grew in place of the lost fake ones. Ina placed her hand on his head and ran it back over his hair to try and comfort him, but only succeeded in pulling away a large handful. She tossed the hair aside in horror as the rest began to fall away in clumps. His already pale skin began to fill with blotchy gray spots.

"What's happening?" Ina cried.

"He's dying, my dear," Ice answered calmly. "The same will happen to you, if you choose to become."

Zeke's skin, now completely gray, was cold to the touch. The fleshy part of his nose caved in and began to fall away. Zeke screamed out in pain again as the metamorphosis continued through his body. His eyes shot open revealing their new gold coloring. His reflection on the floor was beginning to fade as he lost his grip on humanity. His body seized, then became still. His arms fell limp in Ina and Wrack's grasp. Each woman slowly stood up and took a step back from their friend. He now looked exactly as Ice had when they first saw her.

"We have to wait a moment to see if he survives the transformation," Ice commented.

"You mean he could've died?" Ina spat.

"It's a possibility."

Ina spun around and grabbed Ice by the collar of her shirt. Pushing hard, she slammed her former friend into the wall. "Why didn't you tell us?"

Ice stared at Ina intensely. Her gaze slowly softened into bemusement. Reaching up, she grabbed Ina's wrists and squeezed. Ina cried out in pain. Lifting her hands away from her collar, Ice let go. "Don't touch me again," she warned Ina. "Or I might not be so forgiving."

Ina took several uneasy steps away from Ice. She had momentarily forgotten she was a vampire now. Ina rubbed her aching wrists. "How do you know so much?"

"I think the blood not only triggers the genetic alterations, but it also passes information. I know everything, I think, about being a vampire. It's like innate memory to ensure survival," Ice theorized.

"Ina...."

She turned to see Zeke sitting against the wall with his arms folded across his knees. He was staring at her with his new large golden pupil less eyes. "Zeke, are you okay?"

He nodded slowly, his body aching from the change. "I'm fine." He continued to stare at her.

"What?" Ina asked.

"I'm hungry."

Ina's eyes opened wide.

In a flash, he was on her, pinning her to the floor. He pushed her face away exposing her neck. Opening his mouth wide, Zeke bit into Ina's flesh with his new fangs.

Chapter Four

Dawn lifted her camera and began snapping photos as fast as she could. Appliances, furniture and other household items swirled overhead as the team crouched below the dining room table. Cane, Dawn and Bishop had managed to crawl from the living room to their current location with only minor spots of trouble. Bishop was leaning against one of the table legs pressing a white washcloth he had found in the kitchen to a bleeding gash on his forehead.

"Stop bleeding yet?" Cane asked.

Bishop pulled the rag away and looked at it. "It's kind of hard to tell, the rag is so bloody."

"For Hell's sake," Cane grumbled. He ripped the rag away and tossed it into the kitchen. "It's just a little cut, you big baby."

"Well I wouldn't have a cut if you had warned me about that dinner plate!" Bishop pressed his fingertips to the cut to see if he was still bleeding. "I know you saw it coming."

"How you didn't I still don't know," Cane remarked. "It was one of those plates they serve turkey on for Christmas dinner! The bloody thing was huge!"

Bishop pressed his hand against the laceration. "You could've yelled duck, or fore, or something. Anything would have been better than, 'oh, that looked like it hurt'. If you would...." Bishop's words trailed off as something caught his attention. "Cane, move!"

Cane snapped his head to the right just in time

to miss another projectile aimed at the team. He turned and looked down. "What the hell was that?"

Bishop reached around his colleague and lifted a small golden object off the floor. With a chuckle, he showed it to Cane. "It's a goldfish."

"That's just sadistic," Cane laughed. "Is it alive?"

Bishop wiggled it in his hand, "Nope."

"We've got to stop this," Dawn said, pulling the camera away from her face. "It's wrecking the Jenkins' home."

Cane nodded. "Someone needs to talk to Raul."

Bishop tossed the dead fish aside. "Somebody should." He turned to look at Cane, then at Dawn. Both were smiling at him with bright eyes. "Now wait just a damned minute," he protested.

Cane reached over and punched Bishop lightly in the shoulder. "Go get 'em, slugger."

Bishop shook his head as he started to crawl out of their makeshift shelter. "Raul," he said loudly, "I'm coming out. I just want to talk." Making sure he was well away from the cyclone of debris, Bishop warily stood up. He raised his hands in a gesture of good faith. "I just want to talk," he repeated.

"Bishop! Look out!" Dawn yelled.

Bishop caught sight of the projectile, but it was too late. A tennis ball hit him hard in the midsection, just below his rib cage. Bishop felt the air being forcefully pushed out of him as he stumbled back. He grabbed onto the wall to stop and catch his breath. Slowly righting himself, he took a deep, painful breath.

"Knock it off, Raul!" Bishop yelled angrily. "It's not funny anymore!"

He looked up to see everything in the living room fall silent. The debris came crashing down to the floor around them and the room became still. Pushing off the wall, he took an uneasy step into the living room. "Raul?" he asked carefully.

Nothing.

Cane and Dawn warily joined their partner.

"Raul?" Bishop asked again.

"Want to hear my theory?" Dawn asked. "I think Raul is the spirit of a child, and you just hurt his feelings."

"What led you to those conclusions?" Cane asked, somewhat amused.

"Look at everything he's been doing. He's more mischievous than dangerous," she pointed out. "I think he just wants to play."

Bishop glanced around the room. "Is that true, Raul?" He waited.

Dawn took a step back as a pack of chalk lifted off the floor in front of her. They watched as the lid carefully flipped open and a single unbroken piece slid out. In a similar fashion, the lid closed and the box was set back on the floor. They watched the piece of chalk float toward a blank wall.

"Is that you, Raul?" Bishop asked with the slightest hint of a smile on his face. He suddenly realized Dawn was right. He watched the chalk spell out a word on the wall.

YES

Bishop's smile grew. "This is good," he noted. "Why are you here?"

The chalk hovered motionlessly.

"Can you answer me?"

YES

Dawn started to bite her lip out of habit, but quickly stopped. "You can only answer 'yes' or 'no' questions, can't you?"

YES

Cane took a step forward. "Are here to harm the Jenkins?"

NO NO NO

"Okay," Cane said gently, understanding he had upset Raul. "I know you aren't, but I had to ask."

"How old are you, Raul?" Dawn asked after a moment. The chalk paused then slowly began to slide down the wall.

7

"You're seven years old?" Dawn affirmed.

YES

Bishop understood Dawn's train of thought. "Did you come here to play with the other kids?"

YES

"Raul," Dawn stopped. She wanted to choose her next words very carefully. "You do understand you're not like the other kids, right?"

YES

"I know you just want to play," Dawn said caringly, "but you're frightening the family and the other kids. You don't want to scare them, do you?"

NO

"If you frighten them too much, they will probably move away. Do you want that?"

NO

Dawn smiled softly. "I know you're a good kid, Raul, but you can't play here anymore. You need to find friends more like you."

Nothing.

"Raul, did you hear me?"

YES

"Do you understand?" Dawn asked carefully.

NO

Dawn shook her head. "I know you do."

YES

"That's a good boy," Dawn said. "We're going to let the Jenkins back in so you can say goodbye, okay?"

YES

"Thank you."

Dawn turned to look at Cane and Bishop. She motioned toward the front door. Each lifted up their packs as they headed out. Just in front of the door, Bishop felt something hit him softly in the back of the head. He spun around to see the same tennis ball from earlier rolling on the floor. He glanced over at the wall where Raul had been writing messages and a smile crossed his face. He tapped Dawn on the shoulder and pointed at the wall.

BYE, HAD FUN

Dawn chuckled softly as she headed out the door.

* * *

Marcus Specter was alone in his meager hotel room. It consisted only of a bed, one nightstand and a single light overhead. The bathroom on this floor was communal. He sat in the center of his twin sized bed with his legs crossed and his hands folded neatly in his lap. His shirt, along with the rest of his equipment, sat in a pile in the far corner of the room. It was White Guard policy to have a stake near at all times, but he felt no danger from the surrounding city. Ash had been dispatched and Specter knew he always worked alone. There was no one to seek revenge for his death.

He was trying to achieve a deep state of meditation through the use of his chakras, but as of late, he had been unable. Early in his instructions, he was taught a Wraith can survive on little sleep if meditation is achieved daily. It not only opened a window into the soul, it replenished the body. The fact he could not achieve this for the first time in his life was troubling to say the least.

Specter had been an excellent student. He took very easily to the more spiritual aspects of the Guard, but the physical aspects had always been his favorite. There was a certain amount of pride in knowing he had molded his body into the perfect tool. He was taught early on that pride kills, but personally, he saw no harm in a little arrogance in one's work.

A secret sect within the White Guard chose Wraiths. Not much was known about them, only that they used a highly developed sense of clairvoyance to know when a potential Wraith would be born and where. Wraiths were chosen based on their service in previous lives. If they had served as a member of the White Guard in any capacity in a previous life, they were offered the chance to do so again. A potential Wraith would be observed through their formative years until reaching the age of eighteen. They would then be approached by an ambassador of the Guard and told of their "inheritance". This, of course, depended on how they used their early years. If they chose to follow the wrong path that led to violence and crime, they were passed over. All Wraiths must follow the straight and narrow path.

A man named Krieger had been chosen to make contact with young Marcus. It was three days after his eighteenth birthday. At the time, he was living on the outskirts of Belfast with his family and attending school. He was four months away from graduating when the Guard came to him. From a very young age, Specter had shown an almost unhealthy interest in the supernatural. He knew that somehow, some way, he was connected, but through his research, he couldn't find out how. Krieger showed him the way. Krieger was much older than Specter's eighteen years. Specter never knew for sure, but he guessed he was at least sixty years of age at their first meeting. He sported gray hair and a beard with two dark patches that ran down from his mustache to his chin. He used a cane to walk, the remnant of some forgotten battle, but when called into action, he could move like lightning. In keeping with the tenets of the Guard, he always wore black or gray, except for a white shirt he always insisted on.

With what he would later learn were the heavy-handed tactics of the Guard, Krieger gave him his first lesson. After initially turning down Krieger's offer to join the White Guard on the basis of believing the old man to be crazy, Krieger abducted

Specter. The High Guard, the ruling body of the Gwyliad Wriaeth, officially sanctioned this act. Krieger took young Specter to a local cemetery and chained him to an ancient mausoleum. This was a pass or fail test. If Specter failed, he would die. It was as simple as that. As if knowing in advance (in retrospect, Krieger surely did know), a vampire rose from a nearby grave that same night. Krieger had left Specter there alone with only two tools: a wooden stake and the keys to the chains that bound him.

He was bound in a kneeling position with his hands in front of him. This gave him some leeway, but not much. As he watched the vampire rise from the grave in horror, something deep in his mind took over. Leaning forward, he picked up the stake with his teeth. He inched to get the keys that were slightly out of his reach. With the tip of the stake, he managed to pull them over close enough to pick them up with his mouth. Holding them up, he carefully used his hands and mouth to work through the keys until he found the one that fit into the lock. Through this experience, his heart rate remained calm and he kept focused on the task at hand, even though the vampire was almost completely out of his grave. With a twist of his head, he popped open the lock and worked out of the chains. Scooping the stake into his hand, he somersaulted forward and impaled the creature as it struggled to free its legs. The vampire, still wearing his burial clothes, cried out in pain as the wooden stake cleaved its heart in two. In a brilliant burst of blue flame, he was gone, leaving only a troubled young man in the middle of the cemetery.

From then on, he was committed to the Guard. His first lesson had taught him much about himself and who he was meant to be. He moved from his childhood home, the only one he had ever known, to live with the Guard at their compound in Scotland. There he was taught everything he needed to know under the watchful eye of the High Guard. Krieger, now his full-time instructor, made sure he learned the complete history of the Guard, combat tactics, basic education and several languages, including three considered dead. He also learned to be a proficient tracker, something he later learned he was exceptional at in a previous life.

One of the more interesting courses he had taken was that of Past Life Regression. It was through this that he learned about the men, and women, he was before. This also allowed him to unlock secrets buried in his subconscious about the Guard. Specter learned he had been one of the original Wraiths and he had instructed several generations of students. He even discovered he knew several combat methods no longer being taught, and a terrible secret not even most of the High Guard knew. These insights, as well as his diligence, placed him in a privileged group within the White Guard, the Elite Guard, or, as they were more commonly known, the Wraiths. Not everyone who enlisted in the Guard was chosen to become a Wraith. Some moved on to help the High Guard, and even fewer were accepted into the Esgobaeth, which was roughly translated as "those who see". The Esgobaeth were the heart and soul of the

Gwyliad Wriaeth. It was through their psychic thoughts and visions that they provided the Wraiths with valuable intelligence on the enemy.

Specter slowly opened his eyes after taking a long, deep breath to clear his mind. He was not feeling himself at all lately. The lack of meditation was surely doing this to him, but what if it was something else? Something even he couldn't fathom? As one of the best and brightest of the Guard, he had been taught to deal with almost any situation, but there was a nagging feeling deep in the back of his mind he couldn't shake. His training had not covered this.

A knock on his door disrupted his thoughts. Swinging his legs over the bed, he stood up and stretched. Fetching his stake from the pile, he cautiously headed for the door. He stood inside the hinges and braced himself. "Yes?"

"Marcus Specter?" a female voice asked from the hallway with a thick middle European accent. She almost sounded like one of the ever present Transylvanian women in the Dracula movies.

"Yes," he replied hesitantly. "That's me."

"My name is Kiera, I'm the desk clerk."

"What do you want?"

"I have a letter that arrived for you yesterday morning. I'm sorry, but it kind of got lost in the shuffle. Since it was a little slow downstairs, I thought I would bring it up to you and apologize in person."

Specter closed his eyes for a moment, allowing his sixth sense to probe outside the door. He quickly found the woman to be telling the truth. Tossing his stake back to the pile, he unbolted the lock on the door and pulled it open. "Sorry about that," he replied in her native tongue, "can never be too careful."

Kiera smiled when she heard Specter speaking her language perfectly. He even had the accent down. "I understand." She held out the letter. It was a plain white envelope with the bare minimum of text on the front.

"Thank you." Specter accepted the letter and smiled at Kiera. She was young and beautiful with silky brown hair. She was dressed very well—a little too well to fit into this crummy place—and was well kept. If he were any other man, he might try and take advantage of the situation, but he couldn't. He pulled a few crumpled pieces of paper money from his pocket and handed them to Kiera.

"Oh, a tip isn't necessary," she caught herself staring at his muscular chest and getting caught up in the swirling pattern of black tattoos that ran down in a V from his shoulders to just above his abdomen. She tried to hand the money back.

Specter gently wrapped her hand around the money. "Please, take it. You have brought a bit of sunshine to my otherwise dreary world. It's the least I can do."

"I clock out in forty minutes."

Specter was taken aback by the boldness of this woman. "I shall keep that in mind if I require anything else," he said with a nod and slowly closed the door. Placing his back against the wall, he let out a deep breath. Sometimes it was so hard, but he had to remain faithful to her. Even though he didn't know her name. Or, he should say, what name she had in this incarnation.

Looking down at the letter, he quickly recognized the mark of the White Guard in the upper left-hand corner. He checked the time stamp on the opposite side. It had been sent three days ago from Scotland, before he even knew he was coming to Budapest. He carefully opened the envelope and removed the letter. It was written on thick, yellow parchment with a quill pen. The handwriting was lush and beautiful. He scanned over the contents as he began to read.

Brother Specter,

Congratulations on dispatching the vampire Ash. We know he had been one of the few outstanding blemishes on your otherwise perfect record. The Esgobaeth have had a disturbing vision recently that directly concerns you. It speaks of a dark gathering in the land of the ancient god of the Sun (we are fairly certain this refers to Egypt) and also of your death.

We have, at great length, consulted both the Esgobaeth and the High Guard and have come to a decision. You must attend to this matter as we feel it was a prophecy rather than a vision. We have not included the full prophecy in this communication as we are still diligently trying to fully decrypt it. We have wired a small amount of money to the hotel where you are staying. We will be in touch soon. Be careful, Brother Specter.

Signed, High Guardsman Krieger.

Without a second thought, Specter stuffed the letter back into the envelope and tucked it into his pocket. He immediately went to work gathering up his clothes and tools. He had a long journey ahead of him.

* * *

Ina lurched forward as Zeke pulled his bleeding wrist away from her mouth. Her golden eyes were open to the world as if seeing for the first time. Her head fell back slowly, her mouth wide open, exposing her new fangs, still red from Zeke's blood. She glanced at her maker expressing satisfaction in his work. Zeke smiled and took her icy hand in his. He now appeared to her in his human form. She understood this was nothing more than a projection from his mind of how he wanted to be perceived. Vampires could appear any way they wished, but often they chose the guise of their mortal coil. She realized this could be a powerful tool on the hunt, a powerful tool indeed.

Zeke and Ina stood up together slowly. She felt no discomfort in her body. There was no adjustment period or learning curve. Each vampire was born a killer with all the knowledge and instincts of previous generations. Unlike what she had read in novels and seen in movies, there was no "bond" between the maker and fledgling vampire. Much like newborn sharks that must fend for themselves from the moment they enter the world, vampires are born alone. There was no coddling period. They were born with fangs, and they must use them or die.

Ina glanced from Zeke to Ice and then back. "What are we going to do with her?" She pointed a finger at Wrack.

73

Zeke looked over at the woman who had been his friend. He sized her up. She meant nothing to him now, as did many of the things he'd once held dear. She was nothing more than food to him. "She is yours to do with as you please."

Wrack's eyes widened. She took several uneasy steps away from her friends. "Zeke, Ina," she muttered. "What are you doing?" She held up her hands shaking her head. "You can't do this to me!"

Ina smiled terribly. "Thank you." Sprinting across the room, she knocked Wrack to the floor. Before her victim could struggle, Ina was upon her. She dug her fangs into the woman's throat.

Zeke looked away from the display to Ice, who was standing near the head of the sarcophagus. "What now?"

"What do you mean?" Ice asked softly.

"We came here to destroy your coven and steal the vampire," Zeke admitted plainly.

"I know."

"And...?" he asked, somehow expecting more.

Ice smiled. "I have what I wanted. The rest of them can be damned." She paused. "Do you hear that?"

Zeke shook his head.

"A voice, buried somewhere deep in my mind. It's calling to me, to us."

"What's it saying?"

Ice closed her eyes and furrowed her brow. Her human appearance slid off her as if it were water. Zeke knew she was focusing all her mental energy on hearing the voice, so much so that she couldn't keep up her image. He watched her twist her head slowly as if trying to work beneath layer upon layer of genetic memory.

"It's buried deep," she admitted. "It's not an external voice, rather it was given through the blood. It is the voice of our creator," Ice said with astonishment. "I can hear her now, more clearly than before. She is calling to us, beckoning us to come and help her."

"Where is she?"

"I don't know, but I have a strong feeling of a direction." Ice opened her golden yellow eyes and stared directly at Zeke. "We must go to her now."

Zeke opened his mouth to argue, but something stopped him. He let out a long breath and nodded. "Agreed."

Ina stood up with Wrack's dead body in her arms. She turned toward Zeke and Ice as she licked the last bit of blood from the puncture wound on Wrack's neck. Expelling a soft moan, she dropped the body to the floor in a heap. "I like this," she said as she brushed a bit of her blonde hair from her face. "I feel better than I ever have. It's incredible." She leaned over and kissed Zeke on the cheek. "Thank you."

Zeke ran his hand gently across her beautiful face. "You are more than welcome." He glanced down at the vampire still restrained in the sarcophagus. "We need to get rid of him."

Ice nodded. "No one else should be allowed to cheat his or her way into our ranks. You and I have stolen our immortality," she said solemnly. "We can't let that happen again."

Zeke pulled his last cocktail from his deep coat

pocket and carefully removed the fuse. Using his newfound power, he leapt on top of the concrete sarcophagus and began to pour the homemade napalm on the vampire's head. "This should do the trick," he said with a devilish smile. Retrieving his lighter, he snapped open the lid and lit it. He flipped the lighter toward the vampire's head as he jumped off.

As the flame hit the syrupy napalm, the vampire's head was instantly engulfed in flames. The creature's yellow eyes snapped open as it shrieked in pain. Twisting to the left and right, it tried in vain to free itself, but to no avail. The three new vampires watched as the source of their new lives died before them. Its flesh melted away from its bones as it finally came to rest. Taking a step forward, Ice pulled the creature's skull from the concrete and held it up in her hand, the fangs still visible. Rearing back, she threw the skull with all her might against the silvery wall. The skull shattered on impact into a thousand fragments and scattered across the floor.

"It's done," Ice said with finality.

"No," Zeke interjected. "There are still two that know what we came here to do tonight."

"Priest and Seraph?" Ina asked.

Zeke nodded.

Chapter Five

Bishop kicked his feet up on his desk and leaned back in his chair. He was twiddling a yellow pencil in his fingers as he watched Dawn. Leaning over her desk, she was working diligently on the rest of the case report for the Jenkins' poltergeist, 'Raul'. She reached up and scooped her long hair into her hands and twisted it behind her head, pinning it in a loose bun with an errant pencil. Stopping, she glanced at Bishop over the top of her glasses.

"What are you looking at?"

Bishop laughed. "Am I bothering you?"

"Yes," Dawn said quickly. "Why aren't you working on your report?"

"Mine's done," he smiled. "There are these things now called computers that really speed up your work."

"I like doing them by hand," she protested. "They give the report more personality."

"Still can't figure out how to save your documents, huh?"

"Shut up."

"You know, I can show you how to work that expensive laptop you have sitting in your bottom drawer," Bishop offered. "It's really not that hard."

"It's not that I think it's difficult," Dawn countered, "I just don't trust those damned things with important work. If you want to surf the net and look at porn or chat with people you've never met, then fine. They're great for that, but important work should always still be done by hand. They crash too often," she added. "There's the possibility of losing everything in one fell swoop."

"Yeah," Bishop conceded, "but there's also the possibility that a meteor could crash through our office window right now and wipe us all out. You've got to take your chances."

"Maybe later," she said, dismissing him with her hand.

Bishop flipped open his slim, white iBook and launched his web browser. "Speaking of porn...."

"You're incorrigible," Dawn laughed.

"Oh look, 'Showering Asian Beauties'." He started to turn his laptop toward Dawn. "Want to see?"

Dawn held up her hand and shook her head. "Pass."

"Fine, suit yourself." He leaned back in his chair. Looking up, he whipped the pencil toward the ceiling. It stuck in the tile with a satisfying thunk. He surveyed the other ten or so pencils stuck in the roof and decided he should get a new hobby.

The door to the office burst open. Cane billowed in and immediately retreated to the filing cabinets at the rear of the room. Pulling open a drawer, he stuffed the folder he was carrying inside, then slammed it closed. He took a step forward and stopped, leaning up against a cabinet. He glanced over at Bishop, then at his collection of pencils in the roof. "What are you doing?"

"We track a band of Uruk Hai westward across the plains," Bishop answered without a hint of sarcasm.

Cane shot the younger man a puzzled look.

"What the hell are you talking about?"

"'Lord of the Rings'." Bishop pulled his feet off the desk. "You haven't seen the movies or read the books?"

Cane shook his head. "I don't have time for that kind of drivel. Instead, I turn my attention to useful pursuits."

"Like watching hour after hour of Bigfoot documentaries?" Bishop asked.

"It's important research," Cane replied, "and piss off."

"Well, somebody's grumpy."

Dawn looked up from her paperwork. "What's the matter?"

Cane reached over and pulled open a cabinet drawer, then abruptly slammed it shut again. "Weiss."

"I thought you two had patched up your differences," Bishop assessed. "Weren't you guys pals in Seattle after we rescued his daughter, Lexy, and proved her innocent?"

"I thought so," Cane noted, "but apparently that's not how he sees it. He thinks our travel budget is too high as of late."

"That's garbage," Bishop said as he sat up in his chair. "What are we supposed to do, research over the phone?"

"What brought this about?" Dawn asked.

"Apparently, Chairman Weiss' other companies turned in a poor fiscal year, so the Office of Paranormal Research is suffering by association," Cane explained. "He also thinks we need to start charging for our services."

"Seriously?" Bishop asked.

Cane nodded. "If we get called out, then we have to charge. If we're there of our own volition, then we're still free. He's just having a hard time rationalizing the cost of our salaries, especially since he started the new branch office in Seattle."

"Fire Hayden!" Bishop joked.

"No one's getting fired," Cane glanced crossly at Bishop. "We just need to tighten our belts a bit." He ran his hand through his hair.

"What now?" Dawn asked.

Cane sighed. "We have a meeting with the accounting office this afternoon to discuss our new budget and rate plans. They're bringing in all the teams and they want to start with us."

"Great," Bishop shook his head. "We've gone from serious paranormal investigators to the 'Ghostbusters'." He ran his hand through his hair. "I expect to see Bill Murray walk in at any moment."

Dawn laughed. "Who you gonna call?"

"This is really nothing to worry about," Cane assured. "Chairman Weiss gets a new idea or works out a new policy every few months. After a while, he'll forget about it and things will get back to normal."

"I don't know," Dawn interjected. "This is a little more drastic than his usual ideas. We could be looking at a serious change."

* * *

The two watched the sun beginning to set from the window of their third floor loft. This was the first time either of them had done so in a very long time. Priest was sitting in his favorite chair in front

80

of a small wooden desk. Twisting to the right, he kicked his heavy, black boots up on a nearby laundry basket. He watched his lover, Seraph, as she sat cross-legged at the base of the window. Her arms were resting on the sill as she watched the last of the orange and pink light fade beyond the horizon.

"I once read that sunsets deliver a small dose of lithium to the viewer through their eyes," Priest said after a moment. "I have no idea if that's true, but I recall as a child I always felt good when I watched the sun set."

"It's because you were a child," Seraph replied, her gaze still firmly focused on the horizon. "The past is shrouded in translucent gold wrapping. Everything always looks better after it's gone." She took a deep breath. "We should have waited for them."

He flicked his thumb at one of his porcelain fangs. "We couldn't stay any longer. The police were coming and we surely would have been arrested. Hell, even now they're probably finding our fingerprints all over the glass." He kicked the laundry basket away and stood up. Marching across the floor, he slammed his fist against the wall. The drywall beneath cracked and dented, but refused to give way. "Fuck Zeke," he said, pulling his hand away from the wall. "Fuck all this shit."

Seraph stood up and turned around to face Priest. "What are you talking about?"

"Vampires," he hissed. "I am so sick and fucking tired of vampires." He quickly began to tear off his clothes. "I'm tired of what they wear, what

81

they do, what they talk about and who they think they are!" He threw aside his leather garments, leaving only his boots and pants on. "Sera, we are not vampires, nor will we ever be. We are humans. That's it, that's all."

"How can you say that?" Seraph protested. "After all we've been through, after all we've seen?"

Priest took an angry step toward Seraph. "What we've been through? What we've seen? How can you say that? We're nothing more than wannabes. That's it!" He threw up his hands. "So we didn't see the sun for a while and drank blood, a vampire that does not make. We're more like blood fetishists than a creature of the night! We're fucking sick, Seraph, and we need help!"

Seraph took a step back, visibly shaken. She was fighting the tears. "Don't you dare say that! I know what I am!"

"Bullshit," he spat. "You're a scared little girl running away from God. Nothing more."

Seraph fell back, deeply cut by his words. "Get out," she said in a low, angry voice as the first tears rolled down her cheeks.

"We're going down because of Zeke and his bloody plan," Priest continued, undaunted by her command. "You and I are going to jail because we killed people last night!" He reached down and grabbed Seraph by the arms. Lifting her up, he pressed her forcefully against the wall. "We killed human beings last night, Sera! Doesn't that mean anything to you?"

"Let go of me," she hissed through gritted

teeth.

"Zeke fucked us!"

"Let go of me!" she screamed at the top of her lungs.

Anger overtook Priest as he slammed Seraph repeatedly against the wall. "Listen to me!" She hit the wall again. "Fucking listen to me!" He threw her against the wall one final time. He took an uneasy step back as her protests stopped and her eyes rolled back into her head. As she began to slide down the wall, he could see a visible trail of blood. Seraph collapsed to the floor, her body falling limp.

Priest's mouth fell open. Rushing toward her, he knelt down and slipped his hand behind her head. Rolling her head back, he peered into her open eyes. All he could see were the whites. "Don't do this, Sera," he said quickly with a tremor in his voice. "Oh, my god," he breathed. He quickly pressed his fingers to her throat, scanning for a pulse but found nothing. Leaning forward, he listened for breath. "Sera...."

He rocked back, pulling his hand free. Her body collapsed on the floor beneath him. He watched her thick, red blood begin to pool around her head. His emotions were running wild inside him. She was dead and it was at his hand. Stumbling back, he grabbed his leather trench coat off the floor and pulled it on. Pulling the door to the flat open, he glanced back one final time at Seraph lying dead on the floor. It was true, he had killed last night, but this was different. This was someone he had been intimate with, someone he had loved. He had to get away.... Shaking his head, he pulled the door closed.

* * *

Three heavily shadowed figures dropped down in front of the apartment's window as the last rays of sunlight faded behind the horizon. They moved quickly as they slid open the window and entered. Moving lightly over the wooden floor, their footfalls made no sound. The three slowly gathered around Seraph's dead body.

"Can you believe this?"

Ina turned to Zeke and shook her head. "I thought Wrack was the killer of the coven. This is surprising, to say the least."

Ice knelt down next to Seraph's body and lifted her limp head. "So, what's the big deal? That's one less we have to kill." Pulling her hand away, she wiped a bit of Seraph's blood on the wall. "Dead blood," she muttered to herself.

"There's nothing wrong with drinking dead blood," Zeke countered.

"I know," Ice replied with a smile. "It's just disgusting."

Ina turned around and lifted Priest's discarded shirt off the floor. Holding it in her hands, she smelled it. "I want him."

"You had the last one," Ice argued. "I think it's time to share with the rest of the class."

Ina turned toward Zeke. "Tell the overgrown popsicle to piss off."

"Don't look at him," Ice warned. "He has no authority here." She took a step closer to Ina, her green eyes fading to gold. "I never liked you when we were alive. I have even fewer reservations now."

Ina tossed down the shirt and stepped up to Ice. "Let's see what you've got, Popsicle."

Ice smiled, exposing her fangs. Leaping up in the air, she delivered a solid blow to the top of Ina's head that would have killed a normal human. Ina's body hit the floor hard. Before she could move, Ice slammed her open palm into the back of her head, breaking several wooden boards in the floor beneath her. Before she could strike again, Zeke was on her. He quickly restrained Ice's hands behind her back.

"Knock it off," he yelled.

Ice cocked her head to the right and laughed. "She started it."

"But you sure as hell were about to finish it," Zeke added.

Ina slowly pulled herself off the floor. As she looked up at Ice from her knees, she drew the back of her hand across her mouth to wipe away the blood. Her face was full of cuts from the wood, but they were quickly healing. The split lip she had was closing a bit slower than the others. A bead of dark red blood spilled down her bottom lip. She stood up and faced Ice. "Next time—"

"Next time, you'll be dead," Ice warned her.

Zeke threw Ice against the wall as he stepped away. "I said, knock it off! We don't have time for this petty bullshit. You can have your cat fight after we finish our work. Right now, we still have to find Priest." He closed his eyes for a moment, "She's still calling us. It's getting stronger. We have to move quickly."

"Wait," Ina said as Zeke and Ice headed for the door. "I don't understand something."

The two turned and waited patiently for her question.

"Why do we have to find Priest? I mean, who gives a shit if he knows what we went to Ice's coven to do? He doesn't know what happened there."

Ice nodded. "She's got a point."

Zeke shook his head. "I can't honestly say why, but I know he has to die. I just have a feeling," he said honestly. "It's buried somewhere inside my head. I just know we have to kill him." He walked over and wrapped his arms around Ina. "Trust me on this one."

She smiled through a dark bruise forming on her jaw. "Okay. We'll play it your way."

"Good," Zeke hugged Ina then released her. "I think I know where he's heading, but we need to move fast if we want to beat him there."

* * *

Several hooded figures crossed into the light and stopped. Their heads were bowed forward, shadowing their faces while their hands were tucked neatly inside their robe sleeves. They joined nine others, dressed identically in heavy, blood red robes, bringing their total number to thirteen that stood inside the circle of light. All else around them was dark, giving no glimpse of the locale. A musty smell hung heavily in the air, giving the only hint this place was old, perhaps even ancient. In the center of the circle of light, there was a large, lavishly decorated pentagram. A red ring, crafted entirely of rubies, encircled the design.

"Forces are aligning," spoke one of the robed

figures.

"That is why this circle has been called," a second assured. Moving into the center of the circle, the robed figure stood upon the pentagram. "We must not let him fall. He is our only hope in this war. Are we in agreement?"

The circle of twelve nodded their heads.

"We may even be called upon to change the course of natural history," the figure added menacingly. "We have been sworn to observe, but this time, we may have to take a more active role."

"What of our informants?" another asked.

"Useless thus far. We have been forced to gather all our information from prophecy," the robed figure replied. "The ancient texts aren't very clear on the battle that will unfold, but we do know it's coming. Many of us have foreseen it. Without him, we are lost." The figure paused, giving no glimpse of inner emotions. "Tomorrow, we must gather at dawn to begin. Keep this plan secret from all that would interfere, even those you call 'friend'. We must not fail in our endeavor, the fate of our order depends on us."

The remaining twelve passed out of the circle of light into darkness, never once betraying their faces to the light. A lone figure remained in the center of the pentagram. Pausing, nimble fingers grasped the sides of the heavy hood and pulled it back. Her face, for the first time, was exposed to the light. Looking up into the harsh, white light, she opened her golden eyes wide.

Chapter Six

Tick.

Another moment of life that could never be returned was gone. Ironic. While he was pondering the very essence of life, his was slowly slipping by without so much as a whimper.

Tock.

Sinking back into his padded leather chair, he propped his head against the side pensively. To his right sat a half empty glass of beer and a few fragments that used to be potato chips. Lifting the slim, black remote control from his lap, he tapped the power button and began to surf through the channels. There was never anything he wanted to watch; he didn't understand why he even bothered. Settling on a local news program, he tossed the remote on the table next to him. Standing up, he adjusted his shirt and made his way back into his apartment.

Cane wasn't sure why death had been preoccupying his mind as of late. It had been all he could think of. In some way lately, everything led back to the subject. It was starting to trouble him. There had been a few bouts with depression in his life, but nothing this morbid. It had all started a year earlier in Seattle, Washington. After almost losing Lexy Weiss to the Abydos Triad Cult, he had become much more introspective. He had finally forced himself to decide what he wanted out of life, instead of wandering from interest to interest.

Some would say differently, but for him, it was too late to start a family. He needed to choose what his legacy to this world would be when he was finally dead and buried. He decided on his work. That would be the standing achievement he left behind for future generations. He once had a chance for children with Lydia, but at the time, they were both too young and naïve. He had a gut feeling they would've made wonderful parents, but he couldn't take that chance. In today's world of quickie divorces and non-traditional families, it wasn't strange for parents to share custody of the children, but that was something he would never put his offspring through.

Cane quickly stripped away the noble wrapping on the thought. He knew it wasn't for the kids. It was all about him. He couldn't stand the idea of being tied down. What if he had married Lydia and had children? How did he know she was the one for him? What if the one he was meant for came and went without him even noticing her? It was stupid on his part. All his questions and worries were just a way of disguising the fact he was scared of commitment. There wasn't any great mystery; he just didn't want to admit it to himself.

Cane stood and walked to the window. He looked down onto the street, which was empty except for a few stray passing cars. The meeting earlier this afternoon with Weiss and his accounting goons had gone better than he hoped. He, with Dawn and Bishop's help, had successfully sunk the idea of charging for their services in exchange for each team cutting costs. It was a small price to pay to continue the research. He knew people would be less willing to call in a paranormal investigator if they knew there would be a pricey bill attached, seriously hindering the work. Now his research would continue unabated, and his legacy secured.

His eyes wandered to a lone bench near the corner. Two tall elm trees flanked it on either side, as well as a black lamppost that hovered behind it. Late at night, this was the meeting place for a group of troublemakers that lived around the neighborhood, but this night, a lone woman was sitting there. Her wavy red hair was being whipped around her lithe form. She was wearing an ankle length black dress and a thin duster that looked like it was made of silk. She looked ready for bed rather than the harsh elements outside. He watched as the woman glanced up at his window. A thin smile crossed her lips when she noticed Cane watching her. Smiling back, he turned away from the window and headed back for his leather chair.

He stopped.

Something deep in the back of his mind began to sound an alarm. Rushing back to the window, he glanced down at the bench. She was gone. Turning around, he rested his back against the wall and closed his eyes tightly. It couldn't have been. He shook his head and rubbed the bridge of his nose with his fingers. It wasn't her. Opening his eyes slowly, he glanced one final time out the window at the empty bench.

She was dead…wasn't she?

Moving into his kitchen, he grabbed his small, white cordless phone off the counter and held it up. Quickly glancing at the clock on the wall, he verified the time and began to dial the phone.

"It's me," he said slowly. "Can we meet and have a beer or something?" He listened for a moment. "Thanks. I'll meet you there in fifteen minutes." Setting the phone down on the counter, his eyes instinctively moved back to the window. An uneasy feeling crawled up his spine and settled at the base of his skull as he stared at the bench again. Doing his best to shake it off, he headed back into the living room. Grabbing his jacket off a nearby hanger, he moved toward the front door.

* * *

Specter couldn't help but smile as he walked over the cobblestone streets of Sighisoara, Romania. An elderly couple was sitting in the backyard of their medieval cottage watching the bouncing bikini clad women of Baywatch on a small television. Specter followed the black cords from the television with his eyes to the wooden roof where he spotted a small, gray satellite dish. This was why he loved this country. It was clawing and straining toward the twenty-first century, but it hadn't quite made it yet. That was part of its charm.

His journey had taken him south through what remained of the Eastern Bloc as he continued to head for the Mediterranean Sea. He would have to move quickly through Greece and charter a ship that would take him across to North Africa. From there, he could easily find his way to Cairo, but after that, his journey became unclear. Who, or what he was tracking was still a mystery.

He stopped in the middle of the main street. Looking up, he stared in awe at the Old Clock Tower and the Citadel of Sighisoara rising magnificently behind it. This place was ancient, but familiar. His soul had traveled here before. As he looked upon the ancient spires and arches, he felt more than déjà vu, but less than a fond memory. Leaning forward, he pressed his hand against the weathered brick wall and closed his eyes. Using the method he had been taught, he channeled all his energy into his second chakra (the middle of the forehead, between the eyes), slowly allowing himself to be lulled into a deeper and deeper state of meditation. His energy webbed out from his fingers into the cold wall, searching for physical memory.

A burst of white light pulled him from reality and sent him spiraling into the darkness of his subconscious. There, all memories are archived, even those from previous lives. It was dangerous to trek here too often, but the strong sense he received from the building merited the danger. It was generally thought among those of importance that many memories were archived, or repressed for a reason and to delve into them would harm the subject's ability to function in the real world. Specter was of the belief every scrap of knowledge available should be known, even that which had been purposefully locked away.

The overpowering white light slowly receded and he found himself again standing below the Citadel, but this time, it was different. He turned back and glanced down the main street. Gone were the televisions, satellite dishes and the few modern conveniences these people enjoyed, replaced by wood burning stoves, horse-drawn carriages and ragged men and women working the unforgiving soil. Holding out his hands, he glanced down at his attire. He was dressed very much like a noble of the time. He wore a pair of knee-length knickers, well-made boots, and a blue jacket over a finely tailored gray vest. His white shirt collar was held high on his throat by a similarly colored white kerchief, while ruffles hung from the cuffs of his jacket. Running his hand through his hair, he felt a long ponytail being held in place by a bit of ribbon.

Specter turned away from the citadel and began to venture down the street when he felt something sharp jab him in the ribs. Slowly opening his coat, he came upon a familiar sight. It was his wooden stake resting inside a hidden pocket in his coat. The point had burst through the stitching at the bottom, allowing it to prick him. He would have to get that repaired before he left Romania. Letting his coat fall to his side, he patted his trusty friend and continued on.

Several dirty faces looked up from their work with squinted white eyes and stared disdainfully at the finely dressed man. They knew who, and what, he was. To many of them, he was the reason the darkness had come upon their village. Many of them still knew the ancient tales of the Gwyliad Wriaeth and why they were sworn to hunt vampires. Specter hoped the Guard could one day redeem itself in the eyes of the world, but for right now, he had to continue his work. He moved to the right of the road, allowing a carriage to pass by. He had heard of the new horseless carriages, but had yet to see one for himself. Perhaps when he returned to England he would finally get to glimpse this new marvel of technology.

He glanced up at the western horizon. The sun was beginning to set. It was time for him to go to work. Moving briskly through the town, he headed for the cemetery on its outskirts. He could already make out the high iron fences surrounding it. For a place like this, gates and fences were less of a luxury and more of a necessity. Religious beliefs ran rampant through this part of the world creating villagers who held a mixture of new and old beliefs. Many still hung garlic on their front doors and nailed wooden crosses on the fence posts surrounding the gates. It was becoming less frequent, but some still lit a single candle in their front windows to drive away souls of former loved ones feared lost to the darkness. New beliefs were circulating that the candles actually attracted the departed. It was a strange time.

Moving off the cobbled street, Specter made his way up an old, worn path toward the cemetery gates. Stopping just short of them, he adjusted the stake in his pocket for easy access. A noise to the left of the gate caught his attention. Snapping his head around, he widened his stance into a defensive posture and placed the palm of his right hand on the stake's hilt. To his amazement, one of the local village women appeared from the brush carrying what looked like a handwoven picnic basket.

"It's not safe here this time of night, m'lady," Specter warned. "Foul things are afoot."

"I am not frightened," she said bravely, "now that I know we have a member of the White Guard in town."

94

Specter glanced over at the woman. She was wearing a newly made blue dress which looked to be made of material way too extravagant for her meager budget. He let out a quick breath and smiled. Perhaps she and her family had a good crop take this year and she had splurged a bit. That was certainly allowed, he told himself. He scolded himself for being overly suspicious. "Thank you, m'lady." He extended his hand. "Let me help you over those rocks and onto the path."

The woman took his hand graciously. "And a gentleman as well. Thank you."

Specter looked over the woman's delicate features. "Do I not know you?"

"Brother Specter," she said in a playful voice, "how could you not remember me? Two nights ago, you helped my son and I drive one of those awful demons away from our home. If it were not for you, I fear we would have joined my late husband in the grave. My name is Ekaterina."

He nodded. "I remember now. How is your boy?"

"He is fine, and currently in the care of his grandfather."

"I don't mean to pry," Specter apologized.

"It does not bother me to answer questions," Ekaterina answered politely. "Since the loss of my husband, I have had to take over the farming, and many questions are asked of a woman who performs the tasks of a man." She turned her attention to the cemetery gates. "I visit my husband, Adi's grave this same night every year." A bittersweet smile crossed her face. "It is our wedding anniversary."

Specter nodded. "Happy anniversary."

"Thank you."

"You still should not be here this late at night," he said, repeating his warning. He looked into her deep, sad eyes. "At least, not without a Wraith at your side."

Ekaterina smiled and held out her arm. Taking it around his, Specter pulled open the cemetery gates and walked inside. The two moved carefully among the tall, elaborate headstones, most with crosses sitting atop or carved into them. The path was winding and branched out into many directions, but they kept to the center. As they moved further inside, Ekaterina remained quiet, with the exception of a tune she hummed from time to time. He kept his senses sharp as the darkness closed in around them. To the west, he could see the last shred of light being swallowed by the horizon. He placed his hand on Ekaterina's to comfort and warm her.

"He's here."

Specter turned and looked down at Adi's grave. A shock of horror hit him at that moment. The ground was laid open directly beneath the headstone, exposing the wooden coffin Adi was once buried in. Letting go of Ekaterina's hand, he stumbled back from the grave. His eyes gradually moved up and scanned the cemetery. From behind the headstone he could see a bony, emaciated form rising up.

He turned quickly to Ekaterina. "We must go now!"

She looked at Specter through golden eyes and

a horrible smile. "You don't want to meet Adi? Such a pity."

A red flash of fangs and pain ripped Specter from his meditation. He took an uneasy step away from the citadel's wall, pulling his hand back as if it had been scalded. Turning around, he quickly made his way through the town. The cemetery was exactly where he remembered it. The gates, which were once tall and magnificent, had now rusted as vines grew up them. Yanking them open, he followed the main path up through the maze of graves. The cemetery was a very different place today. Large mausoleums were vying for space amidst a sea of broken and dislodged tombstones. The entire area was in a state of disrepair, but he knew where he was headed. He stopped just short of where Adi's grave should have been. Specter paused. This would prove if his vision were real, or nothing more than an elaborate daydream.

He took a deep breath and waded into the tall grass toward the familiar looking headstone. Pushing the weeds aside, he placed his hand on the cold slab and hung his head. He traced Adi's name with his finger and stood up. He had stood in this very place a lifetime ago. Turning to the left, he spotted two graves that weren't in his past life regression. Moving to the first, he pulled away the undergrowth and found a familiar name etched in the stone. It was Ekaterina's. Apparently, what he didn't remember from the regression was he was victorious over both vampires that night.

Turning to the second grave, he stood up. A cold shiver ran down his spine as he moved toward it. He stared at the unmarked headstone. An ornate cross reached from the headstone into the ever darkening night sky. To his dismay, a patch of wild lilies grew at its base. In Guard tradition, this signified that beneath this headstone lay the body of an honored Wraith. Specter slumped down in the weeds and stared at the flowers. Perhaps he wasn't so victorious that night after all.

* * *

Priest skidded around a corner amidst the wet streets. Moments earlier, the sky had let loose with a torrential downpour. Giant raindrops pounded down around him as he sought shelter under a restaurant's multicolored overhang. He was out of breath and shivering, but he couldn't stop. He was running for his life. He had spotted them a few blocks back completely by accident. As he looked up into the completely overcast sky, searching for any hint of the moon's silvery light, lightning arced across the night briefly illuminating everything. In that moment, he saw them, standing on the rooftop above him, only their silhouettes visible. A lump grew in his throat. He knew exactly who they were, but why was still unknown.

He pulled his leather coat tight and took a deep breath. As he exhaled, he watched the water vapor in his breath freeze in the crisp night air. He looked around uneasily. There was nowhere to go. His original destination had been a vampire bar in the downtown district, but they had, in effect, cut him off.

Why are you running?

Priest snapped his head around. There was no

one standing near him. The street was completely empty. He cautiously backed closer to the brick façade of the restaurant.

Where are you going to go, Priest?

He gritted his teeth. "Who's there?" He squinted his eyes and scanned the darkness.

You have no reason to fear. No reason to run.

The realization suddenly hit him. It was her voice. Stepping out from beneath the overhang, he felt the cold rain on his skin. He spun around on his heels looking for the source of the voice, then stopped. His eyes ran up the side of the building. There he spotted three faint forms amidst the dark clouds and rain. They were watching him. "You can't do this to me!" he shouted defiantly.

Trust me.

Priest felt an icy hand slide over his shoulder. With a start, he whipped around. He stared in disbelief for a moment as his mind struggled to comprehend the situation. His mouth fell open as he stumbled back, his hands up in defense. "You're dead."

Seraph stood before him nodding. She was in immaculate condition. No trace of the wounds he had caused were visible on her pale flesh. As the rain fell around her, it seemed not to touch her. Her clothes, her hair and her face were all completely dry. "That's true, and yet here I stand."

"I don't…." He lifted his hand to wipe the rain from his face. "I don't understand."

Seraph smiled softly. "It's all right. Take my hand and I will explain everything." She extended her hand, palm up.

The instinct to reach out was powerful, but he managed to regain some of his composure. "You can't be here. You're dead," he reiterated. "This isn't happening to me. You're some kind of guilty hallucination. My mind is playing tricks on me," he assured himself. "Maybe a bit of undigested cheese…."

"Who are you, Dickens?" she asked with a soft laugh. "You really should hear yourself. You sound like you're going a little crazy."

"A little?" Priest shouted. "You think I sound a little crazy? I'm standing in the fucking rain having a conversation with my dead girlfriend." He took another step away from Seraph. "I think I've gone off the goddamned deep end! What do you think?"

She opened her arms wide to him. "I'm not angry with you. You've opened my eyes for the very first time. I don't look at this as my death, but as my rebirth. You have finally given me the chance to live life as it was meant to be. No more minding rules or social obligations. I can do what I want, whenever I please." Her eyes were bright with excitement. "You have given me an amazing gift."

"What are you saying?"

She flashed her golden eyes.

Priest took a small step toward her. "What are you?"

She tossed her head back and laughed, exposing her new, razor-sharp fangs. "Everything we've always wanted to be."

"Vampire," Priest breathed. "How?"

"That's not important right now," she shook her head. "Take my hand and I can give this gift to you."

Priest looked at Seraph with wary eyes. Something wasn't right, but this was everything he wanted. He pushed his concerns to the back of his mind. The answer to all his hopes and wishes was standing in front of him with open arms. This was the moment he had been waiting for.

Taking an uneasy step toward her, he reached out and took her hand. It was cold and clammy, but powerful. He looked up into her eyes as she drew him close, finally wrapping her arms around him. Seraph glanced up at the two figures on the roof and nodded. Opening her mouth wide, she pushed Priest's head aside and bit into the soft flesh of his throat. He let out a gasp of pain, but quickly began to lose consciousness as his blood was drained. Fear set in then and he began to fight against Seraph's grip, but she was too much for him. Her arms had become like steel. Pulling her head away from the puncture marks on his throat, Seraph took a deep breath and began licking the blood from her lips. She opened her arms and let Priest fall helplessly to the ground.

His head hit the pavement with a sharp snap. Working hard, he tried to focus his eyes on Seraph. "You lied," he managed to whisper.

"No, I didn't," she disagreed. "You were right from the start, Priest. I am dead." Seraph's face and body began to melt away revealing the horrible golden eyed corpse beneath. The vampire squatted down next to Priest and placed its palm on his chest. "I'm not your beloved Seraph at all." Zeke's familiar visage slowly took form over the vampire's face. "It's your old pal Zeke."

Priest's eyes looked past Zeke to see Ina and another unknown woman with startling white hair standing over him. His gaze slowly returned to Zeke. "Why?"

Ina and Ice moved around Priest and each pressed their foot against one of his arms to keep him in place. They smiled viciously at him, their golden eyes burning against the darkened sky. Priest screamed out as he felt the bones in his forearms being crushed under the two women's immense power. Ina giggled in joy as she watched him writhe. Ice nodded in approval at her new comrade. Turning her attention to Priest, she blew him a kiss as she began to grind his arm with the toe of her shoe.

Zeke laughed as he slowly moved his hand around Priest's throat. He abruptly stopped. "Why? It's really very simple." His human face melted away and his gold eyes burned with hatred, "Because we can."

With one motion, he broke Priest's neck.

* * *

Dawn glanced around the bar. Dimly lit areas were in direct opposition to those choked with red, blue and yellow neon. Along the right side, stood the bar with a row of stools accompanying it. In the middle, there were several rectangular tables and to the left, were all the booths. Each had its own light hanging above it, casting a soft white glow. Even though this had become a nonsmoking establishment, she could still detect its lingering odor and several places were still thick with a black film. A woman wearing a floral patterned vest was standing behind the bar wiping down glasses while two men were trying to converse with her. Several of the tables and booths were filled with what she assumed were patrons, she didn't see Cane.

Moving through the doorway, she heard the wooden floor creak beneath her feet. Besides the dull roar of conversation, there was no music to be heard. With every step she took, she became more convinced all eyes were on her. Feeling slightly self-conscious, she wrapped her black trench coat a bit more tightly around her body. The bar was divided into two distinct areas, the upper half, with the bar itself and the tables, and the lower area, with all the booths. A long, gold rail and a set of steps at either end separated the two halves. Dawn walked cautiously through the upper area, keeping a watchful eye out for her partner. She glanced down at her watch and shook her head. She was on time...perhaps he was late. That wasn't too unusual for Cane.

Running her hand along the rail, the ring on her right hand clinked against the metal. She moved down the steps into the lower area and quickly surveyed the booths, hoping she had just somehow missed him. When she came up empty again, she reached into her coat pocket and pulled out a folded piece of paper. She quickly read her scrawled handwriting. This was the right place. Unbuttoning her coat, she slipped gingerly into an empty booth facing the door and began to wait. He would show up, she assured herself, but at the same time, began to worry. He sounded a bit distracted on the phone.

Something was wrong, but he hadn't let on as to what it could be.

She shook her head and glanced aimlessly into the bar. Cane hadn't been himself since last September. After almost leaving the OPR, she hadn't seen the same glimmer in his eyes she used to. His heart wasn't in it anymore. It was only a matter of time before he left the OPR again, and she was sure that this time, he wouldn't look back. Dawn partially understood. The company had been his and Chairman Weiss' baby, and the good Chairman had pulled it from beneath him, but that wasn't the whole story. She had learned later that Weiss had offered Cane a seat on the board and he had outright refused. She smiled. Cane wasn't about business and micromanaging, he was about the fieldwork. He loved getting out there and getting his hands dirty. At least he used to.

Dawn's relationship with Cane was, at best, tumultuous. They had never come to blows over anything, but there had been many days where they both sat in the office quietly, unwilling to talk or apologize. He was the most stubborn man she had ever met, but she knew why. He was brilliant, and he knew it. She had never actually seen his IQ score, but she was sure it was somewhere in the "eccentric genius" range. He was well versed on anything he thought he might need for the job, including ancient history, various mystical texts including the Bible, occultism, psychology, parapsychology, geology and mineralogy, just to name a few. Even after twelve years as his partner, he could still astound her with his knowledge on a

104

subject, but Cane was like that. He enjoyed spending his time reading a technical manual about the Space Shuttle's heat shield, or studying sightings of giant extinct fish in a remote lake in Nevada. It's what he did. He wasn't normal by any stretch of the imagination.

But that was why she liked him.

She wondered what must have been going through his mind lately. She was pretty sure it had something to do with the empty apartment he went home to every night. Since he and Lydia had become reacquainted, he hadn't been the same. She knew the feeling herself. Early in her career, she had almost been married. He was a wonderful man who was caring and warm, but had little interest in the paranormal. That wasn't it though. That had never been a source of contention between the two. She enjoyed having her own little corner of the world she could flee to whenever she needed. The supernatural had become her safety net. She had messed up.

Less than a week before the wedding, she began having serious doubts about herself and the man she was about to spend the rest of her life with. She knew she panicked. In a moment of supreme doubt and weakness, she had called one of her ex-boyfriends. The two went out on the town and ended up back at her place. At this point, she and Charlie, her fiancé, weren't living together, but he had a key to her apartment. Charlie caught her naked on the floor with her ex-boyfriend. No excuse or reason strong enough could be made to ever get Charlie back. It was over. On what was supposed to be her wedding day, she spent the morning in bed crying on her wedding dress.

How's that for pathetic? Running her hand through her hair, she let out a long sigh. That was water under the bridge, though. She had moved past that incident with Cane's help. He had provided a firm shoulder for her to cry on and never once took advantage of her vulnerable state. In those moments, a lasting friendship was forged, one she hoped never to lose.

She wondered for a moment where Charlie was and how he was doing. Last she heard, he was engaged to a woman he had gone to school with and the wedding plans were moving along briskly. That was ten years ago. They were surely married by now with several children. She smiled. It was better for her this way. She wasn't tied to any commitments she couldn't keep. She knew if they had married and had children it would be very difficult for her to leave them behind for weeks at a time while she was working cases. She smiled. Besides, male companionship wasn't all it was cracked up to be. Men break your nice things, leave their garbage everywhere, and have chili and poker nights. The smell must be unbearable.

Dawn glanced up to see Cane wandering into the bar. He glanced nervously around, finally spotting Dawn. He moved quickly down the stairs, almost falling, and sat down opposite her.

"Thanks for coming," he breathed, pulling his coat tightly around him. "It's cold out there."

"It's winter," Dawn confirmed. "It's supposed to be."

"Smartass."

Dawn laughed, "I'd rather be a smartass than—"

"A dumb ass," Cane finished. "I know, I know."

Dawn lifted her hand to signal the lone waitress in the bar. "So what's so urgent you called me down here?"

"Can't two friends just get together for a beer every now and then?" Cane watched the waitress approach.

Wearing a pair of faded blue jeans and a red t-shirt, the obligatory white apron was wrapped around her waist with a pad of paper and pen stuffed in the front pocket. Her blonde hair was pulled up behind her head, exposing the dark tattoo on the back of her neck. A diamond nose ring completed the package. Lifting the pad out of her apron, she looked somewhat preoccupied with other matters. "What can I get you two?"

"Beer," Cane replied.

"Draught or bottle?"

"Bottle."

The waitress turned to Dawn.

"Make that two," Dawn added.

The waitress flipped the notepad closed and slipped it back into her pocket. Without another word, she headed back up toward the bar.

"Why did you pick this place?" Dawn asked quietly.

"I like the atmosphere," Cane shrugged. "No one bothers you here, especially the help." He looked up at the waitress as she returned with their order. "Quick service, though." Lifting the brown bottle by the neck, he tipped it to his lips. Three large swallows later, it was back on the table.

Dawn immediately began to work off the paper label with her thumbnail. She glanced up at Cane, who was currently staring into the bar at the other patrons. She wondered if she should initiate the conversation, or wait until he was ready to talk. Something was obviously bothering him. She could see it in the very way he held his body. Curiosity overcame her. "So…?"

Cane returned his attention to her. He opened his mouth to speak, but snapped it shut again. Lifting his bottle, he took another gulp of courage.

"What's wrong, Cane?" Dawn finally pressed.

He shifted uncomfortably in his seat. "I saw her tonight."

"Could you be a little more specific?"

"Caitlin," Cane whispered, as if frightened by her name alone.

Dawn looked confused. "Who?"

"A woman from my past…" he took another drink of his beer, then pressed the cool bottle to his forehead, "a vampire."

Dawn's eyes widened with interest. "Seriously?"

Cane nodded.

"I remember you telling me they existed," Dawn began. "There's one here in DC?"

"She's hunting me."

The color drained out of Dawn's face. "My God." She took a long drink of her beer. "How do you know?"

"I helped kill her."

Dawn sat dumbfounded for a moment. "Wait, I don't understand. If you helped kill her, then how can she be hunting you?"

"I don't know," Cane admitted. He finished off his beer and signaled the waitress for another, "But I've seen her."

"Have you been getting enough sleep lately?" Dawn asked carefully.

"Don't you pull that psychoanalytical bullshit on me. I know what I saw!"

"I know," Dawn soothed. She pointed a finger at herself, "Scientist."

"Gathering all the facts," Cane nodded. "I know, I know, but this is different. She's real, and she's here."

"Okay," Dawn exhaled, "let's start at the beginning."

Cane took a deep breath. "You remember how Lydia and I met?"

"Sure, she was a newly initiated Wiccan in a coven in Seattle and you were fresh off the boat from your world travels. You were twenty-something, right?"

"We both were," Cane confirmed. "That was thirty years ago. I found work at a small meat packing plant that handled a lot of custom orders for the Seattle area. I was quickly promoted through the company to assistant manager. In that position, I had to deal with a lot of bloody paperwork. It was then I began to notice a lot of orders for large quantities of pig's blood. At the time, I was still very green in the ways of the world, but I had read

109

quite a lot of literature dealing with occult rituals and their use of blood."

"So naturally you assumed it was pagans, or witches," Dawn concluded.

Cane nodded. "That seemed like the only logical answer at the time. So I decided to do a bit of research in my off hours. I jotted down one of the addresses from the paperwork and went to take a look."

"That's the root of all your problems," Dawn suggested. "You're too curious. If you would just leave well enough alone—"

"But I didn't, and you're probably right," Cane smiled for the first time tonight. "Later that night, I arrived at the address. It was a small house with a large, fenced yard. The fence was at least six feet high and wooden, while the house was beginning to look a bit shabby. It had those old gray tiles on the front, you know, the ones that look like sandpaper close up?"

Dawn nodded.

"Anyway, I saw flickering lights from the backyard, so I decided to investigate. Peeking through a hole in the fence, I saw several women chanting naked around an open fire. At that moment, all my suspicions were validated." He paused for a moment to take a drink from his fresh beer. "Unfortunately, one of the witches spotted me."

"What did they do?" Dawn asked, completely taken in by Cane's tale.

"They cast some kind of damned paralysis spell on me."

"Really?" Dawn laughed.

"I couldn't bloody move for an hour!"

"So what happened?"

"These nine naked women took me into the backyard and stood me up in front of the fire."

Dawn let out a snort. "Sounds like the beginning of a great porn flick!"

"I wished," Cane laughed. "They quickly put on their robes after they were sure I wasn't going anywhere. They started to question me after that about what I was doing there, who I was and what I saw. I told them I was just investigating a strange order, and they seemed to buy it, but that didn't make them feel any more comfortable with me. After a while, I finally convinced them I was harmless. They released me only after I assured them I would not return. I did leave and had no intention of going back, but a few nights later, one of the women paid me a visit at the plant."

"Lydia." Dawn said.

Cane nodded as he continued. "She told me that she sensed a kindred soul in me and that her spirit guides had told her to trust me. Later that afternoon, she took me back to the house and showed me what the coven had been working so hard to hide. They had a vampire chained up in the basement."

"Good lord," Dawn whispered. "How did that come about?"

"Apparently, they had captured him in the process of trying to kill one of the coven. There had been a rash of murders that summer in Seattle and they attributed most of them to this vampire. Using, I believe, the same paralysis spell that had caught me, they transported him back to that house and chained him up. Being Wiccan, they couldn't bring themselves to kill the creature, even though he was evil. They kept him alive by feeding him the pig's blood."

"Why didn't they just kill it?"

"First of all, none of them had ever encountered a vampire before, so they had no idea of how to do it. What the movies and television teach you isn't necessarily correct. Secondly, their religion states that everything deserves to live, even the vilest of creatures. So they chained him up to stop the killing, and for a while, it seemed to work, but a few weeks later, the murders started again.

"What do vampires look like?"

Cane frowned. "They can look like anything they want. One minute, you're standing in front of an animated corpse with glowing gold eyes, then it's your deceased grandmother chained to the wall. I don't pretend to know how it works, but they seem to be able to pick any memory out of a man or woman's thoughts and become that person instantly. They can mimic their mannerisms and speech patterns as well. I swore to God I was talking to my Aunt Ruth one evening, even though she had been dead for twelve years!"

"That's incredible. So what did you do?"

"With Lydia's help, I began investigating these new murders to see if they had any connection to our vampire captive. The trail led us to a posh mansion deep in the heart of Seattle. This thing was immense, Dawn. We found our way down to the wine cellar, which had recently been renovated to

112

add space. Practically the entire basement was now part of this cellar, but we found what we were looking for: coffins. Dozens of them."

"So they have to sleep in coffins during the day?"

"I don't know if 'have to' is the right way to put it. As long as they stay out of the light, they're all right, but this particular group had taken on the more romantic qualities of the Hollywood vampire. Lydia and I immediately went to work. All the windows looking into the cellar had been painted black. We broke as many as we could to let in the sunlight, then quickly fashioned two stakes out of a wooden table on the first floor. One by one, we opened the coffins and plunged the stakes into their hearts, killing them immediately."

"So the whole stake-through-the-heart thing actually works," Dawn stated. "That's interesting. What happens when they die?"

"It was incredible," Cane said in awe. "Once their hearts were cleaved, blue flame would burn their bodies from the inside out. All that would be left of the vampire was a pile of smoldering ashes in the coffin. We had gone through at least five when the others began to rise. Lydia and I fought off as many as we could, but their numbers and sheer strength overpowered us. They took us captive." Cane swallowed the last of his second beer and let out a long breath. "Over the next week or so, they kept us locked in the wine cellar chained to the wall. They would torture us and feed off us nightly. Not enough to kill us, only enough to hurt us. I still have a few scars on my chest from where they burned me

with a hot poker. They were sadistic in their work."
He gritted his teeth. "They raped Lydia on more
than one occasion and a few of them ganged up on
me once as well."

Dawn reached over and took Cane's hand.
"You don't have to tell me if you don't want to."

"No," Cane swallowed hard, "I need to.
Toward the end of our imprisonment, we finally met
their leader. She was a slender woman with fiery
red hair that called herself Caitlin. She was the most
sadistic of them all. The things she did to Lydia and
I...." Cane trailed off as his voice cracked.

"It's okay." Dawn squeezed her friend's hand.
"How did you get away?"

"Lydia's coven contacted an ancient order of
vampire hunters known as the Gwyliad Wriaeth. A
team, under the leadership of a man named Marcus
Specter, freed us and dispatched the rest of the
vampires. I personally helped him capture and stake
Caitlin. With two hunters holding down her legs and
arms, we both placed our hand on the handle of the
stake and plunged it into her black heart. We
watched the blue fire engulf her body there on the
floor. Her eyes never seemed to blink. Unlike the
other vampires that screamed and writhed as they
were consumed, she stayed motionless, watching us
with hatred smoldering in her eyes. Before her head
turned to ash, she...she," Cane's hands were
shaking, "she told Specter and I that she would
come back for us, and now it looks like she has."

Dawn took a moment to let the details of the
story sink in and process. "That's incredible," she
finally said. "Cane, do you think the mental trauma

you suffered back then could be a factor in seeing her now? I mean, what if your mind is just playing tricks on you?"

Cane shook his head fervently. "I don't think so. I've been having nightmares about her, and tonight, I saw her outside my apartment. She's back, and she's pissed at me!"

"You saw her die, didn't you? Her body was reduced to ashes?"

Cane nodded.

"Then how could she be back?"

Cane slammed his empty beer bottle on the table. "I don't know!" He quickly lowered his voice, ashamed of his outburst. "I am not hallucinating, Dawn. She's real."

Dawn looked into her friend's eyes. She knew in that instant, he was telling the truth. Reaching over the table, she patted Cane on the shoulder. "I believe you." Tossing a few bills on the table, she scooted out of the booth and extended her hand to Cane. "Let's go home. We can talk."

Chapter Seven

All that remained were ruins. In its glory days, this was a place to behold, filled with magnificence, but at the same time, an ominous air. The spires and walls must have seemed like they reached endlessly toward the skies to the peasants who lived and worked below, while the embattlements must have appeared to be jagged teeth chewing through the atmosphere. Now it had been demolished by time. Bricks and stone from the walls had been stolen to create new buildings for the town after the master had gone. Weeds and vines wrapped their wicked arms around the debris as they reclaimed this place for the Earth.

Specter stood silently and watched the orange sun fading behind the mountains at the mouth of Castle Dracula, his black coat billowing behind him. The orange light was filtering down over the castle ruins giving this once evil place an almost heavenly appearance. It was actually quite stunning. Specter forcefully reminded himself to take a breath. He wondered for a moment about the previous lord of this castle and if the stories were true. Most knew that Vlad Tepes Dracula ("Dracula" is translated as "The Son of the Dragon", or "The Son of the Devil") was a real person, and many had heard how he received his ghastly nickname, "Vlad the Impaler" by impaling his enemies on poles while they were still alive, but none could say for certain if this fifteenth century Wallachian Prince had, in fact, risen from the grave as a member of the undead. To most of the Gwyliad Wriaeth, he was nothing more than a literary character created by Bram Stoker based on the legends of the area, but still…stranger things Specter had seen. He was sure of one thing: no record of a vampire named "Dracula" existed in the Guard's database (which was a shame, Specter would have loved to square off with the legendary bloodsucker).

Specter returned his thoughts to the present. Glancing up, he watched the last sliver of sunlight sink beyond the horizon. He had to move quickly here. There would be a tour group entering the castle in less than half an hour. This area of Romania thrived off the Stoker penned legend of Dracula. It had become a tourist destination for those seeking a bit of the darkness, and perhaps an experience of their own. Specter shook his head. He knew they would be more likely to encounter a real vampire walking to the grocery store around the corner than trekking to the deepest part of Europe. Fishing in his pocket, he felt a cool metal object. He wrapped his fingers around it, holding it firmly in his palm, sensing the power emanating from it.

It was ancient power, built some time before recorded history, yet the science of it was still a mystery and it was only a fragment of the whole. Specter pulled the metallic object from his pocket and opened his hand. He glanced down. It was slightly strange. It had a gleam to it, even in the darkness and yet, it could barely be seen. It was round, but not perfectly so. A row of jagged teeth ringed the topside. These, after all this time, were still razor sharp—a tribute to its original creators. In a ring around the outer edge was a form of pictograph; the language still had not been translated. It consisted of lines, slashes and circles, and at first glance, was quite beautiful. Upon further inspection, the carvings seemed harsh and tinged with evil. Every cut, every line, every circle seemed to have been forged in anger or hatred. The object was a component of something evil and yet it had fallen to the care of the Gwyliad Wriaeth, a noble order. Such was the way of many things in this life.

Holding the disc tightly, yet wary of its teeth, Specter pushed his long coat behind him and moved into the ruins of the castle. He had been here before, so his path, even in the darkness, was well known. Working around the rubble, he came to a clearing that was once the courtyard. Stopping in the center, he knelt down and placed his hand on the cool stones. Rolling up onto his fingertips, he used his fingernails to trace the edges of a circular door. It was a recessed area on the right side just large enough to fit all his fingers inside. Leaning over, Specter blew the excess dirt and dust away from the recess and dug his hand in. Using every bit of his preternatural strength—a gift from the Guard—he pulled the door open amidst the creaks and groans of the rock.

Inside the door was pure darkness, an inky blackness that seemed to move as a liquid, consuming even itself. But Specter knew what was down there. He had been there before and every time it became more difficult for him to enter. This place seemed to call to his soul from time to time, threatening to swallow him whole, engulf him in its darkness. He would usually avoid this place, but this was a dire circumstance. Dropping his legs over the edge, he sat for a moment on the lip. Taking a deep breath, Specter dropped down into the darkness as the stone lid slammed shut above him.

* * *

A lone ceiling fan whirred noisily overhead, casting long, dark shadows across the room. The tables and chairs were bathed in a soft, blue light emanating from several computer monitors left on overnight. This room, known as the "White Room", was the nexus of computer operations for the OPR. Long stretches of computer lined tables ran the length of the room. Everything from data processing to detailed photo analysis was performed here. The White Room contained the most powerful machines in the building. These weren't average Internet surfing or word processing desktop units, they were state-of-the-art computers. This was a geek's wet dream, but for Nick Bishop, it was becoming more of a nightmare.

"Damn!" He slammed his fist against the desktop in frustration. "Why are you not working? I've done everything you've asked, but you still won't work." He stopped suddenly, realizing the stupidity of pleading with an inanimate object. He allowed a brief smile to cross his tired face. It was at least worth a try, he told himself.

Straightening up in his chair, he arched his back in an effort to loosen up tired muscles. Stretching his arms wide, he leaned back his head so a yawn could escape. He didn't want to leave until he had this done. Time alone in the White Room was rare, and he couldn't pass it up. Sure, he could come back tomorrow morning and finish up, but his pride was at stake now. What should have taken no more than an sixty minutes had turned into a four hour adventure.

He cursed under his breath as he returned his attention to the boxy monitor in front of him. It had started out easily enough. All he wanted to do was transfer the audio recording he made at the Jenkins' house into the editing program and analyze it for background noise and possibly EVPs. It wasn't difficult. All he had to do was attach his digital recorder to the computer via a patch cord (the engineers had even gone so far as to cleverly color code all the cords for the computer illiterate), launch the editing software, and record in his audio. That was it. No brain surgery required.

But nothing ever runs that smoothly when working with a computer.

Wading through error message after error message on the screen, Bishop thought he had identified the problem, only to have a new glitch surface. He looked up and smiled with a devilish twinkle in his eye. If the racks of computers along the back wall didn't cost more than he made in a year, he would love to give them his own personal rinse. Nothing at this moment would satisfy him more than just hosing down the entire room, but that wouldn't solve anything…unfortunately.

He licked his lips as his fingers hovered above the keyboard. One more try, he assured himself, was all it would take. Closing everything on the screen, he exited all the way back to the desktop and took a deep breath. Reaching to his right, he made sure his recorder was properly connected to the computer, then launched the program.

To his delight, the program activated and immediately began to download the audio from his recorder. "That's right!" he jumped up and shouted at the box. "Who's your daddy now, bitch?"

After allowing himself a joyous few moments of the happy dance, he slid back into his chair and stared in glee at the green waveform displayed on the screen. "Let's see what we have here." He tapped the volume button on the right-hand side of the keyboard several times and clicked play. He could hear his, Dawn's and Cane's voices on the recording, as well as the background noise that was being created as Raul haphazardly tossed family heirlooms around the room. Nothing seemed out of the ordinary.

During several well publicized cases in the early nineties, several Rogue Ghost Hunters (those not aligned with any group, such as the OPR) had recorded what later came to be known as EVP, or Electronic Voice Phenomenon. These recordings, captured in supposed haunted locales, contained strange, disembodied voices often asking for help, crying out for vengeance, or warning the researchers to clear out. Some could be heard very distinctly, while others had to be "coaxed" out of the audio with the use of filters and editing software. Oftentimes, the EVPs revealed new information about a case that led a researcher in a totally new direction with unexpected results. Electronic Voice Phenomenon had become a welcome addition to many ghost hunters' arsenal of investigative techniques. This is what Bishop was looking for.

Clicking the tool bar at the top, he highlighted the entire wave and added a noise reduction filter. He hated doing this as it gave the audio a bit of a "digital" sound, but he needed to strip away the team's voices. He listened again, but this time, there was little more than a few blips and burps caused by digitally over-manipulating the wave. He quickly undid his filter and tried something different. After a moment of digging through the supplied filters, he came to what he wanted: a high-end cut. It would leave only the tail of the midrange and most of the low end on the wave. He felt a wave of excitement pass over him as he applied the filter. Leaning back in his chair, he watched the progress bar work across the bottom of the screen.

Once finished, he crossed his fingers and pressed play. He listened intently to the wave, which was now a muddy mixture of bass. Suddenly, his eyes opened wide. To make sure he wasn't hearing things, he highlighted a section of the wave and looped it together. He listened over and over again, until he was completely satisfied with his results.

"That's incredible," Bishop breathed as he listened to the sound one more time. Running it through one final filter, he listened to his results. His mouth dropped open. "Oh, crap."

Running the pointer up to the left-hand corner of the screen, he selected 'burn CD' from the drop down menu and stood up. Quickly unhooking his recorder, he slipped it into his pocket. He tapped his fingers on the desk as he waited for the completed compact disk. As soon as the drawer slid open, he snatched the disk and made his way out of the lab. He had to find Cane.

* * *

The sky over Egypt was beginning to slowly lighten as hints of sunlight began to filter over the western horizon. A few clouds dotted the area, but for the most part, it was clear. The city below rose magnificently from the desert sands, much like an oasis of humanity. Ancient spires sat side by side with modern buildings constructed of glass and concrete. Truly, this is where the old world met the new. To the south, the huge stone structures of the pyramids could be seen hovering like ghosts in the morning light. This was Cairo, the capital of this ancient land.

The sound of twin engines cut through the morning air. To the north, a small plane could barely be seen. Random rays of sunlight bounced off the cockpit window, glistening in the low light as the plane drew closer to its destination. Its flaps and landing gear were down as it made its final approach. Smoothly, the plane dipped down toward the exposed runway. Clearance had already been given to the small aircraft. It was on course, looking good and ready to land.

Something went wrong.

The plane's nose dipped down violently as it veered left of the runway. It lurched onto its side, but managed to right itself. The aircraft tried to correct its path, but pulled too far to the right. It was less than ten feet off the ground when disaster struck. The small plane lurched to the right, dipping its starboard wing. The tip scraped against the asphalt runway before biting in, which caused it to cartwheel tail over nose. Instantly, flames erupted from the right wing, engulfing the entire aircraft. As it settled on its belly, it looked like a missile skidding toward the terminal. Gravity and friction finally brought it to a halt. Emergency vehicles were already speeding toward it before it had even fully stopped.

Unseen by the emergency crew, three figures ejected from the fire and wreckage. They moved swiftly away from the flames toward the far side of the terminal. Their moves were fluid and perfectly timed, even though they had just been in a terrible crash. Finally away from the fire, the emergency crews, prying eyes, and most importantly, sunlight, the three stopped. They were not out of breath, or even fatigued from the long run; instead they each stood silently watching the beautiful orange and yellow flames chew through the fuselage.

"Why couldn't you wait until we landed to kill the pilot?"

Ice smiled at Zeke, her golden eyes smoldering like flames, "I thought it would be more fun this way." She licked the last trickle of the pilot's blood from her lips. A jagged cut ran from behind her left ear across her neck and terminated just above her jaw. She had been thrown from her position in the cockpit during the crash against a newly exposed edge of metal. It had sheered through her face like warm butter, but she felt no pain and it would heal quickly enough.

Ina hung to the rear of the trio cradling her right forearm. She pulled her hand away and winced at the charred black flesh that ran from her bicep all the way to the back of her thumb. She could already feel the flesh beginning to heal, but damage this extensive would take time to rejuvenate. As she pulled her sleeve down over her arm, she brushed a singed piece of blond hair from her face. "What now?"

Zeke turned to look at his companions. He had made it through the crash mostly unscathed. Luckily, he had seen Ice bite the pilot and had strapped himself into his seat firmly, avoiding the cuts and contusions the others had received. "We need to find her." He glanced up into the ever brightening sky, his eyes squinting, "But first, we need to get indoors."

As the three moved around the terminal, they kept to the shadows, already feeling pain from the sun. Through their genetic memory they learned, to their dismay, the legends regarding vampires and sunlight were true. If they walked in direct sunlight for more than a few moments, the cells in their bodies would break down and die. The reason for this photosensitivity was still unknown, but most agreed it had something to do with their demon lineage. The best and brightest minds of the vampire world had tried to find the cause, and hopefully a cure, but had come up empty-handed. The problem stemmed from the very nature of the original vampires, the Celtic Fae folk known as the Baobhan Sith (pronounced "buh-vaan shee"). They were attacking this problem with science, when it was

125

clearly of a magical nature.

Even in the shade, each felt painful cracks forming in their flesh as smoke began to waft into the morning sky. Coming around a corner, Zeke spotted a maintenance entrance to the terminal. He stared warily at the twenty foot gap between the buildings. They would be exposed for only seconds, but that would be all it would take. He glanced back at Ina and Ice before deciding his course.

Pulling his jacket up over his head, he charged into the sunlight and toward the door. The sun instantly scalded his exposed fingers and knuckles as flames erupted from his skin. He cried out in pain as the first few flakes of ash floated down past his face. Stopping just short of the door, he focused all his strength and kicked forward. The thick metal door folded in like tin exposing the cool, dark maintenance room. Without hesitation, he dove inside. His momentum flung him into a rack of tools at the back of the room, sending the metal and wood implements raining down around him. Falling back in pain on the floor, he allowed the darkness to cool his wounds. He was unaware of his two companions following closely in his footsteps, their burns much less severe.

Ina dropped down next to Zeke and pushed the tools off him. Slipping her arm around his neck, she cradled her free hand against his cheek. Her thumb brushed a patch of burnt flesh, causing it to flake and fall away. "Zeke?"

He looked up at her through golden eyes.

"Are you okay?"

He nodded slowly. "I feel like a hotdog that

126

was held over the campfire for too long."

Ina shook her head. "Lovely imagery."

Ice danced around the light spilling in from the door and jammed it closed. "We can't all sleep at the same time," she stated. "I think it's best if we take shifts. Zeke sleeps first to heal. I'll take the first watch."

Ina nodded. Sliding her legs under Zeke, she cradled him to her chest and closed her eyes. Zeke was already out cold, his body needing time to rest and regenerate. His burns were far from fatal, but they would take time to completely vanish. Ina opened her eyes for a moment to see Ice perched on the edge of a nearby desk, her eyes focused on the door. She didn't trust her, but rest was more important. Ina felt her eyelids becoming heavy and she slowly drifted off into a listless sleep.

* * *

Cane rolled over and slowly opened his eyes. Suffering from a fierce case of cottonmouth, he tried to work up some saliva to at least wet his lips. His vision still blurry, he rubbed his eyes with the heels of his hands. A long yawn escaped as he slowly sat up and scratched the back of his head. He allowed his eyes to slowly wander around his surroundings as his mind struggled for some coherence. He suddenly stopped. He didn't recognize this place. His heart began to race.

Lifting up the covers, he saw he was only wearing his boxer shorts. He glanced down at the floor quickly searching for his clothes, but they were nowhere to be seen. Pulling the covers a little higher to hide his exposed body, he sank back into bed and glanced nervously around the room. There was a large window to his right with sheer blue curtains hanging over it. The slightest hint of light was filtering through, making it impossible to tell if it was dawn or sunset. A large oak dresser sat against the wall opposite the foot of the bed. The top was littered with personal touches such as photos, but he didn't recognize any of the faces. Turning to the left, he spotted a small table situated next to the door. It held a single potted plant and a set of keys. He wondered for a moment if they were his. Finally, he peered into the open bathroom door across from him. Hanging on a rack inside the door he could make out a bath towel…and a lacy, black bra.

He let out a moan. Bloody hell. What had he done last night? Cane closed his eyes and tried to fight through the fog that had settled over his brain. He remembered sitting in his apartment, a bit of a storm, and then—

Caitlin.

A cold sweat broke out on his forehead at even the thought of her name. Cane closed his eyes and tried to shake her from his mind.

After that, he had called Dawn and they went out for a drink. They had sat and talked and consumed a bit of alcohol. He rubbed the sides of his head. Maybe it wasn't a bit of alcohol…. A sick feeling grabbed Cane's stomach. He hoped that in his condition last night, he hadn't done something idiotic. Above all else, he considered Dawn his best friend, and if that line were ever crossed, there would be no going back. He had seen friendships disintegrate from much less. Besides, he was more or less with Lydia again. Even though they lived on opposite ends of the continent, he still considered Lydia his girl. Pressing his palms to his face, he wished he could remember what happened.

A noise outside the bedroom startled him. She was still here. He wasn't sure if he should call out or wait. He didn't want to face the issue until he had to. There was no reason to rush things. Leaning back, he turned his head to the left, spotting his wristwatch. Lifting it up carefully, he read the dial. He let out a sigh of disbelief as he pinched the bridge of his nose between his finger and thumb. It was almost seven in the evening. Somehow, he had lost an entire day. Looking around, he spotted one of Dawn's robes lying over the edge of the bed. Quickly retrieving it, he threw it on and jumped out of bed. He began tying the belt around his waist as he moved toward the door.

"Bashful this morning?"

Cane looked up to see Dawn standing in the doorway with two cups of coffee in her hands. She appeared to be wearing only a robe.

"You weren't shy last night," she added coyly.

"I'm sorry," Cane stammered. "I just woke up, and I…." he had no idea of what to say. Also, the collar of Dawn's robe was riding a little low, exposing her cleavage. Accepting the cup of steaming liquid from her, he took a sizeable drink.

"How are you feeling?" She began to reach for Cane, but he backed quickly away. "I don't bite," she said softly. "You had a hard night. I just wanted to make sure you were okay."

"A hard night?" Cane asked. "Yes, well…what?" His mind was whirling in a hundred different directions trying to decode Dawn's vernacular.

She nodded. "You were tossing and turning all night. I think you were having nightmares. I had to come in and check on you a couple times." She took a sip of her coffee.

"You had to come in and check on me? So you didn't sleep," he paused, "you and I didn't…?"

"Didn't what?" Dawn asked with a smirk.

Cane sat down on the edge of the bed and placed his cup on the nightstand. "You see, I'm sorry, but I have very little recollection of last night's events," he admitted. "I remember meeting you at the bar, talking about my experience, and then," he shrugged.

Dawn sat down on the bed next to him. She placed her hand very tenderly on his. "So you're asking if we made love last night?"

Cane nodded uncomfortably.

Dawn ran her hand up Cane's arm to his chest. Once there, she pressed her palm against his flesh and shoved as hard as she could.

Cane spilled back onto the bed, unable to find the words to articulate what he was feeling.

"You pig," laughed Dawn. "You think just because you spent the night, and most of the day for that matter, at my apartment, we had sex? Is that all you think about?"

"No, I—"

"We talked. That's all. We both may have had a little too much to drink, but all we did was talk."

130

Dawn walked around to the opposite side of the bed and sat down. Swinging her legs up, she crossed them and leaned back against the headboard. "I called in sick for both of us this morning. I told Weiss a relative of yours died and we were attending the funeral."

"That's lovely," Cane said, shaking his head.

"Would you rather have gone to work with a massive hangover?"

"No, I suppose not." He lifted his cup and slowly began to sip. Another thought popped into his mind. "So, what did we talk about last night?" He asked as nonchalantly as possible, hoping he hadn't opened his big mouth and given away the keys to the castle.

"We talked more about Caitlin, and vampires in general," she said slowly. "Then we moved on to more personal issues."

Cane dropped his head into his hands. "Good lord," he breathed.

Dawn smiled broadly, knowing she had something to hold over Cane. "You told me about Lindsay."

Cane looked up with wide eyes. "Lindsay?"

"Your school sweetheart," she confirmed.

"And the Beetle?" Cane probed cautiously.

Dawn nodded with a grin ear to ear. "I had no idea you used to be so adventurous. Beetles were hard enough to fit in comfortably, but to lose your virginity in the front seat? That takes talent."

Cane became instantly embarrassed and retreated into his trademark British stuffiness. "Well, I...you see, the alcohol...." he took a long breath as he looked at his friend. "Please don't tell anyone."

Dawn reached over and patted him on the shoulder. "I wouldn't think of it. All your secrets are safe with me."

"All?" Cane asked as if something sharp had just poked him in the back.

Dawn smiled.

"Dear lord."

A knock at the door pulled them from the conversation. Dawn quickly stood and moved out of the room with Cane following close behind. Stopping just shy of the front door, she made sure her robe was cinched up tightly. Pushing up on her toes, she peered through the peephole. Her hand moved to the doorknob as she glanced over her shoulder at Cane. "It's Bish."

Cane shook his head. "Don't open the door. We're not here," he whispered.

"Why?' Dawn asked, turning the knob.

"Look at what we're wearing!" Cane protested. "He'll think something's going on between us!"

Dawn rolled her eyes and opened the door, greeting Bishop with a smile. "What's up?"

Bishop said nothing as he pushed past her. Pulling a small pack off his shoulder, he made his way toward the living room. Dawn and Cane followed their teammate curiously.

"Bish, what are you doing?" Dawn asked.

He had already sunk down onto her couch and was moving items off the coffee table in front of him. He retrieved his white laptop from the bag and popped it open. The screen quickly flickered to life

132

as he pulled a compact disc from his bag. Blowing a bit of lint off the back, he fed it into the front of his laptop. An audio program immediately began to launch.

"Bishop," Cane said sternly. "What the hell are you doing?"

Bishop slowly turned around. His air of unease quickly faded to amusement when he noted Cane's attire. "That's a lovely robe, Cane."

Cane glanced down and noticed for the first time that the dark blue robe was imprinted with little, white cartoon cats. He shot a dirty glance at Dawn.

"Hey, you're the one who picked up my robe," Dawn said innocently. "I didn't lay it there for you."

Bishop looked from Cane to Dawn. "Why are both of you in robes?"

"Never mind," Cane said abruptly. "What have you got for us?"

Bishop turned back to his bag and pulled a medium-sized pair of speakers out and hooked them into his laptop. "I took the opportunity to make some recordings during our encounter with Raul. Today, while both of you were quote unquote 'out sick', I had the chance to get lab time and analyze the recording. I found something very interesting."

Cane moved around the couch and sat down next to Bishop while Dawn perched on the arm. "What am I looking at?"

"This is called a Wave Form," Bishop said, pointing to the green lines on a black background. "It is a graphical representation of sound," he explained, "and this program allows me to alter it and play it back."

"Okay," Cane nodded, "I'm not a complete idiot. What I meant was 'what do you have for us'?"

"Oh," Bishop said slightly embarrassed, "sorry." He tapped several keys on his laptop and made sure his speakers were turned on. "The clip is only twenty-eight seconds long, so you have to listen close. Ready?"

Cane and Dawn nodded.

Bishop pressed play. An eerie whine seeped from the speakers filled with static and pops. Several muted noises could be heard beneath the whine, but they weren't easily distinguishable. They sounded like a voice, but it was hard to tell. Dawn felt the tiny hairs on the back of her neck stand up as the first words became audible amidst the noise. The voice sounded deep and demonic, filled with guttural growls and moans. As the voice died out, the whine snapped and finally faded to silence. Each member of the team sat back slightly, their minds chewing on what they had just heard. After an intense few moments, Dawn was the first to speak.

"Did it actually say what I think it did?"

Bishop nodded. "I couldn't believe it myself at first, so I ran it through several filters to try and clean up the track. I must have listened to it at least a dozen times between here and the lab. I can't think of anything else it could be."

Cane rubbed his chin nervously, the hair on his chin bristling against his fingers. "Play it again."

Bishop complied. The recording began again, filling the room with the same eerie whine and demonic voice. A low gurgling sound erupted from the whine, followed by what sounded like several hiccups. From there, a masculine voice began to speak, but as if it were spooled on a tape in reverse. A high pitched shrill sliced through the voice, but quickly died out again. The voice began again, this time much clearer:

Caitlin   is…[garbled words]…coming…[garbled]…from beyond…[more garbled   words,   then   a pause]…Cane…[garbled]…accompanied by death.

Silence fell over the three again as the recording stopped.

"You recorded this during Raul's poltergeist activity?" Dawn asked.

Bishop nodded. "'Caitlin is coming'," he repeated what the voice in the recording had foretold. "Who is Caitlin?"

Dawn turned to Cane. Her eyes widened. He was sitting completely motionless, except for his hands as they shook in his lap. "Cane?" She waited for a response.

Cane slowly turned his head to face her. "She's coming," he breathed. His hand moved instinctively to his necklace. Panic set in when he realized it wasn't there. Cane immediately stood up and started searching around the couch. He flipped pillows onto the floor as he dug his hand down between the cushions. "Where is it?"

"Where is what?" Dawn asked.

"My cross, my necklace," he said, pointing to his throat. "It's gone."

Bishop stood up and took several steps away from Cane. He had never seen him this spooked before.

"I took it off you last night," Dawn said, trying to calm Cane. "I thought I would clean it. It was looking a bit worse for wear."

"That's because I haven't taken it off in thirty years!" Cane yelled, becoming increasingly frantic by the moment.

Dawn's face grew long. "I'm so sorry. I just wanted to do something nice. I'll get your neckla—"

"Yes. Go get it," Cane said abruptly.

"Cane," Bishop said slowly. "What the hell is going on here? What's the matter with you?"

"I don't want to talk about it," Cane said, turning away.

"I don't think I give a damn what you want." Bishop stepped up into Cane's face. His voice became low and intense. "You just threw a temper tantrum in the middle of Dawn's living room!"

Cane's temper flared. "You listen here, you little prick—"

"Who is Caitlin?" Bishop pressed, undaunted by Cane's rage.

Cane shook his head and took a step back. "I, she...." He grew uncomfortable at the mention of her name, almost as if he were in physical pain. That name sliced deeply into his subconscious, conjuring up dark images that had taken three decades to cope with. He wasn't ready for this.

Bishop placed his hand firmly on the older man's shoulder. "Dawn and I are here to help you, but you have to let us."

Taking a deep breath, Cane sunk down in the

136

couch. "It's a long story."

Bishop glanced at his watch. "We appear to have plenty of time."

Chapter Eight

Specter stumbled slightly, but quickly regained his balance in the inky dark. As he moved forward, he kept his hand planted firmly against the wall to guide him. The last time he had been here.... He shook his head. That was a long time ago and there had been a guide present. This time, he was on his own. As he worked through the darkness, Specter tried to remember the sequence in which to activate the device. It wasn't going to be easy and he dreaded having to come this way, but desperate times called for desperate actions. He had to be in Egypt right now. There wasn't time for human transport. He had to depend on something much more ancient.

This place was not of human descent. Since the care of this place fell to the White Guard, several archaeological teams had been dispatched to try and help discern its origins. But this place, as with many ancient structures, held onto its secrets vigorously. Unlike many other structures of similar age, this place had no markings on any surface, save for the device itself. No glyph, cuneiform, or painting was ever found, making it more of a mystery. Several top Wraith archaeologists had advanced the theory that it was older than even the human race, and that it had been built by an ancient order of Gods. Specter wasn't entirely sure he subscribed to this theory, but he had heard stranger explanations.

This was but one of many scattered around the world. All were situated in locations of great temporal importance and were constructed in similar fashion. The entrance was bored into solid rock, while the main corridor was ribbed with long, metallic girders which defied any composition analysis. Each corridor was exactly thirty-three feet long and nine feet in diameter, perpetuating the idea ancient builders had a strong grasp of mathematics. Amidst the ribs, the walls were bare rock, however, the floors were constructed of a substance close to that of marble, although slightly different. This place was powerful. An electrical charge danced between the walls and Specter's fingers as he moved. A blue arc of electricity would pop from time to time, giving him a fleeting glance of the device ahead. Dread rose in him as he drew closer.

The faint red glow that had been emanating from the device had grown into a full-fledged light now. The silvery metal edges of it were in full view. Its outer rim was basically octagonal in shape, with a large, perfect circle inside. Rows of black symbols lined the outer edge that had been meticulously carved into the metal. Specter had the strange feeling he could read them each time he looked at the device, but it was fleeting. Directly below it, there was a similar shape on the floor built into the marble. It was nearly identical, except for a small hole near the front edge.

Taking a deep breath, he stepped onto the device. The hairs on his arms, neck and head instantly stood up. There was a strong magnetic field surrounding the object that terminated within an inch of its edges. It had to be a product of the machine, but a freestanding field this perfect was impossible to create, even with today's technology.

Removing the disc from his coat pocket, he held it tightly between his fingers. He fought slightly against the field, but remained in complete control. Dropping down to one knee, he held the disc teeth down above the small circle on the far edge. As soon as the two components met, there would be no turning back. He would have to immediately key the correct sequence, or....

He didn't like to think about the alternative. He had seen a Wraith stand on the device, insert the key, and then vanish after inputting the incorrect sequence, never to be seen again. It was as if he had vanished off the face of the Earth, which in retrospect, probably wasn't too far from the truth.

The device was something like a teleporter. Through the network of them, matter could be instantly displaced from one area to another. The very mechanics of the device, known as the "Porth Dyfais" (roughly translated into English as the "Gate Device"), seemed to work outside our understanding of physics. Something like this wasn't even feasibly possible at this point, and yet, here it was. He had seen it work, even been through it once himself.

Several ancient vampires had tried to lay claim to the Dyfais on grounds it belonged to their species, but each time, the Guard thwarted them. If they were allowed free run of the Dyfais, they could march armies all over the world in a matter of moments. It was not something Specter liked to think about. Still, if all he knew was true, there was no way ancient vampires could have created the Dyfais. It was in the Guard's care long before they

140

even existed. Its origin had to be much, much older.

Setting the disc gently inside the corresponding circle, Specter quickly stood up. He watched the disc sink slowly into the hole. The once silver object began to glow a deep shade of red as it heated up. The Dyfais actually melted the key back into itself, ensuring proper transport protocols. Once begun, the procedure could not be stopped. He immediately turned his attention to the matching octagon. The center circle split in two and slowly retracted into the wall, revealing a control center of sorts. There were no buttons or levers; rather there were a series of colored crystals set into the same silver metal the outside consisted of. In the proper sequence, these crystals created an area code of sorts, a physical address for the other Dyfais on the network.

It was only a matter of moments now that it had been activated. The steady thrum of energy could be heard building beneath it. Specter had no choice now. As soon as the control panel was opened, a barrier enveloped the Dyfais. This served two purposes: one; to trap those using the gate illegally, and two, to contain the massive burst of energy the device used to initiate transport. Closing his eyes, he blocked out the sounds and sensations and focused. Through years of training, he quickly found his center. It was now only a matter of calling up the correct information, much like a computer. Regressing back to his earlier encounters with the Dyfais, he recalled what his instructor had taught him, and what previous crystal combinations had been used. It was only a matter of seconds before he

141

found the correct sequence.

Opening his eyes, he slowly moved his fingers toward the colored crystals. In all, there were twenty lined up in four rows of five and each was a slightly different shade than the previous one. Using his finger and thumb, he pressed on the first crystal and watched it sink into the panel. He needed to activate four more to create an address. The second and third crystal fell easily into place, while the fourth became slightly harder to depress. Using both hands, he pushed down hard and to his relief, saw it move. Pushing again, he heard a crack.

Immediately, his hands ripped away and his mouth became dry. The Dyfais was humming loudly now, almost at the completion of its cycle. He frantically inspected the crystal, and to his dismay, found a two inch long fracture near its base. Cursing under his breath, he gently placed his hand atop the crystal again. He had to finish. Glancing down, he saw a bright white fog beginning to envelop his feet. Ignoring the distraction, he returned his full attention to the activation crystal. He slowly pushed again and cringed as it cracked and popped beneath his hand. He applied a little more pressure to hurry the process. It was then that the crystal gave way.

Specter stepped back just as the crystal broke loose from its base and fell toward the floor. The purple stone shattered upon impact, sending shards in every direction simultaneously. Specter closed his eyes and let out a slow breath. There was no way to finish now, no way to complete the cycle. He ran his hand over his face and struggled to compose himself. Taking another deep breath, he leaned toward the control panel. A good-sized chunk of the crystal was still visible. His hopes rose. Maybe it would be possible to finish anyway. Pressing his thumb into the hole, he pushed against the remainder of the stone and succeeded in moving it, but it was just too deep for his fingers or thumb. He needed something longer.

His eyes widened.

Throwing his coat open, he retrieved his stake. Pressing the tip carefully into the panel, he slowly began to apply pressure. Another crack startled him, but he didn't stop. Keeping one hand on the handle as a guide, he pressed hard against the butt of the stake until he felt the crystal lock into place. Yanking the stake free, he spun it in his hand and holstered it. Only seconds remained until the Dyfais completed its cycle, leaving no more time for finesse. Focusing his energy, he lashed forward with the heel of his palm slamming the final crystal into place.

The white fog around his feet quickly changed to blue and began to rise up around him. Taking a deep breath of air, Specter held his breath as the noxious chemical surrounded him. It burned his eyes as it began to seep into his nose and ears while his exposed flesh began to itch violently. This wasn't the sensation he remembered at all. Something was wrong. As his body absorbed the chemical, he began to convulse. His head fell back as a tortured scream escaped his lips. Then, in a moment, it was over. The field surrounding the Dyfais vanished, letting the chemical spill out and diffuse in the air. The faint red glow returned, but Specter was gone.

* * *

Ina was the first to wake. Her eyes slowly opened and began taking in her surroundings. It was dark now, she could tell by the sliver of silver moonlight trickling under the shack's door. Glancing to the right, she saw her companions beginning to stir. Zeke was still badly burned from earlier, but the burns were quickly fading. All that remained now were a few bits of wrinkled flesh which would surely fade in time. Her eyes traced over the contours of several tools on the walls as they made their way to Ice. She stopped suddenly and bit her lip. Her eyes caught on several wooden poles leaning in the corner—two of which had been sharpened for unknown reasons. Rolling onto the balls of her feet, she glanced down at Ice. She was still asleep. Ina had no idea for how much longer. This might be her only chance….

She shook her head. This wasn't right. No matter how she felt about Ice, it wasn't right to kill one of her kin. That idea was now coded onto her brain, thanks to the vampire's blood. It was an unwritten law. Vampires could not kill their own kind. She had no idea why, and as she stood up, she found she didn't care either. Her jaws clenched. Moving quickly across the room, she had the pole in her hands and was standing over Ice in a matter of seconds. Lifting the pole, she looked down into the woman's face. It was so peaceful, so innocent. There was no trace of the killer inside, only that of a human being. Ina felt her grip loosen. She shook her head and gritted her teeth. It had to be done. This wasn't an innocent. Ice was a cold-blooded killer, and would do the same to her if she had half the chance...but she hadn't. Ina had fallen asleep before Ice, and she had done nothing, even though she had every opportunity to act.

Guilt weighed heavily on her conscience as her stomach muscles tightened. Glancing over at Zeke, she saw his eyes blink open for the first time, still bleary with sleep and injury. No choice, she told herself. It's now or never.

Ina raised the makeshift stake above her head, holding it firmly with both hands. With one thrust, it would be all over. She wondered for a moment what happened when one of her kind was staked. Would they turn into ashes as she had seen in movies and television shows, or would there be a more dramatic exit? She was about to find out. The muscles in her arms and shoulders tensed.

"Ina!"

She turned her head. "Don't move, Zeke," she growled. "I have to do this."

Zeke was no more than arm's length from her. His hands were up, patting the air. "Don't do anything you'll regret."

An odd look crossed Ina's face. Did he not realize what they were now? Was this some vestige of his mortal coil yet to be shuffled off? They were killers. Nothing more. They served no other purpose in the grand scheme of things. At this point, she could see no difference between taking the life of a human or a vampire. Her expression hardened as her golden eyes gleamed in the darkness. It was possible he could reach her before she staked Ina, but it was unlikely she reasoned. She snapped her attention back to the sleeping vampire and struck. With a motion too fast for human eyes to follow, Zeke leapt from his position and caught the stake in midswing with his hand. Unfortunately, it wasn't enough to stop the blow, only alter its trajectory slightly. The pole dove into Ice's flesh easily and out her back. Her pale eyes shot open and both hands wrapped around the stake as her scream sliced through the air.

Ina exposed her fangs and twisted the pole in an act of defiance and hatred. Ina shrieked again. "That's right, bitch! How do you like that?"

Lifting himself off the floor, Zeke lashed out, angrily knocking Ina on her ass. He stood over her, his true form exposed with his lips twisted up into a vicious sneer. Retribution would be his, but it would have to wait. Spinning around, he fell to his knees next to Ice. Placing one hand on her face, he wrapped the other gently around the still imbedded stake. "Are you okay?"

Ice shook her head slowly. "Do I fucking look okay? I have a giant pole sticking out of my chest!" A trickle of blood ran down her pale blue lips and onto her white face.

Moving his hand down her chest, Zeke carefully probed the area around the wound. Using both hands, he ripped the shirt above it away, exposing her chest. To his amazement, her flesh was already beginning to heal around the stake. "It looks like it missed your heart by a matter of inches."

"I was kind of wondering why you weren't playing a harp," Ice spat cynically. "Get this fucking thing out of me so I can kill that bitch."

Zeke nodded and stood up. Grabbing the pole firmly, he straddled Ice. He gave her one more look. "This is going to hurt like hell."

"Just do it!" She screamed.

"On the count of—"

"Don't make me kill you too," Ice growled. "Just take the fucking pole out of my chest...NOW!"

Without hesitation, Zeke ripped the pole free and staggered back. Ice rolled onto her side in pain, cradling her new wound. She watched as her ruby red blood spilled out like water onto the hard floor below her. She dipped her palm into the blood and held it up, suddenly enthralled by the sight of it. Balling her fist, she regained her focus as anger began to well up. Rolling onto her knees, she glared at Ina. Only one word entered her enraged mind: "Why?"

Ina had pulled herself up against the wall. She smiled and shrugged at the vampire. "You wouldn't do the same?"

"I didn't." Despite the pain, Ice lifted herself off the floor.

Zeke was instantly at her side. "Don't do anything you'll regret," he said again as he placed a hand on her arm.

"Regret," Ice laughed. "That's something I have no use for." She surged forward and pinned Ina against the wall. Pulling her arm back, she held her fist within Ina's sight. "Fuck it." She struck.

Ina fell to the floor and quickly skittered away from the woman's reach. She and Zeke looked up in time to see Ice pull her hand from the hole in the wall she had just created. A shaft of moonlight spilled onto the floor around her, highlighting her body in a soft glow.

Ice glanced down at her bloody knuckles and laughed. She shook her hand as she turned back to her companions. Her face was now solemn. "I still didn't." She moved past Zeke and headed for the door. Throwing it open, she stepped out into the cool night air and took a deep breath, even though she had no need to. "I don't have any more time for this," she added quietly. She looked back over her shoulder. "I'm hungry." With those final words, she disappeared from the doorway.

Zeke turned back to Ina and extended a hand. With some trepidation, Ina accepted the help. Once up, she began to dust herself off. Zeke shook his head. "What the hell were you doing?"

"I just—"

Zeke lashed out with the back of his hand, catching her firmly across her face.

Ina stumbled back, her hand instantly covering the red welt on her cheek. The expression on her face was a mixture of pain and disbelief. He had never acted violently toward any member of the coven before. It just wasn't in his nature.

"What the fuck is wrong with you?"

Ina shook her head. "I...."

His golden eyes were burning with rage. "We're not supposed to kill other vampires. Don't you know that?"

Ina nodded slowly as she let her hand fall from her face. If he started to swing again, she wouldn't let him connect. She steadied herself. "I know, but I don't give a shit. What makes a vampire any different than a human? Why can we kill one and not another?"

"They're our fucking food!" Zeke roared. "It's completely different!"

"Why?" Ina posed again. "Aren't you the one who always said that if we were vampires we could live outside the laws of man? Why then should new laws be applied to us? We are vampires," her voice became little more than a whisper, "we can do whatever we want."

"Yes," he hissed and clenched his fist. "But you still had no right to try and kill Ice. What did she do to you?"

"It's personal."

Zeke slammed his fist against the metal shelving behind Ina. "Don't give me that shit again. Tell me now."

Ina writhed under his glare. She still wasn't used to their real faces or eyes. "I was a member of her coven before joining yours."

"And?"

"She ridiculed me and kicked me out."

Zeke took a step back. "That's it?" he asked, almost in shock.

Ina nodded. "She was a real bitch to me."

Zeke tried hard to contain his laughter. "You were going to kill her for that?"

"She also killed my boyfriend."

Zeke's laughter quickly stopped. "What?"

149

"I was with this guy who called himself 'Drake'. He was a spectacular specimen of a man with short, black hair and a chiseled jaw. No man I have met since could wear black leather the way he could. We were pretty hot and heavy for a long time," her eyes trailed down to the floor. "I always assumed he was the one for me, but Ice had different plans. We joined her coven together, but it wasn't long before she started lavishing special attention on Drake. There came a point where she was seeing him more than I was," Ina admitted. "So, I confronted her about it. She said she understood and would take a step back. At that point, I thought she was being very cool."

"What happened?" he asked, spellbound by this rare glimpse into Ina's psyche. During the entire time they had known each other, she had never opened up like this before.

"She brought me into her chambers the next night with Drake. She was wearing a long, white see-through negligee that didn't leave anything to the imagination. She immediately had two of her goons grab Drake and me. They tied me up to a wall and took Drake before her and bound his hands. She drew a long knife from a nearby table and stood over him. She looked at me and said, 'If I can't have him, no one can'." Ina's head dropped. "She slit his throat and drank his blood right in front of me. It was that same night she removed me from the coven."

Zeke's eyes widened. "Why didn't you alert the authorities?"

"And have the same thing happen to me that

150

happened to Drake? I don't think so."

"So you've been carrying this vendetta around for how long?"

Ina looked up to the ceiling as she did the math in her head. "Almost eight years now."

Zeke rubbed his chin. "She doesn't look like she even remembers you."

Ina nodded, her face sullen.

"I promise, she will get what she deserves," Zeke vowed, "but right now, we have more important issues at hand. We have to find 'her'."

"I know."

"We're very close now. We have to move quickly." He closed his eyes and let his head fall back. "I can feel her calling me." He offered his open hand to Ina.

She carefully accepted the offer. "It's good to know you understand."

Zeke smiled. "We'll kill her ourselves if we have to when this is all over. I'm sorry I stopped you."

Ina returned the smile.

Hand in hand, the two walked out of the shack and into the night. The darkness rolled around them like a fog, quickly enveloping them. Egypt was a place of ancient mystery, they only hoped they could find what they were searching for.

A shadowy figure stepped out from behind the shack with clenched fists. The form moved slowly around to the front and watched the shades of Zeke and Ina fading. She brushed her silvery white hair from her face and sneered. Every word of their conversation was overheard through the new window in the shack. Ice grinned, exposing her glistening fangs. Treachery was afoot, and she liked it.

* * *

Cane looked at Bishop and then at Dawn, his face a mixture of concern and exhaustion. Large, dark bags hung under his eyes while a salt and pepper shadow had begun to cover his jaw. His eyes were a spider's web of red irritation. He looked like hell—well, more than usual. The trio had been up all night, listening to Cane's story and dissecting it word by word. Discussion, by this point, seemed to be endless...and fruitless.

He rubbed his chin as he looked at his two partners. "Do you understand what I've told you?"

Neither spoke.

"These beings are for all intents and purposes unstoppable," Cane reiterated. "If they come," he looked away, "we're dead."

"You can't believe that," Dawn argued. "I won't believe that."

"I'm sorry," Cane breathed.

Bishop shook his head. "You said there were people who could deal with vampires. What did you call them?"

"The Gwyliad Wriaeth," Cane answered.

Bishop snapped his fingers. "That's right. Why can't we contact them? These people are professional Vampire Hunters. They stopped Caitlin once," he smiled, "they can do it again."

"It doesn't work like that," Cane frowned. "We don't flash the Bat Signal in the sky and they come running."

"How did the coven in Seattle contact them?" Dawn asked.

"What?" Cane asked.

"You said the coven of Witches Lydia belonged to in Seattle contacted the Gwyliad Wriaeth," Dawn clarified. "How did they do it?"

Cane's eyes grew bleary for a moment. "I don't know."

"Can we contact Lydia and find out?" Dawn pressed.

Cane slumped back in his chair. Of course, he had thought of this, but it had never held much hope for him. The Gwyliad Wriaeth was almost as mythical as their prey. If it were not for the scars on his body and the shared memories with Lydia, he could play the whole thing off as a false memory—something from a dream that had somehow taken hold. Even more than that, he didn't want to bring Lydia back into that world. He couldn't even fathom the thought of causing her more pain, and taking her back to that place and time, even if only in memory, would certainly do that. He wouldn't. "I'm sorry. That's not an option at this point."

"Why?" Dawn asked, slightly agitated. She couldn't understand why he was throwing away what was his best, and possibly only, chance.

"I said no," Cane stated.

"But this could be your only—"

"No," Cane repeated. "This could be nothing more than my overactive imagination," he posed. "Have we even considered that?"

"In our line of profession," Bishop smiled, "we learn these kind of things are not usually a figment

153

of someone's imagination." He adjusted slightly in his seat. "I think you're scared, and I wouldn't say that to you without good cause. We have to take these visions, these premonitions, very seriously. I don't think it's right to just shrug them off."

"I'm not afraid," Cane stated very seriously. Standing, he began to pace uncomfortably around Dawn's living room.

"Cane," Dawn said with a sigh, "why are you doing this? We have been presented with a very good solution to this problem. Why won't you take it? What have you got to lose?"

"Everything!" Cane shouted at the top of his lungs. His eyes were fierce, his body language angry. "I will not talk about this!" He took a step back from his teammates with clenched fists. "I can't do that. I won't do that to Lydia!" He stopped himself and quickly looked away, realizing what he had said. The proverbial cat was out of the bag. He started to speak, but let the thought fade away. It wasn't worth it. He turned toward a coatrack near the door and removed his jacket. Slipping it on, he gave Dawn and Bishop a final glance and reached for the door handle.

"Where are you going?" Dawn asked carefully.

"I need to get some air," Cane muttered. Stepping through the door, he pulled it firmly closed behind him.

Dawn and Bishop turned to each other in silence. Their eyes spoke volumes of concern and dread. There was no conversation needed, they knew what they had to do. Cane could try to ignore the problem, but they didn't have that luxury. It was

154

time to act, and they had to call in reinforcements.
Bishop reached for his cell phone.

Chapter Nine

The old woman stirred in her seat as the sun began to set. She looked out her balcony window over Cairo and allowed herself a brief smile. She remembered when all this was nothing more than desert; even the great stone blocks that made up the pyramids had yet to be quarried. Her mind wandered to the Sphinx for a moment. She hated that an egotistical Pharaoh had desecrated its original face. It had once been a magnificent shrine to the people it watched over, now it was nothing more than a permanent idol of one man's vanity. She was glad he was dead.

The sun was spreading a golden orange light down across the city in waves. Clouds had rolled in, helping mask the thin line separating the Earth and sky. Never let it be said she didn't enjoy a good sunset, but always from a safe location. A beam of light filtered in through the window and sliced across the floor...just left of her tall leather chair. She pulled her bony fingers off the arm of the chair, just to be safe as she watched the sunlight slowly slip past the horizon.

Spinning around, she stared at her missing reflection in a tall mirror that occupied the wall next to the door. All that was visible was the chair, without even a hint of her form. Turning away, she glanced at her hands. She wished she could see herself, even just once. She was old and withered. She shook her head. "Old" wasn't the word to describe her. She was ancient, predating...almost everything. She could never claim to have been there when Jesus was crucified (if that ever actually did happen, and she had her doubts), but she was certainly older than his silly little cult. She had seen the rise and fall of Caesar, the birth of the super powers, witnessed the Blitzkrieg rampage over Europe and religious followers in the Middle East become zealots for their cause leading to terrorism around the world. But there was no sympathy for this devil.

Time was constantly moving, yet she was not. She remained constant and immovable, ever unchanging, but her time was coming. No longer would she be confined to this place and this horrible city. Her power would be restored. Her plans were finally coming to fruition. Her new apprentices would be arriving shortly, as well as her first live prey. It had been so long, too long.

As the last shred of sunlight drained from the sky, she lifted her hand and clenched her fist. Her bones and flesh popped and cracked in protest. It had been even longer since she had left this chair. As a vampire ages, their bodies slowly solidify. Their skin becomes a thick crust and what lies beneath is unknown. They become more or less living statues, but ones no one would be pleased to look at. Under all the psychic manipulation, they were nothing more than corpses—horrible, decaying bodies.

Caitlin stood and walked tentatively toward the balcony railing. Placing her hands on the metal rails, she peered down into the city streets below. It would be soon now. She could sense her blood in the bodies of her apprentices. It had been mixed with another vampire of her creation and the blood of the humans, but there was still an undeniable trace and it was drawing ever closer.

Soon. It would be very soon.

* * *

The door burst open. Stepping inside, he dropped his jingling keys on the floor. His coat went second. Still angry, Cane moved to his sofa and slumped. He stared at his open hands in his lap, then slowly let his attention drift away. His apartment was dark, save for a single shaft of silvery moonlight that ran across the floor behind him. He could get up and turn on the light, but he saw no point in it. He would actually have to look at himself that way, and he didn't feel like facing that coward. His entire life—except for a period of about ten years in his teens—had stood for reason, and now he was being destroyed by what was nothing more than a memory.

Or was it?

By this point, even he couldn't be sure. He had read of many cases of post-traumatic stress manifesting itself in strange ways, even going so far as to cause a haunting he had investigated a few years back in Jersey, but it couldn't happen to him. Not to Zachary Cane. It wasn't even plausible. Not even remotely.

Why?

He shook his head. He didn't want to admit it could be testosterone holding him back, or it could be something else. It could be the truth. He felt a moment of clarity. It wasn't something he had admitted to himself, or rather wanted to admit to himself. Up until this point, he had been looking for excuses, for alternate explanations, why couldn't it be the truth?

Because it scared the hell out of him, that's why. He didn't want to admit that remorseless demon could still be out there and looking for him. She was dead. She had to be. He had seen her die.

His memories weren't as clear as they had once been—a byproduct of age. Probably both. He knew in most cases like his, memories were unconsciously blocked. He rather preferred it that way. He didn't want to have to think of the slashing fangs, the blood and those horrible golden eyes. The way they had no pupil or iris, just solid color. Solid, hateful color. The way they would peer through to his very soul and use the information contained therein to break him, and those fangs. Those glistening, white, razor-sharp canine teeth were weapons of pain. The human bite produces approximately one hundred and fifty pounds of pressure. When combined with fangs, a vampire could do a lot of damage in a short amount of time.

Cane shuddered. He had endured that pain, and still bore the scars. Letting his head fall forward into his hands, he took a deep breath. The physical scars were nothing compared to the mental ones.

Looking up, he let his hand fall to the crucifix dangling around his neck. He began unconsciously rubbing it between his thumb and forefinger. It comforted him somehow, he wasn't sure why. A member of the Gwyliad Wriaeth had told Cane that crosses meant nothing to vampires. Many of the truly ancient ones predated Christianity, making a crucifix nothing more than a piece of jewelry. Still, it provided some measure of ease in the back of his mind. It was probably a correlation between all the films and books he had read on vampires.

Obsession was a strong word, but Cane used it to describe his connection with vampires. It was something he didn't like to talk about, even amongst his inner circle. It was taboo; a dark secret intended to stay that way. He had poured over volumes of lore and legend, combed through popular culture for any nuggets of truth, but there was nothing concrete to be found. It seemed, as if by design, one legend or story contradicted two others. One reference quoted that they were immortal, while another stated they were only long lived, and yet another spoke of how their life spans could only be measured in hours. It was the same thing throughout all the vampire literature.

He had harbored this dirty little secret for thirty years now, and it had only grown with the passage of time. What was he looking for in those dusty volumes? Even he wasn't sure. He had told himself on many occasions he was looking for the ultimate solution: a way to destroy all vampires, but was it something more? Had he become attached to the very creature that years earlier had tried to kill him? He had studied situations like this, of course. The condition was referred to as Stockholm syndrome, in which the captive began to identify and even in some cases, support their captors. It wasn't rare. When placed in life or death situations, the mind often had strange ways of coping, but was that it?

He could never be sure. Seeking professional

therapy might give him some insight into his scarred psyche, but he didn't want to see the doctor's face when he told them he had been captured and tortured by vampires. Wouldn't that make for an interesting trip to the looney bin? He was on his own. Even his partners didn't understand the gravity of the situation.

How could they? They weren't the ones chained to that wall with vampires sucking the life out of them. It was said you could learn a lot by "walking in another man's shoes", but Cane had always thought that quote was garbage. How could you ever truly know what it was like to be another person? With the millions of individual experiences that make up someone's personality, it would be impossible to say what they would or wouldn't do in any given situation. How could they know? He was trying to protect Lydia more than himself. It was one of the few remaining noble shreds he had.

He let the gold crucifix fall from his fingers as he leaned back on the couch. It had been a long couple days for him, and he was probably reacting badly. Instead of helping his partners, his friends, to understand, he had completely shut them out. That was Cane logic at its finest. Could he really drag them into this though? He didn't want to see them tortured as he was, or worse, killed by those soulless creatures. Was he trying to play the hero here, one man on a crusade to save the world? Or was it something else, something deeper and darker than that? Did he want to become a vampire?

A cold shiver ran up his spine. Cane sat straight up on the couch uncomfortably, his back muscles

161

tensing. Without looking behind, he reached up and unfastened his necklace. Holding it out, he let it fall carelessly to the floor. With a deep breath, he stood and turned around, already knowing what he would see.

A woman, dressed completely in black, stood just behind his couch. She was lovely, with long, slender limbs, and dark wavy hair. Her blue eyes were burning with intensity and her lips were slightly pursed, revealing only a hint of her pearly white fangs. Her dark eyes melted to gold as she stared at Cane. "You know why I'm here." Her voice was unearthly, yet soft and silky.

Cane nodded.

"How is this going to play out?" she asked nonchalantly.

"I won't struggle."

The vampire cocked her head slightly to the right. This wasn't the solution she had been expecting. "You're not going to fight?"

Cane stepped around his couch toward the woman, hands open. "I'm too bloody tired of running. If Caitlin wants me, then she can have me."

The vampire grinned. "Fair enough." Before Cane even had a chance to react, the vampire had knocked him to the floor and was pinning him down. Her icy hands felt like steel shackles around his wrists. She leaned close to his ear, letting out a long sigh of pleasure. "This is my favorite part," she moaned. Tilting her head slightly, she slowly opened her mouth and fully exposed her fangs. Diving forward, she easily pierced the skin on

162

Cane's neck. With her fangs still in the punctures, she slowly pulled to the left, creating two long wounds. Blood immediately began to spill into her mouth and over her tongue.

She drank deeply and began to dream. Much like sex releases endorphins in the human brain, blood had the same, if not greater, effect on vampires. Her mind slipped into a state of ecstasy. With every drop of blood, her mind wandered deeper into its blissful condition. It was only moments before she felt his heart begin to slow. He was dying. She had been a bit overzealous in her assignment. It wasn't her job to kill this man, only to bring him to Caitlin. She let out a brief grunt of dissatisfaction. Pulling her teeth from the wound before she was done, she sat up and looked down at Cane. He was still breathing, but his eyes had rolled back and he was motionless. He was on the very verge of death.

Lifting her left arm, she pulled her sleeve away from her wrist. Bringing it to her mouth, she carefully bit into her own flesh, momentarily enjoying the sensation of pain. Her blood, now mixed with his, dripped from the wound immediately. Holding her wrist over Cane's mouth, she allowed a few precious ruby drops to fall on his lips. She watched as his mouth closed around the blood in satisfaction. That amount wasn't enough to turn him, only to keep him alive. She drew her finger across the cut on her wrist and then pressed it to his neck. The wounds she had just created immediately began to heal. She gazed in amazement, never tiring of that little trick.

Rocking back on her heels, she slowly stood over Cane. She thought momentarily of finishing the job and disappearing into the night, but Caitlin, or one of her minions would find her eventually. She had to complete her task the right way. She could certainly snack on the way back. She smiled as she reached down for Cane. Lifting him off the floor with her preternatural strength, she slung his limp body over her shoulder and headed for the door.

* * *

Specter awoke in darkness. He was lying uncomfortably on a hard floor with his right arm pinned beneath his body. He was in pain. A dull ache filtered throughout his entire body and his head was throbbing. Rolling onto his back, he pulled his arm free. Tingles, like a hundred needles being poked into his flesh, ran up his arm as the blood flow returned. He had no idea of how long he had been out, or for that matter, of where he was. He should've appeared almost instantly in the opposite gate room that was beneath the Great Pyramid in Giza, but instead, he was here…wherever that was.

Fighting through the pain, Specter rolled forward into a sitting position. The motion sent a rush of pain to his temples. Clapping his hands to the sides of his head, he tried to silence what felt like drums behind his skull. Gritting his teeth, he waited a moment for the sensation to pass. At least he hoped it would pass. Seconds seemed like minutes as his head continued to thump, then all at once, the pain subsided. He let out a long breath to relax and center himself as he carefully stood up.

With arms wide, he slowly walked around, taking small steps as to avoid bumping into anything. There was no frame of reference in this place, no dim flicker of light, nothing. He had to depend on his sense of touch alone. Taking a few tentative steps to the right, his hand brushed against something solid. Keeping his hand in place, he added the other and began to feel over the object. It was cold and possibly sculpted, bringing him to the conclusion it could be a statue, or some kind of carved relief. He moved his hands across the object, until he came to the edge. It was definitely a carving of some kind. The corners were hard and sharp, and from his best estimate, at perfect ninety degree angles. He couldn't make out any of the carvings or what they might represent. This first clue gave him no evidence as to where he could possibly be.

He leaned his head back and sniffed the air. It was dry, with a hint of mold and dust. He could be in any number of temples he reasoned, but that didn't solidify anything. He took another breath of the air. He had learned over his travels that every place, no matter how similar it may seem on the surface, has a unique smell. He had been around enough to recognize some countries by smell alone, but this one was eluding him.

The silence around him was quickly becoming deafening. His ears perked up for a moment. A faint sound seemed to be coming from a few feet away from him. He held his breath and listened intently for the sound again, then took a nervous step back. The sound became clear: it was a sharp hiss. There were snakes in here, probably more than a few. It could be anything, but his mind instantly churned out a worst-case scenario. It had to be poisonous. That was just how his luck was going lately.

He held perfectly still against the object. He didn't want to arouse any curiosity from the serpents. Hopefully, they would sense how big he was and not come any closer, but then again, he didn't know a lot about snakes. He knew most didn't have a keen sense of sight; instead they relied on smell and heat sensing pits in their mouth to target their prey. Darkness didn't mean a whole lot to a snake. It wasn't very warm in here, so he knew they couldn't be operating at peak efficiency being cold blooded. They would still be slightly sluggish…and probably grumpy. He realized he was probably standing in a snake's den where they go to escape the heat, or mate.

The feeling in his gut doubled in intensity. There could be literally hundreds of baby snakes slithering around the floor and a couple of angry parents. His situation had gone from bad to worse in a matter of seconds. He shook his head. Maybe he was reading too much into this. There was probably just one, little, harmless snake in here.

He heard three or four loud simultaneous hisses.

Then again, maybe there were more.

Chapter Ten

She enjoyed the sound of her footfalls echoing off the walls of these old buildings. There were many things Ice had begun to savor now that she had new life flowing through her veins. It reminded her of one of her favorite novels, Interview With The Vampire, by Anne Rice. She had always loved the scene where Lestat had just turned the story's protagonist, Louis, into a vampire. 'Lestat leaned close to Louis and said, "Now look with your vampire eyes." The world seemed wholly different than it had moments before; even the buttons on his vest seemed to enthrall the fledgling vampire.' Ice had found her transformation gave her a similar insight into the world. She wondered for a moment if Anne Rice was indeed a vampire, or as stated in the story, a pseudonym for the particular vampire writing the novel. She smiled at the thought. She would have to find out for herself one day.

Glancing up into the starry Egyptian sky, she wandered aimlessly through the old streets, pondering how many other vampires had walked this identical path before her. Her thoughts slowly turned to Zeke and Ina. She had been ignoring the burning in her blood calling to her, but was sure they had not. It was, after all, the reason they were in Egypt: to find their master. Why was that so important, she conjectured? Was it necessary to her survival? She shook her head. There was no reason it could be that way. Being born with genetic memories ensured a fledgling could, and should, immediately leave the nest. There was no wisdom to be gained from her creator. All that she needed she was given in the moment when their blood touched hers.

There was something else at work here. Of that she could be sure.

She came around a corner and paused. To this point, her journey had been relatively human free. She had yet to encounter a group by herself. She hesitated for a moment longer. This wasn't New York City. If a group of pedestrians there witnessed something odd and out of the ordinary, they would probably pay it no mind and continue on their way. Here, by contrast, the people still paid service to the old legends and stories. They were a people still very much afraid of their Gods. She was sure these people knew what a vampire was (or whatever their equivalent was), and no doubt, knew how to deal with one.

She took a step away from the wall into the street. A lone light from somewhere above was shining down on her position, leaving her face in the shadows. A sudden realization hit her: even if they did recognize what she was, she could kill all of them before they had a chance to tell anyone. She was, by far, faster than anyone on the street and ten times as deadly. She was a vampire. She should be scared of no mere human. She was at the top of the food chain. An evil smirk grew across her lips. She continued forward with confident strides.

There were maybe ten merchants selling their wares on this small street. The sun had set only hours before, leaving many of them to break down their stands and talk amongst themselves. Each wore a simple robe, some with colored turbans, others without, but each appeared to be of simple origin. They spoke in their language, which Ice had no knowledge of, and smoked American cigarettes—surely a luxury of their profession. Their products consisted of everything from bootlegged movies and CDs, sacred relics from their culture, to locally grown produce, all spread out on rugs and wooden crates doubling as small makeshift tables.

The first group of men, busily smoking their cigarettes and talking, paid her no attention, but another man looked up with a smile and began to approach her. He carried what looked like cantaloupes under each arm and immediately presented one to Ice. She smiled softly and shook her head. Handing the melon back, she looked into the man's eyes. "No thank you," she said softly.

The merchant started to retrieve the melon, then suddenly stopped. His eyes slowly began to glaze over and his motions became stiff. Ice cocked her head slightly but didn't break her gaze. The man had become transfixed. Did he know what she was? Ice paused a moment. It didn't seem that way. Lifting her hand, she quickly waved it in front of his face. He made no effort to jerk back, or even avoid her hand. Unblinking, he remained focused on her eyes.

"Interesting," she said softly. "What's your name?"

"Sam," he muttered.

"Not a very Middle Eastern sounding name," Ice commented.

"My father didn't want that for me," he spoke as if in a trance. "He wanted me to blend more easily with Westerners. One day, I would leave this country and travel to America, the land of—"

"Okay, enough," Ice said, shaking her head. "I get the point." She bit her bottom lip and started to speak, but quickly reconsidered her question. "Who am I?"

"The one I serve."

Ice was shocked at his answer. "Why?"

The man remained silent.

"Did you hear me?" She snapped her fingers. "Why am I the one you serve?"

Still nothing.

Her mind began to understand what had happened. An evil smirk grew across her face. Her genetic memory had explained what was happening. "I put the 'whammy' on you," she giggled.

The man remained fixed, unblinking.

"It's like one of those old cheesy 'Dracula' movies where I say, 'look deeply into my eyes'," she said, feigning an eastern European accent, "and you have to do what I say." She glanced back up the street at the group of three merchants still smoking their cigarettes. "Go kill those three men," she whispered. She quickly took a step back out of the way and watched in wonder.

Sam dropped both of his melons on the ground and quickly reached into his robe. He extracted a six inch long curved knife from an unseen sheath and clenched it in his hand. His knuckles began to turn white due to the pressure he was applying on the hilt of the weapon. His docile facial expression

170

hardened into one of anger and hatred. With teeth clenched, he leapt at the nearest man and wrapped his arm around the man's neck. With one severe thrust, Sam had drawn the blade through the soft flesh of the man's throat. The man toppled to the ground holding his neck and gasping for air as blood gushed from the wound. The very sight enthralled Ice.

The other two merchants had taken several steps away from their friend and Sam, not understanding what had happened in a matter of seconds. Merchants and pedestrians began to scatter from the scene in all directions. While the first man turned and began to run with the rest of the crowd, shouting, no doubt, for the authorities at the top of his lungs, the second man took it upon himself to stop this crazed killer. Lifting up his robe, he pulled a small pistol from an ankle holster. Lifting the weapon, he cocked back the hammer and shouted a warning in his native tongue. Sam made no movement.

Ice licked her lips. "Kill him," she whispered.

Sam leapt forward with the blade of his knife toward the other man. Without a second of hesitation, the man pulled the trigger, hitting Sam squarely in the chest with the shot. Sam fell to the ground just short of the man, moaning in agony. The man took several uncomfortable steps away from Sam, not knowing what to expect and out of ammunition. He looked up with terror in his eyes at Ice. She was moving slowly toward him. Every movement of her body, every step, seemed to be a part of a choreographed ballet.

171

"If you want something done," she let her eyes fade to gold, "you have to do it yourself."

The merchant screamed in terror and turned to run. He hadn't taken more than a step, when Ice was on him. Grabbing his shoulders, she slammed him up against the nearest wall, instantly breaking several of his ribs. The man cried out again, shouting the name of his god.

Ice placed her finger on his lips and smiled. "He doesn't care."

The man's eyes widened again. He took a deep breath to scream again, but Ice bit into his windpipe. Blood splattered from his gaping mouth as a gurgling sound escaped. With one vicious pull, Ice tore out the man's throat with her teeth. She held the man against the wall lapping at the wine-colored life spurting from his gaping wound. She felt it running over her chin and throat and down onto her clothes. Reaching up to her face, she wiped her chin clean and licked off her fingers. She glanced up into the man's eyes. He was still alive and twitching. If she left him here right now, he would die a horrible, agonizing death, but if she finished the job, he would find a quick end. She allowed her mental projection to melt away revealing to the man the corpse beneath. "You killed my Sam."

She smiled at the man and dropped him to the ground.

Turning away, she wiped the last bit of blood from her face. It didn't matter, she realized. It was all just a mental projection. She could just as easily look like a ten foot tall demon with huge bat like wings instead of a person. She glanced down at her

172

blood stained clothes. With a smirk, she began to peel them off and shred them. She walked completely naked down the street, shreds of white bloodstained cloth trailing behind her. As she rounded the corner, she was dressed once again in a white baby doll T-shirt that exposed her midriff, a white skirt that hung just above her ankles, a pair of six inch "fuck me" stiletto heels and a long, white leather jacket. It was all a mental projection, she realized. No matter how she appeared on the inside, she could look any way she wanted on the outside. She laughed as she tossed her platinum blonde hair over her shoulder and drifted into the night just as the police began to arrive on the scene behind her.

* * *

"She's calling her contact in the Gwyliad Wriaeth," Bishop smiled as he snapped his cell phone shut, "and she's catching the first plane to D.C. with Kelley."

Dawn looked up from her seat and smiled softly. "Finally, some good news. I think it will be good to have the whole team back together, and good for Cane to have Lydia here. It may serve to ease his nerves a bit."

Bishop nodded.

Cane had stormed out a little over two hours ago. Since then, the two partners had remained mostly quiet, chewing on the information presented to them that night. The sun was beginning to peak above the eastern horizon as the sky filled with a soft, orange light. Through a large picture window in Dawn's dining room, they could see the city beginning to wake up.

"Can I ask you a question?"

"Sure," Bishop said softly.

"What do you think of vampires?" Dawn pulled her knees up to her chest and wrapped her arms around them.

"That's an interesting question," Bishop stated. "I assume you mean, do I think they're real?"

Dawn nodded slowly.

"I have to. If Cane told me he'd seen monkeys fly out of someone's ass, I would be inclined to believe him. He has no reason to lie to us. So yes, I believe they are real." He smiled. "I've always had a sneaking suspicion they really existed. There are stranger things in Heaven and Hell, Horatio." He looked carefully at his partner. "Why do you ask?"

"I can deal with ghosts, poltergeists, and all manner of spooky stuff, but this…" she let her words trail off. "This just boggles my mind. I was raised a good little Catholic girl. We were taught not to believe in things like vampires, that they were just stories to scare little kids, and now this," she spread out her arms. "It's a little hard to fathom, you know?"

Bishop nodded. "We've got to be strong for Cane."

Dawn stood up and started for her bedroom. "What time is Lydia and Kelley's flight coming in?"

"They didn't know. They said they would catch the first one out and call us with the arrival time."

Dawn nodded. "I want you to head down to the office and round up one of our tool kits. I'm going to try and track down Cane."

"What do you need a kit for?" Bishop asked as he stood.

"These things are supernatural, aren't they?"

Bishop furrowed his brow and thought for a moment, "I would assume—"

"Then we can find or track them with our equipment."

"I've never heard of anything like this before," Bishop protested. "Shouldn't we find a Slayer or something like that? You know, a vampire cursed with a soul to help us?"

"You watch entirely too much television," Dawn smirked.

Bishop laughed out loud, "Yeah, but you understood the reference!"

Dawn took a moment to remove her foot from her mouth. Shaking her head, she pointed toward the door. "Go. We've got a lot of work to do."

Bishop nodded. "I'm on it." Lifting his jacket off the coat rack next to the door, he quickly slipped it on as he pulled the door open. Taking one more glance inside Dawn's apartment, he stopped. "How can she afford a place like this?"

* * *

Zeke looked crossly at Ina. She had done nothing but complain about Ice most of the evening. Even when they had stopped to feed, she still complained. Typical woman, never stops complaining, even when her mouth's full. He was at wit's end with her. "Can you just shut up for a minute?" he lashed out.

Ina stopped dead in her tracks, her mouth agape. "What?"

175

"All you've done tonight is bitch and moan," Zeke said angrily. "Don't you have something more constructive to do?"

"Like what?" Ina asked, obviously hurt by Zeke's anger. "Walk around Cairo in circles looking for a house that may or may not exist? How many fucking times have we walked around this block? Five? Six?"

Zeke looked down at his feet with a huff. "If I knew where this place was, I would've gone straight there. I don't see you making any suggestions here!"

Ina gritted her teeth, but slowly relaxed her jaw muscles. Taking a deep breath, she moved closer to Zeke. "I'm sorry." She balled her fists and pressed them to the sides of her head. "All I can hear is her," her voice was tinged with a bit of pain. "It's driving me insane."

Zeke reached out and placed his hand on her shoulder. "I know. I hear it too. And it seems like it's getting louder."

Ina nodded.

"I think we're getting close," Zeke stated, "but I don't know exactly where to go. I've been trying to use her voice as a kind of homing beacon, but so far, it hasn't been working that well. I don't think there's going to be some big neon sign that says, 'Master Vampire Here'," he joked.

Ina wasn't amused. Her face was turned toward one of the taller buildings.

"We just have to keep looking," Zeke continued, "and keep our cool." He stopped. Ina wasn't paying any attention to him. He snapped his fingers next to her ear. "Ina! You aren't listening to me."

She quickly waved off his protest and pointed up.

"What?" Zeke spun around and tried to find what his companion had spotted. His eyes immediately focused on a pair of glowing gold eyes on a balcony overhead. "Is that…?"

Ina closed her eyes and took a deep breath. "Yes," she moaned. "I can feel her glory."

"I don't feel—"

Ina quickly silenced Zeke. "Look with your mind, not with your eyes."

Zeke quietly obeyed. Closing his eyes, he took a long breath and relaxed. Immediately, his mind was flooded with images of a striking young woman with fiery red hair and a black dress flowing in the wind. Her skin was perfect in every way, not a single flaw to be found anywhere. Her iris' were emerald, green, and seemed to be as deep as the ocean itself. She was perfect in every way, and she was beckoning to him. He watched in horror as her beauty faded away in his mind's eye, leaving only a dried up husk of a vampire. Slowly, her flesh began to crumble away, leaving only an animated skeleton with fierce green eyes. The skeleton raised both hands to Zeke, palms open, pleading with him to help, but as he reached out, they disintegrated into dust.

Zeke opened his eyes with a start. "She's dying." He turned to Ina and stopped.

A lone tear was running down her cheek. "I know. I think I've always known."

He returned his gaze to the balcony, but the eyes were gone, replaced now with darkness. Zeke reached out and grabbed Ina's hand, immediately charging toward the front door of this rundown apartment complex. It looked as if no one had lived here in a long time, at least no one technically alive. Pushing the rusting gate open, Zeke's feet barely touched the flagstones as he moved toward the front door. Letting go of Ina's hand, he dropped his shoulder and charged toward the entrance. The old wooden door exploded from its hinges in a shower of wooden shards and nails. Stepping inside, Zeke felt a sense of true urgency, as if he didn't make it to her in the next few seconds, he would lose his chance altogether. He couldn't let that happen.

His eyes quickly scanned the dark interior of the building. Much like cat's eyes, a vampire's can see perfectly in any level of light, but unlike a cat, a vampire can see in complete darkness. Zeke spotted a staircase against the far wall of the large foyer. He dashed and leapt over old, discarded pieces of furniture and assorted piles of trash as he made his way to the target. If a human had been standing inside, they would have seen nothing more than a quick blur across the room.

Zeke didn't bother to hit the bottom few stairs, instead he planted both hands on the railing and vaulted into the center. Without losing a step, he charged upstairs and took his first left. Instinct was guiding him now. No emotion, no logic, just pure instinct. He was following the scent of death. He glanced back for a moment to see Ina keeping pace with him. She had just leapt the top step and was rounding the corner behind him. Returning his attention forward, he skidded on his heels and took a hard left. His eyes fixated on a door at the end of the hall.

Within a fraction of a second, he had traversed the entire hallway and was standing perfectly still in front of the door. He enjoyed the sensation of not having to catch his breath after a run like that. Glancing over his shoulder, he saw Ina slide to a stop just behind him. She placed her hand tenderly on his shoulder and nodded. Zeke raised his hand and knocked once on the door. They heard a voice inside bidding them to enter. Carefully, and with the utmost respect, Zeke twisted the old door handle and pushed open the door. He had the feeling he was about to meet royalty.

He didn't know how right he was.

The two fledgling vampires entered the room slowly, side by side. The room was darkly lit, with only a few hints of moonlight spilling in from the balcony door. A lone high-backed leather chair sat in the middle of the wooden floor, otherwise the room was mostly bare. Two or three stacks of books occupied the corners, but there was little more.

Zeke took another anxious step forward. "We were called here," he said in an even tone. "My name is—"

"I know who you are," came a craggy voice from behind the chair. "I chose you to become. I watched the two of you for a long time," the voice admitted, "and I knew you were the ones."

Zeke was about to question her, but it somehow felt inappropriate.

"It's all right to ask questions," the voice replied. "Do not feel ashamed."

"How did you…?" Zeke let his sentence trail off. She had read his mind. She was a much more powerful telepath than he or Ina were.

"It is true I am powerful, but only because of age. Nothing more. When," she stopped and cackled, "if you get to be as old as I am, you too will become this powerful." She felt unabashed about flaunting her gifts. She exposed her long, bony hand and motioned for the two to come closer. "Stand in front so I may look on you with my old eyes."

Zeke and Ina carefully moved around her chair and stopped. Ina quickly tried to stifle a gasp.

"Do I really look that old?" Caitlin asked.

Ina shook her head, but turned away. "No, of course not."

Caitlin cackled again. "Of course I do."

Zeke looked over the corpse sitting before him. She was nothing more than bones with skin pulled tightly over them. The beautiful red hair he had seen in his vision was nothing more than a few wisps of gray that hung down over her face. There was no sign of lips anymore, just an exposed set of grinning yellow fangs. Even her nose was missing, leaving two gaping holes in her face. She was hideous. Even her golden eyes seemed pale and dim, much like a ring that had tarnished. A thin dress of black lace was hanging from her frame hiding what was left of her torso and abdomen, and yet he couldn't see anything but beauty. Even in this weakened, decaying state, she had a powerful aura about her.

He knew that if she wished to, this creature sitting before him could easily kill both him and Ina in a matter of moments.

Zeke dropped to one knee and reached for her hand. "My mistress, my queen," he took her bony hand in his and kissed it gently. "How can I serve you?"

Ina looked down at her companion, but did not follow suit. She couldn't even imagine touching that…thing.

"I have several needs you both can fulfill," Caitlin said slowly, enjoying the respect she was being paid. "First, I need to regain my strength." She inched forward in her seat. "It has been nearly three decades since I have fed," she admitted.

"How can I assist?" Zeke asked.

Caitlin's eyes suddenly hardened. "Restrain your companion."

Ina took a step back in shock. "Wait just a damned minute."

Zeke made no effort to disregard the command. Moving quickly from his position, he was on Ina. He wrapped his arms around her chest and began to squeeze.

She grunted as several of her ribs snapped. "Don't do this, Zeke! Don't let her kill me!"

Zeke said nothing, instead, he tightened his grip.

Ina gritted her teeth as she struggled to break free. In desperation, she threw her head back and hit Zeke squarely on the bridge of his nose. Zeke stumbled back and lost his grip. Recovering quickly, he snapped his hand around Ina's upper arm. Ina swung around wildly with her opposite elbow and hit Zeke just below his bottom lip. She watched as his mental projection faded away when he lost his concentration.

He growled at her menacingly. "You shouldn't have done that."

Grabbing the back of Ina's head, he swung her around full force. Her head hit the wall with a crunch as blood splattered about. Ina stumbled back, dazed and in severe pain. As her projection faded away, Zeke could see the front of her skull had been completely crushed in. Bone fragments and gray flesh hung loosely from the wound.

"Don't waste the blood!" Caitlin screamed.

Grabbing Ina again, Zeke pinned both of her arms behind her back and forced her down to her knees. He looked up to Caitlin. "She's ready for you."

Caitlin slid her bony frame from the chair and stood up. Reaching up, she slipped the straps from her dress over her shoulders and let it fall loosely to the floor. Step by agonizing step, Ina watched the horrible creature approaching her through blurred vision. This wasn't the way she wanted it to all end. She imagined living in Rome, or Paris with Zeke— forever in love. This wasn't supposed to happen. She began to struggle again, but he quickly broke her left arm. Ina gasped in agony.

Caitlin stopped in front of Ina and slowly sunk down to her knees. She lifted her leathery hands to Ina's face and softly caressed her cheek. "You are doing a great service for me, love. You'll never know how much I appreciate this."

Caitlin placed one of her hands on Ina's shoulder, and the other on the side of her head. With strength that surprised even Zeke, Caitlin snapped Ina's neck to the side, breaking her spine and cracking open a long gash in her neck. Her mouth opened wide—at least three times wider than the average human's could—and wrapped around Ina's neck wound. Letting go of Ina's dead body, Zeke took a step back and watched Caitlin in awe. Her frame was quickly beginning to fill out, while Ina's was looking more and more like a skeleton's. Caitlin's dead and rotting flesh began to return to a more familiar gray and her figure became once again that of a woman's. Even her gray hair grew thicker and changed to red. Before he knew it, he was staring at the beautiful, well-endowed woman he had seen in his vision with deep green eyes and flowing red hair.

Caitlin pulled her mouth away from Ina's corpse and slowly let her gaping mouth close. Standing up, she let Ina's body fall to the floor. Zeke watched it smash against the floor and shatter, almost as if it were now hollow. Returning his gaze to Caitlin, he watched her run her hands down her once again youthful body, her face full of pleasure. Walking gracefully across the floor, she marveled in her renewed grace and flexibility.

She turned her attention back to Zeke. "I've been out of the loop," she admitted. Even her voice was renewed. Gone was the raspy cackle of that skeleton. Now it was sweet, smooth and silky. "When last I was out, people were still wearing bell-bottoms and platform shoes. I need to know how to dress." She smiled seductively, "Or would you rather I just walked around naked all the time?"

Zeke smiled, his own mental projection restored. He was now dressed in a pair of black leather pants, a white long sleeved shirt with the cuffs undone and the bottom untucked and a pair of heavy, chunky, black boots. His hair had even changed. Gone was the short, messy look. It was now long, with the perfect amount of wave that hung just above the bottom of his neck.

"I would be happy with either, Mistress."

"Of course you would," she said, stepping closer, "but I plan to leave this place soon, and unless things have changed drastically, I can't go running around naked." She pressed one of her hands to the side of his head. "I need your thoughts." She closed her eyes and pressed her forehead to his.

After a moment, she took a deep breath and a step back. Zeke smiled. She was now garbed in a tight, deep red strapless dress that terminated just above her knees, while a long, black, lacy duster was draped seductively around her shoulders and hung to her ankles. Her lips were painted a gorgeous shade of red that complimented the dress perfectly, while a silver ankh hung round her neck. A pair of red stiletto heels rounded out the new package.

"You are beautiful, Mistress," Zeke breathed.

"Was there ever any doubt?" She laughed softly. "Now I need you to do something for me. I'm expecting a guest soon, but I need a better place to entertain. Find me a lush, new home to call my own." She drew her fingertips across his cheek. "I also need for you and Ice to retrieve something for me."

"Ice?"

"She was the one you were supposed to come here with, not that pile of dust on the floor. She's still in Cairo. Find her and complete these two tasks for me," She pricked her finger with her razor-sharp thumbnail. A drop of blood immediately welled up from the cut. She wiped it across Zeke's lower lip, "and you will be rewarded, Ezekiel."

Zeke licked his bottom lip, felling a surge of energy pass over his body. Her blood was unlike anything he had tasted before. "Thank you." The drop of blood had also transferred all of his instructions directly into his mind. He completely understood her plan and will in the matter. Turning away from Caitlin, he moved quickly toward the door and out of sight.

Caitlin walked gracefully out onto her balcony and once again placed her hands on the cool metal rails. She hoped this was the last time she would feel that sensation. Lifting her golden eyes, she stared out over the lights of Cairo. She had a few matters to attend to, and then she would personally watch all this burn. Every city in every country, she promised herself, then she would rule over the ashes.

Chapter Eleven

"Cane?" Dawn asked as she rapped gently on his apartment door. "Cane, it's Dawn." She paused. "Cane?" More than a hint of worry crept into her voice.

It was closing in on nine in the morning, and she had spent most of it searching. She had visited all of Cane's well-known haunts, and even a few that were not on his usual list. She had even hit the office to no avail. Cane wasn't anywhere. He had to be here. There was no other option. Dawn took a slow, deep breath to calm her nerves and knocked again. Still nothing. She leaned close to the door and listened inside. All was quiet. Reaching into her pocket, she extracted her set of keys and quickly sorted through to find Cane's. Placing her left hand on the doorknob, she stopped. It was already unlocked. A dark shade of fear passed over her face. He never left the door unlocked, even when he was home. It was one of his little quirks. Slowly twisting the doorknob, she peeked in through a crack in the door. "Cane? Are you here?"

Pushing the door open, she scanned the apartment. Nothing seemed out of order, but it was difficult to tell with this place. It always looked as if someone had ransacked it. Cautiously stepping inside, Dawn pushed the door quietly closed behind her. Her senses went on high alert. Moving into the living room, she spotted his coat and keys lying on the floor near the couch. Bending down, she picked up the coat and carefully looked it over. No blood. He probably dropped it there on his way in this morning, she reasoned. Standing up, a small glint of light caught her eye.

Turning toward the couch, she saw something shiny on the rug in front of it. She couldn't tell what it was at first. Crouching down, she pushed the tail of her long coat behind her and reached for the object. Her heart skipped a beat as she drew it close to her face. It was his crucifix. Panic pulled her into a standing position and directed her toward the phone in the kitchenette, but she stopped short. Two steps behind the couch on the hardwood floor, she spotted it: a pool of drying blood.

It was roughly symmetrical, with what looked like a scuffmark through the upper right edge. Her mind instantly jumped to conclusions and she felt her lower lip begin to quiver. Dropping down to her knees, she began to reach for the blood. Inches from the stain, she ripped her hand away. She couldn't do this. She had already contaminated a crime scene. The clues that police would use to find Cane and his assailant were being distorted by her very presence. Lifting her right hand, she slowly unclenched her fist revealing the gold necklace within. It alone would have been enough to know something bad had befallen her friend, but something else was wrong. The necklace wasn't broken, like it would have been if it had been yanked from his neck. Again clenching it tightly in her hand, she slipped into the inside pocket of her jacket and stood up.

Backing carefully away from the blood, she reached into her pocket and retrieved her cell phone. Using the speed dial function, she hit two keys and the send button, then pressed the phone to her ear.

She listened as two rings passed, then another. "Come on, come on," she muttered to herself. Relief hit her when a voice replied on the other side.

"Bishop," she said, nearly out of breath. She listened for a moment. "Shut up," she commanded quickly. "Cane's gone. I found his crucifix and a pool of partially dried blood in his apartment. I'm calling the police as soon as I get off the phone with you." She listened again, nodding her head. "Good, I'll meet the four of you back at the office shortly. We have to get on this before the trail gets cold."

Snapping her phone shut, she realized her panic had been replaced by cool determination. Opening her phone again, she dialed 9-1-1. She would find Cane. Of that she was sure.

* * *

Bishop hit the end button on his slim, black phone and set it on the seat next to him. His expression was emotionless, his eyes unblinking. Then, like the eruption of a volcano, he yelled at the top of his lungs and started slamming his fists against the steering wheel. After a moment, it passed. He cursed himself and Dawn for not taking enough action when they had the chance. This could have been avoided, but now, as far as he knew, Cane could already be dead. He had to move fast. There was no time to waste. Glancing down at the clock on his radio, he shook the steering wheel anxiously. Looking ahead, he could see he was deep in traffic, but inching ever closer to the airport.

Lydia had called him no more than an hour earlier to inform him their flight would be landing just after nine-fifteen. She had somehow managed to wrangle a member of the Gwyliad Wriaeth, who was in Seattle at the time, into accompanying her. Bishop chuckled to himself. With Lydia, it probably wasn't that difficult. She definitely had a way with people. He wondered for a moment if it was some kind of Witch-magnetism, or something like that. Probably a spell she worked to make everyone fall under her thrall. He shook his head as traffic surged another couple of feet and stopped again. He knew there were rules against that sort of thing for Witches, and Lydia was the kind of person who would not disregard something like that, no matter the cost. She was all about balance, in life and with the universe.

The Wiccan Rede states: "And if it harm none, do as thou will", which basically translates to "do what you want as long as it doesn't hurt anyone". He wondered how far that rule applied. If a witch evoked the Gods for a kind of Prosperity Spell to call in old outstanding monetary debts, would that harm another? What if a person gave the witch the money owed without taking into account that they needed to feed their family that week and money was tight? That would surely be harming another, wouldn't it? It would be leaving another in a difficult position at least. What about a Success Ritual to make sure they received that promotion at work? If the boss passed up another, more qualified person who needed the advancement for the raise in pay to give it to the witch because of the spell, wouldn't that be harming another? Bishop shook his head. It was too much to think about. Every action, whether you believe so or not, affects another. It's the Domino theory of life. He didn't even want to go into to the Witch's Law of Threes.

Bishop laid on his horn. It was already ten past nine and he was going to be late. Looking to his left, he noticed the center lane moving faster. Craning his neck around, he saw a brief opening in the line. Gunning his accelerator, he swerved into the lane, barely missing the front bumper of a yellow Taxi Cab. Peering into his rearview mirror, he saw the cabbie practicing sign language in his direction. Bishop happily returned the gesture and piloted his car quickly toward the terminal.

As luck would have it, he saw a car pull out of a space right in front of the doors just as he approached. Hitting his turn signal, he saw another driver making for the same space in an opposite lane. Bishop had no time to waste. Cranking his wheel to the left, he cut the second car off and skidded into the space, stopping only inches from another vehicle's bumper. Slamming the car into park, he ejected his keys from the ignition and threw his door open. Once outside, he saw several angry drivers gesturing in his direction. Spreading his arms wide, he took a bow and slammed his door shut. He knew he would find a key scratch in his paint job when he returned, but he didn't care. It wasn't his vehicle. It belonged to the OPR.

Rushing inside the great building through the automatic doors, Bishop waded through the crowds of people. Pushing others aside while simultaneously apologizing, he spotted the large arrival board on the wall. The flights heading into Dulles had just been updated. The morning flight in from Seattle was scheduled to arrive just shy of nine-twenty. Bishop checked his watch. He still had a few minutes to get to the right gate. He took a breath, and waded into the crowd again.

Finally arriving at the gate, Bishop slumped down in a row of curved plastic chairs that looked out onto the tarmac. He could see the nose of the massive plane rolling into view, its powerful engines still winding down. The walkway began to extend toward the hatch, and several baggage handlers went to work. It would be a few minutes before they started unloading passengers, giving Bishop just enough time to grab some breakfast. Spinning around in his seat, he spotted a small gift shop to his left and a pretzel cart in front of it. Standing up, he dug into his pocket producing a small wad of cash. Flipping through it, he was delighted to find just enough for a warm, buttered pretzel.

Walking across the floor, he stopped midway when he heard the first of the passengers exiting the plane. He glanced longingly at the pretzel cart one last time, then stuffed his money back into his pocket. He cursed the airline for actually being efficient for once. Turning around, he took a position against the wall just to the left of the ramp. He watched several bleary-eyed passengers exit the plane and wander into the terminal. Lydia and Kelley were next off. Kelley's face immediately lit up when she spotted Bishop holding up the wall.

"Bish!" Kelley rushed toward him with arms open wide. The two met in an embrace. "Oh, I missed you," she said sweetly.

191

"I missed you," Bishop said as he reluctantly freed himself from the hug. "How are you feeling?"

Kelley laughed, sending a few stray blond hairs spilling out over her forehead from the messy wrap on top of her head. "Not dead, if that makes you feel any better."

Bishop smiled. "It does."

Kelley was a lovely young woman full of live. In her prior life before joining the OPR, she had worked as a nurse in a local hospital in Florida. Her usually straight blond hair was messily pinned up on the top of her head with what, to Bishop, looked like a chopstick. She was dressed down in a gray cotton t-shirt, a pair of blue jeans and sandals, yet she still looked good. A simple green duffle bag was slung over her shoulder. Kelley was, what Cane liked to call a "brain sucker", meaning she was telepathic. She could read others' surface thoughts through a form of Extra Sensory Perception she said developed early in her teens. There wasn't much you could keep from her, and Bishop on more than one occasion had been chastised for his "dirty" thoughts about her. "You remember Lydia?"

Bishop nodded. "Of course." He reached around Kelley and shook Lydia's hand. "It's good to see you again. I just wish the circumstances were better."

Lydia smiled softly. "As do I. Good to see you again, Nick."

"Please, all my friends call me Bishop."

Lydia nodded. "All right…Nick." She allowed herself a quick chuckle.

Lydia was probably a year or two younger than

192

Cane, but in much better physical condition. On Cane, the years of hard living showed, yet Lydia's face betrayed no such secrets. Her dark, wavy hair was long and hung past her shoulders. Her brown eyes were vibrant with life and joy reflecting perfectly her personality. She was dressed in a long black skirt that hung just above her ankles, and a white, cotton t-shirt, looking nothing like Bishop's mental image of a witch. He always expected her to show up all in black, with a lacy shawl draped over her shoulders. A cane, or wooden staff carved from a dying tree would have probably rounded out the image. A pair of silver sun and moon earrings dangled from her ear lobes, while a gold crucifix hung from her necklace.

Bishop carefully lifted the cross and held it in the palm of his hand. "I understand now."

Lydia's eyes turned away as she nodded. "We don't like to speak about that."

"I'm afraid you're going to have to." Bishop swallowed hard. "Cane's missing. All we found was a bit of blood," he let go of her necklace, "and his cross."

Lydia's eyes raced nervously from Bishop to Kelley as they began to fill with tears. "Oh my God."

Bishop placed a firm hand on her shoulder. "We're going to find him. I promise."

Lydia quickly wiped the tears from her eyes, careful not to smear her mascara. She took a slow breath and remembered the person standing behind her. "Oh, there's someone I want you to meet." She turned to face her companion. "This is Callista."

Bishop extended his hand toward the young woman. She shook his hand firmly. "Pleased to meet you, Callista. I'm Nick Bishop."

"But all your friends call you Bishop," Callista added. Her accent was familiar, but Bishop couldn't quite place it.

"Right," he said with a smile.

Callista could be described in one word: striking. Her eyes were dark brown and had a faint Asian shape to them, and yet she didn't appear to have any more of that heritage in her face. She was much shorter than Bishop, standing only about five and a half feet tall (with her boots on). Her hair was a honey blond with dark highlights scattered through it. It was pulled up in a ponytail behind her head while two strands of hair fell down off her bangs and framed her face. A long, thin braid of hair fell down from her temple, barely touching her shoulder. Bishop counted at least ten colored bands woven into the braid. She looked thin, but athletic. She was wearing almost entirely gray and black, from her formfitting black leather pants, to a simple black shirt. Her long charcoal gray coat appeared to be a blend of silks and billowed around her magnificently. A simple black backpack sat on the floor by her tall, black boots. A black, swirling tattoo started on her neck just behind her left ear and terminated below her shirt collar somewhere.

"You work for the Gwyliad Wraith?" Bishop asked.

"I am Sister Callista of the White Guard," she nodded.

"Just Callista?" Bishop asked with a smile.

"Kind of like Cher, or Sting? Just one name?"

"It's all that was given to me and all that I need," she replied solemnly.

"I can't quite place your accent. Where are you from?"

"The Guard found me in Eastern Russia, then took me to their home in Ireland."

Bishop nodded. "So it's a mixture of a Russian and Irish accent?"

"Russian and Gaelic," Callista confirmed.

"I'm sure you have plenty of good stories to tell." Bishop glanced over his shoulder to see Kelley and Lydia impatiently watching him fawn over this young woman, "But we'll have to save those for another time." He tried to save face. "We have work to do." He turned his full attention to Kelley and Lydia. "We have to meet Dawn at the office as soon as possible. Are you three ready?"

Each nodded.

"Then we're off." Bishop began quickly leading them through the busy terminal.

"We're off?" Kelley asked mockingly. "You've been spending too much time with Cane."

Bishop shot her an off glance as he waded into the crowd. "Well some of us didn't just have almost six months paid leave." He smiled wryly, "Some of us actually had to go back to work after defeating the supreme Egyptian evil in Seattle. Some of us had paperwork to do."

"I died! Remember that, jackass?" Kelley shouted as she stormed after him. "How the hell was I supposed to come back to work?"

Callista moved a few steps closer to Lydia.

"Are they always like this?"

Lydia nodded, "Love is a beautiful thing."

Callista shook her head with a laugh, "Do they know that?"

"Jackass," Kelley yelled again somewhere in the crowd.

"Wench," Bishop replied playfully.

* * *

Zeke spotted his quarry. Moving quickly over several low rooftops, he easily kept pace while remaining unseen. He watched as she stopped at a small, outdoor café and sat down at one of the numerous tables. After a moment, a waiter arrived to take her order. She made small talk with him for a moment, then motioned for him to sit down next to her. The waiter quickly complied. Zeke cocked his head slightly. "What the hell is she doing?" he whispered to himself.

He watched her run her fingers seductively through the waiter's hair as she inched ever closer to him. She was whispering something in his ear, something so quiet, even Zeke's supernatural hearing couldn't make it out. From there, she kissed him on the cheek and leaned into his neck. Zeke stood from his perch in shock. How could she be so brazen in public? Anger swept through him like a wave. He started off the roof, but a sound stopped him. He peered down into the café. The waiter had stood up and was backing away from Ice with his hand cupped over his bleeding neck. Zeke couldn't see the blood from where he was, but he could smell it. Ice leapt from her seat and rushed through the maze of tables toward the waiter. Before he had a

196

chance to move away or scream again, she had completely snapped his neck. The man fell to the ground in a heap. Leaning in, Ice wrapped her hand in the man's hair and yanked. The waiter's head popped off like a grape from the stem.

Swinging around, Ice stared up at Zeke. "Stop following me!" She whipped the head in his direction. It hit Zeke squarely in the chest and knocked him to the ground. He didn't see Ice scale the wall below him and leap to the rooftop. She moved toward him, her eyes melting to gold. "I thought you and Ina made things very clear when you tried to kill me earlier tonight. I don't want anything to do with you, Zeke."

Zeke rolled onto the balls of his feet and tossed the severed head aside. "Ina's dead," he noted without a hint of remorse. "Caitlin killed her no less than three hours ago."

"And Caitlin is?"

"The one who called us here. It was her blood which created the vampire we all drank from in London." He stood up and dusted himself off. "We were hand-picked to be in her service."

"I don't give a crap who picked anyone for what," Ice sneered. "I have everything I want right now." The realization of what Zeke had said first hit her. "Ina's dead?"

Zeke nodded and took a cautious step closer to Ice. "Can't you hear her voice beckoning to you?" He paused, "She wanted you and I, not Ina. She was a mistake on my part, but now she's been dealt with. We need you, Ice."

"I think I mentioned that I don't give a crap."

"You don't understand," Zeke persuaded. "Caitlin can give us everything we've ever wanted, and more. We're either on her team or not, and she's the winning team. I have seen her plans and they are incredible. Consider this," he chose his words carefully, "your personal invitation to join us."

Ice considered. "Or?"

"You die."

She laughed uneasily. "It's as simple as that?"

Zeke nodded.

"I am just as strong and fast as you are," Ice argued. "We became vampires at the same time, remember?"

"That doesn't matter anymore," Zeke said, showing his golden eyes. "I have tasted Caitlin's blood and I want more. You see, I have desire, and that is a powerful ally." The flesh of his hands melted away revealing his true hands. Ice watched his fingernails grow to points in front of her eyes. "Are you with us?"

Ice bit her lip. "No."

Zeke sneered. "So be it."

Ice slowly started to back away. "Don't do this, Zeke. We can find a better way." She glanced behind her to see the ground below. "We don't have to do this!"

"Another whining woman," he growled. "I hate it when they beg." Lashing forward, he dug his claws into her face and ripped three large gashes down her porcelain cheek. Lifting his opposite hand above his head, he hunched down into an attack position.

198

Ice recoiled in pain and shock. "If you're looking for a fight," she let the projection around her face and hands melt away, "you've got one."

Lurching toward Zeke, she caught him in the sternum with a strong right jab. She immediately combined the blow with an uppercut to his chin that snapped Zeke's head back. Recovering quickly, Zeke stopped a third punch with the back of his forearm. Grabbing her outstretched arm, he reversed her attack and spun inside with his claws slashing wildly. Blood poured from the several deep gashes in Ice's midsection. With Zeke's arms wide, she delivered a vicious head butt. Dropping her head, she leapt straight up, catching Zeke under the chin. Landing gracefully, she lunged again with her fangs, but Zeke quickly stopped her. Flipping her around, he grabbed both her flailing arms and pressed his foot directly in the center of her back. Ice screamed as she stared down into the street below. Zeke only laughed as he let go of her arms and kicked.

Ice's body flew like a discarded rag doll over the edge. Wiping the blood from his nose and chin, he cautiously peered over the edge, expecting to see Ice's body on the ground below. Placing both hands on the ledge, he stared in wonder. "What the hell?"

Ice waved up at him, then crossed her arms confidently. She was standing horizontally on the building's wall facing up, her toes dug into the heavy brick veneer, holding her firmly in place. "You didn't think you'd get rid of me that easily, did you?"

Leaning up, Ice charged up the wall straight at

Zeke. The two collided and spilled messily onto the rooftop. Ice was the first on her feet, but Zeke wasn't far behind. She leapt from a standstill with her arms extended beside her. From a height of close to ten feet, she came crashing down on Zeke. The force of her landing crushed him to the ground beneath her and broke several support beams in the roof below. Flipping his legs up, Zeke caught Ice around the neck with his feet. Using his strength and agility, he pulled his legs down and sent Ice crashing through the roof headfirst. All at once, he was standing again and quickly followed her down through the hole.

Zeke hastily scanned the room in which he had landed. An elderly couple was cowering in the corner. Ignoring them for the moment—although they would make a nice snack after he finished with Ice—he tilted his head back and sniffed the air. He could still smell Ice's wounds. She was near, but where? He turned his head slightly to the right and sniffed again. His attention focused on an arch at the back of the room. She was there. Moving slowly, he stopped just outside the arch and peered inside. He could see a small bed with a candlelit shrine behind it. It was the only light in the room. Zeke smiled. It wouldn't help her. Pressing his back to the wall, he started to inch around the arch. Ice was close. Her scent was growing stronger. Turning his head to the right, he stopped suddenly. There was a large swash of Ice's blood on the arch frame next to him.

His golden eyes widened. It's a trick!

Drywall and brick erupted from the wall around

Zeke's head as Ice's hands latched on. Zeke struggled against her grip but couldn't break free. Using all her strength, Ice ripped Zeke through the wall and slammed him against the floor. Immediately striking down, Ice barely missed Zeke's head as he rolled out of the way. Flipping onto his feet as the dust still settled around them, Zeke's hand snapped to Ice's throat. With a guttural growl, he spun Ice around and smashed her head into the same wall he had just been pulled through. Ripping her free again, he pinned her arms behind her back and threw her into the wall again. He repeated the process until Ice's body began to feel limp in his hands. He thrust forward one final time, just for good measure, then let go.

Ice slumped to the floor, her face battered, bruised and bleeding. "Please," she moaned, "no more."

"Will you serve?" Zeke asked, towering over her. His eyes surged with power and hatred.

Ice tried to wipe some of her blood from her face, but remained quiet.

"Will you serve Mistress Caitlin?" Zeke asked forcefully, showing her his exposed claws. He poised them inches from her throat.

"All right!" she shouted. "I will serve," she said defeated. She knew she couldn't take another beating like the one she had just endured.

Zeke slowly retracted his claws and put up his mental projection. "That's all I needed." He reached down and extended a hand to Ice. "Let me help you up."

Ice stared at his hand suspiciously, then

accepted it. Zeke easily lifted her tattered frame from the floor. "What do you want me to do?"

"First," Zeke grinned, "we have to pick up a guest for Mistress Caitlin's party tomorrow evening."

"We're having a party?" Ice asked, still groggy from the fight.

Zeke threw a vicious backhand across her face. "Yours is not to question," he warned her, "only to serve."

Ice rubbed her cheek as Zeke moved out of the room. Anger swelled up in her. Never in her life had she served anyone. That was not going to change. She made a silent vow to herself then and there. Zeke would die for this travesty, and it would be by her hands.

Chapter Twelve

Cane lifted his head and looked around dazedly. His hand moved up to the right side of his neck and pressed gently. There was some pain, but no detectable wound. He slowly started to rub it with the palm of his hand. It felt like he had a kink in his neck, as if he'd been sleeping wrong. Pulling himself up into a sitting position, he pushed himself back against the wall. Bringing up his knees, he rested his elbows on them. He had no idea of where he was, or for that matter, how he had gotten there.

Sporadic rays of light were filtering in through cracks in the walls, giving him just enough light to make out another person. She was sitting on the opposite side of the room, unmoving and staring. Her eyes were like daggers piercing Cane's chest. He felt the undeniable urge to look away. Doing so, he continued looking around the room. The floor was strewn with hay and had the unmistakable scent of farm animals. He heard a loud clanging sound from somewhere outside as the room began to shake. After a moment, his mind began to clear and he realized he was in a boxcar and the train was leaving the station.

He tried to stand up, but found he was too weak. He crumbled back to the floor and slowly took a deep breath. His body was exhausted. He lifted his hand slightly and watched it shake uncontrollably. He was in bad shape...and the reason why was becoming clearer. Reaching up to his throat, he unconsciously felt for his cross, but came away empty-handed. The events that had unfolded earlier suddenly became crystal clear. The woman across from him was a vampire.

Cane shifted uneasily for a moment. "Where are you taking me?"

The vampire said nothing.

"I mean, I know you're taking me to Caitlin, but where are we going now?"

Silence, yet her stare remained unbroken.

"So," Cane breathed, "how do you like being a vampire?"

The woman blinked, yet remained still.

"Listen, lady," Cane said, slightly impatient, "I'm a willing prisoner here. The least you can do is tell me where we're bloody heading."

The woman stood up in one fluid motion and began to walk across the car toward Cane. Standing before him, she pulled back her hand and slapped him across the face. "I don't care if you helped me hop this train, or I had to drag you kicking and screaming, you're still my prisoner. If you don't shut up, I may have to do something drastic."

"You wouldn't dare," Cane said defiantly, not even rubbing his stinging cheek. "Caitlin would hunt you down and kill you."

She reached down and twisted his head to the left. "I've already taken your blood once. What makes you think I won't do it again?" She bared her fangs.

Cane swallowed hard. "Point taken."

The vampire stood up and turned around. Slowly, she returned to her spot on the opposite side of the boxcar. "I don't want to hear another word from you for the rest of this trip. Understand? We'll arrive at our destination shortly."

Cane nodded slowly and sank back against the wall. Crossing his arms over his knees, he passed the time by staring out a nearby hole in the wall. He watched the country speeding by in a blur of browns and greens, bringing him closer and closer to his doom. He was playing the part of the sacrificial lamb, saving those he loved from the same horrible fate. Caitlin would surely torture him again, but this time, she would certainly kill him. That was what he wanted...right?

Cane let his head fall forward in disgust.

* * *

Something slithered over Specter's foot. Quelling his urge to jump back, he remained completely still, hoping not to provoke the snake. Tilting his head back in the total darkness, he rested it against the cool stone behind him. He had no concept of time in this place. Hours, or minutes, or possibly days had passed since he had arrived. He hadn't dared sleep for fear of snake bite and had only a few bits of granola bar to eat from the small ration pack he kept on the back of his belt. His mood was growing grim.

Closing his eyes, he took a long breath in through his nose and exhaled it slowly through his mouth. Repeating the process once again, his body began to relax as his mind found a state of ease. He had to find a means out of this place, and there was no way he would be able to accomplish that with all these snakes slinking about. If this was going to work, he needed total concentration. It was a skill he had been taught by the Guard, but it had been a long time since he had tried it. Now he was glad he knew that particular skill.

Bringing his hands up, he gracefully turned them palms up to the sky, while tucking his elbows into his sides. Tilting his head back, he cleared his mind of all thoughts, worries and concerns. He needed to focus his energy, and after years of training and experience, it had become almost second nature to him. Tensing the muscles in his arms and abdomen, he rolled his eyes toward the heavens. As he felt his inner chi beginning to grow, he placed his left hand flat on his chest, while lifting the right above his head.

He licked his lips. "I gawl am Gwynn," he spoke in the native tongue of the Gwyliad Wriaeth, Celtic. Specter took a breath, "Nos Gwelediad!"

Searing pain shot through his eyes and up the optic nerves into his brain. Reaching behind, he grabbed precariously onto the stone block so as not to fall. Pain erupted from every nerve ending connected to his eyes. Gritting his teeth, he would not allow himself to cry out in agony. He had to bear it for a moment longer for the spell to take full effect. His head snapped back, barely missing the stone block, as his eyelids burst open. Two streams of white light exploded from his pupils and sliced like laser beams through the darkness. Slowly, the pain began to subside.

Taking a moment to catch his breath, Specter kept his eyes closed and leaned heavily on the block. He felt lightheaded and weak, but that was an expected effect of a spell this powerful. He had literally just hotwired his eyes, optical nerves, and the portions of his brain that dealt with sight. It was called "Gwynn's Night Sight" in English and it gave the caster a very unique skill. Opening his eyes, he saw a grayish blur before them. Slowly, it came into focus. Specter smiled as he now saw perfectly in the inky darkness. Everything was bathed in an unearthly silver light, yet he could see clearly.

Looking over the room, he saw every detail and snake. The room, no larger than ten by ten feet, was littered with carved reliefs on the walls, ceiling and floor. Two huge blocks stood behind him on either side of a massive stone altar, while dozens of snakes slithered around on the floor. Their black bodies flexed and strained as they moved. It was worse than he feared. These were King Cobras, one of the most venomous serpents on the face of the Earth, and this was their den. He could see their young speeding around the adults, but more or less coalescing in the far right corner. Moving his attention away from the snakes for a moment, he looked over the carvings on the wall and felt a bit of relief. They were Egyptian. The Gate had transported him to the correct location, but how had he ended up here? Peering over his left shoulder, he saw a small doorway, no larger than about three feet high, cut in the corner. It was his only way out but he was sure it would be full of snakes. He needed a way to repel them.

He couldn't afford to take a bite from any of them, even the young, as their venom was a powerful neurotoxin. Once injected into the human body, the venom seeks out and destroys or impairs nerve tissue, leaving the victim in a very vulnerable position. In smaller animals, the cobra's bite will induce paralysis, allowing the snake to capture the prey with the least amount of resistance, and in some cases, eat them while still alive. For humans, if allowed to spread in the body far enough, impaired motor skills, and in extreme cases, caused the loss of fingers, toes, or arms and legs. He had no idea how far he was away from medical facilities, so getting a bite, even a minor one, would probably kill him.

There were literally hundreds of tombs scattered around Egypt, and he could be in any one of them, even one yet to be discovered. The prospect of digging himself out from beneath feet of sand didn't appeal to him at this point. Opening up his jacket, he began a quick search of his available options. On the backside of each Wraith's belt, there were three small pouches and a canteen of water. These could contain anything the Wraith thought they would need, from food, to matches, to small handheld weapons. Unfortunately, Specter had packed light for this mission. He felt his sunglasses, a pair of brass knuckles, the letter he had been sent by the Guard and a compass. Nothing useful. If he had matches, he could make a torch, but no such luck. He would have to risk it.

Reaching into his pack, he retrieved his sunglasses and pushed them on. This was more for protection than anything else. King Cobras were known as "spitters", and they had the uncanny knack of hitting their prey directly in the eyes, blinding them. Pulling off his coat, he wrapped it around his hands and arms. They would be the most vulnerable as he crawled through the hole. He hoped that enough fabric would stop their fangs or at least keep them from his flesh.

Carefully avoiding the snakes, Specter moved toward the hole. He hit his knees and peered inside. It was as he feared, there were at least three snakes inside, and of good size. Two were pressed up against the cool walls, while the third was coiled in the middle, its head directly facing Specter. Taking a deep breath, he lay down on his stomach and placed his hands in front of him. The hole was tall enough that he could keep his head up, but because of his coat shield, he couldn't see anything. Reaching inside, he heard a now familiar hissing sound. It had to be the middle snake. Carefully lowering his shield, he glanced over the top. The center snake had indeed pulled back slightly, its neck now poised in the classic "S" position, ready to strike. Specter watched uncomfortably as it flattened its throat and flared its hood.

"Crap."

This wasn't going to work. There was no way. Pulling away from the hole, he sat back and tried to rethink the situation. Turning to his left, he remembered the altar between the stone pillars. Excited, he stood up and worked his way toward it. He had found his answer. His hands moved over the contents of the altar, quickly searching for an appropriate sized object. He smiled.

The altar was filled with objects varying from pottery to gold ornamentation used in rituals. This presented Specter with a problem, but he didn't want to address it then. He just wanted to get through that crawlspace and into the adjoining chamber. He would have to deal with this new problem when he came face to face with it. To his left, there were several short jars, each with a lid carved to resemble an Egyptian God or Goddess. He wasn't completely familiar with their numerous deities, but he recognized the animals. Two were hawks, while the other was a dog, and the last was the head of a man. There were obviously the organ jars he had read about. When a person was mummified, someone of great importance, his or her main organs would be removed and placed in these jars to be entombed with them. Kind of disgusting when you knew the organ list included the brain (which they pulled through the nose with a tool resembling a small harpoon).

Setting the jars aside, Specter came to what he was looking for. It was a golden saucer, almost three feet in diameter with handles on opposite sides. It would make a perfect shield, but he needed something more. Glancing to his left, he spotted it. It was a six-foot tall wooden staff with a sculpted golden head shaped like…he sighed…a cobra. Lifting the staff with both hands, he noticed the wood had become slightly brittle. He held it in his hands for a moment before deciding it would have to work. He didn't have any other choice. Moving the shaft over in his hands, he snapped the head off against the stone altar. He hated defacing national treasures like this, but right now, his life was more important than some five thousand year old Pharaoh. As it hit the floor, the sound echoed off the walls and disturbed several snakes. A chorus of hissing erupted behind him.

"Shut up," he said under his breath.

Moving back to the hole, he once again dropped down on his belly and propped the gold platter in front of him. Sliding his hand through one of the handles, he held it tightly to his outstretched arm. The platter was just a bit smaller than the hole, which explained how they got it in here in the first place, but being round, it left the two bottom corners exposed. That's where the staff came in. Setting it inside the tunnel, he slowly scooted it toward the snake on the right.

As the wood touched his tail, the snake quickly moved out of the hole. Specter repeated the process with the snake on the opposite wall with the same result. He turned his attention to the cobra in the center. It was still standing, head poised for a strike. As Specter moved the staff closer, the snake's mouth dropped open. It was warning him not to get any closer, but Specter didn't have a choice.

"Sorry, my little black friend. I have to get out of here," he exhaled.

Pushing the staff ahead, he made contact with the snake's body. The snake hissed in displeasure and lunged at the staff. It struck with full force against the wood, but Specter held his ground, and his shield, firmly. The snake turned its attention to the platter and Specter. Uncoiling, it moved forward slightly. Its mouth still open, it leaned forward and shot two sharp streams of venom at the platter. Specter felt a few drops splatter over and land on his arm and hand. He wasn't sure what effect the venom would have on the skin, but he didn't want to take any chances. Pulling his canteen off his belt, he popped the top open and splashed water over his hand. Slipping the canteen back into its pouch, he returned his attention to the snake ahead. It was a bad move looking away. The snake had moved much closer and was preparing to strike again.

Pulling his hand quickly behind the shield, Specter ducked his head down. He felt the snake hit against the platter with full force, then again. Specter knew the snake was determined to bite him. Gritting his teeth, he drew his knees up and braced them against the wall. It was now or never. Pushing hard forward, he felt the snake strike again. Bringing the platter back against his shoulder, he powered through the tunnel, pushing the snake the entire way. As he neared the egress, he saw the snake's head slip between the platter and wall. Specter became instantly still. If he moved or breathed, the snake would strike.

The cobra spit its long, forked tongue out and tasted the air as it slowly squeezed its powerful black body through the hole. Mere inches from his face, the cobra reared up again and opened its hood. Specter reacted by instinct alone. Ripping his hand free of the platter, he rolled against the back wall of the tunnel, narrowly missing the cobra's strike. Within seconds, the cobra was poised for another attack. This time, Specter threw his hand forward and pinned the snake against the wall, but it had time to spit. The streams of venom hit Specter directly in his sunglasses. Ripping them away from his face, Specter wrapped his hand around the snake's throat, just below the head to avoid a bite. He squeezed hard enough to hold the creature, yet loose enough not to harm him, although his emotions told him to strangle the beast.

With snake in hand, Specter crawled the remaining few feet out of the tunnel. This chamber, compared to the other, was relatively free of snakes. Only the two he forced in earlier could be seen moving away toward their own corners. Standing up, he carefully uncoiled the snake from his arm and tossed it back into the tunnel. Taking a few steps back, he waited to see if the snake would pursue. To his relief, it turned and headed away. It had apparently had enough of him for one day.

Glancing around the chamber, Specter saw a set of steps leading up to a sealed stone door that was set in the wall at a forty-five degree angle. It had to be the tomb's exit. Rushing up the steps, he placed both hands against the door and quickly surveyed the seams. As with most Egyptian architecture, they were tight and well done.

This brought him to the problem he had thought of earlier, now it seemed more and more like he was right. With all the treasures still in place on the altar and nothing broken or defaced, he knew this tomb had yet to be discovered by researchers or grave robbers. It was still more than likely buried under the hot Egyptian sands. Placing his shoulder against the door, he strained with his legs to get the door open, but his strength alone wasn't enough. Taking a step back, he exhaled deeply and tried to catch his breath. He was trapped. He wondered if this was what the prophecy referred to. He was in Egypt, and he was surely going to die in this tomb.

A sharp, but slightly muffled noise caught his attention. He perked his ears up for a moment. It sounded like…scratching, and it was coming from the door. He pressed both hands flat against it and brought his head closer to the sound. He nodded to himself. It was definitely scratching, but what was creating it? A sudden familiar clink filled his ears. Taking a step back, he smiled. Someone was digging with shovels, and they were clearing the door. All he had to do now was wait for them to break through.

He could hear the faintest voices outside. He couldn't make out exact words, but he was fairly certain it was a man and woman. He heard metal hitting the stone door and took another few steps back. He didn't want to be under the door if a ton of sand came flooding in. He watched small streams of sand filter down through the cracks as the door was slowly removed from its seam. After a few minutes, the heavy slab was almost out, so much so that Specter could see slivers of moonlight through the cracks.

A sinking feeling rolled over his body. Why were they working at night? Wouldn't conditions be too difficult for such precise and meticulous work? Something didn't feel right. As the door was finally pulled away, Specter saw no one, only the starry night sky. Taking a few tentative steps toward the opening, he caught a familiar scent on the wind: fresh blood.

Vampires.

Whipping around, he spotted the end of his

staff on the floor. Flipping his foot under it, he kicked it up into his hand and spun on his heels. Twirling it across the left side of his body, he reversed the spin and brought it to a stop in both hands.

"Nice."

Specter glanced up to see two vampires staring down into the tomb clapping for him. He didn't recognize either of them, meaning they weren't in the Guard's database or they were newly created fledglings. His expression turned hard and determined. The two slowly entered and walked halfway down the stairs. The male was leading with the woman two steps behind. Her posture showed her to be subservient, while he stood tall and proud without a hint of fear in his stride.

"Do you know what I am?" Specter asked slowly.

"You're Marcus Specter, Wraith," the vampire replied. "I'm Zeke, and this," he said, pointing behind him, "is Ice." He smiled broadly, his golden eyes glistening in the moonlight. "Ice had her doubts, but I knew you would be here. It was lucky for us that crew of archaeologists had already started this dig, or we might have been cruising around the desert for weeks digging holes." He laughed to himself. "She was right again."

Specter paid no attention to the vampire. Instead, he kept his senses sharp in case of an attack. He was fast, but the vampires were equally so.

Zeke bowed slightly. "You have been invited to a party tomorrow night, Brother Specter. She simply won't accept a refusal."

Specter took the bait. "Who is 'she'?"

"I believe you two have already met. Her name is," he paused dramatically, "Caitlin."

Specter took an uneasy step back at the sound of the name. He remembered her.

"You are to be one of two guests of honor!" Zeke laughed again.

"Caitlin," Specter said, rolling the name around his mouth and over his tongue. It was a name he had not heard in a long time. Not since he killed her. He let his guard down for a moment.

Seeing the opening, Zeke charged. Leaping from the middle of the stairs, he landed with both feet on Specter's chest. The Wraith felt all the air being pushed out of his chest and at least two ribs cracking under the weight. Grabbing the staff, Specter thrust it between Zeke's legs and twisted, sending the vampire crashing to the stone floor. Before he had a chance to recover, Ice was on him. She wrapped her arm around his back, pinning his left arm and began to push his head to the right to get a shot at his neck. She opened her mouth wide, exposing her glistening fangs. Using his right arm, Specter threw a jab that landed on her cheek. With Ice stunned, he struck again, this time knocking the vampire loose. Jumping up, he retrieved his staff and charged for the door. He had to get to a less confined space to finish the fight. Reaching out, Zeke caught Specter's ankle and tripped him. Specter grunted as his chin smacked against the bottom step. Rolling onto his back, he kicked Zeke firmly in the face, twice. Zeke's grip loosened.

Standing up, Specter took a moment to recover. The two vampires did the same.

With his back to the stairs and a vampire on either side, Specter pressed the attack. He swept forward with his staff, hitting Zeke in the chin. The vampire stumbled back. Spinning the staff over his head, Specter smiled deviously at Ice. Stopping in mid-twirl, he brought the staff down with a powerful thrust and connected with Ice's knees. Flipping the staff up, he dropped her easily to the ground. As if possessing a sixth sense, Specter whipped the staff over his head and blocked Zeke's attack from behind. Holding the block, Specter spun on the balls of his feet. Pulling the staff away quickly, he immediately thrust it toward Zeke's nose. The vampire ducked the blow, but was caught flat-footed by Specter's second attack. As Zeke dropped to avoid the hit, Specter threw his knee up and connected with Zeke's nose. The vampire crumbled as a stream of blood poured over his lower face.

To his surprise, Ice was back in the fight. Leaping from the floor, she hit Specter squarely in the back with her shoulder. The blow knocked him off balance. Ice then slashed across Specter's back with her claws, shredding his coat and shirt and cutting two gashes in his flesh. Specter growled and spun around with his staff poised. He dug the broken end into her abdomen, just left of her stomach. Ice shrieked in pain as Specter pushed the staff deeper into her body.

Zeke seized the moment. Leaping up, he wrapped his arms beneath Specter's and pinned him. To Specter's horror, Ice wrapped her hands around the staff and pulled herself closer toward him. The staff broke through her back as she inched closer on the wooden implement. Baring her fangs, she threw several quick punches into his midsection, while another landed on his chin. Under the barrage of attacks, Specter felt himself slowly slipping out of consciousness. Zeke pulled his face back to avoid Specter's wildly bobbing head as Ice struck again and again. Pulling the staff loose from his hands, Ice took a step back and threw a final punch across his face. Specter became limp in Zeke's arms.

The vampire grunted in disgust and dropped the Wraith to the floor. Looking up at Ice, he smiled wryly. "That was a good move with the staff."

Ice took a step back and dropped down to her knees. "If it had been a little higher, I would have been dead." Snapping the staff off behind her, she yanked it back through her wound and dropped it on the floor with a groan.

"Let's get him out of here before he comes to," Zeke ordered. "And before the sun comes up. We've got a lot of desert to cross."

Chapter Thirteen

Bishop led his three companions into the OPR building. Walking through the lobby of marble and glass, he headed toward a bank of elevators at the rear. Lifting his ID out of his rear pant pocket, he slid it through a small black reader in the center of the wall. A red light next to the reader changed to green. Bishop tapped the up button with his thumb and turned to face his companions. Stuffing his hands into his pockets, he waited patiently for the elevator.

"New security measures?" Kelley asked.

Bishop nodded. "Weiss is getting paranoid in his old age."

"Or maybe he just realizes he's really uncovering the truth," Lydia suggested, "and he wants to protect that."

Bishop chuckled. "Yeah, that's it." The elevator doors to his right slid open. He quickly moved for the door and held it open with the back of his hand.

As the foursome piled in, Lydia stopped and glared at Bishop. "Sarcasm never helps a situation."

"But it makes it fun," Bishop smiled as he let the doors slide shut.

Kelley shook her head.

* * *

Caitlin turned and looked over her shabby flat. She hated this place. Every board, every nail, every stain on the walls, this had been her prison for far too long. Taking a few steps inside from her perch on the balcony, she ran her hand over the battered leather chair that had been her world for the past thirty years. This place had not been a refuge for her battered and broken body, but rather a prison for her mind. Placing both hands on the back of her chair, she gritted her teeth in hatred. Digging her fingers into the leather and stuffing, she lifted it easily above her head and tossed it toward the wall. The heavy chair smashed through the termite infested walls, creating a gaping hole. She wouldn't waste another moment in this place. Not one more.

Moving back to the balcony as the dust settled in the room behind her, she leaned on the rails and glanced down into the city. Several tourists were moving along the sidewalk below her snapping pictures and talking about the "ancient wonders of Cairo". Caitlin could hear every word as if they were standing next to her. Closing her eyes for a moment, she took a deep breath and tasted the air. The human's warm, salty flavor washed over her taste buds. Licking her lips, she felt her mouth water for the first time in decades. She had to have them. Leaping onto the rickety metal railing, she perched as lightly as a bird. Her eyes melted to gold as her hands let go of the railing. Falling forward, she watched the ground rush up at her. With a laugh of excitement, she flipped in midfall and landed gently on the balls of her feet. Felling the cool air on her skin only added to her state. She was a predator back in her natural element, and she loved it.

Glancing ahead, she caught sight of the tourists heading around the corner. They were all dressed in khaki pants and shirts as if they were archaeologists from the 1920's. Two were men, while the other three were women. The men were wearing short

220

pants with their white socks pulled up to their knees, while the women had a bit more taste wearing full pants. Changing her projection, Caitlin blended into her surroundings much like a chameleon could. Moving lightly on her bare feet, she approached the group.

"How can you say the pyramids were built by aliens?" one of the women asked. "There is so much evidence to the contrary."

The man leading the group turned around and sized up the woman. "You can't tell me that ancient man, with limited knowledge and tools, built those massive structures on their own. It's just not possible."

Caitlin eased around the corner and stood silently behind them, her body perfectly blended with her surroundings. She licked her lips again and smiled.

The woman shook her head. "They didn't have limited knowledge," she argued. "They had an intricate understanding of mathematics. If you would stop being so pigheaded, you would…." The woman stopped as she looked into the faces of her companions. Their expression had turned from one of bemusement into horror. "What?"

The man pointed behind her.

The woman slowly turned around. Her eyes widened as she took an uneasy step back. It was as if she was looking into the face of the Cheshire cat. A pair of golden hued eyes was hovering before her along with a visible smile of sharp fangs. "Oh fu—"

Before the final hard consonant had even passed her lips, the vampire was on her. Snapping the woman's head back with her hands, Caitlin dropped the woman to the ground. Her projection changed back to her human form as she walked slowly toward the four remaining party members. Stopping in the middle of the group, she smiled broadly. "If you run, you die." Her arm shot out with lightning quick speed and her hand wrapped around the throat of the second man. "But if you stay, you die as well."

The rest of the group turned and started to run.

"That's no fun," Caitlin frowned. "I hate fast food." Breaking the man's neck, she charged off after the group, easily catching up with them. Picking off the slowest first, she grabbed one of the women from behind and wrapped her arms around her chest. Leaning her head in, she bit into the woman's neck and tasted her blood. Tossing her head back, Caitlin moaned in pleasure. It had been too long. Spinning the woman in her arms, she gazed for a moment into her fear stricken eyes. How she loved that look. Leaning in to the opposite side of her neck, Caitlin bit again and savored the blood. He tongue worked in and around the puncture wounds she had created as the blood flowed freely into her mouth. She felt her victim's heart begin to slow as the last drops of blood were sucked from the wound.

Lifting the woman by her throat, Caitlin tossed her away like a rag doll. The woman hit the wall with a crunch and fell to the sidewalk in a heap. Returning her attention to the survivors, Caitlin headed off into the night. They couldn't run far enough or fast enough to escape her. There was not even a chance to hide. It was their scent she was following now.

Coming around a corner, she stopped and became instantly still. Like the Praying Mantis clinging to the leaf ever prepared to attack and devour, she, too, became one with her surroundings. Her golden eyes sliced through the darkness scanning for her prey, but they were not to be seen. Furrowing her brow, she moved carefully against the wall, never betraying her position. The turn had led her into a blind alley, replete with piles upon horrid piles of refuse. All three walls were sheer and she was covering the mouth. They hadn't gotten past her. She could still taste them.

They were here.

Caitlin stepped away from the wall, allowing her camouflage to fade. She wanted them to know she was there...still looking for them. It was torture, pure and simple. In her prime, she had been known to keep a victim alive for weeks, just to break their fragile minds and will. For her, the act of torture became much more satisfying than the kill. She no longer just needed the victim's blood, she wanted their very soul. She craved it. Lifting a long stick from the ground, she tapped it against the wall. Again. Moving slowly into the alley, she pulled the tip along scratching at the surface. The sound echoed off the walls ominously. Sniffing the air, she could smell the sweat running down their faces—liquid fear.

Taking another step, she stopped and smiled. Tossing the stick away, she plunged her hand into a pile of trash and grabbed the woman's arms.

Dragging her kicking and screaming from the trash, Caitlin pinned the woman to her own body. "Who are you?"

The woman muttered something incoherent through her tears and sobs.

"If you don't answer me, you will die. I'm giving you a chance to live," Caitlin said quietly.

"Claudia," the woman mumbled. "Please, don't kill me."

Caitlin pressed her finger to the woman's lips. "Hush," she said softly. "Where is the other man?"

The woman remained silent.

"Is he your husband?"

The woman nodded reluctantly.

Caitlin smiled. "What is his name?"

"Peter," she sobbed.

"Peter," Caitlin called into the darkened alley. "I'm giving you a choice. If you come out right now and give yourself to me, I'll spare your lovely wife."

"Don't do—"

Caitlin wrenched Claudia's head to the side, silencing her. "Listen to me, Peter. I will kill her right now if you don't come out, and then I will dig you out of your pile of shit and kill you as well. So you see," Caitlin relished the moment, "you are going to die anyway, but your wife has the chance to live."

After a moment, a nearby pile of trash erupted as Peter stood up and faced Caitlin. "How do I know you'll keep your word?"

Caitlin dug her fingernails into Claudia's throat. "I've given you no word to keep," she said smugly.

Peter looked longingly at his wife. That he loved her that much was clear. He started to take a step forward, but stopped. "I...." he trailed off. "We...." He couldn't finish a thought.

"What's it going to be?" Caitlin asked, slightly baring her fangs. She inched her head toward Claudia's neck.

Peter wiped the sweat from his forehead with the sleeve of his khaki shirt. Glancing past Caitlin, he tried to size up his chances for escape. She was planted firmly in the center of the alley making getting past her almost impossible, plus her speed was incredible. He wouldn't make it far. He stopped and looked at his wife as tears ran down her face. He couldn't let this happen to her. No matter how vigorously he clung to life, he wouldn't have one without her. She was his everything. He would rather die now in this stinking alley than live without her. "You can have me."

Caitlin lifted her head. "Apparently chivalry isn't dead," she smiled. Stretching out her arm, she offered her hand to Peter.

Slowly, Peter slipped his hand into hers. He glanced one final time at his beloved wife and mouthed, "I love you."

Pushing Claudia away, Caitlin pulled Peter into her arms. Leaning close, she whispered into his ear, "I lied." With an evil laugh, she bit into his neck. From behind, Claudia shrieked in horror as her husband died in another woman's arms. Dropping his dead corpse to the ground, Caitlin wiped the blood from her lips. She turned her attention to Claudia with a sneer.

Claudia's eyes were filled with rage as she stared at the vampire. Pulling herself off the ground, she charged forward and slapped Caitlin hard across the face. "You bitch!"

She threw another slap, but it was easily intercepted. Caitlin tightened her grip on Claudia's wrist, feeling her bones snap. Pulling the woman close again, she pressed their bodies together. "I always get what I want," Caitlin said softly. She licked Claudia's neck. Staring the woman in the eyes, she gently leaned forward and kissed her on the lips. Slowly pulling back, she looked into the mixture of fear, pain and confusion on Claudia's face. Wiping the tears from her cheeks, Caitlin smiled softly. Pulling Claudia's head back by her hair, she savagely bit into her throat.

* * *

Dawn paced back and forth in front of the large windows in her office. Her left arm was wrapped around her chest, while she chewed on the nails of her other, her head down in serious contemplation. She had spent much of the morning being questioned by the police. That wasn't the worst part. How do you tell stern and closed-minded police officers that they should be out looking for a vampire? She couldn't do it. Of course, due to their ineptness, they now considered her a suspect in his disappearance. She felt lucky they didn't arrest her on the spot.

She turned her head toward the door as the sound of the handle being twisted caught her attention. She felt a bit of relief upon seeing Bishop, Kelley and Lydia. She rushed to Kelley and

226

wrapped her arms her. "It's good to have you back. How are you feeling?"

Kelley shot a smug glance at Bishop. "Not dead," she whispered to him.

"You don't let up, do you?" Bishop laughed.

Kelley turned back to Dawn. "I feel fine. Lydia and her coven have been wonderful."

"That's good news," Dawn forced a smile. Slowly letting go of Kelley, she placed her hand on Lydia's shoulder. "Did Bishop update you?"

"He told us everything on the way here," Lydia said, placing her hand on top of Dawn's. "Are you going to be okay?"

Dawn started to nod, but slowly shook her head no.

"We'll find Cane," Lydia reassured her. "We've brought help." She directed Dawn's attention to the woman bringing up the rear of the group. "This is Sister Callista. She's a Wraith with the White Guard."

Dawn reached out and shook Callista's hand. "It's good to meet you. Why are you called a 'Wraith'?"

"It's a modern term," Callista explained. "Because the Celtic language has fallen out of widespread use, many westerners started pronouncing our name as 'Gwi-laid Wraith', instead of the proper way, so several Guards—what we used to be known as—took to calling themselves Wraiths. We've been using that name for a couple hundred years now, I believe. Gwyliad Wriaeth actually translates to 'White Guard' in English."

"That's interesting," Bishop said. "I would love

to know more about the Guard, if we get a chance. It would make for a truly fascinating paper."

"We can't talk much about it to outsiders for just that reason. We have existed in secrecy since before the birth of your calendar. We don't want to jeopardize that now."

"So you can't tell me anymore?" Bishop asked.

Callista smiled sweetly, "Maybe later."

"Good," Dawn broke in. "We need to get down to work here." Moving back into the office, she sat down at her desk. "The police—big surprise—know nothing. They theorize Cane walked in on a robbery and paid the price. What they don't understand is where the body is. It's obvious their theory is fundamentally flawed."

Lydia sat down behind Cane's desk. "What do you think happened?"

Dawn glared at Lydia for a moment before backing off. That was Cane's desk. Shaking her head softly, she reached into the pocket of her jacket. "I found this at the scene." She sat Cane's crucifix gently in front of Lydia.

The witch gasped and sat straight up.

Dawn nodded. "That was my reaction as well."

Bishop started to reach for the necklace, but quickly withdrew his hand. He didn't want to upset Dawn. "Are you sure it's his?"

Dawn closed her eyes and sighed in frustration. "We don't have time for stupid questions."

"Hold up," Kelley interrupted. "I think it's a perfectly valid question. How do we know?"

"I got a good look at it this morning when I was cleaning it. You'll notice the initials 'Z' and 'C' are

228

inscribed on the back."

Lydia frowned. "I had that done when we bought them. Mine has my initials on the back as well. It's his," she stated painfully.

"The bottom line is this," Dawn slammed her fist on the desk, "we have no clues and no leads. The only thing we know the police don't is that a vampire took him, probably one in Caitlin's service."

"Or a warring clan," Callista suggested, "eager to take her prize."

"Well, that puts us back to square one," Dawn said, leaning back in her chair. "Is there anything the White Guard can give us on Caitlin? I mean, you are a mystical order, right?"

Callista nodded. "We know many things, but not all." She had remained standing behind Lydia and Bishop. "Our records show that Caitlin was killed by Brother Specter thirty years ago, and nothing more."

Lydia perked up. "I remember him, a handsome young lad at the time. Probably in his early sixties now."

"You mean someone else actually staked Caitlin?" Dawn asked.

Lydia nodded. "Cane helped, but it was Specter who plunged the stake into her heart."

Dawn leaned back and tapped on her front teeth.

Bishop leaned forward on his desk. "Are you thinking what I'm thinking?"

Dawn smiled.

Bishop turned to Callista. "Does the Guard

know where all their Wraiths are at any given time?"

"We have a pretty general idea," she stated. "We can tell you where a particular Wraith is posted, or if they're on a mission."

Dawn grinned broadly. "Ladies and Bishop, we have our first lead. Callista, can you contact the Guard and find out where this Specter is, or was heading?"

"I will," Callista answered.

"Lydia," Dawn turned to the witch, "we need some firepower. Can you give us a magical edge?"

"I think I have just the thing," she said, standing up.

"Bishop, you're with Callista, and Kelley, I want you to help Lydia."

"And you?" Bishop asked as he stood up.

"I have a few supplies of my own I'm bringing on this case," Dawn smiled deviously.

* * *

Zeke stopped. Craning his neck slightly, he adjusted the dead weight on his shoulder. Specter was folded over the vampire's shoulder at the waist, his arms dangling loosely behind. There had been a few strange looks as the two vampires had entered Cairo, but one quick flash of his golden eyes or a glimpse of his fangs quickly quieted them or sent them screaming into the night.

It seemed that word of a "pale, yellow-eyed demon" was already circulating around the streets, sending shockwaves of fear through the locals. Zeke shook his head. He wished Ice hadn't been so overzealous in her feeding earlier. It was no matter though. Soon the world would know of their kind and once again, they would tremble in fear in their homes at night while they hung useless strands of garlic from their windows and nailed crosses to their doors. He longed for it. To stand over them with blood dripping from his fangs while they realized their pathetic superstitions were useless would be glorious indeed.

He understood Ice more than he wished to admit. He too felt the power coursing through his veins and the calling of the night. How easy it would be for him to disappear into the darkness and wreak havoc over this godforsaken continent. While not as strong as Caitlin, he was easily mightier than any mortal he would meet up with. This world was his for the taking. Isn't that what he always wanted, the freedom to live outside society's rules and regulations? Now it was his, and he was running errands for another vampire. It didn't seem right.

He had spent most of his life dreaming about becoming a vampire, and now he was squandering it. How many nights had he sat alone in bars, just waiting for a creature of the night to pick him out of the crowd and deliver him immortality? He had scoured the literature seeking any kernel of truth that might be woven into the fiction. Ouija boards, ancient rhetoric to contact the devil and sell his soul, and dangerous blood rituals had all marked his path toward vampirism. It had, somewhere along the line, mutated from interest to fascination and finally, to obsession. As he had proven, he had even been ready to take human lives to attain his goals, and yet he was being forced into servitude.

What was this sway Caitlin had over him? Whenever he was in her presence, he was totally and completely under her spell. Perhaps it was because a mixture of her blood coursed through his veins, or because she was so ancient and powerful, she could control every thought that passed through his mind. Whatever the case was, he now belonged to her...like it or not. It just didn't seem right.

He shook his head. He shouldn't think that way. It wasn't for him to decide what was right or wrong. Once his mistress had finished with these few chores, she would start her crusade to rule the pathetic humans, and he would share the power at her side. That was what he was working for, more power than anyone could possibly imagine. He wouldn't be satisfied with raping and pillaging small towns over the world, he wanted to rule them all.

Glancing back at Ice, he started on his way again. He felt a sudden surge of hatred swell up. She wasn't worthy of his mistress' attention. It should be Ina working with him, not that creature behind him. Ice wasn't even worthy of the vampiric blood coursing through her very body. She was nothing more than a thief in the night coveting her new prize of immortality (but then again, what was he?). Zeke couldn't understand why Caitlin had chosen Ice over Ina. It didn't seem like a wise selection to his mind. She would surely stab both of them in the back the first chance she had and betray them. He knew it was coming, it was only a matter of when.

Holding the Wraith's legs, he whipped around a

232

corner and saw his mistress' home come into view. Quickly clearing the troublesome thoughts from his mind, a smile grew across his face. He would surely be rewarded well for this act. That could possibly mean another taste of Caitlin's blood, or something else…a little more substantial.

He smiled wryly.

Chapter Fourteen

Bishop walked a few paces behind Callista. His gaze was a mixture of awe and disbelief. How was it that this woman killed vampires, he wondered. She didn't appear very intimidating or powerful, but that wasn't always the whole story. In many cases, he found big gifts came in small packages. Her dark gray coat flowed majestically behind her athletic frame as she moved lightly through the halls of the Office of Paranormal Research. Even though she wore heavy boots, he could barely hear her footfalls, almost as if she wasn't touching the floor at all. There was something mystical about this woman, although Bishop couldn't quite put his finger on it. She was more human than human somehow.

"Do you know where you're going?" Bishop wondered curiously.

"I do," Callista answered quickly.

Bishop jogged ahead to catch up with her, "And that is?"

"I noticed a payphone in the lobby. I need to call and check in."

"A payphone?" Bishop asked with a twinge of disappointment in his voice.

Callista stopped. "What did you expect?"

"Well…." Bishop said slowly.

"You thought I was going to perform some kind of ritual to contact the Guard," she laughed. "You were hoping I would cut the head off a chicken or something and then dance around naked by candlelight, right?"

"Not that specifically," he smiled, "but close. I just didn't expect a phone call from an ancient order of vampire hunters."

"It's true that our order has many mystical qualities, but communication isn't one of them. We use letters, phone calls and even email to stay in touch." She started down the hall again with Bishop at her side. "We, like everyone else, have had to embrace technology to adapt to the modern world. It's that simple."

"So can I log onto the Net and go to www.white-guard.com?"

"I'm afraid not," Callista laughed. "It's on a private server."

Bishop raised an eyebrow, but continued. "So, how did you end up with the Guard?"

"Genetics," she replied. "I come from a long line of vampire hunters. It's in my blood."

"Is that how most of the Wraiths are chosen?"

Callista nodded as she turned a corner and headed for a bank of elevators. "There have been cases when a potential Wraith is born to parents who have no history with the Guard, but often the traits are passed down through the generations. My mother was a Wraith as well, as was her father before her."

"And your father?"

"A commoner."

"So you're a halfling?"

Callista turned and cocked her head slightly. "I don't think I've ever heard it put quite that way before, but I guess the term is accurate. When I was old enough, my mother sent me to the Guard for training."

"So you really didn't have a choice?"

"Yes and no," she said after a bit of thought. "My mother did tell me about what she did and that it was my destiny to follow in her footsteps. When my mother and father separated, I had the choice of living with either of them. I chose my mother, so in essence, I chose the Guard."

Bishop nodded. "What happened to your father?"

"I don't know," her voice dropped. "I haven't seen or heard from him in close to forty years."

"I'm sorry," Bishop said quickly.

Callista placed her hand on his shoulder. "You couldn't have known," she assured him. "I don't regret my decision."

"Wait," Bishop stopped. "Did you say that you hadn't seen your father in forty years?"

Callista nodded.

"How can that be? You don't look a day over twenty-one," Bishop said in confusion.

Callista smiled. "Among our other gifts, we Wraiths are blessed with extraordinarily long lives. The Wraith you asked about earlier, Brother Specter, is close to ninety years old."

Bishop understood. "Do you mind that I'm asking you all these questions? I don't want to be rooting around in your personal life if it makes you uncomfortable."

"I don't mind," she said with a smile. "I've been with the Guard for so long, I take it for granted. It feels good to be reminded of how truly special it is."

"Okay, I'm apparently feeding your ego here," Bishop chuckled.

"No, you don't understand," she said, waving her hands. "It's kind of like being a movie star. Everyone else thinks what one does is magical, but the movie star sees the inner workings so it becomes less glamorous. One gets bogged down in the little details like contracts and lighting cues, while others only see the finished product, the movie. One quickly begins to forget what they are doing is special, and not everyone can do it. That's all I'm saying."

"So now you're a movie star?" Bishop teased.

Callista let out an exasperated sigh.

"I'm just kidding. I understand," he said with a smile. "You take things for granted when you should be enjoying them."

"Exactly."

"What else can you tell me about the Guard?"

"Actually, very little," Callista admitted. "Some students actually take courses such as the History of the White Guard, but I chose not to. For me, it was enough to know that the Guard was ridding the world of an ancient evil and I was one of the chosen. I didn't have to know anything else."

Bishop nodded, "But what about the training they put you through?"

Callista looked up as the doors of the elevator slid open with a ding. Stepping inside, she punched the appropriate button on the panel. "It's difficult, I won't lie. About two-thirds of the training is physical, while the other third is mental. While our bodies are conditioned to take advantage of our natural gifts, our minds are also prepared for the darkness we must endure."

"How many vampires have you faced?"

She lifted the braid that hung from her temple. "Each of these ties in this braid represents a vampire I have dispatched. I currently have thirteen."

"Lucky thirteen," Bishop muttered.

"The more bands one has in their braid, the more respected they are."

"Thirteen vampires, that's pretty impressive, right?"

Callista shook her head. "It's about average for a Wraith. I met a man during my training who had taken down almost fifty vampires. I don't know what he's at now."

"That's incredible."

"Not if you think about it," Callista answered solemnly. "There are literally millions of vampires walking the Earth and relatively few Wraiths. We're fighting a losing battle, Bishop, and more Wraiths are lost every day."

Her words were like a slap across the face. A cold shiver ran down his spine as he considered the consequences of her statement. "That's rather pessimistic."

Callista shook her head. "To create another vampire takes only moments, but to create a Wraith takes years."

The elevator doors slid open and Callista and Bishop stepped into the lobby. The afternoon sun was filtering in through the large plate glass windows at the front of the building, casting long, dark shadows across the floor. Very few people could be seen as a lone security guard walked the perimeter whistling some unknown tune and twirling his nightstick.

Callista made her way to a row of four payphones toward the rear of the lobby. Lifting the receiver off the hook she began to dial the number. "I need a little privacy here, Bishop."

Bishop nodded. "I'll be over there," he said, pointing to a bench on the far wall.

Callista nodded. "Thanks."

Bishop slowly turned and began to walk away. Stuffing his hands in his pockets, he glanced out the windows at the pale blue sky. It was less than seven hours until dusk, and for the first time in his life, he wasn't looking forward to it.

* * *

"Prophecy has betrayed us."

The other eleven remained silent, but agreed with the first's statement. The twelve robed figures stood motionlessly around the ruby encrusted pentagram. A few wisps of smoke wafted up and mingled in the lights shining down on the crimson robes or the members of the High Esgobaeth. All else was dark. The first stood in the center of the pentagram with her hood folded neatly back and her porcelain white hands exposed. Her features were human, except for her fierce golden eyes. She was obviously of vampire heritage, and yet she stood unabashed in the very center of the Gwyliad Wriaeth's temple.

"Perhaps we misinterpreted it," another offered, their face still shadowed.

"Impossible," the first replied.

239

"He has fallen into the hands of our enemy," a third voice stated. "We will lose him."

The first shook her head. "I do not think that will be his fate. Brother Specter is spoken of in several other texts that follow this prophecy. His role in our future, the very fate of the Gwyliad Wriaeth, cannot be altered."

"This is not true," the second spoke again. "The future has not yet been written." Stepping into the center of the circle, she pulled back her hood, also exposing her golden eyes. "We must accept he has his own destiny to fulfill, and it is possible his fate is to die by the hand of Caitlin."

"I do not accept that," the first argued. "We are missing a crucial piece of information. Something we have possibly overlooked in our haste."

"I know of your affinity for this one," the second offered sympathetically after a moment, "but maybe our original prediction was wrong. Perhaps he is not the one."

The first shook her head. "The scrolls spoke very specifically about the one. He matches all the criteria." She turned and faced the rest of the circle. "Of this, I have no doubt. We must act to save this Wraith."

"At what cost?" the third asked. "Will we assemble an army to fight and die for this one soul?"

"If that is what must come to pass," the first spoke, her position unfaltering. "We must protect our interests."

The second and third looked to each other, then back to the first. "Agreed."

"Then we shall raise an army of Wraiths," the first said with satisfaction.

"And send them to Cairo?" the third asked curiously.

The first closed her eyes and shook her head. "That's not where it ends, but that is where they will be needed. Caitlin plans to grow an army of her own." She dropped her head. "Many will die."

* * *

Dawn stood silently at the door. Lifting her hand from her jacket pocket, she slowly wrapped her fingers around the doorknob. Twisting it to the right, she pushed open the door. A familiar jingle greeted her entrance into the small shop. It had been a long time since her last visit. She hoped the shopkeeper remembered her, but why wouldn't he? On her last visit, she had requested several obscure items. Things like that tend to leave a memory. Shutting the door behind her, she took a moment to allow her senses to adjust.

The interior was dimly lit. From experience, Dawn knew the shopkeeper didn't trust technology, let alone electricity. Shadows cast by flickering candles stretched menacingly across the walls and floor as if some unseen hand were reaching out for her. The place itself was no bigger than her office, but seemed much smaller in comparison. Shelves, which lined the entire shop, were stuffed with relics, books, and magical items of all shapes and sizes. Various jars containing everything from bat's wings to authentic grave dust. The entire store was drowned in brown. From the floors to the hand-built shelves, the walls and counter, everything was

241

dominated by lacquered wood. She detected the faint scent of incense drifting in from somewhere.

The atmosphere was dense, almost soupy in nature. As she waded further into the store, she felt the weight of the world lift off her shoulders. There was a general sense of ease in this place, no hint of malice could be detected. This shop was the very epitome of peacefulness. She took a deep breath, inhaling the sweet smell of incense, allowing it to wash through her body. For the first time in longer than she cared to remember, she felt wonderful and at peace with herself.

Stopping just short of the counter at the rear of the shop, Dawn adjusted her attire. On the wall behind the counter just to the right of a door marked "private", there was a large, beautiful painting. It depicted a nude Adam and Eve standing in the Garden of Eden, with Eve holding a bitten apple in her hand. A large green snake was slowly slithering down the tree behind them, a smile across its reptilian face. She wondered why he would keep the painting in his store, as it was certainly a new addition since her last visit. The owner of this establishment was not a Christian, nor did he hold to any of their values. He considered himself a "heathen" but she would describe him as more of a pagan than anything else.

Dawn had seen this, or a very similar representation of the Expulsion From Eden several times before, but something about this particular painting struck her as odd. She found herself becoming enraptured by it, drawn further and further into the canvas. Images that seemed to be only smudges at first now took on new shapes and forms. Her eyes wandered to the left of the green snake to find a dark area hidden behind the trunk of the tree. She became transfixed on the layers of paint and canvas and slowly the form began to take on the shape of a human.

She shook her head and forcefully looked away from the painting, completely disturbed by what she had seen there. Taking a deep breath, she slowly returned her attention to it, hoping her eyes had been playing tricks on her. To her dismay, the image remained, now easily visible to her. It had to be a fake. It had to be. There was no way the church would sanction this painting. The sound of the door to her left opening startled her. Her nerves were calmed when a familiar visage emerged from the doorway.

"Miss Dawn," the old man spoke slowly and carefully. She could see he was enunciating every syllable and choosing his words carefully. "It's been a long time."

"Gregor," Dawn said with a smile. She reached out and took the man's hand. "It has, hasn't it?" She looked into Gregor's face and understood his new tendency to overenunciate. His left cheek and lower lip were drooping slightly, appearing as if they were filled with anesthetic. Sometime ago, he had suffered a stroke. "How have you been?"

"Fine, and you?" Gregor had to be well over seventy, but didn't look a day over fifty. Excluding the slight damage to his face, he appeared to be in exceptional shape. His frame was lean, but healthy. His once dark brown hair was graying at the temples, but his green eyes were still full of life. He was wearing a pair of dark slacks, a white dress shirt and red tie, with a red vest buttoned smartly on top. He was leaning on a tall, dark cane on his left side, but Dawn wasn't sure if it was more out of necessity or style.

"I've been good," she replied sincerely.

Letting Dawn's hand go, Gregor moved slowly behind his counter and ancient cash register. "What brings you to my humble magic shop?"

"I need a few specialty items." Dawn bit her bottom lip, "My team at the OPR is hunting a very…unique quarry."

Gregor smiled. "What kind of quarry?"

Dawn paused. She knew Gregor was a man of the world. He had regaled her with stories of his adventures across all seven continents before, but this one might catch even him off guard. "Vampires."

Gregor's expression remained fixed. "So, hunting the undead, are we?"

Dawn smiled and laughed to herself. She should have known better than to underestimate her old friend. "How long have I known you, Gregor?"

"Since you were in your teens, I think."

"And you never cease to amaze me."

Gregor smiled sweetly.

"My friend Cane has been taken by a vampire who calls herself 'Caitlin'," she said, suddenly serious. "I need anything you can get me to stop her." Her eyes hardened, "And send her back to Hell."

Gregor was slightly taken aback. He had never

seen Dawn like this before, so full of rage and hatred. She was obviously hurting. Lifting his hand, he pulled it through his hair. "I think I have just what you need." He turned and started back toward the door. "I've been saving this for a long time."

"Wait," Dawn said, reaching out. "Where did you get that painting?"

Gregor pointed his thumb over his shoulder, "You mean the Garden of Eden?"

Dawn nodded.

"I found it on one of my journeys to the Middle East." He smiled. "I liberated it from a personal collection some years ago. I've tried to have the painting dated before, but all I can find out is that it's really old. Why?"

"I just find it," Dawn swallowed hard, "disturbing."

Gregor nodded as he headed for the door. "So, you spotted the vampire behind the tree, did you?" He reached for the doorknob. "That was one of the reasons I took the painting. I had never seen something like that before, and yet it seemed completely appropriate."

Dawn's mouth fell agape and she found herself completely speechless.

Gregor glanced over his shoulder, "Well, where do you think they came from?"

Dawn watched Gregor vanish into the backroom. Taking a step back from the counter, she glanced at the painting once again. She found herself transfixed by the dark creature in the corner. Its outline was barely visible, yet it was unmistakably a vampire. From the gleaming canine

245

fangs to its oddly offsetting yellow eyes, this creature was evil, and yet Dawn couldn't take her eyes off it. The dark creature was as real to her as Adam, Eve, the snake, or even the tree it stood behind. As she stared, the painting became less a visual representation of the artist's imagination and more a snapshot captured in time. She began to feel as if the painter had stood in Eden at that very moment and captured the whole event on canvas. She could see Eve breathing, the snake slithering, and the vampire creeping ever closer to its prey.

Something struck her as odd at that moment. The sky was bright blue. Although no sun was visible in the painting, it was readily evident it was daytime and yet the vampire showed no signs of the light hurting it. From every piece of literature or film she had ever seen, vampires could be killed by sunlight. She knew the creature was a vampire, but there was something else off about it, yet she couldn't put her finger on it. It looked—she searched for the correct word to describe it— inhuman. Not because it was an undead creature, but because of its very appearance. It seemed almost…alien.

"Here it is."

Dawn's attention was ripped away from the image. Gregor stood in front of her. In his hands, he held a rectangular wooden box. Dawn took a deep breath and quickly composed herself. "Sorry, Gregor, I didn't hear you come back in. You startled me."

"It's that damned painting," Gregor confirmed. "I know I've lost myself in it for hours at a time."

Dawn's brow furrowed. "How long were you in the back?"

Gregor checked his watch, "About fifteen minutes."

"I was…." Dawn slowly pulled her hand across her forehead. "Fifteen minutes?"

Gregor reached over the counter and patted his friend on the shoulder. "It happens to the best of us. Don't worry about it." He presented the box. "I have something special for you. Open it."

Dawn reached down and placed her fingers gingerly on the edges of the box. Lifting it carefully, the lid creaked in protest. It had been some time since it had been opened. Peering inside, Dawn smiled.

"This is an authentic Vampire Hunter's Kit," Gregor remarked with pride. "It was made and marketed in Europe during the 1600's."

Dawn scanned the contents. The interior of the box was lined with red velour. The kit contained one wooden stake, a glass vial labeled "Holy Water", a bag of garlic long ago disintegrated, and a wooden cross all nestled neatly inside.

"Good lord," Dawn said, waving her hand in front of her nose. "That garlic went bad a long time ago."

"What can you expect from something that's over four hundred years old?" Gregor laughed. "So is this what you were looking for?"

Dawn nodded. "It's perfect. What do I owe you?"

Gregor patted the air, shaking his head. "Free of charge. Just make me a promise."

Sure," Dawn answered. "Anything."

Gregor's face became stern and solemn. "Promise me that you'll come back alive."

Dawn reached over and pressed her hand on Gregor's shoulder. "I promise." Lifting the box into her hands, she turned away from her friend and headed for the door. She closed her eyes briefly and took a long breath. "I hope," she muttered as she stepped outside.

Chapter Fifteen

Moving through the halls of Caitlin's abandoned apartment building, Zeke still had Specter's body slung over his shoulder. Just before entering, he thought he saw his mistress scaling the outside wall up toward her balcony, but it had happened too fast, even for his vampire eyes to follow. Ice was trudging along some distance behind. He knew she was dragging her feet for a reason. The last woman he had brought to Caitlin was dead now. Would the same fate befall her? Zeke sneered. He could only hope. Turning the final corner, he moved down the hall toward Caitlin's flat.

"I have a present for you," Zeke smiled as he entered Caitlin's rundown apartment. Glancing to the left, he caught sight of the damage to the wall. Spotting her aging leather chair lying broken amidst the debris, Zeke didn't give the sight another thought. Stopping just inside the doorway, he stared at Caitlin, who was standing just inside the balcony, the moonlight caressing her powerful body. Her back was to her two vampire minions.

"Place him on the floor," she said, her voice barely above a whisper. "Has my new home been secured yet?"

"Not yet," Zeke said uneasily as he tossed Specter to the floor. "We thought retrieving this man was a more important task," he explained.

"I did not ask you to think," Caitlin hissed, still turned away from the two. "I instructed you to secure me a more suitable home, and then retrieve my guest."

"I am sorry," Zeke said slowly. "I made a mistake."

"You're damned right you did!" Caitlin spun and crossed the room in a fraction of a second. Wrapping her hand around Zeke's throat, she lifted him easily off the ground.

Zeke didn't struggle against her grip, as he had no need for breath.

"It was by my hand you were created, I could easily undo that." Caitlin's eyes burned a fiery yellow and her face was drawn up into a vicious sneer. "You will follow my instructions, or you will die." With a grunt, she tossed Zeke against the wall, sending his body crumbling to the floor. "Leave me now. Find me a home." She turned away again, "Or don't bother coming back."

Zeke lifted himself up and dusted himself off. "It will be done—"

Caitlin glanced angrily over her shoulder. No words needed to be spoken. Her expression was very clear.

Zeke lifted his hands up in defense and started backing toward the door. Reaching behind, he pushed Ice through the doorway and followed closely.

"Wait," Caitlin snapped.

Zeke and Ice stopped and held themselves motionless. They did not want to invoke her wrath.

"I did not have a chance to welcome the new member to our family," she breathed. Turning around, she approached the two vampires once again, this time, her arms outstretched. "Ice, come to me and let me take a look at you."

Ice glanced at Zeke and then at Caitlin. Taking an uneasy step toward Caitlin, she stopped. Her muscles were tense, not knowing what to expect. She would not go down like Ina had, not without a fight.

Caitlin placed her hands on Ice's shoulders and smiled. She looked down on the new vampire with a mother's love. "You are perfect."

Ice found herself puzzled but slowly started to let her guard down. "Thanks," she stammered.

Caitlin ran her hand through Ice's hair. "I love this look," she giggled. "You look like a vampire should. The white hair, white flesh, icy green eyes, you are a stunning creature." Caitlin leaned close to Ice's face, her mouth only inches from her throat.

Ice jerked nervously, but couldn't break Caitlin's grip.

"I know Zeke has been hard on you," Caitlin whispered, "but try and let that go. You are just as important to me as he is. I chose you for this life. Never forget that."

Ice found some comfort in her words. "Thank you, Mistress."

"Work well for me," Caitlin returned her voice to its normal volume, "and I will reward you well. Work poorly," Caitlin let the thought fade, its message implied. Letting go of Ice, she took a step back. "Now go. Find me a more suitable home."

Ice, now much more at ease, nodded at Caitlin. She turned back to Zeke and slipped her arm through his. Pulling him into the hallway, she laughed. "Better be nice to me now. Mommy likes

251

me just as much as she likes you." Ice laughed out loud as she accompanied Zeke out of Caitlin's sight.

Caitlin returned to her position in the moonlight, carefully eyeing the incapacitated man lying in the middle of the floor. Her anger swelled, but quickly abated. This man lying quietly, motionless, didn't look like the same one who had almost taken her life thirty years earlier. He was older now and seemed almost harmless while she appeared no different and no less fierce. But she couldn't underestimate this man. She caught sight of his trophy braid hanging loosely off the side of his head. The bands now numbered in the fifties. She knew each of the colored bands represented a fallen vampire.

She knew the enemy. It was a necessity. She had spent many years shadowing Wraiths and learning, cracking the code, so to speak. Their customs, their rituals, their techniques, she knew them all. She had studied them meticulously, letting no detail slip her attention. This was how she had survived for so long. Immortality was not simply enjoyed, it must be protected at all costs, and this man had almost ended that. He would have to pay for that indignity, but she still needed to wait for her final guest. Once both arrived, vengeance would be served. Caitlin grinned. She wanted to pick up exactly where she left off thirty years ago.

Walking slowly across the room, she knelt down next to Specter's luscious blood filled body. Running her hand across his cheek, she felt her mouth begin to water. There was no need to feed, but she wanted him, wanted to feel his blood

252

flowing through her veins. To quote a famous fictional vampire, "The blood is the life." She believed this wholeheartedly. After all her years, she still had no idea if humans, or vampires for that matter, had a soul or even where it resided, but she knew it had something to do with their blood. She had experienced what her kind called "The Flash" too many times to deny its importance.

The Flash was a very rare occurrence in vampires. So rare, in fact, most of the newer generation of vampires had never experienced it. Caitlin knew it was linked to age somehow, but knew very little else. When a vampire feeds, they often find themselves in a state of ecstasy, much like during sex. Vampire scientists concluded this was due to the fact they were ingesting human endorphins along with their blood. The blood was not only a necessity to vampires, but it also had many properties similar to a drug. The Flash was an unexplained event whereby the vampire, while feeding, would share in the human's life retrospect moments before they died. It was often said that before a human died, their life flashed before their eyes. It was this the vampire was witnessing. It was rare, but truly fascinating. Caitlin had experienced this phenomenon four times in her life, and she truly hoped Specter would be her fifth. She not only wanted to take his blood and life, she wanted to possess his very soul.

Lifting her left hand, she transformed her thumbnail into a razor-sharp claw. Lifting his trophy braid carefully, she easily cut it from his hair just above his scalp. Holding the braid up in the moonlight, she smiled. This would be her trophy now. Returned from the grave thirty years later, she would claim the life of those who had crossed her. Standing up, she began to weave the braid into her own hair. It would be a constant reminder that she had triumphed over her oppressors. Any Wraith that faced her now would think twice before attacking, and any vampire would recognize the trophy and instantly know her power.

Moving back to her position on the balcony, she saw the eastern sky starting to lighten. It would be morning soon and time for her to rest. Tomorrow would be a special night. It would mark the end of Specter and Cane and her resurrection. It was truly an event to be celebrated. Letting go of the braid, she felt it brush against her face as it hung from the side of her head. It terminated below her shoulder, just above her breasts and stood in stark contrast to her own fiery red hair. She ran her fingers gently over the braid of bands and dark hair. She wondered for a moment how long he had been growing this braid. It didn't matter. It was hers now, as was he.

* * *

The small office was almost completely dark. A few sparse candles flickered in the corners casting odd shadows across the floor. Two figures sat in the center of the room cloaked in darkness, chanting quietly. Both sat cross-legged, their hands resting palms up on their knees with their backs straight. Between them rested a square piece of cloth with several items spread across it. A candle stood in the center radiating a beautiful orange glow across their bodies while four more, arranged to the points of a compass, encircled them.

Lydia and Kelley were naked, except for a few choice pieces of silver jewelry, including two pentacles that hung around black cords from each of their necks (and Lydia's ever present crucifix). It was known as being "Skyclad". Often Wiccans, Witches, and Pagans performed their rituals in the nude, believing clothing blocked the natural energies of the human body. Lydia, a Wiccan High Priestess, chose to practice Skyclad only for special rituals, or occasions where a little extra "magical oomph" was required and this was certainly one of those times. Kelley, a natural psychic, had trained with Lydia during her time in Seattle in the ways of the Witch. She was still in the process of completing her initial year and one day training period, but her natural talents gave her an advantage over other new students. Each was completely still as the chant continued. Only the heaving of their chests as they breathed could be seen. Each took their turn uttering the lines of the spell:

"Goddess and God, we invoke you this night," Lydia breathed. Her voice was subdued, yet commanding.

"To help aid our journey toward a desperate plight," Kelley added, her eyes closed and her head tilted back.

"We ask you for your power and blessing."

"To charge these items upon this dressing."

"Allow us to act under your righteousness and grace."

"So that we may return our friend to this, his just place."

"We act under the Goddess' silvery light."

"Bringing our request to you this night."

Lydia slowly opened her eyes, "Goddess and God, we invoke you this night."

Kelley took a deep breath through her nose and slowly exhaled it through her mouth, "To help aid our journey toward a desperate plight." She looked at her mentor with a crooked smile. "Do you have the same buzz I do?"

Lydia nodded. "We are a perfect whole tonight. Our energies have found harmony."

She looked down at the various items on the white cloth between them. Lying next to the candle was a small, silver dagger with an engraved image of the Goddess on the hilt. No more than six inches long, the dagger had a beautiful design etched up the blade that resembled Celtic art. The hilt was carved from redwood, with a thin silver band spiraling down its length. This was Lydia's personal athame, her magical knife. She used it exclusively for ritual work but this night, was offering it up for a different use. To her left, were several small black bags no bigger than her fist, which she had prepared in advance. Each contained a special blend of ingredients she hoped, when used against vampires, would create a singular effect. Finally, there were four necklaces, arranged horizontally along the top of the magically charged cloth. Lydia had cheated a bit and purchased the charms from a store she found downtown instead of creating brand new ones, but she didn't have much time.

She nodded to her companion. They each held out their right hands, palms down over the items.

Their left hands, meanwhile, palms up, were held skyward to channel the energy. "We must release our energy into the items," Lydia instructed. "Usually, we would channel our excess energy back into the Earth, but this time we can't afford to waste any of it."

Kelley nodded.

"Slowly relax your muscles and feel the power draining out, but be mindful of where it's going." Lydia took a breath. "Ready?"

Kelley smiled. "As I'll ever be."

After a silent count of three, the two women let their bodies relax. Their heads fell forward as they felt the power they had worked to build up exiting their bodies. Kelley's fingertips tingled as the energy worked its way out of them and down into the tools below. She smiled. She felt wonderful. Her body, despite the beads of sweat forming from the heat of the candles, felt clean and rejuvenated. During her time with Lydia's coven in Seattle, she had performed many rituals, but they never felt the same as when she was alone with her mentor. Their bodies resonated with the same frequency, making them perfectly compatible. Taking a deep breath, she felt the last slivers of energy fall from her fingertips. Falling onto her back, she slowly let out her breath with satisfaction. Lacing her arms behind her head, she let the feeling linger a moment longer. They still had to close the magical circle they had created, but that could wait for a moment.

She felt Lydia's warm hand gently resting on her thigh. "I'm afraid we don't have time to waste," she said apologetically. "We need to finish up here and get back to the others."

Kelley sat up with a frown. Lydia didn't move her hand.

The two looked into each other's eyes and at once, were lost. Kelley reached slowly toward Lydia's shoulder, keeping her hand in place, afraid of a reprisal or rejection. No words came. Carefully, she moved her hand up to her neck and finally to her cheek, lightly caressing it with her thumb. Unblinking, Kelley inched closer to Lydia. Moving her hand lower on Lydia's face, Kelley ran her fingertips over Lydia's lips sensually. She leaned in for a kiss.

"Wait," Lydia breathed, "we can't." Her protest was tinged with regret. "We both belong to another."

Kelley slowly sat back and looked at Lydia. She was stunningly beautiful in the candlelight as it worked over her body. She knew in that instant, Lydia was right. They had both been swept up in the moment. "I—"

"No need to speak," Lydia said quickly. "I understand. I felt the same way about my teacher."

Kelley burst out in laughter in spite of herself. "I've got the hots for teacher...."

"Van Halen, right?"

Kelley nodded.

Standing up, the two women hugged and laughed. Pulling away, Lydia kissed Kelley on the forehead and smiled. "Besides, he is a much better match for you than I am."

Kelley looked puzzled. "Who?"

"Bishop."

258

Kelley's eyes widened. "You think Bish and I are," she shook her head, "in love?"

Lydia nodded. "Completely." Crouching down, she blew out the center candle and began gathering up the newly charged items.

"Wait," Kelley said, shaking her hands. She was in awe of Lydia's statement. "How can we be?"

Lydia looked up. "Another mystery of the heart," she giggled. "Come on. We need to get dressed and back to the others." Standing, she headed for the corner where her clothes were piled neatly.

Kelley stood for a moment, her hands still frozen in midair. She cocked her head to the right and stared at her teacher. Looking away, she shook her head as she tried to compute the new information she was just given. She started to speak, but stopped. Taking a quick breath, she closed her eyes and smiled. Maybe Lydia was right. Looking back, she saw her teacher slipping on her shoes, now fully dressed. Lydia started for the door. Snapping herself out of her thoughts, Kelley quickly rushed for her clothes. Scooping them up, she charged out of the office after Lydia. "Wait!" she called after Lydia while pulling on her shirt and pants. "When you say, 'in love,' what exactly do you mean?"

* * *

Cane peered out the small window, resting his head against the cool wall. He could see land looming in the distance, but he was uncertain of their destination. For much of the trip, he had seen nothing but ocean. After a short train ride, the vampire had loaded him onto a small plane. She was sitting about three rows back, the shades on every windows, except his, pulled, protecting her from the sun's deadly rays. She had even closed her eyes for a moment, confident her prisoner had nowhere to go, or perhaps she knew he had no desire to escape.

Cane considered how he was going to explain all this to Dawn...or Lydia. As he neared his inevitable end, he couldn't help but wonder if he was still playing the part of the hero, or the martyr. Was he truly protecting those he loved? He knew by now he had been discovered missing and Dawn and Bishop were surely calling in every favor they had accumulated to aid in their investigation. He smiled. He had taught Dawn well. She would find him, but by then would it be too late? Did he even want to be found?

A knot began to form in his stomach. Sitting back in his seat, he pulled the shade closed. Tilting his head back, he let out a long sigh. He wasn't the hero. That was just wishful thinking. He was being a damned old fool. He was tired of life and he was using this as his escape. When had everything lost its flavor? Had his existence become so bleak he would willingly walk into his own death? He shook his head. Apparently, that was the case. His mind shifted to those who loved and cared about him. They wouldn't understand. How could they? He had lived long enough to realize one of his biggest fears: he was no longer useful.

Dawn was completely capable of handling the team, Bishop was becoming a quality investigator in his own right, even though he was still headstrong, Kelley was still under the watchful eye of Lydia, and Lydia…. He was lost for words. He had lost her once, but had been fortunate enough to find her again. Why was he throwing it away now? How would she feel? Hopefully, they would never know his true motivation. They would learn he died at the hands of a vampire who had sworn vengeance against him thirty years ago, not that he was an old man tired of life. Cane balled up his fist and slammed it against the armrest. He was a bloody coward. That was all.

Leaning forward, he propped his elbows on his knees and buried his face in his hands. They would land soon and it would all be over. He knew he was heading for a bloody, painful and drawn out death. Caitlin would surely torture him before finally sucking that last final ruby drop of life from his body. Not exactly the death he had in mind, but at least those he loved would be safe.

Caitlin would have what she wanted, and hopefully, that would satisfy her bloodlust. After that, the Gwyliad Wriaeth could deal with her. He was, after all, cleaning up their mess in the first place. If they had killed her to begin with, none of this would be happening. Instead, a rookie Wraith had botched the kill somehow and thirty years later, he was paying for it.

How did she survive? He had seen the stake driven cleanly into her heart as he pinned her down. He had watched with his own eyes as her body was engulfed in blue flames. Her death had taken only moments and had left only a small pile of ash on the floor where she stood. Cane had even watched, with some bemusement, the young Wraith fishing his wooden stake from the pile. It was then the Wraith had assured him and Lydia that Caitlin was dead. There were no qualifiers in his statement. There was no "if we do this," or "once the ashes are consecrated." She was dead. That should have been the end of the story, and yet somehow, some way, she had survived to find a method to extract her revenge.

Falling back into the seat, he resigned himself. He was going to die. There was no escaping that now. This was the fate he had chosen for himself and he had to see it through to its bloody conclusion.

Chapter Sixteen

"They have the worst beer here." Taking another swallow from his long necked bottle, Royce leaned back into his padded leather couch. He held the brown bottle gingerly between his finger and thumb as he swirled the amber liquid inside. Wiping a bit of condensation from the label, he held it against his forehead. "I don't even know why we drink this shit."

"Because it still gets us fucked up," slurred his stout friend. Tilting his bottle back, he sucked down the rest of the alcohol. Belching, he dropped the bottle to the floor next to the chair he was sprawled in. "Why don't you get your dad to fly in some good American beer?"

Royce shook his head. "I already asked."

"And the word is?" inquired his other companion, a young, beautiful female.

"The word is no." Royce gulped down the rest of his beer, "Therefore, I am going to do it anyway." He grinned and leaned forward.

The three friends hooted and hollered as they sat around an immense ice chest filled with nothing but beer. The room was decorated with furniture and antiques that were well beyond their means. Lavish rugs lay over the hard wood floor, while a several thousand dollar sound system blared behind them. Each was no more than twenty-five years of age and looked to be in excellent to fair shape. They were each sprawled lazily on either a couch or chair and were all eying another beer. Two men and a woman, the three had been friends for as long as they could remember.

Royce Signet was the leader of the group and the reason they were all in Egypt. His father, Matthew Signet, was a multi-millionaire that had survived the dot-com bust a few years earlier with his matchmaking websites. He purchased a house in Cairo recently but had been unable to use it, so Royce was given a chance to vacation in Egypt with his friends. Royce was one of the few, rare cases where money hadn't ruined him. He still remembered living with his mom and dad in a small trailer park, huddled around a wood stove because they couldn't pay the heating bill. The money provided experiences he would never have had otherwise, but it hadn't changed him. His friends had helped keep him grounded, and he was thankful for that.

To his left, still milking her first beer, was Denise Chang, a spunky Asian American with dyed blonde hair. She had met Royce in second grade, and the two had been friends ever since. There had been some stress through puberty, but their friendship had endured. They loved each other, but in the purest platonic sense. Denise was cool and confident but exuded raw energy. A good time was never far off when Denise was around. She was diminutive in stature, but stood tall in spirit. Royce had seen her stand up to two men twice her size once when her honor had been threatened. She probably would've won too, if Royce hadn't pulled her off them.

The two had made The Agreement about five years ago. After a long night of discussion about relationships (and more than their fair share of alcohol), they had decided that if neither were taken by the time they reached forty, they would marry each other. It was a contract against loneliness, if nothing else, a way to guard from growing old alone.

To Royce's right was Chug Nelson, so named for a party feat yet to be matched. Chug had chugged twenty beers in ten minutes. Why he didn't end up with alcohol poisoning and die, Royce never knew. Chug was built like a football linebacker with broad shoulders and thick neck. His head was shaved bald—no one knew if it was for appearance or necessity. Chug wasn't renowned for his intelligence, but a more loyal friend you wouldn't find. He had joined Royce and Denise in high school during a football game. Chug was on the team, while Royce and Denise were getting drunk below the stands. There had been an altercation with Denise's ex-boyfriend, and as luck would have it, Royce was too drunk to stick up for her. Chug, who was sitting on the bench at the time, heard the scuffle and broke it up (and in the process, thoroughly pounding Denise's ex). Since then, the three were always together. Royce was the brain, Denise was the spirit and Chug was the brawn. For them, it was a perfect combination. Nothing else mattered to them but friends.

As Chug reached into the ice filled cooler, he looked over at his two friends. An odd expression crossed his face. "Let's head out to the pyramids tonight. I want to take a picture of me mooning the sphinx."

Denise laughed, "Pass."

Royce nodded. "I'm with Denise on this one. I'm really not in the mood to see your ass tonight."

Chug popped the top off his beer and took a drink. "You guys are sissies," he said, wiping the excess alcohol from his lips. "Are we just going to sit here and get drunk?"

Royce took a deep breath and nodded. "That was my plan."

"Bah," Chug said in protest. "I'm going to go hit the pinball machine in the den." As he stood up, he took a moment to steady himself. Carefully holding his beer in his right hand, he placed the other on the back of his chair. Taking another hit off the bottle, he staggered out the room.

"Don't break it this time, Chug," Royce called after him. He looked to Denise and shook his head. "He's gonna break it."

"Just like he always does," Denise replied. "Why does your father keep buying those things?"

"The man loves pinball machines. What can I say?" Royce set his empty bottle on the table next to the numerous others and grabbed a new one from the chest. He was a calm drunk, unlike Chug. "So what do you think of Egypt so far?"

Denise shrugged. "It's hot."

"What about the culture? This place is ancient," Royce said with a smile. "Who knows what secrets are still hidden out there beneath the desert sand?"

"I'm just not into that," Denise admitted. "I don't have a place in my heart for old things like you do. Give me modern any day."

Royce dismissed her statement with a wave of

his hand. "No appreciation for the finer things in life."

Denise suddenly perked up in her seat and sat forward. "Did you just hear that?"

"Hear what?"

"Sounded like footsteps outside."

Royce shook his head. "Probably just Chug in the backroom demolishing my pinball machine."

"No," Denise said slowly, "that's not it." Holding her breath, she listened carefully. After a moment, her body relaxed and she slipped back into the chair. "Just my imagination, I guess. Are the doors locked?"

Royce nodded, "And the alarm is set. We're perfectly safe in he—"

THUD.

The two sat straight up, their eyes wide. They had both heard that noise. There was no denying it or mistaking it for something else. It sounded like a fist pounding against the side of the house. Standing, Royce quickly moved to the back of the room and tapped the power button on the stereo. The house became still as they listened again. They became aware of the jingling sound of the pinball machine in the backroom. Chug seemed unaffected by the noise. As each acclimated to the sounds of the house, ease began to return.

Walking slowly back into the living room, Royce sat on the arm of Denise's chair. He placed his hand gently on her shoulder. "Next time my father offers to get me a bodyguard, I think I'll take him up on the offer."

Denise nodded. "That sounds like a good idea."

267

"It was probably a bird flying into the wall or a window," Royce offered. "When I was a kid, we saw an eagle fly into the window of our little house. Big, damned bird, too. So, it can happen."

Denise nodded. "Sure." She was still a bit unnerved by the sound. Something felt a bit off. She couldn't place her finger on it, but something wasn't the way it was supposed to be. She nervously tapped her fingernails on her beer bottle.

"It's okay," Royce assured her. "Trust me."

THUD THUD.

Royce leapt off the arm of the chair and took several steps back. He had clearly heard the noise coming from the front door. Glancing up, he stared into the foyer at the thick, wooden door. "Thief?" he whispered.

"Or mass murderer," Denise countered. Standing, she joined Royce. Slowly, she slipped her arm around his.

Royce glanced down at Denise, then back to the door. "I've got to know."

Denise tightened her grip. "No."

THUD.

"It'll be okay," he patted her on the arm and slowly let go. "We're safe in here."

"I don't like this. Don't go."

"We'll be fine," he stated with a stiff upper lip. "I just want to take a look through the peephole."

Royce ignored the fear in Denise's eyes and carefully started toward the entrance. Glancing back, he smiled bravely. Returning his attention back toward his goal, he crept over the hardwood floors, careful not to make a sound. As he got closer, he heard it again. The hairs on the back of his neck stood at attention. Swallowing hard, he crossed the final few feet. Pressing his hands flat on the door, he kept his head down. He summoned the courage from somewhere deep in his soul to look up. Forcing his head toward the small glass hole, he peered out into the darkness.

Nothing.

Royce turned around and smiled. "There's nothing out there. Whatever it was, it's go—"

The door exploded inward, flattening Royce beneath it. The young man wailed in pain as the doorknob hit him just below the center of the chest and shattered several ribs. Shards of wood and glass rained down on the floor as a tall figure clad in black leather stepped inside. His long coat billowed around him as his wavy, dark hair obscured his face. Only his golden eyes were visible through the dust and debris. Placing his full weight on the door, he squatted down over Royce's face and smiled through glistening canine fangs.

"I know what you are," Royce gurgled.

"Oh do you?" Zeke asked. He leaned closer and lowered his voice. "What am I?"

Royce coughed and wheezed. One of his broken ribs had shattered and punctured his lung. "Vampire."

Zeke smiled. "Very good. You get a gold star."

"I know how this works," Royce sputtered in pain. "You have to be invited in."

"Sorry, kid." Zeke lowered his hand and softly caressed Royce's cheek as a drop of blood erupted from his mouth. Wiping the blood away with his bone white finger, Zeke laughed. "That's just not true." Grabbing the side of Royce's head, he snapped the boy's head to the side, severing his spine. Royce died instantly. "Damned television," Zeke said as he stood up. "What has it been teaching these kids?" He stopped. "What have we here?"

Denise sunk back against the wall. "This isn't happening," she mumbled, "this isn't happening." Tears were streaming down her face.

"I'm afraid it is," Zeke said as he moved toward the young woman. "And you have two choices." He stopped behind the couch and ran his fingers along the leather. Hopping gracefully over the back, he landed outstretched on the cushions. Lacing his fingers together, he rested them behind his head. "Your first choice," he continued, "is to die like your boyfriend there. And allow me to say this, I'm feeling playful tonight."

Denise was too frightened to speak.

"But your second choice is somewhat more appealing. I could make you into a vampire, like me." Zeke propped himself up on his elbows while continuing to stare at Denise. "What do you say?"

Denise began to edge toward the door to the den. Chug should still be in there, she thought. She needed help.

Zeke slowly lifted himself off the couch. "I'm afraid I'm going to need an answer." He started toward Denise, every step calculated.

Denise reached down and snagged a beer bottle from the floor. Cradling it in her hands, she glared at the vampire. "Fuck you!" She flung the projectile and disappeared around the corner.

Zeke easily avoided the bottle and moved toward the door.

Denise ran full speed into the hallway which connected the living room with the den and the bathrooms. Frantically glancing behind her, she saw the massive vampire appear in the doorway behind her. Skittering around a corner, she screamed Chug's name. Slamming the door to the den behind her, she flattened herself against it. Her eyes moved hysterically across the room searching for her friend, but found no trace of him. Turning her head to the left, her gaze settled on the large window that filled most of the far wall. It was smashed in, the silk drapes hanging torn and broken from their rods. Moving down the steps that led into the room, Denise cautiously searched for her friend. She eyed his half empty beer sitting on top of the still active pinball machine. A knot began to form in her stomach. Turning to her right, she saw a dark form on the floor behind a grand piano. Craning her head to the left, she focused her eyes on the form.

Covering her mouth, she stumbled back in horror. It was a woman in a dark coat squatting over Chug's body. His arms were spread wide as she lapped at the blood spilling from his neck like a dog. The female vampire looked up from her prey and spotted Denise shivering in the middle of the floor. She smiled through blood smeared lips and returned to Chug's neck.

Denise felt two icy hands wrap around her shoulders. Spinning around, she stared into the glowing golden eyes of Zeke. Slipping his arm

271

around her waist, he pinned her to his chest. With his free hand, he easily pushed her head to the side, revealing her neck. Opening his mouth wide, he exposed his glistening white fangs. Lunging forward, he bit hard into her throat. A wave of pleasure washed over him as her warm blood splashed onto his tongue. Lifting his head away for a moment, he took a deep breath to savor the moment. Closing his eyes, he could already feel her warmth filtering through his cold body.

* * *

Silence fell over them. Each sat staring into the others' eyes, searching for hope and strength, any shred to hold onto but at this moment, there were none to be found. Desperation gripped them. With the setting sun visible through the window behind them, the team once again returned their attention to Callista. She was standing with her arms folded behind her back, patiently waiting for the group to regain focus and somehow continue.

Taking a deep breath, she continued. "I know this sounds bad…."

"Sounds bad?" Bishop asked from his desk. "I think we're well beyond that point." He started tapping his pen on the desk. "You just told us one of the highest ranking members of your order was on this case, and now he's missing and possibly dead. I don't think that bodes well for us."

"It's true Brother Specter has gone missing. He's missed several of his check-in times, but that doesn't mean he's dead," Callista postulated. "He could just be so deeply entrenched, he can't break away to report back."

"Do you believe that?" Dawn asked.

Callista grimaced. "I have to."

"But that's not the worst of it," Bishop spat, "is it?"

Callista shook her head. She shifted her weight uncomfortably from one foot to the other. "There is a prophecy."

"Great." Bishop let his head fall forward onto the desk with a thump.

Dawn reached over and slapped Bishop across the back of the head. "Knock it off, Bish. You're being a jackass. Let the woman finish."

Bishop sat back in his chair and rolled his eyes.

Dawn forced a smile. "Please continue."

Callista nodded. "The prophecy states a Wraith will go into the land of the ancient god of the Sun to fight an ultimate evil. It also speaks of his death. Members of our order have been working on deciphering this prophecy, but it remains elusive." She ran her fingertips across her forehead. "What we do know is that Specter was sent to Cairo, Egypt. His last reported check-in was in southern Europe, but we assume he made it there."

Kelley tapped her fingernails nervously against her front teeth. "What else does the prophecy speak of?"

"This is only speculation at this point," Callista prefaced, "but we think it refers to your partner Cane as well."

Dawn sat back in her seat. "In what way?"

"Early on, it stated the two who tried to bring down this evil would be targeted by its wrath. It goes on to make vague references about a man who

273

summons spirits and works with the dead. We could take that to mean 'Paranormal Investigator'."

"Does it say what his fate will be?" Lydia asked nervously.

Callista shook her head.

"Great," Bishop stood angrily, "not only are we fighting vampires, but now we're working against fate." He threw up his arms. "What chance do we have?"

Kelley stood and looked angrily at Bishop. "What the hell is wrong with you?"

"With me? What the hell is wrong with all of you? Can't you see what we're up against?" He circled around the desks to stand next to Callista. "This," he said, pointing to her, "is a vampire killing machine. That's all they do. Now, we find out that one of the best vampire killers in the world has fallen by the very hands of the creature that has our partner. What chance does that leave us, a group of normal, average, run-of-the-mill human beings?"

"We have to fight," Dawn said quietly.

"Why?" Bishop slammed his fist against the desk. "Their end has been foretold! Are we going to march in there like glorified cannon fodder just to die? Is that the plan? We could send wave after wave of people against the vampires, so at least Cane doesn't die alone. Is that what you want?" he asked, directing his anger directly at Dawn. "What the hell are we supposed to do? Please, somebody, for the love of God tell me!"

Dawn leapt from her chair, sending it spilling to the ground. "We are going to fight!" she screamed. Reaching across the table, she grabbed Bishop by the collar, nearly toppling him onto the desks. "We have one choice," she growled, "we are going in to rescue Cane. Fate be damned!"

Bishop steadied himself against the desk and stared angrily into Dawn's eyes. Her gaze slowly fell away.

"He's all I have," she whispered.

A single tear welled up in Dawn's eye. Slowly letting go of Bishop, she sunk back. Righting her chair, she slumped down into it and placed her face in her hands. He could see her body shivering as she tried to fight the urge to completely break down. More than anything else, she wanted to crawl into a corner and just cry, but she had to remain strong. She had to find a way to hold it together. They were all depending on her now. She was the leader.

Bishop fell away from the group, feeling as if he had been kicked in the stomach. He looked at his partner, his friend and felt ashamed of his actions and words. It was true, he had meant every word of it, but his intended message had somehow become horribly twisted by the anger and fear. In his pain, he had forgotten everyone else. No longer was this a matter of how it was affecting the group, it was all about how much Cane's loss would mean to him. Rushing around the desks, he placed his hands on Dawn's shoulders. He took a long breath and addressed the group. "I'm," he swallowed hard, "scared. I'm sorry."

The group fell silent once again. Bishop leaned down and placed his cheek against Dawn's as she wiped the tears from her eyes. Each was running the gamut of emotions from fear to anger to depression.

Neither wanted to admit it, but Cane had become like a father to both of them. He was the rock they depended on, and to even fathom a life without him was unbearable. He had always been there for them, now it was up to them to return the favor. They would not let him fall. Reaching down, Bishop held Dawn's hand and in that moment, without a single word spoken, a new bond was forged. The two stood up and hugged, finding security and comfort in each other's arms.

Looking back at her team, Dawn smiled. "Mount up. We have to get to Cairo."

A new sense of energy flowed over the team. Gone were the fears and doubts, they had a mission to complete and a teammate, a friend, to bring home.

Chapter Seventeen

The vampire closed her eyes and sniffed the air. She had missed this place. Over the past twenty years, she had grown accustomed to its smell—it's very taste. This was a city unlike any other she had visited in her long years. Cairo was ancient. She could feel the history swimming around her, even as the city threatened to engulf more of its lost relics, its very heritage. As she moved briskly through the night air, she caught the scent of her master. It was sweet on the cool, desert air as it wrapped her in its arms and caressed her cheek. Slowly opening her eyes, she peered off into the distance. She was home.

Turning around, she checked on her prisoner. He was sitting quietly on a bench with his hands folded in his lap. He had made no effort to escape, not even once. No man heading to his own death would do so willingly, at least not in her experience. Even the oldest of humans who were knocking on death's door didn't go without a struggle. Humans—most anyway—had a built in defense against death. Perhaps it was the fear of the unknown that scared them the most. Throughout the ages, various religions had tried to convince them that something, good or bad, waited for them beyond life. After her countless victims, she was sure none of them truly believed this. To their fragile minds, this was all there was, nothing more, and they would hold onto it with their dying breath.

But this man was different. He seemed to have resigned himself to death. His exterior was calm and collected, showing no signs he was fearful of his impending fate. This troubled her somewhat. It was true she enjoyed watching the light fade from her victim's eyes as they died, but this was something different. The spark, his very essence, seemed to be already gone. His eyes were more like a doll's than a human's. They appeared cold and lifeless, almost as if they had been forged from plastic. She had seen it before, even in some of her kin, he had lost the will to live. She couldn't say how or why, but this man sought death, perhaps as a release.

To her, this was unfathomable. The very reason she had chosen to become a vampire all those many years ago was so death could not touch her. She, unlike those foolish humans, had no preconceptions of an afterlife. This was all she knew and she didn't want to lose it. Life, even in her unnatural state, was all that mattered. Some would say this was a very hedonistic view, and she would often agree. The pursuit of pleasure was all encompassing. She had existed in this form for thousands of years, and in that time, she had been all manner of things. There was still much she hadn't experienced, and that alone was worth living for. Death would not deprive her of any experience, no matter how small or trivial.

In that moment, she began to feel sorry for her captive.

Moving slowly to him, she extended her hand gently. "It's time for us to go."

Cane looked up at the vampire and nodded. He looked curiously at her outstretched hand for a moment, unsure of what he should do. Finally

278

placing his hand in hers, he stood. The two began to move slowly through the streets of Cairo. The vampire was silent as usual, but there was something different about her. Cane could sense it. He decided to take a chance.

"You know my name," he said slowly, "but you've never told me yours."

The vampire glanced at him slowly, then turned away. "Achaica," she whispered.

Cane pronounced the name slowly, carefully imitating her slight accent. "If I'm not mistaken, your name is Greek in origin."

"Greek Roman," Achaica corrected.

Cane nodded. He didn't want to press his luck by asking too many questions, but this was the most talkative she had been. He didn't want to miss the opportunity to learn more about her. "So are you Greek Roman?"

"My ancestors were," Achaica replied without a hint of hesitation. "I was merely born there."

"When you say 'born'," Cane asked, "what exactly do you mean?"

"Are you asking if I was actually born there, or just became a vampire there?"

Cane nodded.

Achaica smiled. "I was actually born there. I didn't become until…."

Cane leaned forward in anticipation of her answer, but there wasn't one forthcoming.

Achaica took several steps ahead of Cane. "I shouldn't be talking to you."

"Why?"

Achaica stopped, but didn't turn around. "Just

because. Let's keep going."

"I'm going to die," Cane said quickly. "Who am I going to tell that you talked to me?"

Achaica turned. "That's not the point," she said quickly. "My mistress instructed me to bring you to her, not to get to know you. I have a task to complete."

Cane nodded and lowered his head.

Achaica watched him stuff his hands into his pockets like a child that had been scolded. She expected any moment for him to begin kicking at the rocks around his feet. She shook her head and bit her lip. She couldn't let herself be taken in by this man. He wasn't hers to have. Caitlin was waiting. Pushing him forward, the two continued further into Cairo.

* * *

Caitlin walked slowly down the steps toward the foyer, her hand sliding along the polished wood banister. Her long red hair was pulled loosely back behind her head with the exception of a few curly locks that hung down on either side of her face. Her style had changed to better reflect what she saw her vampires wearing—a more modern, gothic look. A tight black t-shirt was painted on her chest, terminating just above her waist, revealing her midriff. A pair of loose black pants replaced the skirt she wore earlier, and a long, black, lambskin leather coat hung just past her knees. A silver ankh hung on a thin chain around her neck, while several other pieces of jewelry decorated her fingers. Stopping halfway down, she leaned over and rested on her elbows. She noticed Zeke and Ice waiting patiently in the living room for her verdict.

"You are going to do something about that, aren't you?" she asked, pointing to the pile of rubble at the bottom of the stairs that used to be the front door.

Zeke nodded. "I'll replace it myself, Mistress."

"See that it gets done before sunrise," Caitlin said as she continued down the stairs. Stepping into the foyer, she heard a squishing sound beneath her foot. Glancing down, she saw a man's hand crushed beneath her shoe. "And get rid of the bodies before they start to smell." Walking into the living room, she scraped the bottom of her foot against one of the numerous rugs to clean off the sole. "And what of my guests?"

"The Wraith is resting in the basement," Zeke said with pride. "We found a few nails and boards down there, so we decided to crucify him on the wall."

"Sadistic," Caitlin breathed, "good work. What about my other guest?"

Zeke turned to Ice, then back to Caitlin with a shrug. "We don't know."

"Achaica should have had him here by now," Caitlin muttered.

"Achaica?" Zeke asked.

"She is another of my," she smiled, "children. I tasked her with rounding up Mr. Cane."

Zeke felt a ripple of jealousy. "There are more of us?"

Caitlin tossed back her head and laughed out loud. "You thought you two were the only vampires I had created?" She tried to control her laughter.

"Don't be so damned self-centered, Ezekiel."

Zeke shook his head. "I just assumed—"

"I've lived a long time and made many vampires," Caitlin explained. "You didn't seriously think that the three of us would be enough to carry out my plans, did you?"

"As I tried to say, Mistress," Zeke said slowly, "I just assumed we were all there were."

"Three vampires an army does not make," Caitlin pointed out. "In the same way I called you two, hundreds of vampires around the world have all received my call and are heading here as we speak. Any vampire with even a hint of my blood winding through their veins heard my call and will obey. By nightfall tomorrow, this city will be teeming with vampires," Caitlin grinned, "and all of them will be under my control."

"What are you planning?" Ice asked.

Pulling her hand back, she slapped Ice hard across the face. "It's not polite to speak out of turn," Caitlin glared at Ice.

Ice stumbled back, cradling her face. A mixture of confusion and disbelief painted her pale face.

"Let that be a lesson to you," Caitlin said, rubbing the back of her hand. "Speak when you're spoken to."

Speechless, Ice could only nod.

"Very good." Moving deeper into the living room, Caitlin seated herself on the couch. Leaning back into it, she spread her arms across the back and ran her fingers over the leather. "I do love leather," she smiled. "It's so versatile." She glanced over her shoulder at her two servants. "Well don't just stand

282

there, come and sit down."

Zeke and Ice rushed around the couch, each sitting in a chair opposite Caitlin. They remained quiet for fear of reprisal.

Caitlin leaned forward and smiled. "I want to tell you a secret." She lowered her voice. "I plan to take back what is rightfully ours."

Ice's eyes widened. "You are going to war against mankind?"

Caitlin nodded.

"You'll never win."

Caitlin turned to see Specter standing in the hallway, his wrists torn and bleeding from the nails Zeke and Ice had driven through them. He was leaning against the wall for support and looked to fall down at any moment. Sweat poured down his bruised and battered face as if suffering from a fever. He coughed once, splattering blood over his lips and chin. Lifting his hand, he tried to wipe the blood away, but only succeeded in spreading more across his face from his wrist. Bracing himself, he carefully took a step forward.

"How did you get up here?" Caitlin asked.

Specter slowly lifted his bloody wrists and showed them to Caitlin. "I have the same strength you do, remember? It was just a matter of," he took a deep breath, "tearing free."

Caitlin shrugged. "It's no matter. You are in no condition to fight. Zeke, why don't you show our guest to a seat?"

Zeke nodded and stood. Walking slowly toward the Wraith, he readied himself. Even in his weakened condition, Specter could be a formidable

283

adversary. Placing his hand firmly on the Wraith's shoulder, Zeke led him into the living room and pushed him down into a chair opposite Caitlin.

Specter's head fell back for a moment as his strength slowly returned. Looking forward again, he glanced down at his wrists. The wounds were slowly starting to close. He needed to keep them talking. "Vampires have always been a plague on humanity and the Gwyliad Wriaeth will stop at nothing to wipe them out."

"Oh? And how is that?" Caitlin asked, crossing her legs.

Specter coughed twice, but quickly caught his breath. "Even if it takes us forever, we will find a way," he sputtered.

Caitlin smiled. "That's interesting. Let's face it, Marcus, a few Wraiths with pointy sticks just aren't cutting it. We continue to increase our numbers and spread darkness across all seven continents."

Specter turned away from her gaze.

Caitlin paused, sizing up her opponent. "We were bred to destroy humans," she stated, "and that's exactly what I plan to do."

Specter glanced at his wrists again. The wounds were almost completely gone. Slowly reaching into his jacket, he wrapped his fingers around something flat and rectangular. He only needed a moment longer. "How are you here? I staked you."

Caitlin smiled, "That's my little secret."

"I scattered your ashes," Specter added, his grip tightening on the object.

Caitlin sunk back into the couch for a moment, her eyes focusing off into the distance. "Have you ever wondered if there actually is a Hell?"

"I've never had much time for theological debates," Specter answered honestly.

"That's too bad," Caitlin sighed. "It can be a truly fascinating subject and I think I have a unique perspective." She uncrossed her legs and stared at the Wraith.

Specter paused. "Why?"

Caitlin erupted from the couch and charged. Pinning Specter to his seat, he could see the anger burning in her eyes. Her fingernails began to dig into the flesh of his shoulders. "Because I was there!" she growled. "I went to Hell because of you!"

Specter tried to pull away from her, but her grip was too strong. He forced himself to stare into her fiery green eyes. "You deserved every minute of it," he whispered.

"Did I?" Caitlin slowly took a breath and pulled away. Moving across the living room, she retook her seat on the couch. "Did I deserve to be violently tortured? Did I deserve to relive every single death I had caused from my victim's point of view? Did I deserve to have my arms and legs ripped from my body by unholy demons, only to watch them regrow and the process repeated?" Caitlin paused and looked away, a quiver of pain in her voice. "Probably."

Her honesty shocked Specter. He had to remind himself to take a breath. Remorse was not a trait commonly present in vampires. As the soul leaves the body, it takes with it all shreds of conscience.

"I will not go back there. Not ever." Caitlin sat

forward, "I was rescued from my eternal damnation by my child, Achaica. Using powerful magicks, she ripped my essence from that horrid place and returned me to physical form." She smiled broadly, exposing her fangs. "She nursed me back to health over the past thirty years and made all this possible."

"How?" Specter shook his head.

"She was there, thirty years ago," Caitlin answered, "the night you and that blasted British limey sent me to Hell. She took a small portion of my ashes before you scattered the rest and resurrected me. I wasn't gone from this plane of existence for more than a day, but in that time, I experienced Hell for over three hundred years."

Shaking his head, Specter glanced down at his wrists. The wounds were completely healed, only the oxidizing blood remained. "It's good to know dead vampires go to Hell," he said with a smirk. "We almost wiped out your race once. We can do it again."

"I don't think so," Caitlin sneered. "In the time it takes for you to train one new Wraith, I can create a hundred vampires. You are hopelessly outnumbered."

"We will never give up, Caitlin." Whipping the object out of his jacket, Specter sent it sailing toward Caitlin and was instantly on his feet.

Caitlin's lightning fast reflexes allowed her to catch the object before it hit her. Turning it over in her hand, she glanced at the wooden shard he had apparently broken from one of the boards in the basement. If she had missed it, it would have hit her

286

directly above the heart. Leaping onto the coffee table, Specter kicked forward connecting with the bridge of Caitlin's nose. The force of the impact knocked her back over the couch and onto the floor. Spinning again, Specter lashed out and hit Zeke as he stood. Zeke stumbled back, but quickly regained his balance.

Jumping up, Ice pushed the attack. She dropped down and swept Specter's legs out from under him, sending him toppling to the floor. Rolling up onto the balls of his feet, Specter shook his head. He was still weak. He couldn't take all of them at once. Rolling back just as Ice lunged forward, Specter avoided the attack and recovered. He stopped and sized up the three vampires. Zeke was moving quickly toward his left, while Caitlin and Ice were rushing toward him. Jumping into the air, he spun and kicked Ice in the face with his booted foot. Caitlin reached out and grabbed his leg before he could finish the move. Holding him in midair, she drove him back into the drywall. Pulling away, Caitlin swung him around by his ankle and sent him sailing across the room. Specter impacted the stereo system, destroying it. Amidst the rubble of damaged electrical equipment, Specter rolled onto his back and tried to catch his breath.

Caitlin walked slowly across the room and stood over him. She lifted her foot and dug the heel of her shoe into his throat. "All I have to do is step down and you're dead."

Specter wrapped his hands around her foot and tried to push it away, but she was too strong for him. He struggled for breath as her heel began to crush his windpipe. He clawed vainly at her leg as the hypoxia began to set in. Large black spots began to appear in front of his eyes as his arms slowly fell limp. Closing his eyes, he let his head collapse into the rubble.

"I don't want you to just die, I want you to die horribly." She pressed her heel harder against his windpipe. "I will torture you so you can experience what I did, then I will bring you back and start all over. I plan to make this last at least a month or two." Leaning close, she whispered in his ear, "Welcome to your own personal Hell."

Caitlin snapped her fingers. "Get this Wraith back into the basement," she commanded. "And for Christ's sake, do a better job this time," Caitlin added with a growl.

* * *

Their plane touched down in Cairo amidst the early morning light. The five teammates moved through the terminal and collected their luggage before heading toward the exit. Sleep had been a luxury none of them could afford during the flight. Large, dark bags hung under their eyes and their feet felt like stones as they shuffled over the tiled floor, but they refused to let that bother them. They were on the biggest assignment of their lives and they were determined to complete it.

The conversation during the flight had been sparse and light. Each of them had something to say, but no one had been listening. Words passed lightly from their lips and fell on deaf ears. It was true they were of a singular goal, but each carried their own fears. Each viewed Cairo as their last stand. They would put it all on the line and hopefully overcome, but that was just one possible outcome. They were the cavalry riding in to rescue their compatriot...with General Custer leading the charge.

Dawn wore a grim expression on her face as she moved toward the large, sliding double doors. Her leather jacket was slung over her shoulder and her long wavy hair was pulled up behind her head with a rubber band she had found in her desk before leaving the office. The weight of the mission and the worries of each team member were on her shoulders. She felt like Atlas holding the world in her arms. If she faltered in any way, the world would fall and smash like glass on rocks, as would the hopes and prayers of her friends. She wouldn't let that happen. She owed him more than that. She was determined now. He would come home, even if that meant at her expense. During the flight, she had taken the time to sum up the mission at hand. Not everyone was going to make it, that was the simple truth of the matter. She knew she was heading into the dragon's lair and she would have to order her friends to fight...and die.

A curious thing this was. How does one person order another to their death? Military commanders had to do it all the time, but those were faceless men to them. They sat in their plush offices and moved pawns on a map. It wasn't really real people to them, just pieces on an excessive board game. These were her friends, her family. She knew their names, their faces, and their hopes and dreams. How could she end that with a simple wave of her hand? In one hand, she held Cane's life, in the other, she held the rest of the team's. Who was more important? Was that really the question she needed to ask? She shook her head. This wasn't the way to be thinking right now. She had to tend to her friends...not decide who was going to die. It wouldn't come to that, she convinced herself, but somewhere deep in the back of her mind, she knew it would.

As each stepped out into the dry Egyptian air, they stared over the ancient city of Cairo. For many of them, this was their first journey to the land of the Sun. They wished they had more time to explore the city, to walk beneath the Great Pyramids and to stand in the Valley of the Kings, but this wasn't a pleasure trip. They were here for a purpose. Bishop checked his watch. They had roughly nine hours until dusk. The daylight was their only advantage at this point. They had to utilize every second of it, for once night fell, the vampires would be free to roam.

Callista stepped to the curb and flagged down a dirty yellow Taxi Cab. "We have to hurry. Mac is expecting us."

"Who's Mac?" Dawn asked.

"He is a friend of mine that lives here in Cairo," Callista replied as the cab stopped in front of her. "I called in a favor and he's going to help us."

"What kind of help?" Bishop asked, moving toward the cab.

Callista smiled. "It's a surprise," she said as she slipped inside, "but we can't make him wait. He hates that."

Chapter Eighteen

Achaica dropped to one knee and lowered her head. Behind her, Cane stood silently but confidently. His arms were crossed over his chest while his face showed no expression. If this was truly to be his end, he was going to face it without fear. A solitary light lay on the floor in front of the couch, casting its white glow up into the room creating harsh shadows. Signs of a struggle were evident, but Cane wasn't sure what had happened. This was a large, magnificent home, not worthy of its blood-sucking occupants. Caitlin had obviously stolen it from someone who had probably worked hard to obtain it. This woman had senselessly destroyed another life. She was a disease, a cancer that needed to be excised.

A lone figure stood in the far corner of the room, barely visible in the light. It was a woman, but it didn't look like Caitlin. Something about her was just off. Cane couldn't quite put his finger on it, but it wasn't her. Achaica slowly lifted her head and looked around. She had expected to find Caitlin as soon as she entered. She glanced back at her prisoner with a slightly worried expression on her face, although she was doing her best to hide it. Perhaps her sense of smell had deceived her. She had no other means of locating Caitlin after finding the apartment building she had lived in for the past twenty years abandoned. Her scent trail had been very strong up until this house, but inside, the stench of death was overwhelming. The smells of vampires, mortals, blood and burning electronics filled her nostrils.

Finding her focus, Achaica reached behind and grabbed Cane by the arm. "I am Achaica," she said to the vampire across the room. "I'm here to see Mistress Caitlin. I'm expected," she added.

The vampire across the room didn't respond.

"Hello?" Achaica asked again, a twinge of nervousness in her voice.

"So you're her favorite?"

Achaica glanced up the stairs leading from the foyer to the second floor. A large, male vampire was moving slowly toward her. A long, black, leather jacket was licking at his heels as he moved. "Pardon?" she asked, unsure of what his comment implied.

"I asked," Zeke said, "if it was true that you are Caitlin's favorite?"

Achaica shrugged. "I really can't speak to that," she answered honestly. "I have been with her a long time though."

Zeke stopped on the bottom step and leaned against the banister. "You have brought this man to her?"

Achaica nodded.

"Give him to me," Zeke said, holding out his hand. "I will deliver him to Caitlin."

Achaica stepped in front of Cane. "I don't think so. I was tasked with finding him and bringing him here. It's my job to deliver him directly to Caitlin, not to some," she sneered, "flunky."

Zeke smiled as he stepped in front of her. "I'm going to pretend I didn't hear that. Give him to me now."

"No," Achaica growled.

Zeke whipped his hand up and clasped his fingers around Achaica's throat. She stood almost a full foot shorter than him. His eyes melted to gold. "I said now." He lifted Achaica off the floor.

Achaica's face twisted in anger. Lifting her arms, she brought them down like a sledgehammer on Zeke's elbow. Zeke groaned in pain as he ripped his arm away, his elbow hyperextended. Before he could retaliate, Achaica was on him. Grabbing him by the hair, she whipped him around and slammed his head into the wall. Pulling back, she repeated the attack. As she let go of his hair, Zeke crumbled to the ground in pain. Several streaks of blood ran down his face from the numerous cuts. Reaching down with both hands, Achaica grabbed the larger vampire and lifted him easily above her head. With all her might, she flung the younger vampire into the living room. He sailed across the couch and landed in the center of the coffee table. The weight of his impact shattered the wooden table beneath him, sending shards of wood in all directions.

Achaica charged across the room and scooped up a larger fragment of wood in her hand. Dropping down on top of Zeke, she held the sharp wooden chunk just above his chest. "Don't you dare speak to me like that," she hissed. "I was a vampire before your great grandfather was a twinkle in his father's eye. I will kill you without thinking twice, fledgling."

Zeke held up his hands in surrender. "I'm sorry. Please don't kill me!"

Achaica shook her head. "You're pathetic."

Letting go of the stake, she grabbed his shirt with both hands and delivered a vicious head butt. Zeke fell back unconscious. Achaica dropped the fledgling to the floor and stood. The sound of clapping caught her attention.

"Very impressive."

Achaica turned to see Caitlin entering the room with a large smile on her face. "You have done well, Achaica." She glanced down, "Although I don't think you had to beat Ezekiel quite so badly to prove your point."

Achaica bowed her head. "He was pissing me off, Mistress."

Caitlin stopped in front of her friend. She leaned close and placed her hand on Achaica's shoulder. "He has that effect on people," she whispered with a laugh. Caitlin turned and looked directly at Cane. "My final guest has arrived," she said with a smile. Moving around the couch, her glee faded to curiosity. "Mr. Cane," she said slowly, "why are you standing there?"

Cane glanced around, unsure what the question meant. "I don't follow."

Caitlin stopped just short of him, "Your captor was busy beating the snot out of my boy. Why didn't you turn tail and run out the open door? Why didn't you try and escape?"

"I'm here of my own free will."

The answer shocked Caitlin. "Really?"

Cane nodded.

"Why?"

"I've been running and hiding from you for thirty years."

"Even though you saw me die by your own hand?"

Cane's eyes remained fixed. "I had stopped living some time ago. I was just existing." He took a breath. "I'm not running from you anymore, Caitlin. If it has to end here, then so be it. I can't take wondering every night if I'll wake up the next morning."

Caitlin frowned. "How pathetic you've become. You're just giving in—with no fight." She turned her back on Cane. "I'm very disappointed."

Cane said nothing.

"I would have thought you and the Wraith would have put up more of a struggle. At least the Wraith tried to escape. You," she turned to face him, "you just want to die and are too cowardly to do it by your own hand." An evil smile crossed the vampire's face. "What if I told you that I wasn't going to kill you?"

Cane refused to show emotion.

Caitlin took a step closer to Cane. Lifting her hand, she caressed his cheek with her icy fingers. "What if I told you that I was going to give you immortality?" She pressed her cheek to his and lowered her voice. "That's right, Mr. Cane, you are going to live forever." She laughed, "Forever with me."

Cane stumbled back, his eyes wide.

"Eternal torture," Caitlin licked her lips. "How devious." A look of complete satisfaction spread across her face.

"You can't...." Cane let his head fall forward as his protest died on his lips.

Caitlin nodded. "I can." She lifted her hand and snapped her fingers. "Ice, take our guest down into the cellar with the Wraith." She grinned, exposing her fangs, "But don't harm him too much, he'll be one of us soon."

* * *

Callista had taken the lead through the streets of Cairo. She had been here before and knew the area well. She never understood the vampire's mentality. Why would a creature destroyed by light seek refuge in the middle of the desert? She knew the vampire's shrouded origins lay buried somewhere…perhaps it was here. It was true the Gwyliad Wriaeth had learned much about their adversary, but questions still remained. She shook her head as she rounded a corner. It was not her job to question. It was her task to hunt these creatures down and exterminate them. Nothing else was expected of her. She, like her brothers and sisters in the Guard, were soldiers. It was all they knew, and it was all they were expected to know.

Her long coat billowed behind her as she moved swiftly through the streets. Easily avoiding the various merchants and beggars, she homed in on her target. Stepping left of a man carrying two melons on his shoulders, she spotted her destination. It was a rather uninteresting building with no signs or decorations on the front. Its walls were made of adobe and the only opening in the front was a wooden door. Glancing behind, she motioned for the others to hang back. It had been some time since she had last seen Mac. He suffered from the early stages of Alzheimer's disease, making it impossible to tell if he would remember her or not. He had seemed coherent when they spoke on the phone prior to her leaving Washington DC, but she knew as well as anyone that he had good and bad days. She prayed this was a good one.

Walking up the few stairs to the front door, she rapped heavily with her knuckles and waited. Inside, she could hear movement, but she couldn't be sure exactly what…or who it was. Taking a step back, she glanced into the sky. The sun was heading slowly for the horizon creating a soupy mixture of clouds and color. Callista reached out and knocked again. This time, she was greeted by a gruff voice from within.

"All right, all right. I heard you. No need to knock my damned door down. I'm just an old man, for Christ's sake," he spoke with a thick Irish accent. The muttering continued as he neared the door. "Who is it?"

A crooked smile crossed Callista's face. That was Mac all right. "It's Callista." She listened as Mac undid several locks and finally twisted the door open.

Callista bit her lip as she looked at her old friend. He was dressed in a thin, white t-shirt, a pair of dark blue boxers and a pair of thick black slippers. A robe—that used to be white, but had somewhere along the line been the unfortunate recipient of a pink dye job—hung from his shoulders to his knees. He wore a black bandana on his head and a pair of dark sunglasses disguised his eyes. His face was rough and ragged, sporting a four day old beard and several white nicks and scars. A smoldering cigar was clenched between his yellowing teeth, while a bottle of amber liquor was tucked neatly in his robe pocket. Most would look at Mac and see a complete train wreck, but Callista knew different. This was how he always looked.

"Mac, do you remember me?" Callista asked.

Mac cocked his head to the right. "Why the hell wouldn't I?"

"You know," Callista said slowly, "your condition?"

"Oh, that," Mac waved his hand to dismiss her concerns. "Don't even worry about that. My doctor put me on some new blue pills that seem to be doing the trick. Whenever I start to forget, I pop a handful...or so."

"How do you remember to take the pills when you start to forget?"

Mac pushed his glasses up onto his forehead and stared at Callista. "You know, I have no idea."

Callista opened her arms and stepped forward with a laugh. Pulling Mac into her embrace, she squeezed him tightly. "I've missed you."

He patted her on the back. "I've missed you too, lass."

Callista waved behind her, motioning for her friends to come closer. "I want to introduce you to my teammates."

"I thought you always worked alone," Mac asked.

"It's a special circumstance," Callista replied. "We're tracking some serious game and need all the help we can get. I was pulled off a hunt in northern California for this."

"You don't say?" Mac replied. "Who were you after?"

"A low life named Riddell," Callista said with a sneer. "He's been working his way up the coast killing entire families. He disappeared for a while, but just recently resurfaced. Our records show he's been at this same game for over a hundred years now."

"Savage." Mac shook his head.

Callista nodded. She pointed at the team, "This is the Office of Paranormal Research and their leader, Dawn Lassiter."

Dawn stepped up next to Callista and extended her hand. "Pleased to meet you."

Mac flipped his sunglasses back down over his eyes. "Didn't you tell her?"

"Oh," Callista said with a start. "I'm sorry, Mac. I had forgotten." She turned to Dawn and pushed down her arm. "Mac doesn't like to be touched by strangers."

Dawn nodded. "Sorry."

Mac leaned his head to the left and pulled his bathrobe away from his neck. "I don't want this," he said, exposing two circular scars on his throat, "to ever happen again."

"I'm not a vampire," Dawn replied.

"I don't care," Mac stated quickly. "I let my guard down once. Never again."

"Mac used to be a Wraith like me," Callista noted. "He is one of the few to ever retire."

"After that bloody vampire bit me, they forced me into retirement," he said spitefully. "They said I couldn't be trusted after that. That I may become a vampire sympathizer…." he trailed off. "Leeches…." He pulled a braid of hair from behind his ear and let it dangle down his chest. "I had thirty-two kills," he said, noting the colored ties.

Callista reached over and patted her friend on the shoulder. "I know, Mac."

Mac's eyes became distant for a moment. Taking a deep breath, he composed himself and once again addressed the group. "Well, come inside." Stepping out of the way, Mac motioned for all to quickly enter.

Dawn and Callista stepped inside and stopped. Bishop pushed past them, but also fell dead in his tracks. "Holy crap," he breathed.

As the last of the team squeezed inside, Mac slammed the door shut and relocked his numerous deadbolts. Turning around, he crossed his arms and glanced over his home/office with pride. The main portion of the home was one long room which stretched from the front door to the back wall. On the right side, there was a thin staircase that led to the loft and his sleeping quarters. There was a single desk in the rear of this room with three chairs littered around it. It was surrounded on three sides by bookshelf after bookshelf, each containing some volume of forgotten lore. Amidst the sea of scattered books, several round holes had been hollowed in the wall. Each contained a skull with elongated canine fangs. The only light source in the room was from several tall candelabras. The candles within had been burning for some time as their wax formed stalactites hanging from the arms. The left wall of the room was decorated with every weapon imaginable, from flintlocks and grenades, to ornate wooden stakes and modern machine guns. It was a tribute to his entire life. Every piece of information on vampires and every means to kill them were here.

Bishop stumbled into the room, staring at the vast collection. "This is amazing."

Mac crossed the room quickly and stopped at his desk. "I have something to show you," he said as he searched the desk. Wiping several books onto the floor, he pushed various papers around until he came to the one he wanted. "I think I found something." Running back across the room, he handed the paper to Callista. "Open it."

Callista folded open the paper and glanced over it. "What is it?"

"It's an ancient map," Mac said with a devious smile. "I think it shows the location of a vampire temple in southern Peru."

Dawn leaned in and looked at the map. She tried to make out the characters handprinted on it, but it looked like gibberish to her. "What language is this?"

"It's a lost vampiric dialect," Mac breathed, "I think. I've been able to translate a bit of it, but it's slow going."

"Incredible," Dawn said in awe.

Mac crossed the room again and stood in front of his wall of weapons. His demeanor had changed to that of an excited child showing off his favorite toys. "Now, I assume you are here to gear up. Correct?"

Callista nodded. "We need weapons if we're

301

going to take on Caitlin."

Mac took a step back. "Who did you say?"

"Caitlin," Bishop confirmed.

"That's what I thought you said," Mac muttered. "I'm sorry," he said, moving back toward the door. "I can't help you. You'll have to go now." He started undoing the locks.

"Wait," Callista placed her hand on his back. "What's the matter?"

Mac stopped, his hand still hanging on the latch of a lock. He let out a long sigh. "You can't fight Caitlin, lass. You'll die."

"What?"

"That woman is a butcher. I thought she was dead," he said under his breath.

"So did we," Callista confirmed, "but she's resurfaced and taken their friend and one of our Wraiths captive."

"Oh dear." Mac rested his head against the door. Snapping the locks shut again, he turned and faced the group with a strange expression on his face. "That woman is pure evil. If it is indeed Caitlin, all of you are in for the fight of your lives. You're going to need more than these puny weapons." He charged across the room once again and stopped behind his desk. Looking up, he spotted Bishop. "Lad, can you give an old man a hand?"

Bishop nodded. "Sure."

Moving across the room, he met Mac behind the desk. There he saw a large trunk pushed into its own space in the wall. Several books and papers lay on top of it. Mac pushed the refuse to the floor and grabbed for one of the handles on the side. He

302

nodded for Bishop to do the same. The two men pulled the trunk from its spot and lifted it up. Pushing it forward, they sat it squarely on Mac's desk. Mac moved around the front and undid the latches. Flipping open the lid, he peered inside and nodded.

"These will help each of you," he said, digging inside. "Please, come over here." He turned and watched each member of the party carefully navigate the debris on the floor and stop just short of him. Digging out an item, he turned and sized up the group. His eyes focused on Dawn. "This one is for you. Pull up your sleeve."

Dawn complied. Pulling back her leather jacket, she exposed her naked arm.

Mac reached out and slapped something on her forearm. Reaching under the device, he secured two straps to keep it in place. "This is an old Wraith weapon. It's not used much anymore, but it's deadly."

Dawn pulled back her arm and looked at the device. On top of her arm, twelve small, wooden darts were attached to a leather cuff. "What does it do?"

"Point your arm and flex your forearm muscles," Mac smiled.

Dawn pulled her arm around and pointed at one of the bookshelves. Tightening her arm muscles, one of the darts launched off in a straight line. It impacted the spine of a book and cut through it. Dawn's eyes opened wide. "Wow," she laughed.

Mac nodded. "It takes some practice," he noted. "But you'll get used to it. I have one other tool for you as well." He dug into his robe pocket and produced a small, silver item. "This is my prize possession. Hold out your hand, palm up," Mac instructed her.

Dawn complied. Mac pressed the silver item into the center of her palm. It was no bigger than a silver dollar, but had no markings on it. Dawn lifted the item closer to her face to study it. "What is it?"

"Just wait," Mac smiled.

Dawn took a breath as the silver object began to heat up. It wasn't painful, just startling. She watched several tiny tendrils grow out of the object and begin to wrap around her hand creating a solid band of silver. Dawn looked up nervously at Mac. "What's it doing?"

"This is my most powerful weapon," he remarked. "When in close combat with a vampire, press this band anywhere on their flesh and it will instantly burn them. Hold it there long enough, and you'll reduce them to ash." He looked at the silver band. "This piece was imbued with the same radiation the sun creates; the same radiation that causes vampires to burst into flames during the day. It's like," he smiled, "concentrated sunlight."

Dawn wrapped her fingers around the band feeling its power. "That's incredible."

Mac turned back to the trunk and dug inside. He pulled out dual holsters with pistols inside. Turning to Bishop, he handed him the weapons. "Wear them on your hips like a gunslinger."

Bishop flipped up his jacket and fastened the belt around his waist. Moving his hands down his leg, he started to fasten two small straps to keep the holsters in place. Standing up, he pulled one of the pistols from its leather home and held it firmly in his hand. It was an old fashioned revolver that held six bullets at a time. "I didn't think guns worked against vampires," Bishop said, admiring the craftwork on the weapon.

"They do when you have wood tipped bullets," Mac said with a smile. "Just remember to hit them in the heart or you'll just really piss them off. Around the back of the belt you have several bullets to reload with."

Bishop nodded. "Thanks." Twirling it on his finger, he quickly reversed its spin and deftly holstered it. Looking up at his friends, he smiled. "Hey, who didn't play cowboys and Indians when they were kids?" Laughing, he pulled his coat free of the holster and let it fall around his waist.

Mac turned his attention to Lydia and Kelley. "You two have all the power you need. There is nothing I can give you that will aid you more than what you already possess."

Lydia smiled. "Thank you."

Mac's eyes focused on Callista. "And for my dear friend, I have something special for you." Turning back to the trunk, he dug inside once again. Finding his quarry, he straightened up and turned to Callista. "Here it is."

Callista reached out and took the object from Mac. As she held it in her hands, she knew instantly what it was. She had trained with one at the academy, but had not had the opportunity to take one when she left. This was the Wraith's chosen weapon, but they were in short demand due to their complex construction and magical properties. Callista took a step back from the group and held out the object in her hand. It was cylindrical and no more than a foot long. It was made of a durable alloy and was as slim as a pool cue. Pressing an unseen button on the center, the cylinder instantly quadrupled in length. The ends were sharp metal points with little less than half an inch of wood visible at their very tips. Gold bands wound up from the tips to the handle in a decorative spiral and to add strength. Touching a second button, a long, curved blade sprouted from the top. This was a Wraith's scythe. A weapon built and blessed for an individual Wraith. She could feel power flowing over it. "Thank you, but I can't take this. It's your scythe."

"No," Mac said, holding up his hands, "I insist. I can't be there fighting with you, so I ask you take my scythe. May it bring you better luck than it did this old Wraith."

Callista nodded and bowed her head to Mac. Pressing the buttons in reverse order on the handle, the scythe snapped shut. "You honor me with your gift, Brother MacDougal."

"You honor us all," Dawn added. "Thank you again."

Mac smiled. "Please, rest here tonight. The sun will rise soon and your hunt can begin. I have several cots on the second floor and a case of the finest Egyptian beer in the icebox. Let my home be yours tonight!"

* * *

Ice held Cane by the arm, her fingernails biting

306

into his flesh. Coming around a corner, Ice threw Cane against a wall. The drywall ruptured beneath the impact. Falling back, he slid down to the floor holding his nose. Grabbing him by the hair, Ice held him in place while she threw open the door to the cellar. Reaching around the doorframe, she clicked on the lights. She glanced down the stairs and grinned.

Still holding Cane by the hair, Ice charged down the steep incline. Stopping at the bottom, she flipped Cane around and onto the floor. Curling up in a ball, Cane grunted in agony as his body surged with pain. Rolling onto his back, he tried to take a deep breath. His eyes searched the room. On the far side, there were multiple wine racks made of crisscrossing wood filled to the brim with colored bottles. Above him were two hanging chandeliers crafted from what looked like the finest crystal, and to his left, was a blank wall. Another man was chained to it using the bolts that once held up additional wine racks. He could see a pile of wood and wine bottles behind him in the corner. The vampires must have torn down several racks to make room for their torture chamber.

The man chained to the wall looked very familiar to Cane. Rolling onto his side, he glanced up at him. His arms were bound above his head with thick chains, while his feet were tied together and strapped to the floor. His clothes were torn and bloodied. A moment of recognition hit Cane. "Specter," he breathed the name. The Wraith was unconscious and his face was covered with bruises and cuts from what appeared to be a savage round of torture.

Ice walked around and stood next to Specter. "Bet that's a name you haven't heard in a while," she said with a laugh. "The Wraith arrived just before you did, but his fate will be somewhat," she grinned, exposing her fangs, "different from yours." Ice reached down and picked up a handful of chains. "I—" A noise from behind startled her. She turned to see Zeke emerging from the stairwell.

"I'll take over from here," he smiled.

"Mistress Caitlin tasked this to me," Ice argued. "Besides, I thought you would still be cowering in the corner after Achaica kicked your ass."

Zeke sneered. A bit of dried blood was still caked in the corner of his mouth. "She caught me off guard."

Ice laughed out loud. "She kicked your ass."

Zeke charged and slapped Ice hard across the face.

Ice stumbled back, clutching her face. Her expression hardened with anger as her golden eyes appeared. She looked incredulously at Zeke, her mouth agape.

"Don't ever speak to me that way," Zeke growled, his fists balled and ready for another strike.

"You realize," Ice said slowly, "that I am the older vampire here."

"But I have the Mistress' favor," Zeke said, "I win."

"This is not a contest," Ice argued.

"Sure, you say that now." Zeke laughed. "When you're losing." He reached down and grabbed Cane by the arm. Wrenching him to his feet, Zeke slammed the older man to the wall. "Give me the chains so I can restrain the human."

Cane gasped in pain as his back hit the wall. "Don't you know you're not supposed to hit a lady?" he croaked.

Zeke stared in awe at Cane. Grabbing him by the collar, Zeke lifted Cane and hit him against the wall again. "Why are you talking to me?"

"You should always be polite," Cane managed to say. "It's the gentlemanly thing to do."

Zeke shook his head. "You don't know when to shut up, do you, old man?"

Spinning around, Zeke sent Cane sailing into the wine racks in the rear of the room. Cane's body smashed into the bottles and wood bringing them all to the ground. One of the bottles had shattered directly beneath him, driving shards of glass into his lower back. Rolling off the glass, Cane sliced his cheek open on a chunk of wood. Recoiling, he slapped his hand against the bleeding gashes. Zeke stepped over him and lifted him from the debris. Tossing him across the room again, Cane landed just below Specter's feet.

Zeke shook his head. "I don't need this shit." He glanced at Ice. "Chain him up."

Ice watched as Zeke adjusted his jacket and headed for the steps. Once out of sight, Ice moved toward Cane. Reaching down with one hand, she easily lifted him off the floor and pinned him to the wall. Using the bolts that remained from the wine racks, she wrapped the chain around them, then around his wrists. Moving down his body, she set to work binding his feet.

Cane watched her face as she worked. She was angry, and ashamed. She was muttering under her breath as she completed her task. "You don't have to take that."

"Shut up," Ice growled.

"You are just as powerful as he is," Cane added. "You have every right he does." Cane knew he was treading on dangerous ground. This was a remorseless killer he was provoking. One wrong word and he could be dead. "Why are you subservient to him?"

"I'm not," Ice answered. "I serve her."

"You mean Caitlin?"

"Yes," Ice said as she cinched his ankle chains tightly in place.

Cain grunted in pain. "Why?"

"She is the reason I was created," Ice admitted. "Plus, I don't think she'd hesitate to kill me if given the chance." Ice completed her work and stood up. She looked Cane directly in the eye. She found herself disarmed by this man. Shaking her head, she scolded herself and tried to get her focus back.

"You can help us," Cane said, referring to himself and Specter. "You can free us. You have the power."

Ice rechecked the chains around Cane's wrists, ignoring his comments.

"We'll take you with us."

Ice stopped and stared, but remained silent.

"Help us," Cane asked quietly.

"I...." Ice struggled for words. "I can't." Turning away, she moved toward the steps. Hitting

310

the bottom step, she glanced back over her shoulder at Cane's pleading glance. Averting her eyes, she headed up the stairs.

Chapter Nineteen

The fires burned and the masses gathered. It was exactly as she had predicted. She walked along the balcony looking out over her growing army. Running her fingertips along the rails, she smiled. The moon was beginning to set in the western sky. It would be morning soon and her army would need to rest, but for now, they celebrated.

It had been a day filled with nervous energy as she waited. Moments passing had seemed like hours as she awaited the arrival of her army. Many had come, but many more were expected. This was merely a fraction of those who had heard her voice. Some, who suffered from a more diluted blood lineage, had probably heard her call, but didn't know what to make of it. At this very moment, they were probably wandering lost, knowing they had something to do, but not what it was. Others who had heard the call simply could not make the journey. Her kin was spread far and wide around the world. Still, it was a start.

Caitlin tapped her fingernails on the rails as she sized up her army. There were very nearly two hundred vampires in the courtyard of her new home. They were of all races and creeds, but one thing held true: they all, in some way, belonged to her. She was a Master Vampire, one of such pure heritage, she could trace her bloodline to the very first vampire. No, she wasn't one of the originals, but she was very close. She knew none older, nor had she ever encountered any in her vast lifetime. She watched her children gathered around large bonfires celebrating. The whooped and hollered as they drank any alcohol they could get their hands on. They knew they were among the select that would finally be able to wipe the human plague from this planet and rule. Caitlin had made sure she greeted each and every vampire that had arrived earlier in the night. She wanted to be sure of their loyalties, but in the end, that wasn't important. Their task was to kill every human they encountered; a job they had been performing admirably since their creation.

A small sound behind her shook her from her thoughts. Without turning, she sniffed the air and relaxed. Her eyes remained focused on the crowd below. "Achaica."

Achaica stepped from the shadows revealing her face. "Mistress Caitlin," she said slowly. "I do not want to seem ungrateful to my creator, but…" she paused.

Caitlin slowly turned and faced her progeny. "What is it, Achaica? You know I trust your council."

Achaica nodded. "I question this war, Mistress."

Caitlin cocked her head slightly. "How so?"

Achaica looked her creator directly in the eyes. "We have coexisted with humans for so long in relative secrecy, why threaten that now?" She brushed a bit of hair from her face. "We have it pretty good right now. Our only threat comes from the Wraiths. Shouldn't we be warring against them?"

Caitlin took a long, slow, deep breath and

considered the question before her. "Aren't you tired of hiding from these blasted humans? Hiding your true nature? Don't you wish for a day when you can walk unhindered through the streets of any city and not be afraid of being discovered?"

"I do wish for that, but our immortality has its price," Achaica answered. "They are the rightful heirs to this place. We must find a way to coexist."

"I'll be damned if I have to hide my face from those overgrown monkeys anymore," Caitlin growled. "We are a superior race. We deserve to rule." She turned away from Achaica and once again placed her hands on the rails.

"And when you wipe out the humans, what then?" Achaica pressed. "What are we to feed on? Cows? Pigs?" She took a breath, "Each other?"

Caitlin gripped the rails tightly with her fingers. "There are six billion disgusting humans on this planet. I'm sure we'll be able to slip a few into storage for a rainy night." Releasing her grip on the rail, she turned to face Achaica once again. "What has brought this on? Why all these questions?"

Achaica shook her head. "I wish I knew."

Caitlin sized up her creation. "You're not starting to feel sorry for them, are you?"

"They are just so frail," Achaica admitted.

"That's right," Caitlin said with a smile. "They are frail. They are not born rulers, they were bred to be subjugated. Even now, they are ruled by their religion, their hopes, and their fears. Do you not remember what it was like to be one of them? We were all so afraid to live that most days, we wouldn't even step off our property for fear God

314

might smite us for some past transgression. Take this human you brought me," Caitlin paused, "he is so tired of living, yet he is too cowardly to take his own life out of fear that this is all there is. He craves death, and yet, he will not face it. They claim they have free will," Caitlin continued, "but this is not what I see. They are nothing more than monkeys who found fire. They make grand claims to their own intelligence, even going so far as to hand out awards to the smartest, and yet they won't let go of their antiquated belief systems. They know nothing of what it is to be free. They are weak and deserve to be wiped away with the morning trash."

"But, Mistress—"

"Do not finish that thought," Caitlin's eyes narrowed. "You have been by my side for thousands of years, but I will not hesitate to bind you in the cellar with the human and the Wraith." She took a moment to let her threat sink in. "Right now, I need support. If you're not with me, then you're against me," she hissed. "Do not cross me."

Achaica said nothing.

Caitlin moved close and placed her hand on the woman's face. "You were my first child, and you will always have a place in my heart, dear Achaica." She leaned close and kissed her on the forehead. "Don't let it end this way."

Achaica nodded.

"Now leave me."

Achaica turned and headed toward the door. With one final glance over her shoulder, she was gone. Caitlin was alone once again. Turning back to the railing, she peered down at her army. All was ready for her, but her army needed a new commander and she had the perfect man picked out for the job. A horrible smile spread across her red lips.

* * *

The sun had risen high over Cairo. It was nearing midday. The yellow desert sands glistened in the light as the temperatures slowly continued to rise. Through the modern architecture of the city, the sunlight filtered down over the past. Men and women began to perform their daily routines. The smell of cooked food began to waft out windows and into the streets and mingle with the sound of playing children. If this was to be their last day, it was going to be a beautiful one.

The five walked along a street; beads of sweat already beginning to form on their faces. Callista led the way, followed closely by Dawn, Lydia and Kelley. Bishop thumbed his new necklace as he brought up the rear. All five moved with one mind and purpose. They were close to finding their lost comrade, and nothing would stand in their way. They would trudge through the very flames of hell to recover him. With the charms Lydia and Kelley had provided and the new weapons courtesy of Mac, they were confident in their resolve. Despite the temperatures outside, they were all icy cool inside.

Callista stopped and lifted her head. Closing her eyes, she sniffed the air. A sneer crossed her face as she quickly expelled the foul stench. Taking a step back, she lifted her hand to her brow to shield her eyes from the sun. She glanced across the sun scorched city with her preternatural sight, searching for any trace of the scent she had just encountered. She knew they were close, but she couldn't pinpoint them. She took a long breath and dug into her jacket pocket, producing a pair of dark sunglasses. Turning back to the group, she frowned.

"What is it?" Bishop asked.

"I can smell death on the wind," Callista replied.

"What does that mean?" Dawn wondered.

"It could mean this city is crawling with vampires," Callista conjectured, "or that the ones already here have moved around this city so much, they have spread their scent across everything."

"Which theory do you favor?" Dawn asked.

"It's difficult to tell," Callista said with a sigh, "but I can make out the different scents of at least twenty-five vampires."

"Great," Kelley threw her arms up in disgust. "More reinforcements for their team. What are we looking at now? Twenty-five superhuman beings against, oh, let me see, the five of us?"

"Yeah, that about sums it up," Bishop said with a smile. "Doesn't seem fair, does it?"

"For us, you mean?" Kelley asked.

"No," Bishop laughed, "for them." He flipped back his jacket and sported his dual revolvers on his hips. "Look at me," he smiled, "I'm a badass."

"Well," Lydia chuckled, "at least one of us has a positive attitude."

"I make my own fun," Bishop snickered.

Dawn smiled to herself. It was good for her heart to see her team at ease once again. This had been a trying time for all, but they had pulled together beautifully, despite the odds they faced. After all had fallen asleep last night, she had taken the chance to talk privately with Mac. Cutting through the treacle, she wanted to know what they were facing point-blank. Callista had been a great source of information thus far, but Dawn knew she had also been sugarcoating much of it. Mac had no such reservations. He told her without any hint of reservation they were all facing certain doom. Nothing like this had been attempted since ancient times, and then only with the support of hundreds of well-trained Wraiths. Of course, she didn't mention any of this to the other four. She knew Callista was aware of the stakes, but Bishop, Lydia and Kelley were charging in blind. Lydia, perhaps, understood better than any this monster they sought to destroy. She had been at her mercy before and lived to tell the tale. Dawn hoped they would all live to recount this adventure.

"Wait," Callista held up her hand.

Dawn took a step closer to her tracker. "What is it?"

"A strange scent," Callista answered. She cocked her head a bit and fell silent. After a moment, she pulled her sunglasses from her eyes. "It's an old vampire," she breathed, "accompanied by a human."

Dawn felt her heart flutter. "Can you tell anymore?"

Callista paused, "I'm sorry, no." She pushed back on her glasses. "All I can say is this is very unusual. Vampires do not usually travel with humans by choice. This could be our quarry."

Dawn nodded. "Track it."

Without another word, Callista slipped her sunglasses back on and was off. Her feet moved swiftly over the uneven terrain following the invisible scent. Darting in and out of alleys and doorways, she purposely lost the scent and reacquired it to make certain she was on the right path. The four members of the OPR followed slightly behind her, unable to keep pace with her in the direct heat of day. Coming around a corner, Callista stopped cold in front of a doorway. She quickly took several steps back and pressed herself up against the building's exterior. The other four stopped just behind her. They shot puzzled looks at each other, but remained silent.

Callista pointed at the door, "Vampires."

Bishop's eyes widened, "In there?"

Callista nodded.

"What do we do?" Dawn asked.

Callista smiled. Pushing away from the wall, she spun and headed toward the door. As she moved inside, she pulled Mac's scythe from her belt.

Dawn looked to the other members of her team. "I guess we go in."

Following Callista inside, the four stopped just inside the door. They had wandered into a bar, and from the looks of it, not a very reputable one. The floor was nothing more than plywood with sawdust spread over it. A long bar hugged the back wall with several patrons resting on stools in front of it. Half a dozen round wooden tables occupied the floor with a few scattered men and women at each. A noisy ceiling fan whirred overhead, managing only to spread the lingering cigarette smoke through the bar instead of cool. The entire establishment reeked of vomit and spilled alcohol. The few windows in this place were closed tightly, allowing no light inside. This place was perfect for them.

Several of the patrons glanced up at the five, but quickly lost interest. Callista began to slowly walk through the bar flipping her still closed scythe in her hand. To a casual observer, she was barely worth noticing, but to a more trained eye, every move she made was a calculated decision. She was slowly baiting the hook; calling out her prey. She could smell them, even through the stench of the place. Their scent was unmistakable. She glanced at each person there, but carefully avoided eye contact. Motioning behind, she signaled for the other four to split up and head toward her position.

Zeroing in on a table in the corner, Callista eyed two men sitting there. They were both dressed better than the rest of the patrons. Each was clad in a pair of baggy jeans, a light flannel jacket and a hooded sweatshirt with the hoods pulled up on their heads so their faces were in dark shadows. Both were sitting over a mug of beer, while several empty glasses littered their table. Both men carefully avoided looking in Callista's direction as they milked their drinks.

Slipping into an empty chair at the table, Callista placed her scythe on the table in plain sight. She leaned her elbows on the table and scooted some of the glasses out of the way. "Mind if I join you, gentlemen?"

The men grunted, but voiced no disapproval.

"Sparkling conversationalists I see," Callista joked. She tried to size up her opponents. They were both easily larger than her, but not much else could be determined. Picking up one of the empty glasses, Callista sniffed it. "Good beer here?"

The men continued to ignore her.

Bishop had taken up a position at the bar just behind the men's table, while Dawn had slipped into an empty seat on the opposite side. Kelley and Lydia were leaning against the wall just to the right of Bishop, trying to act nonchalant. Bishop turned, signaled the bartender and ordered a drink. Fishing in his pocket, he slapped several bills on the bar. Turning with his drink in his hand, he raised it to the men and took a long drink. With their attention still on him, he pulled his jacket back revealing one of his revolvers.

"Maybe you two can help me," Callista started again. "I'm in town looking for an old friend. She's red haired, fair skinned, and I think," she smiled, "a couple of thousand years old. Ring a bell?"

The first man looked up at Callista for the first time. His lips peeled back into a sneer. "Filthy Wraith," he growled.

The man's hand shot out toward Callista's scythe, but before he could grab it, she had it in her hand and was up. Clicking a button on the hilt, the scythe snapped open. Callista spun it in her hands, taunting the men. "If you want it, come and get it."

The two men stood up and pulled their hoods away revealing their golden eyes. "Maybe we will," the first warned.

The bartender slammed his fists on the bar. "Hey! We don't want any trouble in here! Take it outside!"

Callista laughed. "I will if they will."

The men glanced at one of the closed windows. A slice of daylight was shining through. Turning back to Callista, each growled and dropped their projections revealing the corpses beneath. The first vampire hissed at Callista and began to work his way around the table, while the second spun and faced Bishop.

Lunging forward, the first vampire attacked Callista. He lashed out with his claws, narrowly missing her midsection. Rocking back, Callista avoided a second swipe at her face. Ducking down, she spun with her scythe and caught the curved blade behind the vampire's legs. The hulking creature spilled onto the floor, but rolled off his back and was quickly on his feet again. Reversing her spin, Callista brought her weapon around for a second attack. The vampire lifted his arm to deflect the blow, but had miscalculated. The scythe's blade dug deep into his forearm. He wailed in pain as he ripped it free. Leaping forward, he caught Callista flat-footed and the two tumbled to the floor.

Bishop quickly drew his revolver and drew a bead on the vampire. Sliding his finger around the trigger he began to squeeze, but before he could pull off the shot, the vampire was on him. The beast, which was almost twice his size, knocked the revolver from his hand and pinned him to the bar. Lifting his hand, the vampire readied the death strike. Kicking out, Bishop hit the creature in the knee to no effect.

Bishop swallowed hard. "Oh, crap."

The vampire laughed out loud. He started the downswing, his claws poised to rip into Bishop's face. Mere inches before impact, the vampire found his arm frozen. Glancing over his shoulder, he spotted Kelley and Lydia. "Witches," he hissed. Before he could change his attack, the two women lifted him off the floor with only the power of their minds. Spinning him in the air, they sent him crashing down into the very table he had been sitting at.

The remaining patrons in the bar began to scatter. Dawn rushed toward the exit and threw it open. Motioning with her arms, she began to direct them outside and out of harm's way. Turning back after the last person was out, she sized up the battle. Taking a deep breath, she pulled back her sleeve revealing the weapon Mac had supplied her. Clicking the first dart into position exactly how the old Wraith had showed her, she charged toward Callista's position.

The second vampire was unable to move. Kelley and Lydia were holding him in place. Scooping his revolver off the floor, Bishop cocked back the hammer and walked toward the immobilized creature. Lifting his weapon, Bishop stared at the vampire. It turned its head toward him and howled in protest, its golden eyes burning with anger. Bishop aimed for the vampire's heart and pulled the trigger. The creature convulsed in pain as the bullet ripped through its chest and punctured its heart. Bishop shot again. Blue flame erupted from the vampire's wound and mouth. An unearthly scream filled the room as the vampire began to burn from within. In a matter of moments, its body was totally engulfed by blue flame. Golden embers wafted into the air as its body collapsed in on itself. Bishop turned and nodded to Kelley and Lydia.

Callista threw a hard punch across the first vampire's jaw. The vampire's head snapped back, but it quickly pressed the attack again. Knocking Callista's scythe away, the vampire ripped its claws across her face creating several cuts. Bringing her legs up, Callista kicked the vampire squarely in the chest. The creature flew back, but landed on its feet. Kicking forward, Callista righted herself and dropped down into an attack position. Flipping forward, she caught the vampire with a high kick. Before she could press the attack again, the vampire wrapped his clawed fingers around her throat and lifted her from the ground. He started to squeeze.

The vampire gasped in pain. His grip loosened. Callista fell to the floor. Turning around, she spotted her scythe and began to scramble for it. Turning back, she stared in awe as the vampire stood motionless, a look of disbelief on its face. Glancing down at his chest, the golden eyed corpse spotted a wooden dart embedded just to the right of his heart. Looking up, he saw Dawn holding her position, her wrist weapon aimed at his chest. Ripping the dart free, the vampire started to charge. Dawn shot again and refused to move. The vampire continued its charge. She shot again. The vampire let out a gasp and tumbled to the floor in front of her. Rolling onto its back, Dawn was able to tell she had finally hit his heart. The vampire howled as blue flame burst from its chest.

Stepping back, Dawn looked over her team. They had performed well. She was pleased. Turning, she headed back for the door. Pushing it open, she spotted the worried bartender waiting outside. "It's okay now. You can come back inside."

The bartender stepped back into his bar and began to survey the damage. "Why did you have to do that?" he asked in broken English.

"You may not believe this," Dawn breathed, "but those two were vampires."

"I know," the bartender said incredulously, "but they were good customers."

* * *

Caitlin stopped just shy of the cellar door and licked her lips. This was her favorite part. All else could wait; this was the moment she had been thinking of "craving" was a more appropriate description, for the past thirty years. As a smug smile crossed her face, an intense feeling of satisfaction filled her body. Revenge was such a beautiful thing when done correctly. Quieting her other senses, she held her ear close to the cellar door and listened. She could hear them; she could hear their fear. Any moment, they knew she would enter and the torture would begin. She could hear the anxiety in every breath they took, in every racing beat of their hearts. It was intoxicating to her. Moving her hand toward the doorknob, she paused a moment longer. It was like her birthday and there were two big presents waiting for her to open. She felt like a schoolgirl again (although, when she was a little girl, there were no such things as schools).

Twisting the handle, Caitlin pulled open the door. She stared down into the cellar. It wasn't quite to her liking. It had been converted into a wine cellar, she assumed by the previous owners. She preferred them dark and dank with a lone bulb hanging from a cord in the center of the room. Dirt floors, spider webs, and shelves of old forgotten knick-knacks would complete the image. She knew it was stereotypical, but some things just didn't need to be changed. Shaking her head, she stepped onto the carpeted stars. Bright white fluorescent lights dotted the ceiling, vanquishing every shadow and dark corner. The walls weren't dank and dirty, rather clean and tiled. It didn't matter. The blood would splatter just the same.

Hitting the bottom stair, Caitlin turned and stopped. Pressed against the wall, their arms and hands bound with chains were Specter and Cane. Their hands were tied separately well above their heads, while their feet were chained to the floor. Each man's head hung forward, almost painfully. Specter's face was a mess of black and purple bruises. Zeke and Ice had been somewhat overzealous in their task of returning him to the cellar. He would recover she knew, but it took some of the fun out of his torture if he was already half dead.

It was then she noticed another figure in the room. Standing in the corner, watching over the two captives was Achaica. She stood with her arms crossed and one of her feet lifted and pressed flat against the wall. Her normally dark attire had been somewhat brightened. She had eschewed the black coat and leather for a softer, red cotton dress. Her dark hair was hanging loosely around her face, framing her high cheekbones and stunning blue eyes. Her vision was trained on the two captives. Caitlin couldn't discern which she was more interested in, but she had a pretty good idea.

"What did he do to you, Achaica?" Caitlin asked quietly with a tinge of concern in her voice.

Achaica looked up at her sire with a long face. At any moment, it looked as if tears were about to fall from her eyes. Her mouth was drawn into a deep frown. Closing her eyes for a moment, she took a long breath. Ignoring Caitlin's question, she pushed past her and made her way up the stairs and out of the cellar. Caitlin heard the door quietly click shut behind her.

Caitlin disregarded Achaica's strange behavior and continued with her task. Taking the final step into the cellar, she circled in front of her two prisoners and stopped. Both men were breathing, but neither appeared to be conscious. Their bodies hung limp from the chains. The iron filled scent of blood was heavy on the air. Glancing up, she saw the chains had cut into Cane's wrists and blood was trickling down his arms. Her senses became drunk with the sight and smell for a moment, but she quickly brought herself back from the brink of blood lust. She didn't want to just tear into them…she wanted to savor it; every moment, every drop of blood and every scream of pain, she wanted it all.

Stepping in front of Cane, Caitlin reached out and caressed his cheek with her fingers. Cane slowly lifted his head and opened his eyes. Three long cuts ran down his face over his left eye and onto his cheek. They were crusted with blood, and bruises were forming around them. The beginning of his torture hadn't been severe, by Caitlin's standards at least, but it was about to get worse. Flicking one of the cuts with her thumbnail, she broke open the fresh scab. Blood welled up and began to run down his face. Running her finger through it, she lifted the warm, red fluid to her mouth and licked it off.

"You taste sweet," Caitlin smiled.

Cane slowly opened his eyes and lifted his head. His eyes slowly focused on the woman before him. "I'll have the prime rib, medium rare," he mumbled.

Caitlin looked crossly at him. "What the hell are you talking about?"

"Yes," Cane nodded, "I'll have the soup and salad."

Caitlin slapped him hard across the face, opening his wounds further. Pulling her hand back, she struck him again. Blood flowed freely down his face now.

Shaking his head, Cain's eyes started to focus on something distant in the room, but he quickly snapped his attention back up to Caitlin. "Bloody Hell," he breathed, "I'm still here."

"Welcome back, love," Caitlin cooed.

Cane glanced to his right to find Specter still out cold. He was alive, but just barely at this point, his breathing shallow and his body beaten. Closing his eyes, Cane let his head fall forward cursing under his breath. He was in a prison of his own design, there was no denying that, but things were moving out of his control. "Just kill me," Cane growled.

"Not yet," Caitlin smiled. "You will die," she assured, "but then you will reawaken to a new life."

"I won't be like you."

"I don't really see that you have a choice." Caitlin took a step back and stared at her captive. "You see, when you die and become a vampire, you lose your soul. No more regrets, no more remorse, no more caring," she noted. "The very thing that makes you a compassionate human being is gone. The only thing that remains is pure unbridled evil."

"What if your blood doesn't take?" Cane asked, vainly searching for options. "What if there's a problem?"

"That very rarely happens," Caitlin assured him, "and in those cases, the person doesn't die, they become something different...."

Cane looked oddly at Caitlin.

"Did you ever see the movie 'Nosferatu'?"

Cane nodded.

Caitlin giggled with glee. "When the transformation goes wrong, you still become a vampire, but a grotesque, mindless killer like the vampire portrayed in that movie." Caitlin grinned, exposing her fangs. "So you really have nothing to look forward to, love. You'll be a vampire either way." She took a step closer and pressed her body against Cane's. "Shall we begin?"

Cane felt complete revulsion at her touch. He pulled his head away with a sneer. "No," he pleaded quietly.

Caitlin's green eyes melted to gold as she opened her mouth wide. Her fangs seemed longer somehow, too big to even fit in her mouth. Leaning forward, she pressed Cane's head to the side and licked up his neck. "Are you ready for eternity?"

"Please no," Cane mouthed.

Drawing the tips of her fangs up Cane's neck, Caitlin savored the moment. She had been waiting thirty years for this. Rotating her head slightly, she pressed her fangs sharply against his throat. Closing her eyes, she administered the slightest amount of pressure with her jaws. She felt her fangs pop through the soft flesh. Cane tried to recoil in pain, but she held him firmly in place. Pushing harder, her fangs sliced deeper. Cane's blood began to gush from the wounds. Pulling her teeth from the wounds, Caitlin ran her tongue in and over the holes, his warm blood shooting into her mouth. She pressed her body against his, feeling his warmth draining into her. Wrapping her left leg around his, she began grinding her hips into him. Again and again, she slid her fangs into the wounds, opening the holes further, then pulling them free. Cane groaned in agony as he felt his life starting to slip away. Caitlin easily drew Cane's blood from his wound. She could feel the rhythm of his heartbeat in his blood flow beginning to slow. His body couldn't take much more. She felt his muscles beginning to relax. He wasn't fighting anymore; he was about to die.

Pulling her mouth away from the wounds, Caitlin forced herself to stop drinking. Tossing her head back, she wiped the excess blood from her mouth and moaned in complete satisfaction. She could feel his life racing through her body. Running her hands over her face and chest, she could feel the warmth of his blood. Looking up at Cane, she stopped. She could easily let him die right now. His body had only moments left to live, but that was what he wanted. She couldn't allow that. His torment would not be so quick and painless. He still had much to pay for.

Lifting her hand, she pulled her razor sharp thumbnail across the right side of her neck, opening a deep cut in her flesh. Sliding her fingers through his hair, she maneuvered his mouth toward her open wound. Both had to move quickly. If they took too long, Caitlin's wound would close and Cane would die. She felt his cold lips against her neck. No movement. Perhaps she had waited too long, she thought. His body was cold. Caitlin forcefully ran Cane's lips through her blood. "Drink," she instructed him.

Her pleasure turned to anger. He was fighting her. He was forcing himself to die. He would not drink. Caitlin growled. She wouldn't let him go that easily. Lifting her arm, she bit into her own wrist. Flexing her wrist to increase the flow, she lifted it above his head. The blood from her wound dripped down onto his face. Moving his head back, she pressed her wrist to his mouth. She could feel her blood starting to pool inside his mouth. Knowing one good swallow would be all it would take,

Caitlin realized there was still no movement. Still holding her wrist to his lips, she reared back and punched him squarely in the gut. Cane's head fell back as he gasped for air. Struggling for breath, he gurgled through the blood in his mouth.

Pressing his eyes closed in agony, Cane swallowed.

Chapter Twenty

Five figures stood on a rooftop as the sun began to fade behind them. The air felt heavy, as if it were beginning to close in around them. The western sky was a concoction of pink and orange clouds, giving way to the blackness encroaching from the east. Cairo was slowly beginning to shut down. In the wake of news of a "golden eyed demon", a citywide curfew had been implemented. No one was to be on the streets after sundown, while extra police had been added to the patrols. A wave of hysteria had gripped the city. In this place of ancient curses and long forgotten lore, the news of an inhuman killer washed over the city like a plague. Every place the five had traveled that day, news of additional sightings were being reported. Windows and doors were quickly being locked as the sun faded away.

Somewhere along the journey, the five had slipped from reality into legend. People spoke in hushed voices as they passed and quietly offered their prayers of hope. They were Vampire Hunters now. They fought for those who could not, defending the weak and powerless. Wielding the tools of the trade, they came armed with something much more powerful: goodness. No longer fearing death, they walked into the dragon's lair. They were the righteous few, chosen by an unseen hand to be champions.

Resting his foot on the ledge, Bishop stared down over the rooftops. Callista and Dawn stood next to him quietly contemplating, while Kelley and Lydia slowly moved up from behind. Callista had followed the scents to a home on the outskirts of the city. This place reeked of death. It had been a home for the living, now it was a haven for the dead. Large walls surrounded the entire mansion, but they would be simple to breach. The sounds of dozens of voices echoed up off the steep walls of the city. They could see the orange glow of fires burning in the courtyard. A moment of fear gripped them then. They were vastly outnumbered.

Kelley placed her hand on Bishop's back. Turning, he looked into her eyes and found a bit of relief. "Thank you," he whispered. "Can you and Lydia tell if Cane's in there?"

Kelley looked at Lydia, "I think so."

Lydia nodded. Kelley stepped back and took the elder witch by the hand. The two closed their eyes and focused. Their power grew and washed over them. Turning their attention toward the house, they looked inside with invisible eyes. Lydia led the way with Kelley channeling and focusing her energy. Peering from room to room, the searched for their friend. Lydia took a sharp breath. Again. Letting go of Kelley's hand, Lydia opened her eyes and took a step back. Pressing her hands to her temple, she struggled for clarity.

Kelley reached out and placed her hand on Lydia's shoulder. "What is it?"

Lydia ripped away from the touch, "Don't touch me." She stumbled back from the group further. Closing her eyes, she gasped in agony.

"What's the matter?" Dawn asked, stepping forward.

Lydia shook her head. "It can't be."

Bishop and Callista moved closer, their hearts beating wildly. Bishop tried to reach for Lydia, but she pulled further away. "Lydia," he said slowly, "talk to us. What did you see?"

"I found him," Lydia breathed.

"Is he alive? Is he okay?" Dawn asked in a blur.

Lydia looked up at her friends and shook her head. "He's not himself anymore." She swallowed hard. "They made him a vampire."

Dawn stumbled back as if she had been kicked in the gut. Reaching behind for something to steady herself with, she missed and tumbled to the floor. Her heart throbbed in her chest, feeling as if it would burst free at any moment. She bit down on her lip to hold back the tears. Lifting herself into a sitting position, she drew her knees to her chest and balled her fists. Anger began to well up inside her. Clenching her teeth together, she threw her head back and screamed into the approaching darkness.

Bishop dropped to his knees next to her. Placing his hands on her shoulders, he worked to get her attention. "Dawn!" Her eyes were brimming with rage and hatred. "Dawn!"

She snapped her head around to face her friend, her bottom lip quivering.

"We still have a job to do," he said quietly. "Do you understand?"

"He's gone," she whispered.

Bishop nodded. "I know."

Dawn reached up and grabbed him by the shoulders. "We failed! He's dead!"

Bishop fell speechless as he stared into the pain and anguish in Dawn's eyes.

"What the hell do we have left to do here?" she asked angrily. "We're beaten."

"We may not have been able to save your friend," Callista offered, "but we can still save others."

Kelley nodded and stepped forward, "She's right. If we don't stop these vampires, more innocent lives will be lost."

Lydia took a deep breath and wiped the tears away from her eyes. "It's what Cane would have wanted us to do. We have to fight."

Dawn lifted herself off the ground and rushed toward Callista. "He can't be gone. There has to be something we can do," she reasoned. "Is there a way we can bring him back? If we kill Caitlin, will he be human again? You know, kill the Master Vampire?" Her eyes pleaded with Callista.

"I'm sorry," Callista said slowly. "Once a human becomes a vampire, they're gone. In the thousands of years the Guard has fought them, we have never found a way to reverse the process." She took a long, deep breath. "He's gone."

"No," Dawn said. "I won't accept that. He wouldn't give up on one of us, so I'm sure as hell not going to give up on him. There has to be a way." She turned to Lydia, a wild look in her eyes. "You can do it. I know you can. You're a powerful witch."

Lydia shook her head.

"You're all worthless," Dawn growled. "How can you give up on him so easily? We have to find a way!"

Bishop grabbed Dawn by the shoulders and

spun her around. He stared into her grief stricken eyes. "Dawn, stop," he barked. "That's enough!" He slowly relaxed his grip. "We still have a way to save him," he offered.

Dawn's eyes widened.

"We have to find him," Bishop paused, "and release him."

Dawn ripped free of his grasp and stepped away, shaking her head. She fell to her knees. Running her opposite hand through her hair, she took a deep breath. Looking up at her team one by one, she knew they were right. Standing up, she glanced into the ever darkening sky at the multitude of stars. Through the anger and anguish, she struggled to find a moment of clarity. Her friend was already dead. All that remained was a dead husk. Taking another deep breath, she walked over to Bishop and placed her hand on his shoulder. Moving down his arm, she took him by the hand. Looking into his eyes, she saw the same grief and anger she was experiencing. She was not alone.

Turning back to her team, she nodded. "We have to finish this." She swallowed hard. "One last thing," pulling a wooden stake from her jacket, she spun it in her hand.

The group turned to hear her request.

Dawn frowned. "Cane's mine."

Bishop turned to see the last shreds of daylight fading. "Let's go."

* * *

Specter opened his eyes. Groggily, he glanced around the room. Running his tongue over his mouth, he tried to work up enough saliva to whet

337

his dry palette. Swallowing, memories came flooding back to him along with a throbbing pain in his skull. He lifted his head. He was no longer chained to the wall, instead a long table had been set up in the cellar. He found himself strapped to it with heavy leather bands. His clothing, except for his pants, were sitting in a pile just to right of the table. Glancing to his left, he saw a small table filled with various cutting instruments, including knives, scissors and razor blades. He knew his torture was about to begin.

Looking up, he spotted another man chained to the wall where he had previously been. His head had fallen forward, but he could still easily make out the man's features. He seemed familiar somehow, yet Specter couldn't quite place him. The man didn't seem to be faring any better than he was. Staring at his face, his recollection became clear.

"Cane? Zachary Cane?" Specter struggled against his restraints, but they were too tight. Even with his strength, he was unable to break free. "Cane!" He called out again.

He realized it then: Cane wasn't breathing. There were no signs of life there. Specter closed his eyes and uttered a silent prayer. Caitlin had claimed another soul. He glanced over Cane's body. An odd sensation washed over him. There were no signs of torture or abuse. His skin appeared to be perfectly healthy…. Specter shook his head. "Vampire."

Cane's head snapped up and his now golden eyes shot open. Opening his mouth, Specter could see his enlarged canine fangs. Rolling his eyes over the room, Cane spotted Specter and hissed.

338

"Blood…."

"Fight it, Cane," Specter urged. "You still have time to fight it. The transformation may not be complete."

Cane cocked his head to the right and popped his neck. A horrid smile grew across his face as his projection faded away. "Why would I want to fight it?" Cane licked his new fangs with glee. "I like it."

"I see you two have reacquainted yourselves."

Specter glanced across the room to see Caitlin resting against the wall with her arms crossed. Zeke and Ice were standing next to her, while Achaica was hovering in the shadows of the stairwell. Unfolding her arms, Caitlin walked across the room. She ran her fingers up Specter's body seductively. "I wanted you to be the first to know," she said slowly. Leaning close, she pressed her lips to his ear. "The war begins tonight," she whispered. She turned and motioned toward Zeke.

The young vampire moved across the room with purpose. Stopping in front of Cane, he began to undo his bindings.

"I also wanted to introduce you to the new Commander of my army," Caitlin smiled.

Zeke pulled the last chain free. Cane stepped away from the wall rubbing his wrists. Dropping down to one knee, he bowed his head before Caitlin.

Caitlin shook her head. "There's no need for that, my friend." She placed her hand on his shoulder, "Rise."

Cane stood next to his creator, his golden eyes burning within his skull. "Can I have this one?"

Caitlin smiled, "No, this one is mine. There will

be others for you." She ran her hand gently across his cheek. "I promise." She slowly returned her attention to Specter, "And as for you," she lifted a rusty knife from the nearby table, "it's time to die."

"Others will come," Specter warned her, "and they will stop you."

Caitlin pressed the blade of the knife to his chest. "Let them come." Digging the blade in, she pulled it from his collarbone down to his abdomen creating an angry, bloody gash.

Specter clenched his teeth, not allowing her the satisfaction of a scream.

Caitlin smiled. Setting the knife aside, she pressed her finger into the wound. Dragging it the entire length, she lifted it to her mouth and sucked off the blood. "I've heard a Wraith's anatomy is slightly different than a normal human's." Caitlin laughed. "I think I'd like to find out." Lifting a razor blade from the table, she pressed it deep into his flesh.

As the other vampires moved around the tortured Wraith, Achaica grimaced. Retreating further into the shadows, she headed for the cellar door. Once outside, she moved through the numerous vampires occupying the living room. Hitting the foyer, she pulled open the new door and stepped outside into the early evening. Slinking around the large porch, she slipped into a patio chair and pulled her long coat tightly around her chest. Looking down at the floorboards, her hair fell over her face.

"What are you doing?"

Surprised, Achaica looked up to see Ice leaning

against the wall. "I just," she took a breath, "needed some fresh air."

Ice nodded. She turned her face slowly and glanced into the darkness. Moving slowly across the porch, she leaned her elbows on the wooden railing. "Can I ask you something?"

Achaica nodded.

Ice bit her lip. She wasn't sure if she should air her concerns. She decided to take a chance. From what she had seen of this vampire, their motives seemed similar. "What do you think of Caitlin?"

"She is my creator," Achaica admitted. "I owe her my life."

"That's not what I asked."

Achaica studied this young vampire for a moment. "She's gone too far," she said quietly.

Ice nodded.

"I have little love for the humans," Achaica added, "but I don't want to see a war."

Ice stood up and moved to Achaica's side. Crouching down, she glanced nervously over her shoulder then back to the elder vampire. "We can stop her."

"What do you mean?" Achaica replied in surprise.

"We have it within our power to bring this war to a quick end."

Achaica shook her head. "I don't think you understand. Caitlin is millennia old. She could easily dispatch both of us before any coup could be executed."

Ice remained firm. She licked her lips deviously and smiled.

Achaica sat up in her seat and stared at the young vampire. She couldn't believe she was even listening to this woman. Her creator was all that she knew anymore. She was her everything. Closing her eyes for a moment, she took a breath of the cool night air. She slowly turned back to Ice. "What did you have in mind?"

Chapter Twenty-one

Dropping down into a patch of bushes, Bishop moved slowly to reach the other four members of his team. Crouching low, he carefully avoided the moonlight. From the rooftop, the team had slowly made their way toward Caitlin's mansion. Moving steadily through the brush, they came within sight of the house. Tossing his black leather jacket back, Bishop placed his palm on the handle of the revolver and stopped. There, barely visible in the darkness, were two guards standing watch at the front gate. Tapping Callista on the shoulder, he pointed to the two vampires. Callista nodded. Turning back to the group, she motioned with her hands for the team to split up into two groups. Pointing toward the rear of the house, Callista motioned for Bishop to take Kelley and Lydia. She would take Dawn and go in the front. As each member of the team nodded in agreement, they quickly split up and headed off.

Sticking to the brush as much as possible, Bishop, Kelley and Lydia headed toward the rear. They hoped to find the back gate unguarded. Stopping for a moment, Bishop drew his revolver and snapped open the chamber. Double-checking that he had a full load, he snapped the revolver closed again and holstered it. Glancing over his shoulder, he saw a mixture of anticipation and concern on Kelley's face. This had turned from a rescue mission into a full frontal assault. Understandably, she was worried. Bishop smiled deviously at her and winked. As a smile crossed her face, he took off again through the brush.

* * *

Cane grabbed his stomach as he stumbled away from Caitlin. Glancing over his shoulder, he could see the blood spilling from Specter's wounds. She had no intention of killing him…just inflicting as much pain as she could. It was torture for Cane. He needed to feed. His body craved it. He could feel the hunger pangs in his body; he needed blood. Placing his hand on the wall, he tried to steady himself. He was weak and tired. Every muscle ached as it cried out for sustenance.

Stumbling forward, his mind was flooded with images. In seconds, he had lived the past lives of millions of vampires. He knew the knowledge of a thousand generations instantly as it passed down to him genetically. Dropping to the ground, Cane pressed the meaty part of his palms to his temples as they throbbed in pain. Rolling onto his back, his eyes moved erratically over the room searching for something, anything, to anchor him in reality. Reaching out, he felt the bottom stair with his fingertips. He had to get out of there. The blood was driving him mad. Rolling onto his stomach, he pushed himself off the floor and looked up. Grabbing for the handrail, he started to slowly make his way up the steps.

He suddenly doubled over in pain. The urge to vomit gripped him, but he fought it. There was nothing in his stomach to expel. Biting his lower lip, he looked up to see the door. White light from the hallway above was filtering in, hurting his eyes. Propping himself against the rail, he pulled his free hand down his face. Taking a deep breath, he pulled himself up using the rail. His feet felt like brick slabs beneath him, threatening at any moment to drag him down into the depths of perdition.

This isn't who you are.

He stopped and struggled for a moment of clarity. He chased the thought, but as quickly as it had appeared, it was gone.

You must fight it!

Cane gasped in agony. Only the hunger remained. Wrapping his fingers around the rails, he started to pull himself toward the door. He needed to find blood. He didn't care who it came from.

* * *

A six foot high fence surrounded the entire mansion. It was constructed of single black iron bars that seemed to wind up from the bottom and through each other. Sharp barbs lined the top, not so much for security, but for aesthetics. Still, it would make it difficult, if not impossible, to climb. Their only option was to get through a gate.

Through the fencing, they could make out the meticulous landscaping of the front yard. High hedges encircled the entire property, while lighted fountains and sculpted bushes were tastefully scattered about. Amidst the foliage, they could see several figures moving. Each was dressed similarly in dark clothing. The sound of their voices carried over the flat terrain as they partied and celebrated what they felt would be an easy victory. Several large, round garbage cans had been placed around the grounds with a fire burning in each. Vampires gathered around the flames, continuing to revel in their own egos.

Stopping across the road from the front gate, Dawn and Callista surveyed their opposition. Beyond the gate and two guards, there were several more vampires. They seemed to be carousing with each other, but that made them no less dangerous. Callista began to rethink her decision. Even if they got past the guards, they would have to deal with all the vampires in the courtyard, and then with any inside the house that stood in their way. She shook her head. There was simply too many of them. No Wraith had ever attempted something like this alone before. Even with all her skill and training, she would be no match for ten vampires simultaneously. She needed another option, but what?

* * *

Kelley reached out and grabbed Bishop. Stopping him, she crept up next to him. "We're not alone," she whispered.

Bishop instantly dropped to the ground and drew his pistol. Slipping his finger through the guard and around the trigger, his muscles tensed. "Where?"

Kelley glanced nervously about. "I don't know, but I can sense them."

Lydia nodded, "As can I."

Kelley closed her eyes and took a deep breath. "They are many," she said slowly, "and powerful."

"I need to know where." Bishop asked urgently, "Where are they?"

Kelley opened her eyes and straightened up. Fear passed over her then. "Everywhere," she whispered.

346

Crawling onto the hardwood floor, Cane sprawled out on his stomach. The coolness felt good against his burning flesh. Lifting away from it, he propped himself against the nearest wall and closed his eyes. The hunger had subsided for a moment. Taking a deep breath, he tried to relax his aching muscles. Lifting his hands, he pressed them to his face. Glancing into the living room, he could see several vampires moving around restlessly. They were waiting for something, but he didn't know what. Although black was a predominant color in their dress, each reflected their own style, and in many cases, the time in which they were brought over.

Fight it, damn you!

Cane snapped his head around. There were no others standing in the hall with him. He was completely alone. Balling up his fists, he pressed them firmly against his ears.

This isn't who you are!

Cane shook his head. He was going mad. Doubling over in pain, he felt the hunger return. He imagined a mouth inside chewing at his stomach. Closing his eyes tightly, he buried his face in his knees. Clenching his teeth, he could feel his fingernails beginning to dig into his palms. Lifting his fists, he watched a drop of blood form on the bottom and fall away. Blood.... Snapping his head around, his golden eyes blazed with hunger. He spotted a young female vampire sitting alone on one of the couches in the living room. As Cane stared at her, he felt the color drain from his vision, leaving only her highlighted. Lifting himself off the floor, he savored the first few moments of the hunt. Staring at her, he spoke quietly, "Hey."

The young woman glanced up and scanned the room. She was lovely, swathed in a dark blue silk dress. Her skin was a creamy white. Her hair, styled in loose ringlets, was pulled up behind her head. Her body was long and lithe, creating beautiful lines and curves. As her eyes moved over the room, she finally focused on Cane. She pointed to herself.

Cane nodded and smiled slightly. He beckoned to her.

As she stood, she adjusted her dress. Moving slowly across the room, she stopped just shy of Cane. "Who are you?"

"That's not important," Cane replied. "Mistress Caitlin has requested your presence."

The young vampire smiled.

"Follow me," Cane hissed.

Leading her down the hallway, Cane pressed his hand to her back. He could smell the blood within her. His senses reached out as they moved, searching for other vampires. The woman glanced back nervously, but refused to turn away. She wanted to meet Caitlin more than anything. Cane could sense it in her. He could taste her longing in the air. Stopping, Cane directed the woman toward a closed door. He could tell there were no other vampires in the room. This place would do nicely for his purposes. Reaching out, he twisted the doorknob and pushed open the door, revealing a darkened bedroom. Guiding the woman inside, Cane pressed the door closed behind him.

"Where's Caitlin?" The woman asked.

"I have no idea," Cane growled.

"What the hell is this shit?"

Without another word, Cane lunged forward catching the woman by the wrists. The hunger was overwhelming. Pushing her down to the floor, he felt the small bones in her wrists shattering beneath his grip. The woman screamed out in agony, but it was of no use. It would be over soon enough. Pressing his knee into her chest, Cane bent down over her. He could feel her ribs breaking beneath his weight. With her arms spread wide, he opened his mouth and dug his fangs into her throat. She screamed again, but it was quickly drowned in a gurgling noise. Cane dug all his teeth, not just his fangs, deeply into the flesh of her neck. Pulling them free, he began to lap at the wound. Her warm blood spurted into his mouth and ran down his chin. Throwing his head forward again, he bit once more, creating a new set of holes. Pressing his lips to her neck, he began to feed.

Stop! This isn't who you are!

Cane pressed his eyes closed and pushed away the voices. As her blood flowed into his body, he began to feel her quieting. Her heart was beating slowly now. She was on the edge of death. Flexing his muscles, he drew every drop of blood from her. Pulling his head away, he lifted up and ripped her left arm from her body. Flipping the limb over in his hand, he licked the jagged flesh trying to find a final drop of blood.

Standing up, he dropped her arm onto her dead body. He wiped the blood from his chin and glanced down at the broken husk on the floor. Only moments ago, this was a vibrant young vampire, now she was nothing and he had enjoyed killing her. It was the sheer power to take life whenever it pleased him. With a laugh, he stepped forward and pressed his foot against her skull. Pressing down, he felt it crunch beneath his weight. Stepping back, he opened the door and glanced into the hallway. No one had heard them, or no one cared. Lifting his shirt, he wiped away the last bit of her blood from his face. Looking down at his hands, he lifted them to his lips and licked her blood from them. Taking a deep breath, he smiled in complete satisfaction.

* * *

Specter clenched his teeth as Caitlin dug the razor blade deeper into his chest. Pulling it down and free, she smiled at her handiwork. She had created an almost perfect square on his right pectoral muscle about the size of her fist. Dipping the razor blade into one of the corners, she worked up an edge.

With a laugh, she set the blade aside. "Now this may hurt a bit."

Grabbing the raised edge, she ripped the flesh away with one violent tear, revealing his muscle beneath. Specter grunted in pain, but refused to cry out. Blood spurted from an exposed vein.

She tossed the square of flesh aside and giggled in delight. "You don't look so different beneath all the weapons and clothes." Leaning forward, she opened her mouth and let some of his blood spurt inside. "So sweet," she sighed after gulping it down. Looking up at Specter's face, she saw a lone tear running down his cheek. "I won't think any less of you if you scream."

Specter clenched his teeth, "You won't get the satisfaction."

"Very well." Grabbing a small silver container from the table next to her, she flipped open the lid. "You know what I like with my drinks?" She dug her fingers into the container and produced a thick lemon wedge. Holding it up to Specter's face, she smiled devilishly. Setting the container aside, she held the lemon just above the patch of exposed muscle. "If you scream, I'll stop," Caitlin bargained. "I made the same offer to your wife and daughter before I killed them years ago."

Specter turned his face away and closed his eyes.

"Your loss," she sighed. Pressing her fingers against the side of the lemon, she squeezed the juice into his wound.

Specter's body arched up in pain as the acids in the lemon juice worked on his exposed flesh. His lips curled back in a sneer of hatred and pain. Turning his head slowly, he stared directly into Caitlin's eyes, unflinching. As the pain began to subside, he felt his body relax for a moment. Sheets of agony ran down his body from the numerous wounds Caitlin had created. Each felt like a canyon in his flesh, the edges ringed with pain. Taking a deep breath in through his nose, he held it and tried to focus his energy. There were no means of escape he could see. His only victory now would be not to break. He wouldn't let her hear him scream. He would not.

Caitlin shook her head. "Poor baby," she ran her fingers down his cheek. "She looked so much like you. It's a shame."

Specter's face was racked with guilt. "Do not speak of them."

"Your daughter would have grown up to be a lovely woman," Caitlin offered. "It's too bad you had to sign their death sentences."

"No!" Specter growled as a bead of blood rolled down his chest. "You tricked me and killed them in cold blood! Elsa and Isabel were precious to me," he moaned. He strained against his restraints, but could not break free. "Damn you!"

Caitlin smiled and shook her head slowly. "We've been chasing each other in circles for a long time, you and I." Caitlin laughed, "Longer than I care to admit. You kill my vampires; I suck your brother dry. You try to kill me, I kill your family, but I tire of it all. I have bigger concerns to attend to now. You were nothing more than an incentive for me, Marcus. Nothing more than an added bonus."

Specter was shocked to hear Caitlin use his first name. Closing his eyes, he refused to play her game.

Caitlin leaned close and whispered in his ear. "What do you say we end it tonight?" Her feigned look of concern quickly faded into a sneer as she dropped another lemon wedge into his wound. Using the butt of her hand, she ground it into his exposed muscle.

* * *

It didn't look like they had much of a choice after all. Pulling her scythe free of her belt, Callista

352

laid her thumb gently on the trigger. Looking back at Dawn, she nodded. Dawn lifted her hand and looked at the Wraith with a forced smile. Reaching out, Callista grabbed the other woman's hand. Staring into Dawn's eyes, she saw fear and hatred. They were two emotions considered useless and dangerous by the White Guard. Fear slowed your reaction time, while hatred clouded your judgment. She knew Dawn's need for revenge, and while Callista could respect her reasons, she knew if Dawn continued to hold this emotion, it would most likely become a one-way trip for her.

Callista reached out and pressed her hand against Dawn's chest. "Fight because it is right," she whispered. "Not because you are angry." Focusing her energy, she attempted to transfer her calm to Dawn.

Dawn looked down at the Wraith's hand, and then into her eyes. She felt warmth radiating across her chest from Callista's fingertips. As the tendrils of warmth snaked further into her body, Dawn found herself in a growing state of ease. Letting out a long sigh, Dawn became at peace with herself. The events of the past hour remained, but now, somehow, she felt better equipped to deal with them. Her hatred and sadness were gone, leaving only the desire to fight for what was right, to fight for Cane. Understanding Callista's words, and her gift, Dawn nodded in appreciation.

"Let's circle around," Callista whispered. "You take the guard on the left, I'll have a go at the one on the right. Ready?"

Dawn nodded.

Callista grinned and activated her scythe. "Let's go."

* * *

Bishop glanced nervously around. He couldn't see what Kelley and Lydia were sensing. Straining his eyes, he peered into the darkness. Lifting his revolver, he cradled it gently in his hand. The hair on the back of his neck and arms began to stand up. As who or whatever they were moved closer, Bishop felt a chill run down his spine. It felt like someone was standing over his shoulder; so close in fact, he almost imagined he could feel their warm breath on the back of his neck. Shifting uncomfortably, he drew his second revolver and glanced at Kelley.

Kelley and Lydia were peering in different directions. Alarms were sounding in their heads, but they couldn't understand why. They could tell something was out there in the darkness, and it felt as if it was closing on their position from all directions. Rocking onto the balls of her feet, Kelley carefully moved closer to Bishop's position. She reached out and placed a hand on his shoulder to calm and steady herself. Reaching into a satchel that hung across her shoulder, she slowly wrapped her fingers around one of the spell balls she and Lydia had created. Lifting it from her bag, she held it tightly in her hand. She didn't want to have to use it this soon as they were very limited.

A sharp noise to her right quickly caught their attention. All three snapped their heads around to see several tall figures standing around them swathed in black. As Bishop looked at each figure, a smile slowly crossed his face.

* * *

Dawn glanced down at her wrist as she approached the gates, visually reaffirming her weapon was loaded and ready. She didn't want to take on two vampires, even with a wraith at her side, without certain assurances. Stopping just short of the fence, she spotted several tall, brick pillars the iron was tied into. They were spaced about seven feet apart giving her little cover, but at least it was something. Staying low, she moved quickly across the ground holding her breath as weeds and grass crunched beneath her feet. Pressing herself against one of the pillars, she paused, trying to determine if she had been detected.

Glancing over her left shoulder, she could see the outline of the first guard. He was a hulking individual that looked as if he had just stepped off the football field. His white skin was almost luminescent in the pale light. She could see he was holding some kind of weapon, but she couldn't quite determine what it was. Hopefully, she thought, she wouldn't have to. Crouching down, she moved slowly along the ground toward the next pillar. She was now standing less than five feet from the guards. Slowing her breathing, she listened into the darkness. The guard's voices could be heard, but their subject wasn't clear. Peering around the pillar, Dawn scanned for Callista, but found nothing. She didn't want to charge into battle without her, and yet she didn't want to be late either. She would have to take a leap of faith. That scared the hell out of her.

Taking a deep breath, Dawn dove to the next pillar. Her heart was racing in her chest as acid churned in her stomach. She could feel her muscles beginning to spasm slightly from the excessive adrenaline charging rampantly throughout her system. Lifting her face skyward, she stared into the heavens hoping to find her courage but found only uninterested twinkling lights observing from a distance. Clenching her teeth, she decided it was now or never. Pulling back her sleeve, she took one more deep breath and spun around the edge of the pillar.

Bringing her arm down, she aimed her weapon quickly at the nearest vampire. Across the gate, she saw Callista erupting from the darkness, her scythe spinning in her hands. With a devious grin on her face, Dawn tensed the muscles in her arm. One of the wooden darts rocketed away from the weapon.

The linebacker vampire spun on his heels toward Dawn. With a sound that could only be described as a squeal, he stumbled back, clutching at his chest. Dawn's eyes went wide. She had missed his heart. The dart was lodged in his chest, about three inches to the left of her target. With a grunt, the linebacker pulled it free and snapped it between his fingers. His projection quickly faded away revealing the corpse beneath. His golden eyes glowed ominously in the darkness as he crouched down and hissed. Dawn felt her heart sink. Dropping her wrist, she quickly tried to reload the weapon just as Mac had shown her. Her fingers fumbled over the firing mechanism as the vampire leapt toward her. Hearing a click from the weapon,

356

she lifted it again and fired. The vampire fell from midair, as if impacting an invisible wall. Looking down at her opponent, Dawn saw the first few wisps of blue flame erupt from his body. She hadn't missed that time.

Dawn looked up at the other vampire. He and Callista were warily eying each other, waiting for the other to make the first move. Dawn lifted her arm and aimed carefully at the second vampire. "Callista!" Dawn shouted.

"This one's mine," Callista responded without looking up.

Callista whipped her scythe around her body with lightning speed. The weapon was no longer an individual item, it had become a part of her body. Bringing the spinning weapon to a halt horizontally in front of her, she tapped a button on the hilt releasing the blade. The curved, silver blade shimmered in the moonlight. Her opponent wielded a similar weapon, but she could easily see that his proficiency was much lower than hers. His weapon was a long, metal staff with five barbed tips at each end. Moving it to his right hand, he spun it around his waist, doubled back and finished with a flurry around his shoulders. Cradling the weapon in both hands, the vampire smiled exposing his glistening white fangs.

The two combatants charged. Their weapons met in the center with a pronounced clack. Whipping the bottom of her scythe up, Callista broke the stand-off. Stepping back, she avoided a swipe at her head, then another aimed at her torso. Dropping down, she swept the blade of her scythe back around the ankles of her opponent and easily dropped him to the ground. As she moved in for the deathblow, the vampire somersaulted backward and righted himself. Spinning his weapon gingerly in his hands, he taunted the young Wraith.

Callista smiled and shook her head. "You're only prolonging the inevitable."

"Am I?" the vampire growled.

Thrusting his staff forward, he narrowly missed Callista's head. Blocking the attack, Callista spun on her heels and brought her scythe around. Broadsiding the vampire in the chest, she heard several of his ribs crack. Twirling her scythe up and out, she dug the hilt into his chin and pulled free. The vampire staggered back, but quickly regained his balance. His playful attitude was gone. His eyes burned like fire in his skull as he whipped his staff back into position. Lurching forward, he swung his staff around like a bat. Callista blocked the first blow, but couldn't avoid the second. One of the barbs on his staff dug into the soft flesh of her face as the vampire reversed his attack. Ripping his weapon free, he dug an angry gash in the young Wraith's face.

Dropping down to her knees, Callista cradled her wounded flesh. As the blood ran over her fingers, she glanced up into the lust filled eyes of her attacker. Rage gripped her then. He had no intention of finishing her off. He was going to feed from her. Her hand slid away from her face and wrapped around the hilt of her scythe. Twisting it in her balled fists, she pressed her attack. Leaping to her feet, she spun her scythe over her head and

358

brought it hard across the vampire's nose. As his head snapped back, Callista continued her sweep and dug the blade deep into his chest. The vampire gasped in awe at the young woman. Callista drew a deep breath and spit in the creature's face. Pulling her blade free, she spun it in her hands and flipped it up. With one fluid swing, she brought the blade up through the vampire's groin and through his head. As the two halves of his body began to slide apart, blue flame engulfed him. Taking a step back, Callista spun her scythe in a flourish around her body. Bringing the graceful move to an end, she bowed to her defeated opponent. Looking up, she let out a gasp of pain and fell back to the ground. Her hands instantly shot to her face.

Dawn, amazed by the battle she had just seen, rushed to Callista's side. Dropping down to her knees, she pried Callista's hands away from the wound. Wiping some of the blood away with her coat, she stared at the gash. "You'll need stitches."

Callista shook her head, "I'll be fine. I just need a minute here. I don't think we—unghh...."

Callista's body fell hard to the ground. Glancing up, Dawn's eyes met with another vampire holding a baseball bat in his hands. Glancing past him, she could see the gates open and others rushing toward her. Dawn felt her heart sink into her chest.

The vampire tossed the bat away and reached for Dawn. Grabbing her by the shirt, the vampire lifted her into the air and moved toward her throat with his fangs exposed. As Dawn struggled against him, she heard a dull thud. The vampire's eyes widened as he let go and fell backward. Dawn scrambled to her feet and stared down in awe at the blade of a Wraith's scythe embedded in his skull. Snapping her head around, she saw several men and women charging out of the darkness toward the other vampires. Dawn clenched her fist and smiled. Dropping down next to Callista, Dawn slipped her hands around the young woman and lifted her onto her lap.

"It's going to be okay," Dawn assured her as the first of the Wraiths met the vampires in combat.

"What's going on?" Callista asked as she pressed her hand against an ever growing knot on the back of her head.

"The cavalry has arrived," Dawn smiled.

Chapter Twenty-two

Leaning over slightly, she kissed him on the forehead. Her full lips pressed gently against his flesh. Standing straight, she ran her fire red fingernails through his wet hair. She looked at him, not with hatred or vengeance, but with love. He was the culmination of her plans, the fruition of her second existence. He had given her the strength to fight for life and how she loved him for that. A small part of her wished she could share her gift with him, but she knew it would be fleeting. He would never accept her, no matter what form he took.

Specter had passed out moments ago probably, she guessed, from a combination of the blood loss and shock. He was indeed a powerful warrior. Others wouldn't have survived this long. Caitlin silently thanked him for his strength. She was truly enjoying this, and was glad it didn't have to end yet. Her fingers danced along the dark black tattoos on his neck and chest as she slowly moved down his torso. It was odd, she thought, this man was made of nothing more than flesh and bone, yet he contained such stamina and potency. It was a product of his magical bond with the Gwyliad Wriaeth she knew, but he was much more. Even if he were a mere mortal, she knew he would be much the same.

Lifting her hand to her mouth, she bit into her index finger. Blood instantly welled up from the wound and began to flow freely down her hand. Turning her hand down, she placed her finger on Specter's lips. She watched her crimson life flow over his lips and into his mouth. Pulling her hand away, she watched intently for a moment. She smiled as Specter's tongue licked off the blood. It wasn't enough to turn him, just enough to keep him alive a bit longer. She wasn't finished with her torture yet. He still had much to endure, much to pay for.

Shaking her hand, she glanced down at her fingertip. Within a matter of seconds, her self-inflicted wound had healed. Lifting a moist towel from the table, she slowly wiped the dried blood from her fingers. Satisfied, she tossed it away and took a step back. Relaxing her neck, she twisted her head slightly to both sides, stretching her tired muscles. She had been without sleep for three days now and her body was starting to feel it. She rubbed her temples with her fingers. There would be time for sleep once she was dead. She still had much to do. Glancing back at her captive, she made sure he was still tied to the table. After a quick visual examination, she was satisfied. Caitlin turned toward the stairs.

"Mistress?" a voice called out from the darkness.

Caitlin stopped. It was Zeke. She was quickly beginning to regret bringing him over. She knew he would be loyal to her, but she didn't realize he would turn into such a gutless kiss ass. "Yes?"

Zeke charged down the steps, stopping just short of the bottom. He glanced from Caitlin to Specter, then back. "Mistress Caitlin," he breathed, "we have a problem."

Caitlin's gaze remained unwavering. "What is

362

it?" she asked impatiently.

Zeke swallowed hard. "We're under attack."

"What?" Caitlin roared. "By whom?"

"The White Guard."

"You'd better be damn sure before you make that statement," Caitlin spat.

Zeke nodded. "We're sure."

Caitlin looked away from her soldier for a moment. "This is an unwelcome event," she breathed, "but not totally unexpected. What's the state of my army?"

"From what I can make out," Zeke said slowly, "we're holding our ground, but more Wraiths keep appearing out of the darkness. We have no idea how many we're up against."

Caitlin smiled deviously. "This couldn't have worked out any better."

Zeke was slightly taken back by her statement. "Pardon, Mistress?"

"We could have the entire Wraith army on our doorstep right now," Caitlin pointed out. "If we can wipe them out here, we'll have little to no resistance during our upcoming campaign." She reached out and patted Zeke on the shoulder. "We're at war! Send out every vampire in this compound. I want the Earth to be stained blood red in the morning."

* * *

A tall, well-built man stopped and extended his hand. In his opposite hand, he held his scythe at the ready. His long, black coat billowed around him in the crisp night air, while the moonlight shimmered off his shoulder length golden hair. He was dressed all in black, from his shirt down to his thick boots.

A bandolier was stretched across his chest with several wooden stakes tied to it, as well as numerous small containers of holy water. His braid, swaying gently from the left side of his head, hung down barely past his shoulder and was tied with at least ten colored bands. His bearded face showed a mixture of concern and anticipation.

"I'm Brother Barkley," he said with a thick Scottish burr. "We need to move quickly."

Bishop reached up and took the man's hand without a second thought. Rising to his feet, Bishop flashed a crooked grin at the Wraith. "Am I glad to see you." Bishop turned to see several other Wraiths helping Kelley and Lydia to their feet. Turning back to Barkley, Bishop cocked his head to the right, "But why are you here?"

"We were sent to rescue a member of our order," Barkley replied, "as well as bring down Caitlin and her minions."

"To the point," Bishop smirked, "I can respect that. How did you know?"

Barkley smiled, "The Gwyliad Wriaeth know many things."

Bishop nodded, "Cryptic."

Barkley laughed. "Come. We must hurry. Our forces have already engaged the enemy at the front gates. We have to provide backup."

Bishop took a step back and motioned toward the gates with his hands, "Lead the way, Bark."

Barkley glanced at Bishop oddly, but let the conversation die. Whipping his scythe around his body in a flourish, he nodded to the other Wraiths and shot off toward the front gates.

"What do you think of this?" Kelley asked, taking a step closer to Bishop.

"I think our odds have just vastly improved," he stated as he watched the Wraiths tear off into the darkness.

"But what about Cane?" Lydia asked.

Bishop turned and looked at the witch. He hadn't noticed earlier, but her face was drained of color and her hands were shaking. Will appeared to be the only thing holding her up as her body looked to give out at any moment. He quickly rushed to her side and offered support. Placing his hand on her back, he shot a concerned look toward her.

Lydia brushed off the look with her hand. "I'm fine," she said.

"No, you're not," Bishop corrected her. "We need to get you out of here."

Lydia placed her hand on her forehead. "I need to get in there," she stammered. "I can reach him."

Kelley's mouth fell agape. "I knew it!" She rushed toward her mentor. "I could feel it, but I didn't know exactly what it was!"

Bishop glanced curiously at Kelley. "What? What am I missing here?"

"She's bonded herself to Cane," Kelley answered as she placed her hand on Lydia's shoulder. "I could feel her power building earlier, but I didn't know what she was doing." She turned to Lydia. "Why didn't you tell me?"

Lydia shook her head as she took a deep breath. "I couldn't. It was mine to bear alone."

Bishop looked confused. "I don't understand. What are you doing?"

"I," Lydia sighed, "I thought I could bring him back by tapping into his essence." She wiped a bit of sweat from her face with her sleeve, "But the vampire presence in his body has become too strong too quickly." She looked up at her student with tears in her eyes. "I lost him."

"You have to sever the connection," Kelley urged. "He's taking you down with him."

"Will someone explain what's going on?" Bishop growled.

Kelley took a quick breath, "As Cane's essence is dwindling, so is Lydia's. She bonded her spirit with his," she looked back at her teacher, "he's dying and taking her with him."

The gravity of the situation gripped Bishop. He turned to Lydia again, "You have to let go!"

Lydia shook her head. "I can't."

"You can't die," Kelley pleaded.

Lydia's eyes were wide. "I still sense some good in him."

"All right, Luke," Bishop said in frustration, "Cane has gone to the Dark Side and become Darth Vader. There's no bringing him back."

"They did in Return of the Jedi," Kelley replied.

Bishop closed his eyes and shook his head. "You're not helping." He slowly returned his gaze to Lydia. "Callista told us there's no way to turn him back. He's gone," he lowered his voice as it bubbled with emotion. A lump welled up in his throat, "He's dead."

"I—" Lydia's eyes started to roll back in her head as she toppled to the ground.

Dropping down, Bishop caught her before she hit. Cradling her in his arms, he brushed her hair from her face. Running his fingers down to her throat, he checked for a pulse. He glanced up with terror in his eyes at Kelley, "We're losing her."

Kelley hit her knees. Pressing her hands to the sides of Lydia's face, she focused her energy. "We have to sever the link."

"I don't know what to do," Bishop admitted.

Kelley lifted her hand toward Bishop. "Just take my hand and focus."

Bishop slipped his fingers along Kelley's palm as he slowly took her hand. He could instantly feel the electricity between them. It surged up his arm, through his neck, and into his face. It was warm and creamy as it bubbled through his body. A sense of ease settled in. Taking a deep breath, he closed his eyes and focused on Lydia.

"Very good," Kelley whispered. "Keep focusing on her well-being and safety. I'm going to try and break the link." Leaning over, Kelley placed her forehead on Lydia's chin. Using every method Lydia had taught her, Kelley sank deeply into a meditative state. The darkness in her mind was slowly replaced with shimmering, dancing colors as her mind began to visualize the problem. Through the colors, an image of Lydia and Cane began to emerge. She saw them both, withered and old, walking away hand in hand. Kelley began to reach for the two, but stopped. There was no pain here. This is what they both wanted. She slowly began to withdraw from Lydia's mind.

A tidal wave of color washed over Lydia and

Cane as they disappeared into the distance. As Kelley drew her hand back, she watched the two go; knowing full well that two of the most important people in her life had just died. The landscape around her changed instantly. The colors drained away leaving only blackness. Kelley felt a sharp pain surge through her mind. As she reached out, she realized it hadn't come from her or Lydia. Much like a swimmer surging toward the surface after a dive, Kelley struggled toward consciousness. A sense of fear gripped her as another wave of pain washed over her.

Snapping her eyes open, she glanced to her right. Bishop was gone. Reaching down to Lydia, she checked again for breathing and a pulse. She closed her eyes quickly. Lydia was gone. Turning away, Kelley leapt to her feet and searched the darkness. To her dismay, she spotted a body stretched out on the ground about ten feet away. She instantly began rushing toward him, but skidded to a stop. There was another form hunkered over him. Her eyes widened. She knew instantly what had happened. During their meditation, a vampire had snatched Bishop and drug him away. Reaching into her satchel, Kelley wrapped her fingers around one of the small magical bags Lydia and she had created. Winding up like a baseball pitcher, she whipped the black bag over her shoulder toward the vampire.

The creature looked up at Kelley with blood on his mouth just as the bag hit. It impacted the vampire just above his left shoulder and burst open. Its contents sprayed over the vampire and began to mix with the air. A chemical/magical reaction happened then. A burst of white light erupted from the bag and tore through the vampire. As it tried to lift its arms in defense, the light obliterated the creature. Its skin began to peel and crack as it burned. Wisps of cinder flew up into the air as its body was reduced to nothing more than a pile of ash.

As the light began to subside, Kelley moved quickly toward her fallen friend. Crouching down, Kelley pressed her hand to his cheek. There she detected life. The vampire had not had enough time to feed completely. "Bishop?" Turning his head, she saw two deep puncture wounds on the right side of his neck.

"Shit," she gasped. "He didn't drink the vampire's blood," she muttered repeatedly. "Bishop?"

Tearing a strip of fabric from the bottom of her shirt, she wrapped it around his throat to quell the bleeding. Slipping her hand under his back, she lifted him into a sitting position. "Bish?"

Slowly at first, his eyes opened. He glanced around in a daze before settling on Kelley. "What...?" His hand slowly moved up to his neck. A look of shock and fear grew across his face as his fingers glanced over the painful wound. In a panic, he tried to stand up, but found his body too weak. He toppled back to the ground.

Kelley placed her hands on his shoulders, "Sit still. You're going to be okay. You just need to rest for a moment."

Bishop shook his head furiously. "We need to

get in there."

"You're not going anywhere," Kelley commanded him.

Bishop let out a grunt as he rubbed his fingers over the bloody wound on his neck. His mind suddenly became aware of what they had been trying to do. "Lydia? How's Lydia? Did we do it?"

Kelley placed her hand gently on Bishop's cheek. Closing her eyes, she slowly shook her head.

Bishop's head fell forward in defeat. "We can't let them take anymore," he said angrily. "We have to draw the line here. No further!"

Kelley nodded.

"Help me up," Bishop grunted.

Against her better judgment, Kelley stood and helped her friend onto his feet. Bishop swayed uneasily for a moment as he tried to catch his balance. Gripping onto Kelley's shoulder, he was finally able to steady himself. Taking a deep breath in through his nose, Bishop slowly exhaled it through his mouth. He turned to Kelley with an intense look of determination on his face. No more words needed to be spoken. Kelley understood. As the two started for the front gate, Kelley pulled another black bag from her satchel. Stopping a few feet away from Lydia, she tossed it on her body. As the bag broke open, her body was instantly engulfed in flame. Kelley would not let her teacher, her mentor and her friend, be fed on by a vampire, even in death. As she watched Lydia's body burn, she felt a single tear fall from her eye. Turning, she pulled a wooden stake from her bag. She nodded at Bishop, who had drawn both his revolvers. The two charged toward the front gates.

* * *

Dawn watched in awe as thousands of Wraiths cut a swath of death through the center of the vampires. They looked like nothing more than dark blurs on the landscape as their long coats blew behind them and their scythes whipped through the bodies of their enemies. The courtyard was awash with an ominous blue light as the vampires fell and burned. Moving ever deeper into the compound, the Wraiths found thicker resistance. Their pace slowed as hundreds of vampires swarmed from all sides. Quickly, what was an offensive push, had become more of a defensive stand as the vampires circled around.

Dawn found herself near the center of the Wraiths with Callista at her side. She watched two Wraiths fall in a shower of blood to her right, their scythes clattering to the ground. Spinning on her heels, she scooped up one of the fallen scythes and reactivated it. The blade sprung to life as Dawn flipped it in her hands. She could instantly feel the power of the scythe. A warm sensation washed up her arms from her fingertips to her shoulders and quickly crept into every corner of her body. This was no mere weapon, she realized it was as if the scythe had a soul and personality of its own. It wasn't just a Wraith's weapon, it was their partner in combat, guiding and helping them. Wrapping her fingers tightly around the decorated hilt, she felt powerful and yet nimble. Snapping her head up, she rejoined the battle with a new sense of resolve.

Dancing to the right, Dawn avoided the

downswing of a vampire's sword. Moving her scythe around lithely, she pressed the creature's weapon to the ground. Bringing her arm around, she fired a wooden bolt point-blank into the vampire's heart. The creature shrieked in pain as blue flame erupted from the impact. Clutching its chest, it fell to the ground. Lifting her scythe, Dawn spun around and easily took the head of a second charging vampire. Glancing to her right, she saw another Wraith fall under the attack of several vampires. Blood splattered from the warrior onto her face. Dawn's gaze hardened. Screaming, she charged toward the vampires with her scythe raised. Cutting through a third vampire, she joined the fray.

Callista, meanwhile, had a problem of her own. After striking down a nearby vampire, three had taken its place. She looked into the golden eyes of the two men and a woman. Behind her, she could hear the clink of the other Wraiths' weapons. Lifting her scythe, she spun it in her hands like a baton, taunting the vampires. With a smirk, she slammed the butt of her scythe into the ground and drew a line in the dirt. She nodded to her opponents, daring them to cross it.

The first vampire charged. Bringing her blade up, she caught him in the midsection and cleaved him in two. For good measure, she stabbed the sharpened wood butt of her scythe deep into his torso as he fell. Spinning, she pulled her weapon free. Cradling it horizontally in her hands, she whipped it up and caught the female vampire in the nose. As she stumbled back, the male vampire pressed his attack. Slashing with his claws, he tore through Callista's coat, but narrowly missed her flesh. Pulling her coat free, Callista whacked the vampire up the side of his head with her scythe.

Spinning, Callista brought her scythe around and buried the blade deep in the female vampire's torso. The woman screamed in pain as she wrapped her hands around the hilt of the weapon. Callista struggled to free her weapon but out of the corner of her eye, she saw the male charging again. Reaching her hand into her jacket, her fingers snatched a silver ring on the side of her belt. Letting go of the scythe, she pulled on the ring exposing the piano wire it was attached to. Pirouetting, the Wraith brought the wire up and around the creature's throat. Clenching the opposite end of the wire, she pulled away. The wire tightened and easily severed the vampire's head beneath her enhanced strength. His body erupted into flame and cinder as it toppled.

Reaching through the flame, Callista grabbed her scythe again and tore it free of her opponent's abdomen. Spinning it over her head, she brought it down just as the last of the cinders cleared the air and sliced through the female's throat. Blood spurted out like a geyser as the vampire fell to the ground. Walking casually forward, Callista lifted her scythe as she stood over the vampire. Her golden eyes grew wide. With one powerful strike, Callista brought her scythe down and cleaved its heart.

* * *

Cane ambled through the almost empty house. His thirst quenched, he found there was no need to

373

hurry. Walking into the living room, he stopped and fell into one of the padded leather couches. He lifted his feet and propped them on the remains of the glass coffee table. Tossing his head back, he started to wonder where the other vampires were. This room had been a den of activity just moments ago, and now it had fallen almost completely silent. Turning his head to the left, he spotted a blue glow outside the window.

Standing slowly, he moved to the window. Pressing his hands against the glass, he watched the battle raging outside. He knew instantly his kin were fighting against the Wraiths. His new genetic programming told him he should hate these people, but he couldn't seem to care. He watched Wraith and vampire fall amidst a sea of flashing blades, but felt no compulsion to render aid. This was not his war.

Pushing away from the window, he heard footsteps behind him. Moving quickly across the room, he ducked down behind a chair in the corner. He would not die for some ancient vampire or Wraith's ideology. Peeking out from behind the chair, he watched Caitlin and Zeke move into the living room. His gut instinct was to stand at his sire's side, but something deep in the back of his mind kept him from revealing his location. Both vampires should be able to sense his presence, but Cane hoped they weren't paying enough attention. He stared at the face of his creator. It seemed to be filled with doubt and anger. The events unfolding outside must have caught her off guard, he thought. It was this distraction that would allow him his escape. While others were busily fighting their ancient war, he could slip into the night unnoticed. Cane smiled as Caitlin and Zeke retreated from the room.

As Cane stood from his hiding spot, a hand reached out and grabbed him by the shoulder. He quickly spun around and stared into her eyes. All at once, he found himself very calm. With a mere beckoning of her hand, he followed her out of the room.

* * *

Bishop and Kelley moved quickly behind a pack of Wraiths as they chewed through the opposition. His holsters drawn, Bishop took aim on every vampire that threatened to break through the Wraith line, but was careful to conserve his ammunition. Mac had only provided him with so many bullets. Kelley was situated slightly ahead and to his right. Still clutching her stake, she had a look of grim determination on her face. As Brother Barkley cut a swath of death ahead of him, Bishop saw the circle of Wraiths come into view. He could see Dawn and Callista fighting near the edge of the pack.

Spinning to his right, he pulled the trigger just as a pair of golden eyes appeared out of the darkness. The vampire clutched its chest and fell forward as blue flame overcame it. Glancing over his shoulder, he saw the first of his team of Wraiths fall to a vampire. The line tightened and continued to move, intent on helping their brothers and sisters trapped in the center. As the vampire leaned in to feed on the Wraith, Kelley threw herself on its back.

The vampire reared up and clawed at Kelley, trying desperately to throw her. Leaning back, Kelley plunged her stake into the vampire's back. The creature screamed and bucked, but it was already too late. Jumping away, Kelley watched the creature fall. Rolling onto her feet, she turned and looked around in fear. The Wraiths hadn't stopped and waited for her. She and Bishop were alone.

Moving to Bishop's side, they saw the wall of fangs and claws folding in on them. Drawing his second pistol, Bishop began firing wildly into the crowd taking out as many vampires as he could. With her back pressed to Bishop's, Kelley dug her fingers into her satchel. She needed to wait for the right moment. Her muscles tensed. Reaching his arm over her shoulder, Bishop fired in two directions simultaneously. His advantage was quickly fading as his revolvers held only six shots each and he didn't have time to reload. Firing again, he saw another vampire fall shrieking to the ground. Glancing over Kelley's shoulder, he dropped another, but there were just too many. Three shots remained between both revolvers.

Snapping his head around, he spotted another vampire charging in from the crowd. Bishop tried to pull the trigger, but the vampire was too fast. Thrusting Bishop's arm into the air, the revolver fired wildly into the air. As Bishop pulled his other arm around to fire again, the vampire pulled the revolver free of his grasp and tossed it away. Now holding both of Bishop's arms, the vampire opened his mouth and leaned in. Struggling to break free, Bishop delivered a vicious head butt to the bridge of the vampire's nose. As the creature instinctively recoiled, Bishop seized the moment and kicked the vampire directly in the groin. Letting go of his arms, the vampire dropped to his knees and doubled over. Quickly popping his knuckles, Bishop balled up his fists and threw a right across the vampire's chin, knocking him bleeding to the ground.

Kelley pulled her second light grenade from her satchel. Holding it tightly in her hand, she stared unblinking at the mob of vampires streaming toward her. She knew the range on her magical weapon was limited, but it should kill enough, and drive back even more so she and Bishop could rejoin the rest of the Wraiths. Out of the corner of her eye, she saw one of the vampires make his move. Claws outstretched, he dove in and knocked Bishop and Kelley apart. Kelley stumbled to the ground, the light grenade knocked from her grasp. The small black pouch tumbled to the ground, but didn't burst open. As Kelley lifted to her hands and knees, a swarm of vampires followed the first. A female hit her squarely in the back and knocked her to the ground. As Kelley struggled toward the grenade, she felt the vampire's hands on her shoulders.

Bishop toppled over the monster in front of him. Somersaulting onto his feet, he came face to face with a second swarm. Swinging around, he connected with the first vampire's face. It stumbled back, but the second took no time in retaliating. Grabbing Bishop's outstretched arm, he swung the young paranormal investigator around into the waiting arms of another attacker. Snaking his arms around Bishop's neck and waist, it lifted him easily off the ground. Dropping down to one knee, the creature brought Bishop crashing down. Bishop howled in pain as his spine twisted unnaturally over the vampire's knee. Rolling Bishop onto the ground, he then leaned in for the kill.

Kelley cringed as the claws of the female vampire dug into the flesh of her back. Her mind instantly flashed back to a set of glowing red eyes in the darkness. She could feel the Phantom clawing at her chest as it toyed with her and her girlfriend…. Rage gripped her then. Pressing her palms to the ground, Kelley pushed off and flipped the vampire from her back. Grabbing the legs of another vampire, she toppled him to the ground. On her hands and knees, she skittered ahead and reached for the grenade, but the female vampire knocked her to the ground again.

"I have had," Kelley growled as she snatched the grenade up in her hand and rolled over, "enough of you."

Grabbing the woman by the throat, Kelley dug her fingers into the vampire's soft flesh. The vampire instinctively opened its mouth and gasped for air. Stuffing the grenade into her mouth, Kelley pulled her hand away and punched the vampire sharply beneath the chin causing her to bite down. The woman's eyes widened a moment before she exploded.

Kelley looked up to see dozens of vampires around them being incinerated by the light. Jumping up, she grabbed Bishop and helped him to his feet. Lifting his arm over her shoulders, she made her way through the folds of burning vampires toward

378

the Wraiths. Stopping just short of the Wraiths, a burning hand reached out and grabbed her by the ankle. Spinning around, she spotted the disfigured vampire holding her. Kicking hard, she easily knocked its head off and sent it rolling along the ground. As the vampire fell to dust, Kelley moved into the center of the Wraiths and dropped. She cradled Bishop in her arms, pressing her forehead to his.

"Can you feel your legs?" she asked quickly.

Bishop nodded. "They hurt."

"That's a good sign," Kelley said with a sigh. "I thought I'd lost you."

Bishop laughed quietly, "I'm not that easy to get rid of." He lifted one of his hands to hers. "Listen, I know this may not be the right time, but—"

Kelley shook her head, "I know."

Bishop's heart was pounding in his chest. He couldn't tell if it was from his wounds, or Kelley's touch. "Where do we go from here?"

Kelley ran her hand over his forehead and through his messy hair. "I," she stammered, "I do love you, but I'm not ready for that kind of relationship."

"What does that mean?"

"I just can't," Kelley sighed. She pressed her lips to his head. "After all you've done for me..." she felt her words stall in her throat. "I owe you my life."

"But?" Bishop swallowed.

"But," Kelley started, "I have responsibilities I can't ignore. Lydia helped bring me back from the brink of death and taught me a new way to look at the world. I owe it to her to continue the traditions she instilled in me. I have to go back to Seattle and take over her coven."

"You're choosing her over me?" Bishop asked incredulously.

"I'm not choosing anything," Kelley quickly corrected. "I'm doing what I feel is right. I'm sorry."

Bishop let his head fall forward with a long sigh. "I love you too, and I want you to be happy. Do what you need to do." He squeezed her hand tightly, but continued to look away. "Let's finish this."

Kelley nodded with a soft smile. Looking up, she saw the tide beginning to turn in the Wraith's favor. The warriors pushed deeper into the vampires, all the while stepping over the bodies of fallen comrades. Digging into her satchel, Kelley grabbed her remaining two light grenades and flung them into the surrounding vampires.

Chapter Twenty-three

Caitlin watched the battle disintegrating from her second floor balcony. Wringing the rails with her hands, she cursed under her breath as vampire after vampire fell to the blades of the Wraiths. Turning away from the battle, she slammed her fist through the wall as she moved inside. Grabbing a nearby table, she flung it angrily across the room into a cabinet of fine china. She suddenly stopped. She wasn't alone. Holding her position, she licked the air but couldn't tell if it was a vampire or Wraith. She wondered if Zeke were possibly standing guard outside her door, or if the Wraiths had broken through and gained access to the house. Carefully, she began to move toward the door. Pressing her ear to the wood, she listened to the hall outside. Nothing. Pushing away, she carefully retreated back into the room. She had to find a way out. This location was no longer safe for her, but she would not leave without her prizes. She had to round up Cane and Specter. A war was pointless without the spoils, she told herself.

Moving quickly toward a second door in the room, Caitlin felt a twinge of recognition in her senses. There was definitely someone near, and it was someone she knew, but with all the scents in the courtyard wafting through the house, she had a difficult time discerning who it was. She steeled herself. It made no difference that she was more than capable of taking on anything thrown at her. She had lived far too long and survived far too many battles to go off and cower in the darkness.

Puling open the door, she stepped into the adjacent room and stopped. There, standing in front of her, was Achaica. Her hands were clasped behind her back. Standing behind her was Cane, looking vacant and unaware of the situation. Achaica took a step forward, "Mistress."

Caitlin took a cautious step toward Achaica. "What the hell is going on here?" Something was wrong.

"I wanted to have a word with you," Achaica replied. "In private."

Cane cocked his head to the right. "Beware the Ides of March," he muttered almost as if in a daze.

"What do you want?" Caitlin's senses were on high alert.

"A few of us find your war very distasteful," Achaica replied. "We do not think you, or any of us for that matter, should be warring against the humans. There is no logic to this. We feel it is nothing more than warmongering on your behalf. You remember the old saying 'absolute power corrupts absolutely', don't you?"

"You have no right to question my actions!" Caitlin yelled. "Yours is but to follow."

"Not anymore," Achaica replied coolly. "You've gone too far this time, Caitlin."

"Why are you standing up for those glorified monkeys?" Caitlin growled. "We are superior!"

"That may be true," Achaica nodded, "but we don't want things to change. All we have to do is retain the subterfuge we don't exist and the humans pay us no mind. We are free to do what we want. We will not allow you to throw that away."

"Insolence," Caitlin spat. "How dare you? I created you!"

"It is true I owe my immortality to you," Achaica replied, "but you do not own me."

Caitlin's eyes melted to a bright yellow. "I will tear you limb from limb for this, Achaica. You don't realize what you have cost yourself here tonight."

Achaica shook her head, "Look out your window! Your war is over before it even began! You have failed!"

Caitlin started to charge for Achaica in a blind rage. It was exactly what Achaica had hoped for. Glancing across the room, she nodded to her accomplice. As Caitlin threw the first punch into Achaica's midsection, Ice appeared out of the shadows wielding Specter's scythe. She had crossed the floor and was starting her downswing in less than a second thanks to her preternatural speed. The blade of the scythe dug deeply into Caitlin's back. The ancient vampire howled in agony as Ice worked the weapon deeper into the wound.

Caitlin doubled over as she glanced behind her. "Et tu, Ice?"

"What?" Ice asked quickly.

Caitlin shook her head. "What are they teaching you kids in school today?" In one motion, Caitlin had spun around and lifted Ice from the floor by her throat. "It's Shakespearean," Caitlin replied. Reaching her arm around, Caitlin ripped the blade from her back and tossed it across the floor. "I'm very disappointed in you, Ice. I thought you would be my new right-hand. I could have offered you things you never dreamed of."

Ice struggled in Caitlin's grip, but could not respond.

"It's a shame," Caitlin added. "Well," an evil grin crossed her face, "goodbye."

Pulling her hand away quickly, Ice fell to the floor. Her hands reached for her throat to find her windpipe missing. The young vampire toppled to the ground in a heap, her blood washing over the hardwood floors. Stepping forward, Caitlin pressed her foot against the back of Ice's head. With one step, she crushed the young woman's skull.

Turning, she watched Achaica lifting herself off the floor. "What did you do to Cane?"

Achaica stood and took several uneasy steps back. "Trance," she answered. "Nothing more."

Caitlin rushed across the floor and pinned Achaica to the wall. "Why?"

"He was an innocent. He did not deserve this," Achaica said, turning away from Caitlin. "I wanted him to be here when you fell, then I would take his life myself and ease his pain. I wanted to give him redemption."

"Still passing judgment," Caitlin whispered, "even where you are so close to death."

"I have nothing else."

Caitlin nodded. "That's right." Opening her mouth, she bit into the flesh of Achaica's throat and began to drink, taking back the immortality she had once given. Tossing her head back, she licked the last bit of Achaica's blood from her lips. Stepping back, she watched her friend slide to the floor, dead. They had spent many lifetimes together. It was a shame to lose her this way, but all things must end.

Caitlin turned to Cane. Snapping her fingers in front of his face to get his attention, she stared deeply into his eyes. "Come back," she commanded.

Cane stumbled back and pressed his hands against the wall to find balance. Glancing around nervously, his eyes finally settled on Caitlin. "What's going on here?" He looked down to see the bodies of two vampires.

"It doesn't matter," Caitlin said quickly. "Come, we have work to do."

* * *

Callista and Dawn stood near the edge of the Wraiths. With a click of a button, both retracted their scythes. They watched the bodies of vampires writhe as they burned. Kelley's light grenades had obliterated everything inhuman in a twenty-meter radius, and those still alive were retreating rapidly. Squads of Wraiths had broken off and were pursuing the stragglers. Turning back to the Wraiths, the two women surveyed the aftermath. Scores of Wraiths lay dead throughout the courtyard, while the once well-kept yard and shrubberies now burned. It had become a war zone. In the distance, they could hear the approaching sirens of police and fire crews. Their time was dwindling. They had to finish this now.

Glancing through the remaining Wraiths, Dawn spotted Kelley and Bishop sitting on the ground near the center. Kelley was cradling Bishop in her arms. Dawn felt her heart jump. Stowing her scythe on her belt, she rushed toward her teammates.

385

Dropping down next to Kelley, Dawn placed her hand on the young woman's shoulder. "What happened?"

"Same thing that happened to everyone else," Kelley replied as she ran her hand through Bishop's hair. "We took casualties."

"Is he okay?" Dawn asked nervously.

Bishop glanced up and nodded. "I'm going to be okay."

Dawn let out a long sigh of relief. Leaning over, she hugged her partner.

"Just a little battered and bruised," Kelley said with a smile.

"Thank God," Dawn breathed. She glanced up at Kelley, "Oh, and thank the Goddess."

Kelley nodded.

"Where's Lydia?" Callista asked.

Kelley turned away. "She didn't make it."

Dawn bowed her head, "I'm so sorry."

"Thank you," Kelley forced a smile as a tear fell from her eye.

"We're near the end," Dawn said slowly. "I don't ask any of you to go with me."

"We know," Kelley answered, "but we are anyway."

Dawn glanced down at Bishop.

"Count me in."

Then she turned to Callista.

"Can't go without a Wraith at your side."

Dawn smiled. "Thank you all. The sacrifices we've made here have been great, but we came this far, we have to finish it."

Just as her words were spoken, two Wraiths

erupted from the house. "She's gone!"

Callista turned and looked at her brethren. "Who?"

"Caitlin," the Wraith replied, "and there is no sign of Brother Specter! The house is empty!"

Dawn quickly turned to Callista and placed her hand on the Wraith's shoulder. "She couldn't have made it that far. Can you track her?"

Callista nodded and set off through the courtyard with the remaining members of the OPR in tow.

Chapter Twenty-four

The three vampires moved quickly into the night. Caitlin, Zeke and Cane made no noise as they avoided the edge of the city and turned into the desert. The sun would be up soon and they needed a place to rest. Reaching the top of a dune, they spotted the Giza Plateau and the three great pyramids rising majestically from the desert sands. This was not the first time Caitlin had set foot in Giza. She had witnessed great empires of the sun rising and falling, even stood in the presence of the great boy-king, Tutankhamen, on one hot, windswept night. She could recall great cities stretching out over the plateau, their inspired architecture reaching toward the sky and the gods they held so dear. All of that was gone now. Time had a way of washing away entire civilizations, no matter how great or prosperous they were in their own time.

Caitlin turned and glanced back over her remaining soldiers. Cane was standing directly behind her, making no effort to hide his vampire nature. His golden eyes glowed ominously in the moonlight. Zeke brought up the rear with her prize slung over his shoulder. Specter had made no movements thus far, and his breathing had become shallow and weak. She wondered if she had gone too far in her earlier torture sessions. His life was hers alone to take. She would not allow time to take its course. Patting Cane on the back, Caitlin pointed down the hill toward the pyramids. Cane nodded and started down the slope with Zeke directly behind him. Caitlin took a moment to revel in the glory of the ancient buildings. They were basked in a yellowish hue thanks to giant floodlights situated at the bottom of each. Even in the middle of the night, the Egyptian government wouldn't miss a chance to exploit these once great monuments.

Carefully moving down the dune, Caitlin followed her companions onto the plateau. As she moved closer to the pyramids, she was careful to avoid any human contact. The last thing she needed right now was to run into one of the overgrown monkeys. Her mood was foul enough as is. She would probably have to tear them apart just to satisfy herself. Maybe she would have to anyway. That would make her feel better. She cursed under her breath. Her insurrection ended before it even had a chance to begin. Most of the vampires with even the slightest hint of her blood now lay dead or dusted on the ground around her compound. It would be difficult to raise another army in such a short amount of time. Nevertheless, she had the time. She would wait and try again.

Hitting the bottom of the dune, she skidded to a stop. Zeke and Cane were holding steady just outside the perimeter of the floodlights. There was security on the grounds protecting against exactly what she was trying to do. It would be simple to charge in and force her way into the pyramid, but that would set off too many alarms and probably draw the Wraiths. No sense fighting a battle she couldn't win. She would have to use cunning and guile to achieve her goals now. Tapping Zeke on the shoulder, she pointed to a visible gap in the security.

The young vampire nodded. He easily altered his mental veil to match the surrounding sand and sky. He looked like nothing more than an odd reflection of light standing before Caitlin. Reaching over, the ancient vampire took Cane by the hand, altering his projection as well.

Now shrouded, the three raced across the desert floor toward the Great Pyramid. Caitlin knew this area intimately. During her stay in Cairo, Achaica had taken her on walks around the pyramids under the full moon to help aid in her recovery. It was during those nights that Achaica had become much more than just a nursemaid; she had become a true companion. Caitlin had confided in her creation all the lost secrets of the vampire world while trying to impart her knowledge to a new generation. Achaica, in exchange, had helped Caitlin recover her health and strength and in many cases, given her the will to go on.

Achaica....

Caitlin lowered her eyes to the ground. What had she done? The woman she was most indebted to was dead by her own hand. Caitlin returned her gaze forward. She would not waste time or tears on a woman who threatened treason and preached revolution to others in her order. No matter who this woman was to Caitlin, her punishment fit the crime. There would be no new world order as long as women like Achaica stood in her way.

Reaching the towering temple, Caitlin led the way toward the entrance. Coming around the corner of the pyramid, she climbed up on the first of the great stone blocks. Pressing her back to the wall, she waited as a member of the security force walked directly under her. Pushing back his cap, he glanced up in her direction, then moved on without hesitation. Moving further up the pyramid, Caitlin stopped just short of the entrance to the Great Hall. A lone guard stood there silently reading a magazine under the bright floodlights. Caitlin motioned for Zeke and Cane to stay put while she took care of this.

Moving up the last stone block, Caitlin dusted herself off and moved around to the back of the guard. Lifting her hands, she wrapped one around his mouth and the other around his chest and arms. The guard struggled, but it was to no avail. Still invisible, Caitlin dug her fangs into the man's neck and drank. Two trickles of blood ran down his throat from the puncture wounds. Caitlin felt him go limp in her arms. Dropping him to the ground, she quickly motioned for her companions. Zeke was first inside the pyramid, while Caitlin and Cane stood guard. As Caitlin moved toward the entrance, she pointed down at the dead guard. Cane nodded. Grabbing him by the wrists, he pulled him inside the pyramid.

Dropping their mental projections, the vampires walked slowly up through the Grand Hall. In modern times, stairs and handrails had been installed, as well as work lights along the ceiling. They moved slowly toward the King's chamber at the top. Cane marveled at the craftsmanship of the hall. During his life, this had been one of the many places he had wanted to experience. Now he found himself walking through the hall dragging the dead body of a guard. Dropping the man's hands, he stared down at the corpse. There was no need to carry it further. Caitlin had only wanted it pulled out of sight. Turning, he moved quickly to catch up with his companions.

The three stopped at the top of the hall and stared back down. Finally away from the approaching sun, Caitlin breathed a sigh of relief. She knew in recent years the pyramid had been closed off to tourists, so she and her companions should be able to find rest in this ancient place. She found herself slightly concerned about renovation crews, but it was nothing she couldn't handle if pressed. Turning, she stared at the door into the King's chamber. Pushing inside, she gazed at the half built pedestal the Pharoah's sarcophagus would have rested upon. A lone light in the ceiling shone down over the flat surface of the stone, creating an almost heavenly appearance. The rest of this large chamber was dark, concealing any secrets it might yet keep.

"Took you long enough."

Caitlin snapped her head around and scanned the darkness. Sniffing the air, she detected the presence of several humans...and a Wraith. Caitlin growled in anger.

"We were beginning to wonder if you were going to show up," Dawn said, stepping out of the shadows. "We hate to wait."

Caitlin cocked her head slightly and smiled. "I apologize," she said slowly. "I had no idea we were expected."

Bishop, Kelley and Callista moved out of the

shadows to join Dawn. Each held their weapons at the ready with a stern look upon their faces. Callista snapped open her scythe as Bishop folded his leather coat back behind his holsters. Kelley held her stake tightly in her left hand while her other was deep inside the satchel that hung over her shoulder.

"We tracked you to the Giza Plateau," Bishop smiled. "Once there, it was just simple logic that you would pick the largest and most grand place to hide out for the night. You're very predictable."

"Am I?" Caitlin asked with a bemused grin. "At least I have good taste." She glanced over her shoulder to see Zeke laying Specter on the ground. Cane was inching toward the exit. She returned her attention to Dawn. "Is this the best you could do, a boy, a Wraith child, a Witch Apprentice, and you? You truly expect to defeat me?"

"I've seen stranger things," Dawn smiled. "Is that enough witty banter?"

Caitlin nodded, "I think so."

Dawn snapped open her scythe and charged toward the ancient vampire. The two met with a resounding thud in the center of the room. Whipping her weapon around and up, Dawn sliced through Caitlin's left knee. Ignoring the pain, Caitlin struck back. Throwing a punch across her body, she knocked Dawn hard to the ground. Recovering quickly, Dawn kicked forward and landed her foot directly on the wound she had just created in Caitlin's leg. The ancient vampire stumbled back clutching her bleeding limb, her long red hair spilling over her face. Snapping her head up, she glared at Dawn with burning yellow eyes.

Callista turned her attention to the other two vampires in the chamber. The third, a man she recognized as Cane, was heading quickly for the exit. Apparently his loyalties lie somewhere other than with Caitlin. Bringing her scythe over her head, she whipped it hard across the room. The blade hit the wall and dug in, blocking the exit. Cane stumbled back and turned his attention to Callista. Growling in protest, he charged into battle. Stepping around Bishop and Kelley, Callista stepped forward and intercepted Cane and easily knocked him to the ground. Dropping down on top of him, she pulled a stake from her coat and lifted it into the air.

Bishop snapped his head around to see Callista. "No! Wait!" he shouted. "Don't kill him!" Diving forward, Bishop knocked the Wraith to the ground.

Cane leapt to his feet and spun on his heels. Baring his fangs and yellow eyes, he hissed angrily. Lashing out, he drew his claws across Bishop's face. Bishop fell back coddling his bleeding cuts, while Callista worked under Cane's next attack and got to her feet. Standing tall, she dropped her shoulder and charged the vampire, sending both into the king's pedestal.

Zeke had moved quickly across the room. Changing his appearance in midstride, he now wore an ankle length black leather trench coat and black leather gloves with silver spikes on the knuckles. Lifting Bishop from the floor, he tossed him across the room and into the far wall. Bishop hit and crumpled to the ground. Snapping his head around, Zeke zeroed in on Kelley, who was still standing in the corner clutching her stake. Zeke easily charged in and pinned the Witch against the wall. As Kelley struggled, he opened his mouth and showed his fangs. Leaning in, he bit forcefully into her throat. Kelley moaned in agony as he pushed his fangs deeper. The stake fell from her hand. She felt her heart beginning to slow as her life was drained away.

Scooping her scythe from the floor, Dawn charged Caitlin again. Spinning it around her body, she brought it powerfully down and sliced through Caitlin's midsection. Reversing her attack, she brought the blade down toward Caitlin's head. Reaching up, Caitlin stopped the blade between her hands and moved it away from her head. As the two combatants struggled for control of the weapon, Dawn saw the hilt beginning to bend. Letting go with one hand, she quickly popped her hand under the weapon and knocked it out of Caitlin's grasp and into the air. The weapon flipped end over end above the two. Grabbing the hilt as it came down, Dawn ripped the blade down and into Caitlin's chest. The vampire stumbled back as blood spurted from the new wound. Reaching up with a grunt, Caitlin tore the blade from her flesh. Holding the scythe in her hands, she stared up at Dawn with a sneer. Standing straight, she snapped the scythe over her leg and tossed it to the floor.

Trying to shake the stars from his eyes, Bishop pressed his hand against the wall and stood up. Glancing across the room, he watched in horror as Zeke fed from Kelley. Drawing his revolver, he held his breath and squeezed the trigger. The bullet whizzed across the room and exploded into Zeke's skull. The force of the impact knocked him away from Kelley and into the wall. Both he and Kelley slid to the floor. Charging across the room, Bishop pressed his foot against Zeke's chest and stared down at the vampire. The entire right side of his head had been blown open by the shot. Blood, skull fragments and brain matter oozed down the wall above him.

Bishop pulled his foot away and turned his attention to Kelley. Dropping down to his knees, he pressed his fingers to her throat and searched for a pulse. He breathed a small sigh of relief as he found one. Pulling the makeshift bandage away from his own throat, he gently wrapped it around hers. Leaning over, he kissed Kelley on the forehead. Bishop's head suddenly snapped back in pain. Looking down, he saw the pointed end of a stake jutting from his abdomen.

Callista pressed Cane hard to the pedestal. She knew she couldn't claim this kill, but she had to restrain him and keep him from hurting anyone else. Lifting up on her knees, she rolled Cane over and pulled his arms behind his back. Digging into her coat, she retrieved several zip ties and tossed them on his back. Grabbing two, she wrapped them around Cane's wrists and pulled them tight. Cane grunted in protest. "Shut up," Callista snapped. "I know I'm not cutting off your circulation because you don't have any." Lifting herself out of the pedestal, she spotted Caitlin pushing Dawn into a corner. Digging a stake out of her pocket, she charged the vampire.

Dawn surged back, narrowly avoiding Caitlin's strike. Reaching back, she felt the cool wall of the chamber. She was out of room. Thinking quickly, she lifted her arm and shot off a wooden bolt. Caitlin easily intercepted the projectile and snapped it in her hand. Reaching out, she slapped Dawn's arm down. Lunging forward, she pressed Dawn to the wall and grinned. Lifting her hand, she pressed her fingertip against Dawn's shoulder. Pressing and twisting, she dug her finger into the flesh of Dawn's shoulder. The woman screamed out in agony as Caitlin worked her finger deeper into the wound. Pulling her hand free, she lifted her bloody finger toward Dawn's temple. Just as she was about to break the skin with her finger, Callista leapt onto the vampire's back. Spinning around, Caitlin easily threw Callista to the ground and knocked the stake from her hand. Stepping forward, Caitlin's foot landed directly on Callista's outstretched arm. As Caitlin pressed down, Callista felt her bones being crushed.

Bishop glanced over his shoulder to see Zeke smiling broadly. As blood poured down his face, he twisted the stake deeper into Bishop's back. Fighting the pain, Bishop threw his right elbow back and connected with Zeke's nose. The vampire's head snapped back for a moment, but it was long enough for Bishop. Drawing his revolver, he rolled onto his back and pressed the barrel into Zeke's chest.

"Suck on this."

Bishop pulled the trigger. The wood tipped bullet ripped through Zeke's heart. As the vampire fell back clutching his chest, a plume of blue fire erupted from the gaping hole in his head. He screamed in agony as it began to rip through his body. As he clawed the floor in agony, his body exploded, leaving only ash and cinders floating in the air.

Rolling onto his side, Bishop dropped his revolver and crept toward Kelley. With the last remaining bit of his strength, he pulled himself forward letting his head fall on her lap. He quickly fell unconscious from blood loss and shock.

Caitlin lifted her foot away from the bloody patch she had created. Callista gritted her teeth, but refused to cry out. Reaching over her body, she scooped her crushed arm to her body and tried to scoot away as Caitlin walked forward. Callista gasped as pain shot up her torso in waves.

"It must be something about you Wraiths," Caitlin commented, "Specter refused to scream as well." Stepping forward, she placed her hand in the center of Callista's chest. "You are about to die. How does it feel?"

"My soul is ready," Callista croaked.

"That's good!"

Stepping down, Caitlin watched her foot break through the ribs of the Wraith and down into her chest cavity. Callista tried to scream, but found herself unable to breathe. As her head fell back, her life quickly faded away. A lone tear ran down her cheek as she struggled to hold on. Glancing up at Caitlin one final time, Callista's eyes rolled back into her head.

"You bitch!"

Caitlin spun to see Dawn charging toward her. Dropping her shoulder, Dawn plowed into Caitlin at full speed. Both women careened across the floor, finally skidding to a stop against the far wall. Flipping onto her knees, Caitlin grabbed Dawn by the throat and slammed her head against the wall. Bringing her arm up, Dawn pressed her fist beneath Caitlin's jaw and activated her wrist weapon. A wooden bolt ripped through Caitlin's jaw and lodged almost an inch deep in the palette of her mouth. Falling back, the vampire grabbed the bottom of the bolt with her hand and tried to rip it free as blood poured down her neck. Seizing the opportunity, Dawn lunged forward and snatched the broken head of her scythe from the floor. As Dawn jumped to her feet, she brought the scythe blade down and sliced cleanly through Caitlin's left forearm.

Shocked, Caitlin stumbled back from her limb as it twitched on the floor. Unable to open her mouth, Caitlin pushed herself away from Dawn shaking her head.

"You took Cane from me," Dawn said slowly as she approached Caitlin.

Caitlin's eyes were wide with fear.

"I don't know how old you are, or how many significant events you have lived through," Dawn said frankly. "Nor do I really care. You killed Cane," she said angrily. Reaching into her pocket, she recovered the silver coin Mac had given her. Centering it in the palm of her hand, she watched as the silver tendrils shot out and quickly formed a solid silver band around her hand. Glancing up,

Dawn stared at Caitlin. "You're going to die now," she assured Caitlin, "and this time, I'll make damn sure its permanent."

Dawn flung the scythe down at Caitlin, burying the blade deep in her chest. Caitlin fell back to the hard stone floor beaten and unable to speak. Kneeling down next to the ancient vampire, Dawn pressed the silver band to Caitlin's forehead. Instantly the flesh around it began to crackle and sizzle as if being burned. Caitlin tried to struggle, but Dawn pushed the blade of her scythe deeper into her chest. Caitlin's eyes closed as glowing embers began to fall away from her flesh. Blue flame erupted around her hand and began to chew into the vampire's flesh. Pulling her hand away, Dawn slipped off the silver band and watched it revert to its coin state. Standing up, she dropped it on Caitlin's throat. The tendrils sprang to life and instantly began wrapping around her neck. Caitlin moaned in pain as her body burned. Cinders and smoke were thrust into the air by the flames as her body fell to ash and disintegrated.

Stepping back, Dawn pressed her hand to her wounded shoulder and limped across the room toward the king's pedestal. Peering inside, she found Cane still restrained. His eyes were wide, but he made no sound. He stared at Dawn oddly.

"Do you recognize me?" Dawn asked.

Cane remained silent, unmoving. His eyes seemed to focus on her, but through her at the same time.

"I don't know if you can hear me, Cane," Dawn said slowly, fighting the urge to cry, "but I love you." Leaning on the edge of the stone pedestal, she placed her hand in the center of Cane's chest. He made no move to fight her or pull away. "I know it's selfish, but I don't want you to go." A tear slipped from her eye, "But you can't go on living like this. I know that."

She glanced up to the ceiling as she let out a long sigh, then back to her friend. His gaze remained fixed on her. "There are so many things I wanted to tell you, but I always thought I had plenty of time. I just wanted you to know," she wiped the tears from her face, "that I don't know if I lived up to your expectations, but I am proud to be your friend. You were always so much more to me than just a partner, you were my confidant, you were my ally, and you were the father I never had." She took a long breath. "I know I never said it, but I idolized you. You were the standard by which I set my life. I knew if I could be half as strong as you, I would have a fighting chance.

"I watched you suffering over the past year. I don't know why, but I saw you lose your zest for life. It was as if you just gave up, expecting the end to come. You can't imagine how much it hurt me. I can't say for sure what you were going through," Dawn felt a lump well up in her throat, "but I hope you know that I was always there for you. I felt weak and powerless watching you like that, but I knew there was ultimately nothing I could do. I was there for you. I hope that was enough."

Cane's face remained bereft of emotion.

"I love you, Cane. I hope you can find peace." Dawn leaned back her head as the tears flowed freely now. Reaching into her jacket, she pulled out a wooden stake and held it tightly in her hand. Placing it in the center of his chest, she stared deeply into his eyes.

"Goodbye, Cane."

With one thrust, she pushed the stake into his heart.

Chapter Twenty-five

The halls of the Office of Paranormal Investigation in Washington were quiet. News of Cane's death had spread like wildfire through the personnel. Many had opted to take a personal day to grieve for their lost friend and mentor leaving only a skeleton staff on hand. The air seemed to be thick with grief, and yet lacking something so basic, no one could put his or her finger on it. The building seemed empty and cold. This place had irrevocably changed.

The elevator doors chimed twice as they slid open on the second floor. A moment passed before anyone stepped out. As the doors began to slide shut, a hand reached out and forced them open again. Pushing forward, Bishop rolled out into the hallway in his wheelchair. Working the wheels with his hands, he maneuvered the chair into the center of the hall. Leaning back for a moment, he took a breath as pain shot up from the stitches in his abdomen. The last thing he wanted was to tear one of them. He didn't want to go back to the hospital after being there for three weeks already.

Pushing his chair forward, he headed toward a confrontation he didn't want to have. A yellow envelope sat in his lap with Chairman Weiss' name carefully written on it. Bishop glanced down at the letter then ahead again. Slowing to a stop, he reached out and knocked three times on the heavy wooden door.

"Come in."

Bishop twisted the doorknob and pushed open

the door. Swiveling his chair, he rolled into the office and up to the desk situated in the center.

Chairman Thomas Weiss, the head of the OPR, immediately stood up and walked around to greet Bishop. "I had no idea you were out of the hospital," he said, extending his hand.

Bishop shook the Chairman's hand and nodded, "They let me out yesterday."

Weiss, an older man with graying hair, adjusted his glasses and leaned back on his desk. Quickly straightening his tie, he returned his full attention to Bishop. "What can I do for you, Mr. Bishop?"

Bishop lifted the envelope from his lap and handed it to Weiss. "I just wanted to present my letter of resignation in person before I packed up my office."

Weiss looked surprised. "You're resigning from the OPR?"

Bishop nodded.

"There's no reason for me to stay," Bishop replied coolly. "There's nothing keeping me here."

"But you would be the head of your team now," Weiss countered. "You would lead all investigations."

"Thanks, but I'm not interested," Bishop smiled.

"I read your report," Weiss commented, "but you omitted several details."

"Like?" Bishop asked.

"You never mentioned what happened to the vampire hunter, what was his name?" Weiss snapped his fingers, "Specter."

Bishop nodded. "I was on heavy doses of pain

killers when I wrote that. I must've just forgot. Specter is expected to make a full recovery. He's in the hands of the Wraiths now."

"Are you planning to stay in touch with Dawn and Kelley?"

Bishop nodded. "If I can. Kelley moved back to Seattle to take over Lydia's coven of witches, and I have no idea where Dawn is. She told me that she also tendered her resignation last week, but never said where she was going or what she wanted to do."

Weiss placed Bishop's letter on his desk carefully. "What do you plan to do with your life now?"

Bishop shrugged. "I have no idea, but I need time to heal, both physically and mentally."

Weiss nodded. "We're all still in shock from the loss."

The two sat in silence for a moment, staring vacantly off into space. Everything that needed to be said had been. All that remained now was to sever the tie, and neither man was eager to do that.

Finally, Bishop broke the silence, "Well, I better be off." He extended his hand to Weiss, "Thank you for giving me the chance to work for the OPR."

Weiss shook Bishop's hand and nodded. "It was my pleasure, son. If you need anything, let me know."

"I will," Bishop said with a smile. Turning in his chair, he rolled out of Weiss' office and closed the door behind him.

Weiss moved back to his desk and sunk back

down into his chair. Spinning around, he watched the sun beginning to set over the Washington D.C. skyline. Running his eyes down to his windowsill, he stared at the picture of himself and Cane taken shortly after they had started the OPR. Taking a deep breath through his nose, he exhaled slowly and let his head fall forward. Grabbing Bishop's letter, he pulled open his desk drawer and slipped it inside with the others.

* * *

Rain poured down over Paris. Men and women ran with their coats pulled up over their heads into cafes and stores to get out of the drizzle, yet two figures walked unhindered in it as the moon peeked in and out from behind the heavy storm clouds. One was a man dressed entirely in black, while the other was a young woman wrapped in a fur coat. They walked arm in arm as they lifted their faces into the rain. Smiling and laughing, the two disappeared in an alley. The man gently pushed the woman against the wall and began kissing her neck. He ran his powerful hands up her sides and over the wet silk dress that clung to her curvy body.

"Not here," the woman protested in French as she giggled. "We could be seen."

"That's not all you have to worry about," the man replied. Pulling away from the woman's neck, he blinked his golden eyes and showed his fangs.

The woman screamed in terror as the man bit into her throat. Running his hand up over her mouth, he drank deeply. Suddenly, a twinge ran up the back of his neck. Pulling away, he wiped the blood from his mouth with his sleeve. Glancing toward the mouth of the alley, he saw a figure standing there draped in shadows.

"Wraith," he hissed. Pushing his victim aside, the vampire readied himself for battle.

Tossing her long leather coat back, Dawn activated her scythe and charged into the alley.